Beware of Chicken

— BOOK 1 —

CASUALFARMER

First, to my parents, for inspiring and encouraging me.
Next, to Kevin Blue, for his endless kindness and support.
To Tsuu, whose art has helped the characters come to life.
To Drew, for his work.
And to the ever kind people who have supported me on Patreon,
for making all this possible in the first place.

It's been a dream come true.

Cover and interior art by Tsuu

ISBN: 978-1-0394-4809-4

Published in 2022 by Podium Publishing
www.podiumentertainment.com

Beware of Chicken

Cultivation. The Taoist concept of extending one's lifespan by cultivating Qi and practicing mystical martial arts techniques. Through the power of Qi, a cultivator can ascend beyond all limits and reach immortality.

It is a long and bloody road, rising above the masses and climbing the Realms of Cultivation. Spirit Beasts stalk the lands. Demons and Demonic Cultivators murder and pillage. Wars can rage for a thousand years. Lives are snuffed out like candles, as experts do battle with powers that leave both the heavens and the earth trembling.

It is a lifetime of brutality and hardship, yet these things are transient. The reward for reaching the peak forgives all sins in the pursuit of power.

It is a journey only the most stalwart are capable of making.

CHAPTER 1

HE BRAVELY TURNED HIS TAIL AND FLED

You wish to leave the Sect?" Senior Disciple Lu Ri asked, repeating the disciple's request. He had to make sure that some trick was not being played on him.

He stared at the young man before him wearing the blue robes of an Outer Disciple of the Cloudy Sword Sect. The boy had a black eye and his arm in a sling. Lu Ri could see the telltale signs of wounds hidden behind his robes, and the boy was favouring one leg. Quite a pitiful sight, all told.

"Yes, Senior Brother," the disciple responded. "This Jin Rou's abilities are lacking. I was defeated by disciples who are two years junior to me. I would leave before I bring greater shame upon our Cloudy Sword Sect."

Lu Ri sighed internally. It was natural for one who was older to be stronger, for they had been cultivating longer—but this had been a Young Master of the Cloudy Sword Sect against an Outer Sect Disciple. The battle would have had a foregone conclusion, even if the Outer Sect Disciple was a hundred years older than his opponent. And Jin Rou was the *weakest* Outer Sect Disciple currently within their halls, not even into the Profound Realm. Such a bout was deeply, deeply shameful. The Honoured Founders spoke of the correct way to trade pointers. How to properly train your juniors instead of this brutalization. Lu Ri wished he could have put a stop to it . . . but he had no authority over the Young Master. The Inner and Core Disciples were beyond his purview.

The Senior Disciple considered the brown-haired young man, the prominent freckles on his cheeks barely peeking out through the bruising on his face. He was tall, taller than most Lu Ri had seen in his many years, and his body bore signs of hard physical labour, rather than the sculpted body of a cultivator. Indeed, Jin Rou was not powerful, but he *was* diligent and always willing to tend to the Sect's less desirable tasks. He always reported for work details. Losing his attention to detail in caring for the compound and Lowly Spirit Herbs would be a blow . . . although not one of any significance. The boy had no *real* training or knowledge of the techniques of the Sect.

If this was enough to crush his spirit, to abandon this life, then he was not meant to be a cultivator in the first place. The Cloudy Sword Sect was no place for the weak of heart.

At least he was polite enough to attend to the formalities instead of just disappearing. It was the first time in over three hundred years that somebody had paid the exit fee—disgruntled Sect members normally just disappeared. Lu Ri considered attempting to dissuade him from leaving, but he felt the *certainty* in the boy's actions and words. He was set on leaving, and nothing Lu Ri could do or say would persuade him.

"What is your intent after leaving this place, Disciple?" he asked out of idle curiosity.

"Perhaps I shall become a farmer, Senior Brother," the boy replied. "I had some luck in growing the Lowly Spiritual Herbs, so such a thing should be within my minor talents."

Lu Ri raised an eyebrow at the absurd statement. A mere farmer, from a boy who had—even barely—passed their Sect's initiation? It would be a complete waste of talent. The devastating defeat must have completely demoralized him. How unfortunate.

Lu Ri sighed, not looking directly at the boy, and instead gazed out at the stark beauty of their mountain.

"I see. I shall mark down your leaving. From this day forward, you are no longer a disciple of the Cloudy Sword Sect, Jin Rou."

Jin Rou bowed his head and clasped his fist in front of him, wincing as he moved his still broken arm. "This Jin Rou thanks you for your time and consideration. I shall darken the compound's halls no longer."

Lu Ri stood and inclined his head. He gave the gesture of respect back to the boy. "Then go into the world, Jin Rou." Lu Ri looked at the boy's face. His solemn nod. He was going out into this world with nothing but the clothes upon his back and the small bag of items at his feet. Lu Ri may not have been able to rebuke the Inner Sect Disciple . . . but he could do this. He picked up the pouch of money Jin Rou had given him and held it back out to the young man. "Here. I shall mark it down as paid in full. Diligence and proper courtesy deserve a reward, and the Sect does not need this sum." It was probably all the money the boy had, anyway. Lu Ri did have *some* kindness to him, and Jin Rou would need the luck of the heavens in his new life.

Jin Rou's eyes widened with shock. Hesitantly, he reached out, like Lu Ri was going to snatch the coin purse away from him. It fell into Jin Rou's hand with a small clink. The young man bowed his head in gratitude. "May Heaven be kind to you, Lu Ri," he said with a crooked little smile.

And then Jin Rou was gone from the Sect.

□

I came to in the middle of getting my ass beat. From darkness and terror, I suddenly *woke up*, only to receive a fist to my jaw and a bunch of mocking laughter. Then I had gotten pulled to my feet and slapped around for another twenty minutes. My first experience in this world was the feeling of my ribs giving in, my arm shattering, and then passing out.

Let me tell you, that was absolute *horseshit*. Jin Rou was kind of an idiot for not getting out of the way in time when the little shit wanted to fuck somebody up, but at least he hadn't crippled me. Or torn off an arm or something, just because "the commoner was so beneath him" or whatever.

A few of the other disciples were kind enough to drag my—Jin's? *my?*— twitching body back to my little room . . . then ransacked some of the herbs I—*he'd* grown as "payment" for their good deed.

Dicks.

It certainly didn't endear the place to me. It only really hit me that I was in magical xianxia land while I was moaning in pain. Apparently, one of the chest-shots had hit poor Jin Rou hard enough—and in just the right way—to stop his heart and kill him.

And before he'd even fallen over dead, I'd gotten shoved into his body.

At least I'd gotten his memories of the language along with how to actually use the remaining herbs to deal with the worst of the damage. It meant mashing and grinding the herbs—which was *extremely painful* with how many injuries I've got.

Jin Rou himself had been fairly respectable from what I could tell about him from memories, I suppose. He was an orphan—after his Gramps disappeared—and he'd managed to join a Sect through hard work. Kind of.

His admittance had only happened because one of the instructors flipped a coin when deciding his fate, since he just barely squeaked past qualifying. The instructor had said something about heaven favouring him or something when he was inducted.

Jin Rou had wanted to become a powerful cultivator, a master among masters, and do whatever it is the dickbags who run this place did. Which was presumably to be dicks, dickishly.

I kinda . . . didn't care about his motivations, his goals or ideals.

My body now, buddy. Sorry, not sorry.

Dear old Jin Rou had been a servant anyway and had to do any task that the other people at the Sect offloaded onto him, while he harboured vengeance and hate and angst against them for being entitled dickbags. I kind of got where he was coming from, but I wanted *none* of that shit.

I shoved Jin Rou's memories to the side, so I couldn't see them. Or have all his emotions rattling around my head. I declared any revenge fantasies and ambitions null and void. I wanted none of the little fuckboy who'd wasted my ass. Most importantly, I wanted *nothing* to do with the politics of this world, because *holy shit*. There was way too much line extinguishing and murdering each other for "face."

You know, the usual.

So, I'd looked up the methods for leaving the Sect when I was mobile the next day, grabbed one of Jin's hidden pouches of money, and gone to the guy in charge of this kind of stuff to get the hell out of there.

I wasn't expecting to get the money pouch back, but I was okay with losing that one. Jin Rou was actually reasonably good at saving: He had been saving to purchase a few spiritual pills, after picking up so many extra chores.

What was his, is now mine, and I'm using it to get the fuck out *of here*. Far away from all the sword formations and Grand Demonic Dick-Punching or whatever the fuck these chuuni bastards spout.

Some might call me a coward. I'd say I have a healthy sense of self-preservation. What kind of moron would hang around the people who'd *killed* him? Why would I pal around in this wretched organization where I was little better than a servant?

So, I packed up and left. No real direction, all I knew is that I had to get out. I *had* to leave. I felt like I was drowning up here, among the spartan stone buildings, though that may have just been the fact that we're literally above the clouds. I had no idea *how* high up I was, but a flash of memory showed me a rising platform that was used specifically for the entrance exams.

Right now? I would have to take the stairs. So, I walked out of the main gate. Enormous slabs of stone the size of ten-story buildings, and carved with depictions of the Cloudy Sword Sect's founders.

The gate guard casually placed a single hand against a door and pushed what had to be hundreds of thousands of tons aside like it was easy. He gave me an appraising look but otherwise ignored me as I left.

I swallowed and started marching down the spiraling stairs, flanked on every side by solid grey stone and frost. It was bitterly cold, and I probably would have just died instantly if I wasn't a cultivator. Instead, it was merely horribly uncomfortable as I descended down from above the clouds heading towards Crimson Crucible City, far, far below the Cloudy Sword Sect's lofty perch. My journey took me past the cloud barrier and away from the stark mountain. I marched down the seemingly endless flight of stairs, into a forested path, heavy with fog. I could feel the air getting thicker with each step I went down. Maybe it was the fact that there was more oxygen down here, but each step I could breathe easier.

It took me two days of walking at a decent clip before I could even really *see* Crimson Crucible City, surrounded by waterfalls that would put Niagara to shame with their size, all flowing down into thousands of rivers. The sound was a dull roar that I thought had been distant wind at first. It was a spectacular, breathtaking sight. The other noticeable landmark was just as breathtaking but also gave me the creeps just looking at. The Demon's Grave Ravine seemed to have a permanent shadow around it. The guard towers on the edges of it were bristling with defensive emplacements, ready to fight off the *things* that occasionally poured out. It really, *really* hammered home that I was someplace else, in addition to the enormous, sprawling, walled thing that was Crimson Crucible City. It was a place I knew nothing about, and I had no GPS or handy map app to guide me. But I did have the memories of somebody who'd lived there all his life.

I took a break on a rock, just staring at everything, my view finally unobstructed by the clouds or the mist. I felt like hell. Sleeping on the forest floor and being plagued by nightmares, waking up with every little sound . . . it *sucked.* But I wasn't just going to lay down and quit. I took a deep breath, then pulled on the other guy's memories, trying to tease them from the metaphorical box I had shoved them into. I needed something concrete. Not just the sudden flashes of comprehension explaining what I was looking at, but detailed memories of the city he had grown up in.

I immediately regretted it, as that was all the memories needed to flood into my mind.

The feelings were intense. Recollections of gangs, sickness, and a *demon assault*. Love of his long-dead parents, and the times he had with "Gramps" learning how to cultivate. The shock of it all sent me to my knees, holding my head, on a lonely mountain path.

I shoved them all away from me. All of Jin— *Rou's* memories. *The other guy*. I shoved them back in their little box, spat the taste of bile from my mouth, and shook off the phantom pains.

I really had no desire to stay in the city. There were too many memories. I needed someplace *else*. The city was safe enough, if you knew which alleys not to go down. The memories of Rou thankfully did, but I couldn't live here.

→

First, I needed information. Rou had lived his entire life in Crimson Crucible City and didn't know too much about the world outside it. Hopefully, I could find a nice, quiet place away from things. On the outskirts. Some place without a lot of fighting, if that was possible. And for that I went to the library. Okay, it wasn't *really* a library, it was "The Archive," and you needed a pass for anything that wasn't common knowledge. But it was smack dab in the middle of town, and any citizen could make use of it. The technology level was that of perhaps the iron age for the most part, but they also had things that didn't quite fit. A free library was one of them, and I think I saw some kind of mall, complete with advertisements.

Just to hammer home that this was a place touched by the magic of Qi, there were a bunch of glowing crystals about this part of the city. Some served as light bulbs, some emitted cool air, and still others spewed water into fountains.

There was even a reception area. The clerk seemed a bit surprised at my questions, but he directed me to where I wanted to go.

It was a collection of *twenty* five-story-tall shelves, all packed with scrolls.

I got to work, pulling a couple off. It was surprisingly quick work, and soon enough, I found my prize.

The Azure Hills. Little to no Qi. Weakest province in the Crimson Phoenix Empire. Of limited value.

Not a lot of Qi meant few spirit beasts, and more importantly, it meant barely any cultivators.

I had my destination. It was kind of far away. And by kind of far away, I mean "several days in a car, on a highway." *At least.* And without any cars or planes, and not really a lot of money to my name . . . I'd have to walk it.

At least cultivators have good endurance, right?

I went back out into the city and got some supplies for the long road ahead.

I glanced up once at the giant mountain, where the Sect was. I couldn't see anything. The Sect and the cultivators above were hidden behind the clouds. With one last sigh I left the city of Jin Rou's birth, marching north towards the Azure Hills, determination in my heart.

→

"One Dandanmian up!"

I raised a hand, and the kid carrying my bowl of noodles put it in front of me. I was in a noodle shop in a gorge, splurging a little. I had been getting tired of the rations I had after three days and decided to treat myself.

Digging my chopsticks into the bowl, I slurped up the spicy noodles and looked around. It was pretty busy here, with lots of people laughing and joking. I felt the tension that had built up start to drain out of my shoulders as people just talked and laughed. Maybe this world wasn't quite as bad as I had been expecting.

Aside from the place's location right beside a hundred-story-tall waterfall . . . everything seemed pretty normal.

Just as I thought that, the door burst open, and a man wearing gaudy red clothes stormed in, his eyes blazing with fury. "Tao Gui, you honourless bastard! You're courting death!" he thundered, and the rest of the patrons were silenced.

Another person, one wearing travelling clothes, stood up, brushing off his rice hat. He had a nasty, cocky smirk on his face. "Yuanjun! You dare interrupt my meal? Kowtow a hundred times before this daddy, and I'll let you off with a spanking!"

The hell? This daddy? What kind of speech pattern is that? I thought to myself. I saw quite a few people make moves for the exit, as the two men marched towards each other. Qi swirled around their bodies. Were they *really* about to have a fight in a noodle shop—

Yuanjun's fist pulled back, and I dove behind the counter with my noodles. I nodded to the owner, who was also behind the counter, and slurped my noodles as two men started to reenact a crappy kung-fu movie. Except oh so *very* real. We both flinched as wood smashed and people shouted. There was the sound of breaking bones, and a few flecks of blood splattered across the wall.

I hope this dude had a good insurance policy, because shit's *fucked.*

There was another roar and a detonation of Qi as the front half of the building *disintegrated.*

I really, *really* wanted to be anywhere else right now.

→

The trek so far had been . . . *mostly* peaceful. The majority of the month had been just day after day of steady forward progress. Raging Waterfall Gorge was aptly named. There were thousands of waterfalls, spewing mist in the air, and the entire place was crisscrossed with bridges. There was a kind of sheer verticality to the land that was breathtaking.

I wished I could stop and enjoy it, but fate had it out for my sorry ass.

It was one thing to read about a rampaging monster attack. It's another thing entirely to be caught in one, as the trees snapped and a giant beastie hurtled after me. The "Earth-Crushing Devil Serpent"—*what the* fuck *kind of name was that*—roared with fury, smashing apart the road. People were screaming and crying and hollering.

I just ran, my legs pumping as fast as I could make them, while I thanked whatever deity existed that the creature was kind of slow.

I ran like the hounds of hell were after me, repeating a single mantra.

The Azure Hills has none of this shit. The Azure Hills has none of this shit.

Oh, gods, I hope *I live through this.*

→

Each day drove me onwards to my destination. Each reminder of the danger of this world made me go just that bit faster. I made, quite frankly, obscene time, my feet carrying me onwards far quicker and with more endurance than I'd thought possible. I wasn't sleeping too well, and sometimes I'd just wake up, pack up, and start walking, even in the middle of the night.

I walked through the giant and breathtaking Howling Fang Mountains with barely a pause to admire them. The Azure Hills beckoned. The safest corner of the safest place. And then, I wouldn't have to deal with anybody.

There, I'd start a new life. I was going to be a farmer. I'd get a wagon, some rice, maybe a few chickens or something, and then live on my own, like a modern pioneer.

Maybe I was building that idea up a bit too much in my head . . . but my thoughts and plans were a nice respite from the hell that was this world.

→

It was a rainy, overcast day that matched my still sleep-deprived mood. But even with that, the Azure Hills looked . . . less harsh than other places I'd seen. Gentle rolling hills, flush with green grass. Coming out of the stark Howling Fang Mountains, it looked like paradise.

I passed through the capital of the province, Pale Moon Lake City. Situated on a giant, perfectly round lake, the city was home to over a million people.

It was considered small.

I stopped briefly to use the Archive in the city to find a good spot to settle. There were a few choices. The Grass Sea sounded appealing . . . but that was apparently where all the Sects were, so I crossed that off the list. "Blaze Bear infestation" were the words used to describe the Ash Forest. The area around Pale Moon Lake had millions of people, and nearly all the prime farmland was already taken.

That only left one place. North. To where barely anybody lived. I tapped my finger on the map, on top of a symbol that denoted a settlement. *Verdant Hill* sounded like a nice name for a town . . .

→

I arrived at my new home in the middle of spring pulling a covered wagon. It was a recent addition to my journey, and I had brought everything in it that I would need from the town a few days away. Three months on the road, three months full of terror and nightmares were finally at an end. I smiled down at my new plot of land. It was a few rolling hills, covered by a forest, and had a lovely little river winding through it. It was fantastically picturesque, as were most places in the

Red Phoenix Continent. It had taken me months to travel this far, but right now it was looking worth it.

The town's magistrate considered the land mostly useless, as there were some minor monsters around. And it needed a *lot* of clearing, but hopefully nothing I couldn't handle. Rou knew how to throw a punch at least, and I had tested it out by putting my fist *through* a tree—which had honestly scared the crap out of me.

The land had also been extremely cheap. I had gotten this place for a steal. Five hundred acres of land for less than a year of Rou's savings. Man, fuck property prices back home. *This* was where it's at! After I'd been told the price I'd considered the possibility I had been screwed over and asked the locals about this place, but nope, no sleeping dragons or ancient curses, as far as anyone knew. Just out of the way and more trouble than it was worth.

People rarely came up this way, since it was so far from the town and the surrounding villages. Nobody would bother me here.

No Spirit Beasts, no cultivator fights, no nothin'.

I breathed in the fantastically clean and invigorating air and slowly let out the breath, my shoulders sagging as the tension finally bled out of them. Enough lazing around. I had some work to do.

I reached into my packed wagon and grabbed my axe, causing my chickens to cluck in irritation at me and the young rooster to crow at the sudden jostling, puffing up his red feathers. The large, sturdy cart was full to the brim with supplies and a few tools. Everything else would be made from scratch. I'd have to get creative, but for just one person it would be enough. The rivers were full of fish, and the berry bushes should let me live off the land for a while, along with the rice seed, of course.

I gave my chicken a little scratch under his developing wattles, and the little guy calmed a bit.

Well, time to get to work. Operation "No Cultivator Bullshit" is a go! There would be no fights here, no mad scramble for resources. Just me, a plot of land, and *peace.*

→

There's a certain sort of *zen* you reach when you engage in heavy physical activity for long enough. My axe hewed through trees, my saw made planks, my hammer drove in nails, and my plane made things level. All fuelled by the supernatural strength of a cultivator—even if I was an exceptionally weak one. It was surprisingly calming and invigorating at the same time, and I must confess I heartily enjoyed the heavy physical labour since I had the strength of ten men. Fragments of memory guided one part, while my own experiences in the Before, growing up on a farm, guided the other. My breathing was a perfect rhythm, and my Qi circulated around inside me. I felt so at peace and refreshed!

Also, being able to tear a stump out of the ground with nothing but brute strength would never get old.

The first task, as always, was *shelter.* There was absolutely nothing here, so that was the priority project. A simple one-room affair that didn't take me too long to build, with how strong I currently was.

It wasn't anything spectacular, but it would keep the elements off me and the bugs at bay, with its thatch roof and pounded-dirt floor. Apparently, the survival classes I had . . . *before* came in handy for this lifestyle, though wiping my ass with leaves was an annoying novelty. At least the river was right there. I'd built my shack right against my chicken coop, so I could hear if there were any predatory interlopers during the night. The foxes and the wolves had yet to notice my intrusion into their territory or the tasty treats that were clucking away, curious about their new home.

I was proud of the little things I had built.

I woke to the call of my rooster, who I had named Big D. An incredibly childish name, but it amused me greatly. My young lad would follow me around during the day, hopping around and often sitting on my shoulder. From his lofty perch, he proclaimed his dominance to the world, the cheeky shit.

"Cock-a-doodle-doo!" he'd screech.

"You tell 'em, Big D," I'd reply.

My hoe bit the earth and never dulled, reinforced as it was by my Qi, and it tore into the ground with more speed than any ox could ever accomplish. My chickens eagerly followed behind me, pecking at bugs and plants I unearthed with my efforts, bucking and clucking all the way.

Yes, get good and fat, my pretties, and you will be delectable in the future.

Ah, even now the thought makes my mouth water.

Up and down went the hoe, up and down went the hoe, until I noticed something. A strange root poked out and had a vague sense of Qi about it. Interested, I picked up the lumpy and nondescript tuber.

In novels, this was where the protagonist would immediately identify the plant, spouting that it was some rare so-and-so "Root of Six Elixirs" or something. But quite frankly, I had *no clue* what it was. I'd have to go to the town Archive at some point, but considering it was here, it probably wasn't very rare or important.

Shrugging, I put it in my house, then got back to work. After this field—which was going to be my vegetable garden—I'd start on the rice paddy. There were lots of rocks to clear out of the way, but they were no match for my mighty shovel!

It sucks that I haven't been able to get any wheat yet, but whatcha gonna do?

→

That night, I had an absolutely delicious egg fried rice, with Big D sitting on my shoulder. Maybe it was a little morbid to eat eggs right in front of your pet chicken, but he didn't seem to mind. There were eggs from my chickens, rice from the stuff I had brought to get myself set up, some sesame oil that I had splurged on when I bought my land, and some of the leftover Lowly Spiritual Herbs I had, uh . . . "liberated" from the Cloudy whatever Sect. They tasted pretty damn good once I'd stir-fried them. A little spicy, a little sweet, a little savoury—I would definitely have to grow more of them. They weren't that hard to grow, according to Rou's memories. I'd just have to baby them for a bit.

Sure, I could convert them into pills, but I was *extremely* suspicious about all the pills these people choked back. I'm half convinced that every cultivator is so damn nuts because of all the drugs they did.

I shook myself out of my introspection and turned to the pleased clucking sounds coming from my "kitchen." Big D was eagerly pecking at the little nubs of spirit herb I had cut off that looked a bit wilted.

They *probably* wouldn't kill him. They were supposed to be good for thc body.

Eh, if he likes 'em, he likes 'em. Not going to deny the little man his treat.

I got ready for bed, with Big D jumping up onto the perch I'd made him by the window.

Man, if I was still in the Sect, I'd be doing shitty chores or sitting in a corner cultivating for months on end, instead of actually *making* stuff.

I smiled when I looked up at the grassy hills that led to the back of my new home, the sunset warming my body. Then I wandered into my house and collapsed on what I was charitably calling my bed. It was just a frame with some blankets on it, but it was mine and I'd made it! I curled up and went to sleep, my mind already whirling with what I would do tomorrow.

My eyes drifted shut. I didn't have any nightmares. It was nice being able to sleep through the night again, with a warm spring breeze caressing my face.

CHAPTER 2

RICE FARMING 101

I jolted awake to Big D's furious battle cry and the angry snarling of a fox. I had my shovel in my hand and was out the door as fast as I could. It was an extremely pleasant night. The stars formed ribbons of light that shone brightly, uninterrupted by any light pollution. But I had no time to admire the view.

Big D was flapping around the fox's head, kicking at it furiously. His spurs, the little blades of bone roosters have on the back of their legs, struck and slashed. He was too small for them to deal any real damage, but he was trying his little heart out.

I was transfixed for a moment as David challenged Goliath. They were two streaks of colour in the night. The other chickens were cowering and clucking nervously, watching the battle unfold.

With a burst of speed, the fox managed to hit him with its paw and knocked him down and away. Big D's footing was fouled. His fate was sealed. The fox pounced, its razor-sharp teeth going for the kill, trying to end my little warrior.

Oh? You dare trespass into this Daddy's domain?! . . . I couldn't believe I'd just thought that. I really was going native, using that turn of phrase. I snorted to myself.

The fox's teeth clamped down on iron instead of flesh, and it looked up, shocked at the shovel I had put between it and Big D.

It was then the fox realised it fucked up. It turned and tried to run.

My shovel whirled, and with a *clang*—the fox died.

I looked back to my little warrior. He had managed to get to his feet and was glaring hatefully at the fox's corpse. I gave him a once-over, and he was fine, as were my girls—just a fright.

I didn't blame the fox; it was their nature to hunt. I hoped he didn't blame me for braining him with a shovel in retaliation.

I also hope he forgives me for selling his fur because I'm totally going to do that. I think *you can eat fox.*

→

You can, in fact, eat fox. I . . . just wouldn't recommend it. Tasted like ass. I forced myself to swallow the grilled meat. It was a measly, dry offering, as predators don't tend to have much fat. The gaminess was really off-putting too. Food wasn't scarce at the moment, but that was no excuse to waste any. I had to take what I could get . . . and what I'd gotten was a fox.

I reserved the right to complain, though.

I grunted as I moved a pot full of dirt to its proper position, then got things ready for the second part of rice planting.

Growing rice *properly* involves a bit more than just chucking your seed into the ground and hoping for the best. I had witnessed the farmers' techniques from the village, and they were a bit . . . lacking. Or at least lacking by modern standards; they seemed to be able to feed themselves just fine.

For example, the first thing you do before planting is soak the rice in a one-to-sixteen ratio of salted water. Rice seeds with the greatest amount of endosperm—those with the best chance of a yield—will sink to the bottom of your barrel. Filling the barrels was pretty easy, they barely weighed a thing to me, but the salt was a bit trickier. It wasn't as expensive as I'd thought it would be, which I was thankful for. The lighter rice will then float to the top and is easily skimmed out. Those I would pound a bit more and eat, getting off the husks and boiling them for brown rice.

Then, after soaking, you plant the desirable seeds in wide buckets for the first part of their life as they sprout. That was what I was doing at the moment.

Then, finally, you transplant them to your paddies. I always found it rather strange that rice does better when you rip it out of the soil and stuff it somewhere else instead of leaving it be.

The funny thing is that I'd learned most of this from reading manga. Thanks, Shizuko. I had no shame cheating by using techniques from the

1860s when the technology level was mid- to pre-thousands level, like all *true* Isekai heroes!

Except some of the technology stuff wouldn't really work. Guns would be pretty much useless against cultivators and Spirit Beasts, and I had no desire to conquer the world. *Eh, rice is more important than that stuff anyways.*

But enough about that. I examined the buckets one more time and then turned to the paddies, walking over to continue working on them. The paddies themselves were underway, carved into the side of one of the hills in a terraced style. It would be fed by one of the small rivers when it finally came time to flood them. Want me to be honest about something? The reason it was done like this is because that hill had the fewest rocks I needed to clear. Some of the damn things were twice my height, even if I could get them out of the way, mindlessly crushing rocks got boring after a while.

Cultivator strength and endurance always did turn tasks that should have taken months or years into a matter of days, but sometimes I had a sneaking suspicion that my "zen" modes lasted for longer than I thought they did. I was always *super* hungry when they stopped, and occasionally Big D gave me the gimlet eye when I got back home.

Cultivation be whack, yo.

I finished examining the terrace wall for any potential defects. It looked pretty good, but just in case, I pushed some more of my Qi into it. Lending my spirit to help reinforce the wall and strengthen the grass's roots to keep everything steady.

The masters at the Sects would probably have an aneurysm about how much Qi I was "wasting," but I didn't see it as a waste. It was a resource. If you got it, use it. Besides, it didn't take *that* long for it to come back. At the start of the next day, I was usually feeling fresh as a daisy. Maybe if I was a better cultivator or had more extensive reserves, it might have taken longer to recover, but I didn't know and quite honestly, I didn't care.

Yawning, I wandered back to my little house, and Big D greeted me with his signature screech.

"You tell 'em, Big D," I said as I scratched his head affectionately. His defeat hadn't made him skittish, so that was good. He was still a little ball of piss and vinegar.

My Lowly Spiritual Herbs were growing in their buckets beside my sprouting rice. The Spirit Herbs needed Qi to grow properly, and I figured, why not just infuse the rice with Qi too? It couldn't be any harm.

I had also replanted the strange root I'd found. I couldn't just run off to a local archive, so this was the only way I had to store it. It had some Qi to it, so it got a dousing too.

I carefully infused my spirit into the water. I then picked up my watering can and got to work, with Big D sitting on my shoulder, occasionally hopping off to snap up a bug that dared try to assault the vulnerable shoots.

Good boy. More spirit greens for you after dinner.

→

So, things went. I had to brain a few more foxes and a starving-looking wolf, but otherwise things were mostly peaceful.

Day after day I worked. A little house rose. My bed got just a bit more comfortable. Rocks were ground down into gravel, and a tangled forest gave way to cleared land. It was like watching a movie in fast forward. Those half-primitive technology videos and my own farm-boy upbringing helped a bit, but I wasn't *really* a normal human. I could start a fire in a single twist of a dowel and hew entire trees down in two swings of an axe.

So, I worked. I let myself go and learned to love the routine. Learned to love the land as I pushed more and more of my Qi into the soil, reinforcing and nurturing it. It was a careful act, because too much Qi could cause things to explode, but the land drank it all in without complaint.

Chop the wood.

Break the rocks.

Plant crops.

Nurture soil with Qi.

Eat food.

Sleep.

Months passed by.

I awoke to each new day with a smile, feeling whole and happy.

□

The Great Master had given him the name *Bi De*. He knew not what it meant, but he knew the name was his. He knew it was powerful.

But *he* was not.

Not yet.

Awareness was a fickle thing. It came and it went. But he *knew* during those times. He *thought*. And he was elevated above those who were beneath him. His senses were refined to better alert the Great Master to interlopers during the night, those of red fur and sharp teeth.

But every time he failed in something he knew was his duty, like defending the females, he felt great shame. His Great Master nurtured him without reservation, treating him like a favoured son and not the shameful thing he was.

He was *weak*.

He had to grow in strength and fulfill his destiny!

He rode upon the Great Master's shoulder while his Lord infused their food with his very essence and struck from above upon the base creatures that dared to sup off his energy.

He stood the night watch while the Great Master slept. He guarded the coops while the Great Master completed his great wonders, commanding the land and taming the forest.

He watched as the Great Master moved in the morning, his body flowing with tremendous skill. It was the same set of movements, every morning, before he started his work.

And so Bi De sought to improve himself. He ran through the Great Master's lands. He jumped over the hills and onto the giant branches of trees. He shoved his body against the Great Pots of Growth until he could finally move them.

And now, he stood upon the Great Pillars of *Fa Ram*—another name with an unquestionably sublime meaning—and gave it his all to imitate the Great Master, to achieve some pale imitation of his wondrous skill.

His body soared through the air. His legs lashed out with strength unknown to his lesser kin. He danced as the Great Master danced. He drew breath as the Great Master drew breath.

Something swirled around him.

Within him.

□

I smiled at Big D as he hopped and kicked along my fence.

Cute little guy.

CHAPTER 3

BENEATH THE CRESCENT MOON

Bi De knew fury. One of the red ones had *vexed* his Great Master. One of the foolish creatures that never learned, even as their kin died by the score to his Lord's mighty spur, his "shovel." Yet it was different from the others, somehow managing to sneak past Bi De, nearly slaying one of the Great Master's flock. It was fortunate that he had that ill feeling and thus gone on patrol. He had barely sounded the alarm in time, his voice berating the foul interloper.

But this red one, this vile beast, was skilled. It danced around Bi De's blows, as he called upon his Great Master. His Lord had appeared from his coop to bring death upon the interloper. Yet, horror of horrors, the monster had evaded the Great Master's mighty spur, the one that he used to tame the earth. In all other cases, his iron spur had been a command of death. With a single contemptuous blow, he had smote all others.

But not this one.

At first, Bi De was stunned nearly to the point of spitting blood. Why did his Great Master not pursue it? He could have easily slain the interloper, this demon, if he directed his full and terrible wrath against it.

He did not understand, but he knew his Great Master had wisdom that far eclipsed his.

Thrice, the *foul spawn* did attempt to take what was rightfully the Great Master's. Its guile, cunning, and luxurious pelt surpassing all its kin. Thrice, did the Great Master's mighty blows miss.

The Great Master even gave it a name from the very pits of hell: *Basi Bu Shi*. Bi De shuddered whenever he heard it. His Great Master's words of power contained both virtuous and fell wisdom.

Each night, he contemplated his Great Master's wisdom and methods while staring at the moon. The great celestial body was calming to gaze upon, and when he was not alert for interlopers, he found himself drawn to its sublime radiance.

But now, he understood. He had deciphered the conundrum his Great Master had set before him. His Great Master had once more brought out his mobile coop, the thing with wheels that could be pulled behind his Lord. He remembered vaguely, before he was enlightened, travelling to these blessed lands upon the mighty fortress from . . . *another place* that was . . . hazier.

Some of his Master's supplies had run low. He wished to return to the other place, so that the people there might give tribute to his glory.

But to travel outwards, the Great Master would have to leave his home with only Bi De remaining to serve as Fa Ram's guardian.

And he was not strong enough. His weakness was preventing the Master from living how he wished. It was unacceptable.

He had been issued a challenge in Basi Bu Shi's continued existence. A mighty task to prove his worth against the wicked.

The Great Pillars of the Fa Ram called.

He redoubled his efforts.

His kicks took on new energy.

His dance, new grace.

He would slay this mighty enemy and earn his Great Master's trust.

□

Well, just a bit more 'til I head back to Verdant Hill, I mused as I worked. I'd have to take the chickens along with me, so they didn't all get eaten. I knew I should probably finally deal with Basil Brush. I had been kind of lazy about it, just chasing him off and hoping he would get the message, but he was becoming persistent.

I couldn't blame him. The chickens were growing big. Big D had basically reached adulthood, he was now much more solid-looking than the string bean he used to be. His plumage was a lovely red colour and his tail a nice green. The classic rooster.

I squinted at Big D as I finished dressing a fox pelt. I tilted my head to the side, trying to make sense of what he was doing.

Is—is my fucking chicken doing a training montage? I watched his incredibly crisp kicks for a little longer.

I shook my head. *Nah, I've just spent too long alone and I'm humanizing him a bit too much. Or maybe it's just cultivator world bullshit.*

I returned to my work while humming. I had a few good things to sell, and these fox pelts were really nice.

All right, next time I see Basil, I'll hunt him down. The damn fox puppet always annoyed me in the Before, and I'll be damned if I let him laugh at me.

□

It had taken three days. Three days of diligent, nonstop training. Refining his kicks. Sharpening his spurs. He was ready. The image in his mind of the wicked one's movements were set. He knew how it would fight.

Tonight, he, Bi De, would slay the wicked Basi Bu Shi.

Tonight, it would be either glorious victory or his death—either were acceptable. If he fell in battle, it merely proved that he was unworthy of his Great Master's continued sufferance.

He went into the night, hopping from tree branch to tree branch in silence. The lands of Fa Ram were impossibly vast, yet he persevered. Into the northern forest he ventured, where the wicked one had fled every night, scampering away from his Great Master's wrath. There, he found his quarry.

Basi Bu Shi. Rage seized his heart at the beast, walking upon the Great Master's domain like it owned it. It was utterly unacceptable. He would have the beast die a thousand deaths for its arrogance!

And arrogant it was. It stalked but did not realise others could stalk it.

In silence, Bi De descended from his perch, striking from the heavens against this beast from hell. His legs lashed with great strength and his enemy snarled in pain. His spurs bit deep, penetrating flesh, but it was no killing blow. The creature's fur and pelt deflecting some of the damage.

He struck again to press his advantage, but Basi Bu Shi was worthy of his hellish name, the lithe creature shot away with the deep scar in its flesh leaking blood profusely.

Bi De saw it in his mortal enemy's eyes. The spark of *awareness.* The spark of *fury.*

This one . . . this one *knew* too. It was not as the hens were. It was as Bi De himself was.

His foe did not run.

It *knew* he had not called his Great Master.

It *knew* it could lay him low here.

Their silent dance began.

His legs and spurs cut through the night air as he flipped and dashed around his enemy's razor teeth and tearing claws.

It tried to strike him with its paws, to foul his footing and drive him to the earth, but he had grown wise to these beast's tricks, dodging around its wicked claws and leaping away from its snapping teeth.

The two whirls of red chased each other through the forest, bouncing off the mighty trunks and leaving gouges on the forest floor.

Bi De felt triumph. He was equally matched with the beast though all his instincts screamed it was his absolute superior. Its nose was slashed open, one of its ears a ragged mass. His spurs ran crimson.

But the wicked one had more tricks. It raised its limb to strike another blow, sending Bi De's wings snapping out to redirect the momentum.

He saw the gleam of satisfaction too late.

The paw slammed down instead, launching the wicked one forwards, and the vile Basi Bu Shi became a streamer of red trailing behind an open maw.

Teeth crashed down upon his wing. The wicked one shook its head savagely and then threw him across the clearing to slam into a tree.

It was pain like no other. He nearly cried out—he nearly summoned his Great Master.

But he refused.

This was his test, and he refused to fail.

He staggered to his feet, his legs shaking with the effort.

Basi Bu Shi drove him to the earth with a mighty paw. His head slammed into the forest floor, the smell of blood and dirt filling Bi De's nostrils. Basi Bu Shi laughed over besting the Great Master's disciple. He savoured his victory.

Bi De knew only shame as he lay there, pinned to the base earth. He could not return his Great Master's blessings. He could not ever repay him. All Bi De could do is stare up at the night sky in torment.

The enormous crescent moon loomed in his vision. It was his favourite phase of the celestial object. He always contemplated it when it showed its most perfect form. It looked somewhat like his master's mighty spur—or his own useless, weak ones.

Ah, how he wished for a mighty weapon to slay the wicked.

The Crescent Moon loomed.

Bi De, in his last moments, contemplated the lunar glory.

Bi De, in his last moments, *understood.*

He guided his energy and intent true. Blades of light, pure as the moon above, sprung from his limbs.

[Rising of the Crescent Moon]

His body rose from its prone position, and he ascended as surely as the moon. The wicked one could not contain him, its paw hurled back from the force. The blade struck true, gouging out one of the *foul spawn's* eyes as he flipped in the air.

The enemy shrieked in pain, its very soul burned by the righteous, heavenly blades he now bore.

He hung in the sky, under the moon's celestial light, gazing down upon his enemy.

All things that rise, fall.

[Descending Lunar Fangs]

It was inevitable, as true as the sun, the moon, and the stars set in the sky, so too did he once more descend to the base earth, carrying the weight and glory of heaven with him.

Both of his glimmering spurs buried themselves in the neck of the red one—this unsightly *Basi Bu Shi.*

[Wheel of the Crescent Moon]

His legs split apart, once more throwing him into a flip, the white energy formed a ring-like afterimage around him and parted his mortal enemy's head from its shoulders.

He landed gracefully once more upon the earth.

His enemy's head thumped to the ground behind him. Then, Bi De collapsed onto his side, exhaustion overcoming him. His breath came in great gasps, as he greedily tried to suck in air. He turned once more to his enemy—as if the monster would rise again, even without his head.

The wicked beast did not move. His body remained still.

He—he had done it. Bi De had completed his Master's task!

He roared his victory to the heavens, praising the moon for its guidance. The air reverberated. His own females burst into surprised clucks and began calling too when they heard his victorious voice.

His Great Master burst into the clearing a moment later, worry and fury in his eyes.

↔

I stumbled to a stop after once again being called out of bed. Big D being this far away when he screamed was worrying. Had he been taken by the fox? I moved as fast as I could and found the source. The small clearing was cut up from something, and there was Big D, looking pleased as punch, standing on the mangled and beheaded form of Basil Brush.

What the fuck?

↔

His Great Master, as always, lavished affection upon him. His broken wing was bandaged, his disheveled feathers combed, and his wattles rubbed in a most pleasing way. His Great Master praised him, commending his strength in no uncertain terms, while his Lord carried him in his arms.

He was delivered back to the coop and fed full sprigs of Heavenly Herbs. His Great Master commanded him to rest and heal.

He was a good disciple of his Great Master. He had passed his test and was now granted guardianship of Great Fa Ram, trusted to hold faith for his Lord while he braved the world.

CHAPTER 4

NOTHING BUT A HOUND DOG

A warm wind blew through the little village of Hong Yaowu, at complete odds with the cold chill going down the young woman's back.

There were many ways Hong Meiling had expected her day to go. As the village chief's daughter, she had many tasks to fulfill. Watching over the children, collecting herbs, making medicine, tending to whoever got hurt. It was often a hard job, but it was one she enjoyed. She loved her village and her family.

She had not been expecting . . . *this.*

She had been reading a medical scroll when the scent came to her, seemingly carried on the breeze. The fragrance belonged to a young man. It was a strange quirk of birth that a mortal girl like her could smell Qi, but she'd had the ability all her life. He had the stench of Qi about him, thicker and headier than she'd ever smelled before. He was even more powerful than the last time she had smelled him—when he'd shared a meal with her father after inquiring about how they grew their rice.

That had been a strange visit. She had only caught the tail end of the meeting, as she was off in the forest collecting mushrooms. He'd seemed tired and twitchy, with bags under his eyes. A curiosity. He was gone that very day, headed off to the end of the road, far past where anybody else from the Empire had settled.

But he was back again now. Curious, she had gone to see the young man, wondering what he was doing out here. Had he come to meditate in the hills and now was leaving? She couldn't imagine any cultivator staying out here for long. There was nothing of value to them here in the Azure Hills.

When the children's ball struck the tall, broad-shouldered boy pulling a loaded wagon with more ease than an ox, her heart had leapt to her throat. Mud coated his clothes. All knew that cultivators did not suffer such things. She still remembered many years ago, when she and her father had travelled to the city, the contemptuous ease with which a cultivator had slain a beggar child for having the gall to get in his way.

When little Xian had rushed to retrieve his ball, she rushed after him, desperate to beg for her little brother's life.

Instead, the young man had started laughing. He looked so much different than when she had first seen him, his eyes wide open and sparking with merriment.

He gave back the children's ball . . . then joined them in the mud pit.

The cultivator, for that was the only thing the young man could be, cackled as he danced through the mud dodging the children of the village who threw themselves at him in an attempt to knock him into the wallow. He gently diverted them into the muck with wet splats or picked them up and carried them around the pit, tickling them all the while.

Meiling was *very* confused.

He had steadily drawn an audience and more children. At first, the adults were wary, but now most had wandered off or sat around the edges smiling at the silly lad and the kids.

"Ha-ha! You're a thousand years too early to defeat me!" he laughed at them, hands on his hips. "My *chicken* is mightier than all of you!"

The children shrieked in outrage, and her dear little brother turned to her.

"Meimei! Meimei! Help us, Big Sister Meimei!" he pleaded. The cultivator's eyes snapped to her.

Which sealed her doom.

Not in the traditional sense of a girl being doomed by a cultivator, for she was no beauty, thin and freckled as she was. Many had commented on the unfortunate speckles that spread across her nose and cheeks, or the sharpness in her violet thistle-flower eyes.

Instead, a massive, gleeful grin spread across the cultivator's face, and he approached her.

"Oho?" he asked, leering down at her. "Another challenger?"

"So, what if I am?" she demanded of him, unable to back down under the pleading gazes of the children. She had never been very good at refusing when someone baited her. Everybody enjoyed her dagger-like tongue

. . . when it was directed at somebody else. She glared at him and dared him to challenge her again. It was stupid. He was a cultivator, and she was a mere mortal. But she glared back defiantly anyway, for the sake of her little brother.

Then he did something unexpected. He scooped her up, one hand going under her legs and the other cradling her back. There was no effort to his movement—it was as if she weighed nothing.

She flushed as she was brought into strong, firm arms . . . and then the cultivator unceremoniously jumped into the mud pit with her, holding her tightly enough that she couldn't get away. She normally liked the feeling of the squelching mud. She enjoyed catching frogs with her little brother, especially the way their little cheeks puffed up.

However, that was something she prepared for. She rarely just *jumped* in. Especially in her clean clothes.

After she had just taken a bath yesterday.

She had no idea what "*Ca Wa Bun Ga*" meant, but as she felt the mud slop into her clothes, she saw red.

"You wretched, pig-headed *shit monkey*!" she howled, ignoring the fact that she was surrounded by children, and launched herself at the boy, who was laughing so hard he had doubled over. Meiling slammed into a solid body, and there was a brief moment where she was paused, unable to shift him. Then the moment passed, and she shoved him over backwards and into the mud. The adults, including her own father, found the entire situation hilarious.

The children cheered for their champion, and the cultivator dashed around the mud pit while she chased after him.

→

"Meiling the hellion!" her father teased her as she prepared dinner, bare hours after managing to wash most of the mud off in the river. She stuck her nose up in the air contemptuously, refusing to rise to the ribbing. He kept chuckling, and the rest of the ladies tittered at her expression.

They were to have dinner with *that bastard*, and she was mightily displeased. Well, most of the village was going to be having dinner with him, but they, as the chiefs of this small village, would have to host *the bastard* in their *home*.

At least *that bastard* had provided two deer and several rabbits for them.

Gods, she hated the cultivator and his strong arms and his cute grin—geh! No! She shook her head to clear away the treacherous images her mind provided for her.

What was worse, nobody believed her that he was powerful either. "Sure your nose isn't off, Meimei?" they'd asked. For no cultivator got into a *mud fight with children* or went and made friends with peasants.

Everybody else, at first vigilant, slowly relaxed. Even her father had calmed down, but she could still see that her father's eyes flicked towards the cultivator occasionally.

She had started to doubt herself. Did he just have some kind of Qi-filled plant on him? He smelled earthy and pure, but her nose had never steered her wrong before. She briefly contemplated attempting to dose him with a laxative. Hong Yaowu was known for its medicine, and she was a dab hand at her craft. But if he was a cultivator, she stayed her hand. He might not mind the mud, but that might be too far.

He would expose his wicked nature soon enough, like the one from the city—or worse, the reaving bandit Sun Ken.

Aside from her scattered thoughts, the dinner preparation was fortunately uneventful. There were tables set up in the middle of the village, and a great amount of food would be there for everyone to enjoy. Her family too would be setting out on their regular visit to Verdant Hill, once every two months.

Meiling kept a close eye on him, but the cultivator spent most of his time playing go with the men and losing spectacularly. The white stones on the table were dominated by their black counterparts. She had never seen somebody quite so *bad* at the game.

She had felt uneasy when her best friend, Meihua, had brought them tea. Meihua was everything she wasn't. A classical beauty, with flawless pale skin, midnight-black hair, and full red lips. Meiling, being the younger by a year, was even stuck with the diminutive nickname Meimei, while Meihua was never called by anything but her name. When she went to Verdant Hill, men stopped and stared, struck dumb by Meihua's loveliness. She had received marriage proposals from over fifty men but was determined to marry the clerk Tingfeng.

Surely, the cultivator would accost her. In all the stories, they were as beasts upon beautiful women!

"Oh? You're getting married soon? Congratulations! Wait a sec—here. I don't know If I can make the wedding, but that's no excuse not to give a gift!"

Instead of accosting her, he gave Meihua a beautiful fox pelt, congratulated her on her upcoming marriage—

And then turned back to the go table, laughing as he lost again. Weren't cultivators supposed to be skilled at everything, true geniuses? Old Man Lao, the cultivator's opponent, was *terrible* at go.

"Hey, Jin, Jin! Come catch frogs with us!" Her little brother demanded, as soon as the game was done.

"Frog catching, huh?" The cultivator asked, rubbing an imaginary beard. "Behold, you witness a master of the frog-grasping palm!" He rose to his feet, his arms crossed, and the children cheered.

Then the cultivator dropped to all fours, hopping like one of the amphibians they were about to torment. The children eagerly copied him, croaking and hopping all the way to the stream. It was absolutely absurd. Any tension lingering within the adults and her father dissipated as the men and women shook their heads in amusement.

. . . Maybe her nose *was* playing tricks on her.

↔

Man, that Meimei girl was glaring really hard at me, like an offended cat. It was pretty cute, the way her freckled nose scrunched up. *Maybe* I had gone a bit too far, but I had been happy to play with other people. It was fun to actually talk to someone who wasn't a rooster.

The look on her face had been hilarious when I dumped her in the mud, though.

Totally worth it.

These dumplings were really good too. Super tasty, and I was scarfing them down. The food I ate on the farm was passable, but with all of my stuff still growing and barely established, it hadn't been particularly tasty fare.

This was my first meal not made by my hands in nearly six months. I closed my eyes and chewed contentedly, savouring it for a moment . . . before shoving in another mouthful.

→

It was the dead of night when Meiling woke up, drenched in a cold sweat.

There was something out there. It stunk of old blood and death. The scent lingered mixed with hate and malice. The terror was nearly overwhelming, sending shakes down her back as the wicked Qi invaded the village. She felt like she was about to vomit. She curled into a ball, wheezing and choking like she was drowning.

And then, it was suppressed. She smelled the cultivator's Qi as it shoved the bestial Qi backwards, repelling the blood and rot with the scent of freshly tilled soil and harvested rice. It surrounded her, overwhelming her senses, and dispelled the fear and dread as if they were never there.

She heard the stirring from the cultivator as he rose from his rest. Then came the rattling of the door when he went to confront whatever was coming closer to the village.

Meiling, her legs shaking, followed. Just what was he up to? What was he going to do?

She had to know.

↔

I woke up with an itchy feeling crawling down my spine. I could feel *some* sort of predator nearby, but without Big D to sound the alarm, I hadn't acted. Groggily, I rolled myself off the futon and stretched.

Eh, might as well take care of it. It was pretty close, and while I was confident these people would probably be able to handle it, I was awake now anyway. I grabbed my shovel from my possessions, wandering out of the house. The fires were still smouldering a little, and I smiled at them. Today had been fun. Childish as hell, but fun. And those dumplings Meimei had made were *really* good.

Although, when I told her that, she scrunched up her nose at me. That girl was too easy to tease.

I ambled into the forest, following my gut feeling, until I found a wolf. It was a big, mangy thing, with red skin showing through the gaps in its fur.

Oh man, he's a biggun, ain't he? Needs his toenails trimmed too. I thought to myself.

It snarled and pounced.

↔

She followed the cultivator through the winding forest, the scent of blood battling against the smell of earth. She could barely hear because of how hard her heart was pounding, but the cultivator didn't seem to notice her footfalls.

At last, he came to the source of the horrific Qi, and her blood turned to ice.

A Reaper Wolf. It was unmistakable, with its razor claws and slashing teeth. But what truly horrified her was the black mane it sported, ridging its back with midnight fur.

It wasn't just *a* Reaper Wolf; it was *the* Reaper Wolf. The ultimate form of its kind. The Butcher of the North. The Caravan Reaper. *The Wicked Blade.*

It had been around these parts for nearly three hundred years and had even killed *cultivators*. None who had tried to slay it ever came back.

What was it doing *here*?! Were they all to die tonight?

She cowered behind a tree and prayed for Jin's soul, for him coming face-to-face with a monster that had songs written about its terrible deeds.

The Reaper Wolf moved faster than her eyes could see, pouncing on him in a storm of bladed claws.

The shovel met it.

Klang!

It struck the fell beast in the center of the head. The wolf's eyes exploded out of their sockets. Its forehead caved in, as its head was driven into the soil.

It twitched once on the ground and stilled, dead in a single strike.

She gaped stupidly at the scene. The cultivator yawned. "Bad dog," he muttered and rubbed at his eye.

The Wicked Blade hadn't even whimpered as it died. A life that ancient and that foul . . . simply ended in an instant. Her village was saved from a monster that could butcher them all like it was an afterthought.

Meiling watched as he took no blood, nor its teeth, nor the Wicked Blade's Qi laden core. Instead, his shovel went to work digging a hole big enough for the corpse, which he used to bury it in moments.

"No hard feelings, okay, buddy?" he muttered to the mound, while green Qi swirled around his hand and disappeared into the soil. She thought she could hear a wail for a brief moment in her head, and then the lingering scent of blood vanished.

She was still standing there in shock when he started walking back to the village. The cultivator squinted at her crouched form when he passed the tree she had been hiding behind.

"Need a ride back?" he asked her.

Her mouth moved before she could think it through. "The last time you gave me a ride you threw me into a mud pit," she shot back, sounding more annoyed than terrified.

Jin chuffed in amusement and then gestured forwards. "Well, come on, dangerous wildlife out here," he said. "You can make me some dumplings again, as thanks for escorting you home."

She scoffed as if she found the idea distasteful, much to Jin's amusement. Her legs were rattling like windblown branches, yet she managed to stand, wobbling after Jin.

She turned one last time to look at the overturned dirt.

There were fresh grass shoots already sprouting out of it.

Her father was waiting for them when they got back to her house, worry clear on his face. "What happened?" he asked, his eyes shooting to the cultivator. "All of the animals kicked up such a fuss!"

"Eh, just a wolf," Jin replied with a shrug, sounding unconcerned.

"Yeah," Meiling agreed. "Just a wolf, Father."

He looked at her, his racing heart calming down. He glanced between the two of them, at the fact that neither looked particularly concerned, and nodded.

Just a wolf *indeed.*

CHAPTER 5

VERDANT HILL

Jin, contrary to Meiling's expectations once again, did not leave first thing in the morning to run ahead to Verdant Hill. He could have just left them in the dust.

Instead, he helped stack crates of mushrooms with her little brother clinging to his back like a monkey. Meihua's father had even given him an ox to borrow for their trip to the town so that he wouldn't have to pull his own cart. Thanks to his help, the preparations were sped up considerably, and they were on the road, a caravan bound for Verdant Hill.

"So, what *did* happen last night, Meimei?" a boy with an unfortunate resemblance to a monkey asked as they walked.

"A wolf, Gou Ren," she replied bluntly. Of course, nobody believed her. Even her father was giving her pointed looks and smirking whenever he caught her looking at Jin.

He hadn't believed that they had *just* found and chased off a wolf. He thought they'd snuck off to do . . . *other* things, like kissing in the moonlight or something equally ridiculous. It didn't help that Jin had just completely ignored her when she told him her proper name and just continued to call her Meimei.

"Ah, our darling *Young Mistress* has finally discovered the joys of womanhood," another boy gasped with exaggerated pride. Yun Ren, Gou Ren's elder brother, wiped an imaginary tear from the corner of his fox-like eyes. His ponytail bounced with every step. "After flaying every man she's ever met, she's finally found one that can tame her cold heart."

She glared viciously at both of them. Gou Ren held up his hands in defeat, fleeing to the front of the caravan, while Yun Ren just kept laughing at her. The ass. The Xong brothers were nearly family— but family only in the annoying little-brother way, the both of them.

And over the years, she had spent entirely too much time patching them up after their bone-headed schemes.

"Watch your drinks," she told him pleasantly, flashing him a smile that promised painful retribution. Which one should she go with? The laxative? Or just the bitterroot?

Yun Ren smirked . . . until his eyes took on a more serious cast. "Do . . . you want us to take care of him?" he asked, eyeing Jin, who probably outmassed him twice over— in addition to being a cultivator. Yun Ren had never even used his sword outside of training with it.

That was a fight that he certainly wouldn't win.

"It's fine," she grumbled, knowing that saying that just made her look more guilty. Yun Ren shrugged and sped up, following his younger but taller brother.

"You could have helped me," she said blandly to Meihua, who throughout the entire exchange had stayed silent, focused on her sewing. Her friend was as prim and proper as always, looking fresh out of some sort of painting, not a single hair out of place.

Meihua just smiled a little knowing smile that said she didn't believe a word of her denials and said nothing.

"I like him!" her little brother opined. Of *course* her little brother liked him— he'd played in the mud and caught frogs with them. As far as Xian was concerned, he was family already.

She snorted and buried her face back into the medical scroll she'd been reading. As if any man would want to do *that* with bony and freckly Meiling.

She saw—out of the corner of her eye—as a wagon began to tip when its rear wheel got stuck in a hole. Her eyes widened, and she opened her mouth to shout a warning to Gou Ren, but she never needed to. Casually, Jin shifted his position from where he was talking to Meihua's father over to the loaded wagon, and with one hand lifted the back end out of the hazard without breaking his stride. He'd made it look like it weighed nothing at all.

He winked when he caught her looking.

She scowled and looked away, hints of red blossoming on her cheeks. *Bastard.*

□

For two days had the Great Master been gone, and for two days had Bi De kept his Great Master's coop safe. None had so far dared to challenge him, and no more of Basi Bu Shi's ilk slunk around in the shadows. He held a twig in his beak that had been split many times to form bristles and used it to sweep away the dirt that threatened to invade where it wasn't wanted. Soon, he would be able to use his wings for this, but not yet. His Great Master's medicines were most potent, turning what should have been a life-ending injury into a mere inconvenience. Loathe as he was to have consumed such rare reagents, his Great Master's beneficence was impossible to refuse.

He stalked among his master's crops and tried to empower them as his Great Master did. His efforts were laughable compared to his Lord's. That only revealed the truly vast gulf between them. On the first day, merely attempting to infuse the herbs with his Qi had sent him to the ground, gasping and dizzy from exertion, with barely enough strength to eat the lesser beasts that came to try and eat them. His master could work the entirety of Great Fa Ram without effort. Truly, his Great Master's power was beyond his ability to comprehend.

He stalked back to his own pavilion, in the place with all the females. They were . . . *disappointing* to him in some ways. They held not the same spark as he, despite being in the Great Master's presence and occasionally consuming some bit of Heavenly Herb.

He wondered why, yet could not come up with a satisfactory answer. It was something to meditate upon, certainly.

He shook himself and attended once more to Great Fa Ram.

□

Verdant Hill crested the horizon. It was a town of about two thousand people, on top of a hill. Unlike Meimei's little village of about fifty, Verdant Hill had some impressive walls and a palace-looking administrative building in its center.

The people of our little caravan were surprised that we'd made such great speed. Usually, they arrived late on the second day, but this time we'd gotten into Verdant Hill early in the morning of the second day. The distance itself wasn't too far, but you had to cross an extremely hilly section to actually get here. Though to call them merely hills was a disservice. They were damn near mountains, and the carts had to travel single file on the road.

Thinking on it, the geography here was really *weird*. Impossible landmarks were the norm. Lots of potholes on the road too.

I may have to fix that, if only for my sake.

Our party was composed of Meimei, her little brother, Xian, and her father, who was *also* named Xian. They were the village chiefs, and they made medicine. Their village's name, *Hong Yaowu*, even translated to something like "Medicine Warehouse." The girl who was going to be getting married soon was Yao Meihua. Her dad, Yao Che, was the village blacksmith, a monster of a man who was as tall as I was. The last two with us were the Xong brothers, Yun Ren and Gou Ren. They were the sons of the village's best hunter; they were supposed to help unload the mushrooms and other goods.

It was nice to talk to people again. Everybody was pretty friendly and seemed interested in what I had been up to. I actually enjoyed the trip. It was a nice walk through the countryside.

The guards seemed to know Meimei's father, and so they waved us in without any trouble. I bowed to Hong Xian in thanks for letting me borrow the ox . . . even though I hadn't actually needed it.

It was the thought that counted though, and I greatly appreciated his generosity. We all agreed to meet up at the inn later. We would be staying a night at least, and maybe another night too. We all departed at the same time after stabling the animals and locking away our carts. Meimei was instructed to bring a bottle of what I assumed was alcohol to "Brother Bao" by her father, while the rest of the group went off to sell mushrooms at the exchange.

Well, first things first. Time to—hopefully—find out what the weird root was. It was still back at the farm, but I had drawn a reasonably good rendition of it.

I could feel Meimei's eyes on me as I set off. We were heading in the same direction.

"You're headed to the Archives too?" I asked her.

She looked at me suspiciously for a moment, then nodded.

There was a pause in the conversation as we walked. Meimei was looking at me with a considering glare, until she spoke. "What are you looking for at the Archives? I may be able to help you find it," she offered.

"Trying to get out of making dumplings for me, Meimei?" I teased. The girl rolled her eyes, but I could tell she was amused. "I take it you're familiar with the Archives, then?"

"Father used to be an Imperial clerk before he had to go back to the village and take Grandfather's place when he passed. I spent a lot of time in the Archives, when the Xong brothers didn't need tending," she replied, and once more she had her "watching cat look" on her face, gauging my reaction.

"Great!" I replied, and for some reason she looked shocked at my statement. "I don't know what *exactly* I'm looking for, but I sketched it down. A root of some kind. I wanted to know what it is."

I took out the picture and the notes I had made and handed it over to Meimei.

She was still looking a bit confused as she accepted my drawing as we reached the Archives. It wasn't particularly large, but his Imperial Majesty had decreed that every town and city have one. Along with a collection of standardized books, scrolls, and some more local knowledge, it also had all land and tax records along with everything else an archive should have.

"Well . . . come on, then, I know the First Archivist, so we can start with him," Meimei muttered, looking at my drawing. "I'm not *supposed* to be able to look at the advanced scrolls, now that my father isn't part of the Imperial clerks anymore . . . but Uncle Bao lets me anyway."

"Ah, Lady Hong Meiling, she with friends in high places," I sang to her, putting on my most "courtly" voice, and Meimei actually laughed out loud, smiling brightly—before she realized what she was doing, and her smile dimmed. She kept a cute little smirk, though. *Score.* I wondered if she would have dinner with me—although dating here worked kind of different, I think. If people dated at all.

We ascended the stairs, the guards once more just waving Meimei through. They gave me an odd look, then just shrugged and resumed their watch with bored expressions.

"Uncle!" Meimei called, and we were rewarded with a happy gasp from a man behind a desk.

Uncle Bao was . . . well, *bao* shaped. He was a very rotund, balding man who looked jolly, with many smile lines on his face.

"Mei'er! Daughter of my brother Xian! It's so good to see you again!" he exclaimed and waddled around his desk so he could embrace Meimei, who—contrary to my expectations—seemed happy with the treatment.

"It's good to see you too, Uncle. Father sends his regards and prays that you meet him at the usual place."

Bao beamed at her, accepting the alcohol jug she handed him. "I shan't miss it, my little Mei'er!"

He then turned to me, his eyes suddenly piercing. "And who is this, standing before me here?" he demanded of me.

I smiled at him and made the proper gesture of courtesy. *Thank god for Rou's memories. Otherwise, I would've fucked up which hand went where.*

"This one's name is Rou Jin," I said, using the reversed name I had on my documents. "I greet you, First Archivist, and hope that you are in good health."

"He's a friend of the family, Uncle," Mei whispered to him. "Father trusts him."

The piercing quality of his stare suddenly went away, and Bao's smile came back.

"Well, for my brother to trust you with his daughter, you must be a man of virtue!" Meimei's face went red, but she didn't say anything. "I'm guessing you want to use the archives, Mei'er? You know I can't let you into the advanced scrolls. But I'll be here in the back room if you need me, and I'll be joining your father tonight! Mark my words well!"

Bao winked at her and then waddled away. Meimei picked up a key he put on the desk.

"To the Archives?" she asked.

The guards ignored us again as we walked up and opened the locked door. The room was both big and cramped at the same time, with shelves absolutely stuffed with scrolls lining the walls. The organization threw me for a loop, because it was all written in some kind of shorthand that I didn't know. The difference between the stuff open to the public and the things locked away, I guess.

"The ones for herbs are over here," Meimei said, expertly navigating the shelves and rows. With a shrug, I followed her lead, to a large section near the back.

Over fifty scrolls lay lined up neatly on the shelf.

This is going to take a while, isn't it?

We grabbed the first of the scrolls on herbs and sat down to read.

↔

Jin is strange, Meiling thought as she looked at him from the corner of her eye. Not even "strange for a cultivator," but just odd. This was the most pleasant interaction she had with a man not from her village in years. A lot of the men willing to look past her reputation and meet with her grimaced when they found out that she could read the Courtly Characters or scoffed when they heard about her time in the Archives. Useless for a woman to know, they said.

Never mind that she was the best at making medicine within fifty li. Never mind that she knew how to cure the shaking fevers, to set broken bones, and to drain a cut to stave off infection. *And* she knew how to cook and clean and mend, so she *knew* her womanly duties. She had taken care of her household ever since her mother's passing.

But the Archives just sealed the deal. Wasting time, people called it.

They saw only gloomy Meiling. An impudent woman with a tongue like a knife spitting metaphorical, and sometimes *literal*, poison at their "good sons." The itching powders didn't even last that long! She made sure to retaliate only *after* they insulted her appearance or scoffed at her knowledge.

Jin had looked *impressed* by her. *Happy* even. And he'd willingly sat down with her amongst the mass of scrolls as they got to work.

Now they were sitting shoulder to shoulder.

He smelled of earth and the harvest to her.

The memory of the Jin in the mud pit warred with her memory of him slaying the Wicked Blade.

He was surprisingly good company. He seemed to trust her judgement.

Maybe . . . maybe he isn't *like those other cultivators?*

□

I yawned and stretched. It was starting to get dark out, today had been a bust so far. Nothing in the scrolls looked even remotely like what I had, and we had gone through most of the scrolls on herbs.

"C'mon, Meimei, we'll look again tomorrow. I've got some stuff to do in the morning first, though. Gotta sell my furs and pick up some more supplies."

Meimei yawned too. She seemed annoyed that we hadn't found anything.

We started putting the scrolls away, but I stopped when something caught my eye. A scroll Rou had read before. *Contemplations of the Flame Bud*, it was titled.

It was a tale of two men.

They each find a Pearlescent Flame Bud. It had taken a thousand years for the flower to bloom, gather its power for the sole act of reproducing, and spread its pollen on the aetheric currents.

One of the men, upon finding the flower, is struck with its beauty. He contemplates the flower and the way it delicately draws in energy. He considers the way its seed disperses on the currents of the world, travelling far and wide to find a partner. He observed the cycle of its life, and when it finally withered and began storing energy to make its seeds, he thanked the flower for its wonderous life and left, gaining little from the encounter.

The other man, upon finding this flower, cackles with joy. He tears it out of the ground, root and all. He shoves it into a spirit furnace and burns away everything of the flower he deems superfluous, concentrating a sole aspect of its essence. He then makes a pill out of it to consume, greedily devouring its essence to slightly improve his resistance to fire.

Obviously, this wasn't the way it was really told. It had lots more flowery language, and to cultivators, the moral of the story was basically "YEAH, SNORT THAT MAGIC FLAME FLOWER, THE OTHER GUY IS DUMB AND WEAK."

Rou had agreed with that particular interpretation.

My only thought after remembering the story was, "Maybe all those contemplation guys *actually* ascend. While *you're* all stuck down here."

I shook my head and finished putting away the scrolls. Meimei returned the key to the Archivist, and we wandered back through the pleasant night to the inn together, just as her father was about to go out.

A massive, shit-eating grin spread across his face when he saw the two of us enter together.

"Did you two have a good day together?" he questioned in a leading tone, loud enough for the rest of the people of their village that were there to hear. They were all sitting together at a table, and when Hong Xian raised his voice, it went dead silent. Meimei flushed crimson, and the two guys, Gou Ren and Yun Ren, *immediately* started asking how her day was.

CHAPTER 6

"YOUNG MASTER," TYPE 19

While a lot of stuff I'd seen wouldn't look out of place in ancient China, the Exchange was not one of those. At least I thought it looked strange. The Exchange was a building where all the merchants gathered, like some sort of ancient mall. The Exchanges were in every town with more than a thousand people, filled with businesses and merchants plying their trades.

I was expecting a marketplace the last time I came here, like something from a history book, instead I got something a lot more structured.

But I guess faster travel and communication—in the form of Artifacts or transmission stones—could make something like this possible.

Shaking my head, I went about my business. First place I went to was Tan Gong's Heavenly Furs. That was a super fucking pretentious name for a dude who dealt in mortal furs. But it was none of my business. There was a small line of people selling things. Some people got shouted out of the line for bringing something of poor quality, while others completed their transactions quickly as if they did this all the time.

The man sitting behind the booth wearing a uniform met me with a frown on his face.

"Ugh. *Another* dirt farmer. Yes, yes, boy. Make it quick. I'm sure you *think* your pelts are worthy of being purchased by our Heavenly Furs company, but we have exacting standards and—my word!"

I had, naturally, ignored his speechifying and brought out the pelts. His eyes bugged out, and he swallowed.

Hey, xianxia tropes were in fine form today. I had some transcendent fox pelts here. Now, the clerk was apologizing for being hasty and wringing his hands, calling me "Good Sir." I guess this was the part where I should start face slapping, for being rude to this expert, but I *really* don't care about all that.

Whatever, dude, you're practically drooling over my stuff. You want to buy it or not?

Of course, I actually just kept my mouth shut with a slight smile on my face while nodding along appropriately while he simpered, even as I imagined just shutting him up. There was nothing to be gained from insulting some random dude manning a counter—

Then he brought his manager out. Who *also* started calling me "Good Sir." And they started making noises of wanting me to have a contract to supply them.

I declined as politely as I could and just sold them the pelts I had.

"If you ever have any other furs to sell, please think kindly of our Heavenly Furs company!" both men said while bowing to me as I made to leave.

Of course I'm going to "think kindly" of you. You're the only gig in town.

The man who bought my planks of wood was considerably more polite. He was a good bloke.

I then went shopping for my own supplies. More sesame oil, sesame seeds, and then I found a guy with some wheat. Apparently, I just hadn't been looking hard enough the first time. *Ah, bread, how I've missed you.* Wouldn't be able to plant it now because fall was going to start soon. After that I got a bunch more veggie seeds, some more barrels, a few more chickens, and a lovely set of cast-iron pans.

I briefly debated getting a pig or a cow but decided against it for now. *Gotta establish the farm a bit better, I think.*

I'd probably be meeting up with Meimei soon, so we could go through the last of the herb guides.

Today was a good day.

My back started itching a little bit as I stepped out of the Exchange and back into the town again. I scratched it absentmindedly.

□

Meiling *had* been having a good day.

Emphasis on *had.*

It had started out well enough. Jin had some business to take care of, so Meiling had decided it was about time to invite Meihua out into the town. They had walked together, arm and arm, enjoying the sights together. Meihua had even brought her a lovely new hairpin, and now they were sitting down to have tea together.

But her sister, in all but blood, uttered foul betrayal.

"So, when is Jin marrying you?" she asked conversationally, just as Meiling had taken a sip from her tea.

Meiling choked as her drink went down the wrong way and started coughing.

"Wha-uh? Not-maybe-nev—*Meihua*!" Meiling gasped, and her friend laughed merrily, the sound like tinkling chimes. She glared at her friend. "Not you too," she whined. "I'm getting enough of that from Father! We haven't done *anything* either, so wipe that knowing look off your face, you vile woman!"

"Oh, but you snuck out in the night with him," Meihua sing-songed.

"Meihua, *please*," she begged, her face red.

"All right, I'll stop. All attack, no defence with you. You *do* like him, though, don't you?"

Short, brown hair. Vibrant green eyes. That stupid grin. Her lips quirked up into a tiny smile.

"Oh, dear," Meihua said, looking at her fondly. "You are *smitten*, Meimei. Almost as bad as I am for my darling—"

"Shaddup," she grumbled back and drained the rest of her tea. Meihua giggled again, but obligingly finished up as well and needled her no further.

"Come on, I can't deal with you anymore," Meiling griped, but Meihua just smiled knowingly. "Let us get you to your *darling*—"

Suddenly, there was an acrid tang on the wind. The foul odour slid under the smell of earth she'd grown accustomed to. Blood and oil. An insidious, slimy thing, full of ill intent.

Qi.

The third time she had smelled it *not* coming out of a plant in so short a time.

Her head whipped around, and she saw the man. He was dressed in fine clothes, with two men standing on either side of him.

Her gut churned, and her spine tingled, as she got a very, very bad feeling about him. The same feeling she'd gotten, just before the man in the city killed that beggar child. His head started turning in her direction, and she looked away.

"Meihua. This way." Meihua noticed her discomfort and obliged. They exited the small outdoor seating area swiftly. Meiling practically dragged her friend behind her through an alley on the way to the palace.

"Meimei, what's going—"

"Qi. Cultivator. I know you think my nose is off on Jin, but *please* trust me on this," she interrupted Meihua.

Meihua sighed. "All right. But I think you've read too many stories. Would someone dare do something like that?"

Meiling grimaced and kept walking to the palace.

"I hope we never find out."

□

Meimei was looking off when we met up again at the Archive, all tense and angry. I asked her what was wrong but got a snappy "nothing" in response and decided to leave it.

The next few hours passed in silence, and we didn't find anything on my root. I wasn't bothered, and the hours of reading had bled some of the tension out of Meimei's shoulders.

"It . . . wasn't nothing."

I gestured for her to continue.

"I can smell Qi."

Huh, so that's how she followed me.

". . . and there's a cultivator in Verdant Hill. He smells like oil and blood. He had nasty, almost evil, eyes too."

Well, that's not good.

"I'm probably just being paranoid . . . but I'm worried about Meihua. She's in the palace right now, so there should be no problems . . . but . . ."

What? Sure, Meihua is kind of pretty, but would some asshole really try to just . . . take *her?* I poked at Rou's memories. The memories painted an unpleasant picture in my head.

Meimei looked stressed and worried.

"C'mon," I said after we put the scrolls away. "Let's go pick up Meihua and . . . Tingfeng? We'll have dinner together."

She seemed surprised at my offer, her eyes widening a bit at the implied promise of protection. I didn't know if I would be able to fight, but . . . well . . . I'd try, if something did happen. It's the least I could do.

"Fine," she muttered, still looking stressed. That wouldn't do.

"My Lady Hong Meiling, would you do me the honour of dining with me tonight?" I asked with an exaggerated bow.

Her lips quirked up this time, and she gave me a half-hearted glare.

"Of course. Rou Jin, I would be *honoured* to dine with you."

Ouch, I can feel *the sarcasm.*

It didn't take long to reach the palace. Meihua seemed delighted to see us and immediately clasped arms with Meimei while I greeted Tingfeng.

We set off for dinner soon after.

→

"And then she called me—what was it again? Ah! I remember, it was a 'wretched, pig-headed shit monkey?' It was great!"

I slung my arm around Meimei's shoulders and pulled her close while Tingfeng howled with laughter. Meimei rammed her elbow ineffectually into my side. She was turning so red, I thought she might have a stroke.

Okay, maybe I was being a bit overly familiar, but the girl was cute when her face turned red. Besides, while she was elbowing me, she wasn't actually trying to pull away.

"Ah, I remember when she called me a worthless slug, sniffing around a lotus flower!" Tingfeng mused. "She was right, back then, and those words gave me the strength to earn my position if only to prove her wrong."

Tingfeng grinned at Meimei, walking with Meihua arm in arm as they headed back to the inn. Sunset in the town was nice. There was a wonderful breeze flowing through the streets, and I was having fun with new friends for the first time in months. Maybe I was a little drunk on the atmosphere.

It was nice. People were nice. Not everybody was some power-obsessed asshole looking to defy the heavens. Meimei had given up trying to escape and was now just glaring half-heartedly at me—

She suddenly froze and paled.

My back itched.

Three men suddenly appeared in front of us, clearly looking for trouble. We were in a side street, and they'd come out from around the corners, cutting us off beside a small fruit tree and a couple of houses.

Are we getting mugged?

The leader, a man in silks, smiled. "I am Zang Li, Young Master of the Shrouded Mountain Sect. You, girl," he said, pointing to Meihua. "Be honoured. I shall allow you to warm my bed tonight."

I gaped at the sheer audacity. *Seriously? People seriously did this shit? What the hell?!* I could feel myself getting angry just looking at the smarmy fucker. He wanted to pull this shit? But I didn't just launch myself at him. That would be stupid.

Something didn't feel right. My ability to sense other people's Qi wasn't the greatest, but I could tell something was off.

"Do his lackeys have Qi?" I whispered to Meimei. She sniffed and nodded. I could feel how tense she was, from where my hand was on her arm.

"Not much, compared to you," she bit back tersely.

Well, that settled it, then. If these assholes had less Qi than me, then they were *definitely* not part of the Shrouded Mountain. I could remember some of the Sect names, and those guys were supposed to be strong. Besides, I don't think any member of Shrouded Mountain would be caught dead in the Azure Hills.

I took my arm off Meimei.

"No, she won't be doing that," I said simply.

"You dare oppose the Shrouded Mountain Sect?" the cultivator sneered, as if saying that would make me back off.

I scoffed. "You aren't from the Shrouded Mountain Sect. And I doubt they'll be happy about you using their name, buddy."

The cultivator seemed stunned that somebody would openly defy him, freezing at the implied insult and glaring hard at me. What I said seemed to have cut pretty deep, because he grimaced, snapping his fingers. His buddies grinned and drew swords, stalking towards us menacingly.

They twirled their weapons and jumped at me, but hell, even I was more than a match for them. They were certainly slower than that big wolf I'd brained in Hong Yaowu—that poor pup had the mange or something, and it was *still* better than these guys.

I stepped forwards and grabbed both of their heads, weaving my arms around their blades. They barely had time to process the fact I had grabbed them before I slammed them together, their skulls making nasty cracks as they met. I tossed them towards their boss, and he didn't even *try* to catch them. They hit the ground hard and twitched for a moment, before going still. I waited for them to get back up, but they just laid there, out cold. I shook my head and started towards the fuckboy playing at being a Young Master. He was glaring again, his eyes full of anger at my swift defeat of his stooges.

A breath later, Qi exploded around him. It flowed around his body, a sheath of lightning and little drops of darkness.

I paused, a bit worried at the development. Even I could feel that. Hell, I could *see* that.

"You bastard, you're courting death!" he roared. "Behold the technique that slew a cultivator in the Profound Realm! My ultimate spear!"

A chill ran down my spine at his words. The fear came rushing back. But there was no running away now.

[*Heaven Piercing Lance!*]

Oh shit, he's fast—I didn't have time to block. He moved quickly enough that he was just a blur, his fingers aiming for my heart. I gathered my Qi in defence for the first time since I came here. Rou's memories on how to reinforce my body properly came easily.

I *pulled*. I pulled my Qi from my core, from my dantian, and formed a lattice of interconnecting threads in my chest.

I felt solid. Sturdy. I hoped it was enough.

Zang Li came in like a meteor, trailing lightning and black fire. His eyes were deadly and focused. He hit me in the chest, fingers swirling with sharp Qi. My feet dug into the cobblestone street. My Qi . . . it felt like a pump connected to a deep well. My Qi surged and gushed like a broken fire hydrant, swelling up to block the blow.

Zang Li roared, pushing forwards.

His fingers hit my chest and bent backwards—like, *the wrong way* backwards. The Qi sheathing his hands guttered out.

We both stared at his hand for a moment in incredulous shock. There wasn't a mark on my chest. Just his palm and broken fingers pressed against my skin.

He fell back and started screaming, holding his wrist.

The fuck?. . . how much of a shitter can you be?! Profound my ass.

I gave him a good smack for being an idiot, sending him slumping down to the ground. Then I walked forwards and collected his lackeys, slinging them all onto my shoulders. They were pretty light.

"Hey, Tingfeng?" I asked.

"Y-yes?" he choked out.

"Where's the jail?" It wouldn't be able to hold a proper cultivator, but none of these guys were proper cultivators. The man quickly gathered himself.

"Right this way, Brother Jin!" he called out, taking the lead. I raised my eyebrow at the term of respect but didn't say anything otherwise.

I hope I can convince the captain of the guard to just say I was a wandering cultivator. Say I left town after this. I don't want any douche nozzles to come and try to find me in case he has friends.

□

Meiling stared around the street with incredulous eyes as the men went off, heading towards the jail. What was once pristine and well maintained had changed. Grass and flowers had sprouted from around every stone. The tree nearby, preparing for the fall, had grown and blossomed. The wooden buildings closest to the impact point had started growing branches with tiny leaves poking off them.

It looked like the town had been abandoned for nature to reclaim over the course of a hundred years.

Meihua seemed just as stunned as Meiling was. It wasn't every day somebody challenged a man who moved faster than the eye could track to defend your virtue.

"Told you my nose wasn't off," Meiling said, feeling a bit faint.

CHAPTER 7

COUNTRY ROADS

"It was an honour meeting you, Brother Jin." Tingfeng clasped his hands before him. "I pray that you will do us the honour of attending our marriage after the harvest."

I made the appropriate gestures. "I will not miss it, Brother Tingfeng," I said, and I meant it. Meihua and Tingfeng were good people. "But are you sure about these?"

By these, I meant the two young pigs I had been gifted. I had been planning to build some actual pens and maybe a barn first, but one does not refuse generosity lightly. Especially after a man swears to be your brother for the rest of time and then pledges if I ever needed his services he would answer without hesitation. It had been a bit awkward. I had never really been one for grand oaths or displays.

Eh, at least I found the music shop while he'd been haggling with the person who sold him the pigs. A pipa was *kinda* like a banjo . . . right?

"Brother Jin, for what you did for us, I would buy you a thousand more, and it still would not be enough repayment."

I sighed internally. *Well, all right then. I hope Tingfeng doesn't beggar himself by repaying* everybody *as extravagantly as he says he would. He did it even after I said he didn't need to do anything for me.* Fake boy was in prison and shackled with about ten "Spirit Restrainers," some kind of Qi-suppression artifact that only worked if people were low level in their cultivation. People, like me, in the Initiate's Realm. Rou had often been called "barely a cultivator" when he was in the Sect because he'd been so low. Personally, I thought it was a bit overkill for such a weak person, but eh, better safe than sorry I guess.

We were all in reasonably good spirits as we set out back along the road to Meimei's village. Xian Jr. was all over my back again, asking me to show him how I'd defeated the bad guys, and I obligingly showed him several kung-fu moves I remembered from badly translated movies.

He laughed at my "Hooahs!" and "Whatchas!" and little flips.

↔

It was a beautiful night. The moon was bright and full, and lightning bugs danced in the air for what would likely be one of the last times before fall truly set in. If she was a poet, she might have been inspired by the scene. As it was, she was just content with what she could see. They were camped at the foot of one of the hills, and Jin had climbed higher up to get a better view.

"Meimei . . ." her father ventured.

She looked at him, absentmindedly stirring the stew she was cooking for their dinner. "Yes, Father?" she asked.

"I wanted to apologize to you, Daughter. I did not take your words with the consideration they were due and have shamed myself." He bowed his head slightly to her in regret.

While a part of Meiling was hurt that nobody had believed her, the other part understood that what she had said had been simply unbelievable. Jin certainly did not act like any cultivator she'd heard of. "I forgive you, Father."

"What did he get up to, that night in the forest?" he asked after a moment. "*Was* it a wolf?"

Meiling looked up at the sky. "It wasn't a wolf. It was . . . the Wicked Blade."

There was silence as her father stared at her. "The Wicked—are you sure?" he asked anxiously.

Meiling nodded. "I recognized the size and coloration, as well as its patchy fur."

Her father paled and then let out a shaky laugh. "Well, we are truly blessed by heaven, then."

They sat in silence until the stew was done. Meiling scooped up two bowls full and turned to her father. "I'll take this to Jin." She gestured up the hill nearest them. "He isn't too far."

Her father nodded but spoke up when she started to walk away. "Be careful, Meimei. Although . . ." He sighed. "He seems like a virtuous man."

There was an odd inflection to his voice. Half resigned, half hopeful. Years of matchmaking had already failed . . . and this sounded like *permission.*

Her cheeks tinted red at the thought. "We barely know each other, Father," she objected, but her heart wasn't in it. She was curious. Curious about what could produce a man like that.

Her father, however, simply raised an eyebrow at her.

The trek up the hill was relatively easy, even with the trees and rocks in the way while she held onto two bowls of stew. She filled her nose with the night air and opened her ears until she found him. He was sitting on a large rock, instrument in hand.

He had his tongue stuck out in concentration as he tried to play a tune she'd never heard before on a pipa. He was holding the instrument wrong, to the side over his knee, rather than upright, and kept hitting bum notes or messing up the chords.

"Jin, I brought you dinner," she said quietly.

He started, surprised to see her, and then put his instrument to the side. He hopped off the rock, quite a distance, and landed effortlessly. "Thank you, Meiling," he said earnestly.

"So you *did* remember my name," she mock-scolded, and he grinned at her.

"Of course I remembered, Meimei," he said with a smirk, reaching out to take the bowl from her, though he paused and glanced back up at the rock. He chewed his lip. "W-want to come up top with me?" he asked after a moment, seeming suddenly bashful. His face was a little red from the embarrassment.

It was kind of cute.

"I'd love to," she replied, a bit bashful herself. She had little experience besides stories for this kind of thing. He smiled brightly at her acceptance, and he was once more his more sure self. He scooped her up, cradling her against his chest, and jumped. He alighted on the rock with far more gentleness than she'd anticipated.

The view from the top of the rock was spectacular. It jutted out from the hillside into a gap in the trees, allowing one to see out across the rest of the hills, illuminated by the full moon.

They sat in companionable silence on the rock, eating their dinner and taking in the view. She was rather gratified by the small sounds of enjoyment coming from him as he ate.

"What song were you trying to play? I've never heard it before," she finally asked, and his face flushed thoroughly this time.

"It's a song I heard in my . . . *childhood*," he explained. "It's sung in a language, not of the . . . Empire."

"Truly? I thought there was only one language men spoke." Meiling was intrigued, but she supposed it made sense.

"Mmm. The man who taught me this song was from somewhere very, very far away."

There was a cool breeze through the trees, and Meiling leaned up against him for warmth. Jin's arm settled around her waist and pulled her slightly closer.

"Sing it for me?" she asked.

"I'm not a very good singer," he demurred.

"Can't be any worse than your pipa playing," she teased.

Jin laughed. "All right, all right. It's your ears on the line here, anyway."

"Almost heaven, West Virginia . . ."

His voice wasn't beautiful or grand. It did not stir the soul nor cause the land around him to weep. But it was nice enough.

Meiling closed her eyes and relaxed, her fingers entwining with the hand on her stomach.

She didn't know when she went from leaning on him to in his lap.

She also didn't know who started kissing who, but she realized her father had been on to something.

Kissing under the moonlight was *very* nice.

The knowing grins they got when they returned were embarrassing, though. And Meihua wanted *all* the details.

→

I was finally alone again, on my way back to my farm. I would have been home last night, but Meimei insisted that she make me the dumplings she had promised me.

Let me tell you, angry cat Meimei was cute as hell. Meimei, in an apron, smiling and serving me a home-cooked meal, *did things* for me.

She was cute. She was spunky. She had a wicked sense of humour, and I kind of had it bad for fiery girls like that.

But . . . well, I couldn't just ask her out for a date or a fling, things didn't work like that here. I had to court her properly. Which meant thinking about marrying her.

Was I ready for that? Was I ready to just dive headfirst into something like that?

Warm smiles. Laughter. Companionship.

Months of isolation had taken their toll. I had tasted for a brief moment having other humans in my life, and there was no going back. This . . . this was my life now. I was stuck in this world. What was I gonna be? A hermit, or a person? I steeled my resolve. It was a big decision. It would either end in tears or happiness. And if this was to be the rest of my days? I was going to make it a whole and fulfilling life.

But my farm isn't ready for another person, let alone kids. I've got work to do.

That meant so many things. A house. Clothing, more food— I felt a fire in my gut, and I lifted. The cart came off the ground as I just started carrying it. The chickens squalled, Chunky and Peppa oinked in shock, and the miles disappeared under my feet.

Maybe she would say no . . . but I had a project. I had something to work towards.

□

Bi De's eyes snapped open. His Great Master's presence was near.

He swept off the Great Pillars of the Fa Ram. He checked the coop, only to find it spotless. He plucked the few interloping parasites from the Heavenly Herbs. He arranged the seeds he had collected that felt of Qi upon the table within the coop as tribute for his Great Master. He hoped his prizes would be well received as repayment for his Great Master's generosity.

He arranged the corpses of the wicked ones on Great Pillars so that his master would see the trophies he'd acquired. There was a small—yet long—member of Basi Bu Shi's ilk. Another creature was a beast that shared the same form as him but was far less noble, with a hooked beak and grasping talons.

Now he stood, a sentinel at the entrance of the Fa Ram. His females were arranged behind him, clucking and wandering as was their habit.

His Great Master crested the horizon, moving at speed.

Bi De swept into a bow, kowtowing before his Lord, as was only proper.

His Great Master scratched his wattles in greeting and took a deep breath of this Blessed Land's air.

"Good to see you, *Bi De*. Let's get to work," he declared, and brought his disciple up to rest upon his broad shoulder.

CHAPTER 8

EXPERIMENTAL PROCEDURE

Bi De's Great Master was a generous Lord.

He had praised Bi De for the contributions he'd acquired for the Great Fa Ram. The slain enemies were sown back into the earth. His seeds were put away for safekeeping, for there was something known as "winter" on the horizon, and they would be unable to be grown for a while. For his diligence, Bi De was awarded a prize directly from his Great Master's hand.

The Pelt of Basi Bu Shi, fashioned into a powerful artifact. It increased his nobility and majesty tenfold and kept the rain off his feathers. It even imparted a portion of the beast's ferocious speed unto him . . . or at least he thought it did. He was *certainly* faster now than he was when he had killed the wicked thing.

It was also most pleasing to his females.

The Great Master had brought new females for his flock as well as two new potential disciples, or so he assumed. Chun Ke and Pi Pa were odd, hairless things that rooted around and squealed in a most displeasing manner. Pink and wrinkled, they were offensive to his senses. They stank, waddled, and ran around, oftentimes spooking his females.

But the Great Master fed them his leftovers and threw them the dried-out nubs of Heavenly Herbs, treating them well. So, he stayed his spurs and watched to see if they were worthy of ascending past their base selves.

He held no great hope. They were obviously dullards of the highest order, dung upon the land, and unworthy of the Great Master's time and care. But he did not doubt his Great Master. They obviously had *some* use, else his Lord would not have taken them in.

His Lord had also redoubled his own efforts, and once more Bi De watched in awe. Trees fell, one after another, and were transformed into logs and planks.

The rice was swiftly reaped and then set out to dry, the fat heads of the foodstuff looking unbelievably tempting. His physique shone with sweat as he worked with a fire in his eyes, toiling with such speed and prowess Bi De could only stare in awe, wishing for a fraction of that might.

Now, the Great Master was acting with his overwhelming wisdom again, and Bi De was lost.

His Master had built great fires, placing selected stones within them. Bi De could only observe the great work, for whenever he got close he felt the heat overwhelm him from the mere proximity. His Great Master was, of course, not so limited. So, the flame swelled to temperatures Bi De had never experienced. It was so hot it required several days to cool after the fires were quenched, and when they were taken from the fires, the stones were white and brittle. With his bare hands, he crushed them to powder, with the ease Bi De could now crush interlopers. The Great Master collected the powder and added water, clay, and smaller rocks to produce an odd grey sludge, one that flowed sluggishly. The Great Master then moulded and poured the sludge into the shapes he desired.

Several squares were created, as well as tiles. Thus, they were left to dry under the sun.

The next day, when he examined them, he was enlightened.

His Great Master had made liquid stone. Bi De was dumbfounded. Stone could be transmuted to liquid and back again? Truly, his Great Master's wisdom surpassed all others!

↔

I examined the brick carefully, noting the cracks and imperfections. I pulled, and the brick easily came apart in my hands. *Well, let's chalk this one up to a bust.*

Even *with* Qi, my concrete was shit. I would need to do some more testing with ratios. I knew how this was supposed to work . . . mostly. So, I figured I'd probably succeed *eventually* if I kept trucking at it. The Romans used seawater and volcanic ash to get what they wanted, and they'd made some of the best concrete in existence, even when compared to modern materials. I knew where a volcano was . . . but there's no way

I'd be able to get there now. It just wasn't worth it. I'd see how far I could get with Qi and some experiments.

Until then, it looked like we were starting with stone. I'd hoped to get the new house finished before the snow hit . . . but that *probably* wasn't going to happen. I had my drawings, so I knew what I wanted. I had started measuring out foundations, and I had superhuman strength and endurance . . . but I was still only one guy. These things *always* took longer than you thought they would. I had worked on a couple of houses in the Before, and every single one was overtime and over budget. It just happened.

I sighed contentedly, sitting down and dipping my feet into the water of the stream. I took a moment to enjoy the feeling of the setting sun on my bare skin and the sensation of the cooling water to wash away the fatigue of the day.

Man, this place was just perfect. The wind and the sounds of the countryside drifted on the breeze. The grass swayed in the wind. A fish decided to nibble my toe. It was a little carp, with an appetite bigger than his brain. I gently shooed the little fellow away, chuckling at his persistence.

Big D joined me and shouted his usual "Cock-a-doodle-doo!"

"You tell 'em, Big D," I muttered, scratching my guard chicken's head. We sat together as I cuddled my companion, grooming his feathers and scratching his belly, until I found a spot that made his leg start kicking. He was like a guard dog, but just *way* meaner. Really, what kind of chicken could manage to kill a hawk?

I paused. Guard dog. Guard *chicken*. The thought took me. I grinned and got up, getting a plank of wood, a chisel, and some ash.

I debated writing it in English, but I kind of wanted to see how people would react to this. I selected the characters and drew them out on the wood, then took my chisel to the plank. I finished it off with the ash, painting the characters dark black.

I stared at my new signpost.

I couldn't help it. I started laughing.

This is going to confuse visitors so *much.*

I placed my work proudly on the fence's gate and then went for dinner.

I had fish from the river, with Spirit Herb and asparagus. I was trying to experiment more, after experiencing good food again after months without it. It was fun to cook. It was fun to try and make new things, and if anybody ever came over to visit, well, I'd show them some hospitality!

Sure, it took longer and was far more work than the extremely simple meals I'd made before, but I wanted to do it. I *needed* to. I had enough food now; it was time to live a little.

It was delicious. Peppa and Chunky got the leftovers, the little sweethearts clambering into my lap afterwards, nuzzling affectionately.

I eventually crawled into bed and wished for the next day to be just as good as this one.

□

". . . as quoted by witnesses, the travelling cultivator declared that such weak cultivators couldn't be a part of the mighty Shrouded Mountain Sect, much less that one could be a Young Master of it," the guard declared, obviously trying hard not to quake in his boots as he stared at the larger man.

Jian Li Wei's face was stony as he studied the mortal before him. His rage was a quiet thing, gently bubbling beneath the surface. The irritation was compounded by the lack of Qi in this place. His breaths were slightly heavier, and his eyes felt like they were drying out. Both were repulsive experiences.

To be called upon by mortals, claiming that they had captured someone with the gall to declare that they were a part of my Sect? It defied belief. Yet they *had* captured someone from his Sect. He glared at Third Brother Zeng's youngest, Zang Li, chained as he was in suppression seals. Li Wei had nearly exploded at seeing one of their own detained like that, but after hearing the story, he could only conclude it was a kindness visited on them by the unknown cultivator. His rage transferred to the brat who was defeated in the Azure Hills. He could understand the boy's joy at breaking into the Profound Realm, and having a bit of fun exploring, but soiling himself by travelling this far into this weak place to gallivant around the countryside? And then to be caught by mere mortals?! To lose the Shrouded Mountain Sect face like this, this little brat dared?

At least he had the sense to keep his damned fool mouth shut and hadn't compounded his failures.

"We thank the Verdant Hill for so swiftly informing us of this egregious plot against our Shrouded Mountain Sect," he said, lying through his teeth. "We shall take these . . . *imposters* elsewhere."

The mortal bowed his head. "We release them to you, then, Elder of the Shrouded Mountain."

Li Wei gave the pathetic boy a once-over as he was unchained from the suppression seals. His lightning Qi was intact. The Wandering Expert who had defeated him had shown *remarkable* restraint, and for that reason alone he decided not to interrogate the mortals over who they had seen. It would be uncouth to strike at a man after such an altercation. The only thing truly wounded was the boy's pride . . . and his fingers. Barely worth thinking about. If all went well, the Shrouded Mountain would not truly lose face over this incident.

He heaved the boy up over his shoulder, then gestured to the Inner Disciples he had brought with him. They grabbed the other ones, nodding. The boy's lackeys. They'd claimed to be of the Shrouded Mountain, but he didn't know them. These ones were disposable, and they would not speak a word of the Shrouded Mountain Sect's involvement.

The group departed, leaping into the air and bounding over so much land they may as well have been flying. The Inner Disciples peeled off, going to dispose of the two unknown faces. They would have been unable to keep up with him anyway.

In a day, he could cover more distance than a mortal could in a month.

"Before you even open your mouth, you brat, I will not be fighting your battles for you. You have shamed *yourself*," Li Wei snarled at the boy. Zang Li looked appropriately contrite, if slightly ill. It served the little bastard right. "Get revenge on your own, or look away from this matter on your own. Either way, you *will* be returning to the Shrouded Mountain."

"I apologize, Uncle," the little shit mumbled. Good. He would be humbled further later.

□

Internally, it was not Zang Li who was considering his uncle's words. Lu Ban was sweating and concentrating his hardest on stabilizing his technique. At the same time, the expert carried him like a sack, purposefully making the journey uncomfortable. It had been hard enough under the suppression seals, but he was a dragon amongst men and destined for the heavens.

If the expert had done a deeper examination, he would have found out Zang Li was *not* Zang Li. On a cursory glance, his Qi was that of lightning.

Underneath, oil and blood bubbled. The slayer of the Young Master of the Shrouded Mountain squirmed in his stolen skin and rummaged through stolen memories. His Qi worked quickly and subtly, fully consuming the other. The reason he had travelled to the Azure Hills in the first place was to complete his consumption and stabilize his power. The fools who had previously travelled with Zang Li hadn't even noticed the change.

Finally, *finally*, he felt the shroud complete. He let out a breath. *The Twilight Cuckoo's Triumph* settled. Now, only the most powerful of experts, using the most skillful examinations, could decipher his true origins.

His plan was at fruition, though faster than he'd thought would happen. Now, he would have the resources of the Shrouded Mountain, as he'd originally intended when he slew the Young Master and devoured him. He might have gotten a bit carried away while stabilizing his technique, feasting upon his lessers and enjoying the Azure Hills, weak as they were, but now . . .

In the safety of his own mind, Lu Ban swore that he would slaughter all those who stood before him.

This "Jin" would pay dearly.

CHAPTER 9

TITLE DROP

Rice. The staple of the world.

White rice is delicious, but like all grains, it takes a supreme amount of effort to cultivate. After you husk it, you needed to pound it more to get the bran and germ off.

White rice *also* lacks several essential vitamins. By removing the rice's hull, you rid it of vitamin B_1, essential to the human body's process. And then, with a lack of B_1, you get beriberi. Shortness of breath, swollen legs, nerve damage. And finally, death.

A nasty way to go, if you ask me. Like all those infomercials say, a well-rounded diet is key!

I was perfectly capable of swiftly husking and polishing my rice; however, I held myself back, deciding only to do half white and half brown rice. That should give me a good mix of the two for nutritional requirements.

Even with my cultivator-enhanced constitution, fully harvesting my rice was a *lot* of work. Threshing, husking, polishing . . . I was three days in already and still had a lot to go, but then again, my yields had *vastly* exceeded my expectations. I had half an acre of rice on the hill, and I was about half-done preparing it, yet I had already filled *forty-two* 40-kilogram bags—the standard measure here. I would need to make more bags just to hold my stuff!

Truthfully, I didn't know how much I would need for the winter, so it was better to have too much than too little, but *holy hell was this going to be a lot.*

Still, nothing was wasted. The husks and the stalks I would turn into fertilizer or occasionally kindling. I was actually looking *forward* to winter. From Rou's memories, it was significantly milder than the ones I was used to. But then again, I'm used to -20°C with dips down into the -40°Cs, and massive amounts of snow. The snow was even off the ground before this world's equivalent to April!

The wonder of wonders!

Oh man, I was going to build the biggest snowman ever! It would be the General That Commands the Winter, Bane of Cultivators!

I giggled to myself at the image. I just hoped one of my carrots would be big enough for a truly giant schnoz. You can't have a snowman without a carrot.

I inhaled deeply and exhaled the pent-up excitement and random nervousness I'd been feeling. My first harvest in this world. My first winter. And . . . well . . . I was happy. Happy with my work. Happy with everything.

The sounds of the farm washed over me. The oinks of Peppa and Chunky, the clucks of the hens, and the chirps of the newly hatched chicks. The little ones had come into the world just last week, and already they were making nuisances of themselves and running Big D ragged making sure none of them died.

They were insanely cute. A good amount of them hatched too, especially considering I didn't have an incubator. There were only a few rotten eggs, and my pigs and chickens polished those off with gusto.

I smiled at the little ones trailing in a line behind their dad, yellow fluff and shaky legs.

Ah, this is the life.

□

"Brother Jin certainly lives far enough away," Gou Ren complained. They were walking to where Jin had said his home was to deliver the few tools he had requested. Gou Ren's thick eyebrows were drawn down in annoyance, his scowl nearly reaching his bushy sideburns. "And does he even need help with his harvest? He's only been there seven months; he can't have *too* much to bring in."

Gou Ren had been grumbling about the walk since the start—but the boy who looked vaguely like a monkey always grumbled, it was just something everybody in Hong Yaowu put up with. He always ended up doing what he was tasked with, though, so it was tolerated by most people.

"Ah, but, Brother, if he's already done, then all we've done is take a nice walk and enjoyed another's hospitality," Yun Ren chirped, ever the pragmatist. His eyes were locked in a perpetual vulpine squint, his ponytail bouncing with each step. "Besides, we need to escort our young and delicate flower here, to keep her purity safe as our illustrious Chief has commanded." He tapped the sword he carried, and Meiling rolled her eyes. It was a joke. After all, he had never actually had to use it.

"Meiling? Delicate? A *flower*?" Gou Ren scoffed with a teasing grin, retreading an old game between them. "The only plant she resembles is a bunch of thistles. If you embraced her, you'd only get pricked."

Meiling scowled. "I'll remember that remark the next time you beg me to cure your ills, Little Gou. I seem to remember *somebody* moaning in their bedroll over a stomachache and begging me to save them from certain death—when it turned out to be built-up gas."

Gou Ren's face flushed while his brother started laughing. "Hey! You said you wouldn't tell anybody about that!"

"Oh, did I?" Meiling pretended to ponder. "I remember no such promise; after all, I'm just a bunch of thistles."

Yun Ren pretended to sigh and shook his head. "You should know better than to go to a battle of wits when you're unarmed, Brother."

Gou Ren spluttered at his brother's betrayal, while Meiling and Yun Ren shared a smile. Sensing no path to victory, Gou Ren huffed and started walking faster.

Meiling was certain they were close because she had started to smell the faint scent of earth and the harvest that came with Jin's presence. It was an invigorating smell, full of life, and had none of the faint acrid tang most Qi did.

"Ah, I think I see a fence!" Gou Ren declared, and indeed they were swiftly approaching a barrier at the end of the road. "I think we're here."

It was a sturdy fence at the bottom of a hill, composed of large logs, stripped of their branches and driven into the earth and then cross-hatched with planks. It was taller than they were.

Meiling looked bemused at the sign hung prominently beside the open gate at eye level. It proudly proclaimed something absurd in bold characters.

"'Beware of . . . *Chicken*?'" Yun Ren asked. "Am I reading that right?" He asked Meiling, and she nodded, a bit surprised that he got it. Beware was one of the harder characters.

Both brothers laughed. "Brother Jin has an odd sense of humour," Gou Ren declared. "Why would anyone fear a chicken?"

Something thumped to the ground in front of them. They paused, looking down at the vaguely round object.

It was the head of a hawk, its eyes plucked out.

As one, they looked from the hawk's head back up to the top of the fence. A magnificent rooster—wearing a fox fur vest—cocked his head to the side and *stared* at them. His breast feathers were vibrant orange and red, his tail green and teal, and his wings were a bright blue. The spurs on his legs were long and wickedly sharp. His gaze was piercing and far, *far* too intelligent for a rooster. He stared down, judging them, eyes narrowed with consideration.

The brothers yelped, staring up at the imperious thing regarding them closely.

Meiling gaped. It was half hidden by the scent of earth, but the rooster smelled like . . . the moon?! *How is* the moon *even a smell?*

The chicken seemed to decide something and hopped down from the fence to land in the middle of the gate. He considered them a moment, then he swept into a graceful bow, his wings splaying out to the sides. He stayed that way, watching them.

Meiling realized what it was looking for.

"Yun Ren, Gou Ren, bow," she muttered to them and dipped into a bow of greeting.

"What, to the *chicken*?!" Gou Ren asked.

"It's a *Spirit Beast. Bow.*" Meiling bit out.

They bowed.

The rooster rose from his position, satisfied, and nodded his head. Then he walked to the side of the fence and held his wing out to beckon them in through the gate.

Gou Ren looked at it warily.

"Who's afraid of a chicken," Yun Ren mockingly whispered to him as they walked onto the land.

"Shut up!" Gou Ren hissed.

The Spirit Beast bowed once more, when they were inside the fence, a quick dip of his head, and then walked in front of them as they travelled up the small hill.

And that was where the real surprise lay.

"Gods above, this was all forest and stone last year! Some of the rocks were bigger than a house!" Yun Ren gasped.

They gazed upon gentle, rolling hills and fields, flush with verdant grass. A river wound its way down a hill filled with terraced rice paddies, some with still drying rice in them. It would not look out of place in a land that had been cultivated for *decades*, not mere months.

A small house and a larger storage shed sat on top of the hill, along with another smaller fence. Chickens clucked, pigs oinked, and they could hear the steady pounding of a person husking rice.

Meiling breathed in the air. It was *heavenly*. It smelled clean and pure, mixed with something lightly spiced and fiery, and the ever-present smell of life.

"Look at that rice," Gou Ren muttered. "I've never seen that much rice in one field before, and it's only half done. What kind of man is Brother Jin, to do all of this himself?"

Their musings were interrupted by the chicken letting out a mighty cry.

The pounding stopped, and Jin's voice came from within the house, speaking in another language, the one he had told Meiling about.

"*You tell 'em, Bi De!*" she heard Jin say in that strange language he knew.

The rooster crowed again, and Jin stepped out.

Meiling stared.

His shirt was off, exposing tanned, rippling muscles slick with sweat. Jin's look of contentment changed to happiness, and a bright grin overtook his face.

"Meimei! Brother Yun Ren, Brother Gou Ren! Welcome to the *Fa Ram*!" he shouted with genuine joy, happy at their visit.

"Brother Jin! We've come to see if you need help with the harvest!" Yun Ren called, ambling over.

Jin looked surprised and then touched, his eyes going misty for a moment before his grin returned with full force.

Meiling stared.

Gou Ren poked her in the back, and she jolted. "Stop drooling, Meimei," he scolded in amusement. Patches of red crawled up her face.

Jin laughed. "I wouldn't say no to some help, but what about your own harvest?"

Gou Ren shrugged. "They'll be fine, I reckon, or else Elder Hong wouldn't have sent us."

"Well, if you're sure, I should be done in a day or two at this rate."

A day or two?! Meiling thought incredulously.

"I was planning on heading up to the village anyways after I was finished, so I didn't miss Meihua's wedding," Jin continued, smiling brightly at them.

"Well, then, we're at your disposal, Brother Jin," Yun Ren declared.

Jin shook his head. "You've just arrived! It's not much, but I'll give you the grand tour of the place!" Jin walked over to where a shirt was lying folded up and put it on, after wiping some of the sweat off. Meiling studied the ground with great intent.

And so, they trekked over the land, looking closer at his rice paddies, the stones carefully arranged by size, a gravel pit, and the beginnings of a bridge over the river. While they walked, they regaled each other with stories from their time apart: a mere month, but there were still things to talk about.

Even if some of it was needling each other.

"A thistle, huh?" Jin asked with a smile. "I can see it. Medicinal. Tough enough to grow anywhere. And really, they are beautiful flowers, the same colour as her eyes."

The brothers looked at each other in shock, while Meiling covered her face with her hands, such was her embarrassment.

Yun Ren gasped in exaggeration and respectfully clasped his hands together. "Brother Jin, your skill with compliments humbles this Yun Ren."

"Brother Jin, your tongue is silver and quick! Teach this unworthy Gou Ren your ways!" the other brother jokingly demanded. Meiling made a sound like a dying fox at the words.

They laughed as they continued walking, wandering down the small river, while Meiling lagged behind, trying to compose herself.

"What about that? Brother Jin, are you raising another house?" Yun Ren asked, pointing to slabs of stone and planks of wood over the first, smaller river.

At that, *Jin* flushed.

"Ah . . . th-this place isn't big enough for more than one person," he muttered, his eyes flicked to Meiling before darting away again.

Meiling swallowed thickly, her heart pounding in her chest. *He's building a house for a family.*

"Yeah, building a house! Anyway! Here are the Lowly Spiritual Herbs—" he said, clearly desperate to change the subject by starting up his tour again.

Meiling forced herself into motion, following along behind Jin, even as pleasant images danced in her head. She hoped when she lived here that the Spiritual Herbs would be a bit farther away from the house, though. They smelled rather overwhelmingly of fire and cinders.

Then she realized what she was thinking and pinched her leg. When *I live here*?

→

Jin was tireless. He did not work that much faster than they did, it's just that he *kept working*. His hands moved at the same speed. His breathing was steady and even, and the work that needed doing just *disappeared*.

Meiling weaved more bags to pack away the rice in, while Gou Ren transported the dried rice to him, and Yun Ren helped harvest vegetables.

And then Jin made dinner for them. There were strips of chicken filled with the strange herbs that smelled spicy to Meiling. Spiritual Herbs, squash, mushrooms, and some spices, which were then crusted in leftover rice, and fried until crispy. It was served with baked carrots, radish, and freshly harvested rice.

It was the most delicious meal any of them had ever eaten.

↔

Bi De knew he was vindicated when those that shared the form of his Great Master had come. He had treated them as guests, as his knowledge demanded. A strange set of actions he *knew* to be right, so ingrained in his mind they were. He gazed upon them and noted his Great Master's immediate superiority. None of them had the power and majesty of his Lord. They were inferiors, and obviously here to give tribute.

Still, there was no reason to be rude. He *knew* guests were to be respected and cared for, unless they did something to forfeit that right. They had arrived at the opening to the Pillars, as was proper, and exchanged proper courtesies, so they were allowed upon his Great Master's Blessed Land.

They had been similarly appropriate in their awe, for the Great Master was peerless upon this earth. He gave them face by bowing to them, for his master bowed to them too. If he had not, he would have been greatly shamed. To not have the Disciple bow to honoured guests of his Great Master was utterly unforgivable.

With his Great Master, they too toiled in the land. They were utterly inferior to him, of course, but they worked with skill and heeded his Lord's words well.

They were worthy of respect in that regard.

And then, as the time for the evening meal came, the Great Master took the plumpest of the females—one from the beginning—and slew her, just as he slew the other creatures that he ate. Like she was not something of his.

Bi De was shocked, his beak open with horror.

His master had slain one of his own!

He was shaken greatly by the act—so greatly shaken, in fact, that he fled to the Great Pillars of the Fa Ram to contemplate this development. His energy, his Qi roiled, unbalanced by his Great Master's action. It threatened to go out of control, and he barely managed to clamp down on it.

Would he be next? The thought was traitorous. It was ludicrous. He sat on the pillars and closed his eyes.

He contemplated deeply the reasons for his Great Master to consume one of the females and found that such a thing was not as shocking as he first believed.

They were all his Great Master's. They lived upon his Blessed Land, and they dined upon his benevolence. But the female had made no use of his Master's overwhelming generosity. She had grown fat and had a tiny amount of Qi, but she had not ascended. She was as the interlopers that invaded mindlessly, that ate of his Lord's essence.

This was merely the Great Master's essence returning to him, to once more nourish the new generation. Those who possessed skill, and the luck of the heavens, would ascend as Bi De had. Those that did not would return to the Great Master.

Bi De nodded to himself, satisfied with his understanding. He would not be callously killed by his Lord. The sky had darkened completely, and the moon was gleaming in the sky.

He returned to his Great Master and was given his measure of Heavenly Herbs, and he had affection lavished upon him.

Then, his Lord vacated his coop and gave his female guest a great amount of face by allowing her to lay in his bed. He went to lay under a storage area, and the other males lay upon bedrolls outside.

Bi De prepared himself to assume the night watch, yet his attention was seized when the female stole out of the house and headed towards his Great Master. At first he thought treachery, for only wicked beasts slunk around at night.

He followed her, and his Heavenly blades formed. The silver energy sheathed his spurs, a powerful and holy light that was the bane of the wicked. She approached his Great Master's prone form. He watched carefully for any threat, for there were no good reasons to approach his sleeping Master.

Her hand reached towards the Great Master, and Bi De prepared to intervene. "Jin?" she asked, and Bi De's Master awoke.

"Meime—?" he began to ask, confusion on his face, when the woman leaned in, their faces pressing close together. His Master leaned back and pulled her with them, both laying together under the bedroll's sheets.

Bi De's blades guttered out as he comprehended the circumstances.

She was not just *a* female.

She was the *Great Master's* female.

He spared one last glance as the woman lay on his Master's chest, the two of them talking quietly. He turned and once again took his post.

This had been a night of many revelations. He felt like he had comprehended the barest fraction of his Great Master's unmatched intellect. He puffed his chest out with pride. Such a feat showed just how much he had grown—

A happy squeal shattered his concentration, and Bi De stumbled, whipping around to glare at the pen. He preened his ruffled feathers back into order. He hoped Chun Ke and Pi Pa would not ascend and instead be eaten.

They were most annoying creatures.

CHAPTER 10

LIFT TOGETHER

The day was done.

They all sat, exhausted against the wall of Jin's hut. Even the tireless Jin had started to falter towards the end, but now they sat together, hot and sweaty. Yun Ren and Gou Ren were down to their loincloths, slumped to the side and greedily drinking water. Meiling was stripped to the waist, with only her dudou preserving her modesty, and she groaned at the state of her sore fingers and rubbed at her aching back. Big D had been enlisted, carrying Meiling's completed bags to Jin, and getting more stalks so that she could weave.

But they were done. True to Jin's words, the last of the rice had been harvested at the end of the second day. It had been long hours and back-breaking work, but they had done it.

Eighty-three 40-kilo bags of rice. An extraordinary number for the small amount of land Jin had put to the plough.

Yun Ren sighed with contentment after he finished his drink, running his hands through his matted sweaty hair before grinning at the vessel. It was a bamboo tube with a groove cut in it, so that a lid could be screwed on. Meiling was having trouble opening hers, her red, overworked fingers shaking and slipping—Jin reached over and opened it for her.

"Brother Jin, this is quite the vessel. It's certainly easier to work with while out in the fields," he said, leaning over to hand the empty thing to Jin.

Holding up a hand in refusal, Jin shook his head, "Keep it, Brother Yun Ren. They're easy enough to make. I actually broke a couple of gourds when I first started and spilled a lot of water. These were more durable and easier to clean."

Gou Ren moaned, pushing himself up into a seated position. "Brother Jin, you worked us like oxen," he complained. He looked with pride upon the many baskets. "But to see the work done is always a pleasure."

"It is, isn't it?" Jin asked with a soft smile. They sat in companionable silence, the cool breeze a balm upon their sweaty bodies, and the setting sun bathed the world in warm light.

Eventually, Jin got up and stretched. "Come on, let's get cleaned up, and then I'll start dinner. We are having crayfish tonight!"

→

The river was still warm at this time of year, though fall was rapidly approaching, with the occasional gust of cold wind. With the small bar of soap Jin had, the dirt and grime were easily washed from their bodies. Their exhaustion was telling—the normally quarrelsome brothers did not even try to dunk each other once nor attempt to start any splash war.

Instead, Yun Ren simply handed his brother a comb. Grumbling, Gou Ren dutifully brushed first his elder brother's hair and then Meiling's while Jin prepared them a meal.

First, he dredged up the baskets along the river. Then, Jin split the crayfish in two, removing its gut, and in his wok he added peppercorns and oil, as well as leek, ginger, and garlic. He fried the crayfish until they were red, then served it over rice.

Big D dined on the leftover crayfish shells, picking at them with great enthusiasm.

This time, everybody camped out in Jin's little house. It was cramped. They were squashed together and a bit uncomfortable, but the shoving and elbows were part of the fun. Meiling did not even offer a token attempt at subtlety, simply pulling Jin into the bed with her, much to the brothers' amusement.

"Oh no, Brother! We must act to preserve Brother Jin's purity!" Yun Ren japed. "No wonder Elder Hong sent us along; his daughter is a lusty beast!"

Gou Ren snorted looking at them with tired eyes. "I think he's fine. She's already asleep."

Yun Ren barked out another laugh. "Indeed," he said and sat down. He'd seemed to be pondering something before finally making up his mind to ask. "Brother Jin?"

"Yes, Brother Yun Ren?"

"Take good care of our Meiling, yeah?" It was a voice of honest concern, for a woman that may as well be his sister.

Jin nodded and pulled Meiling closer to his body.

"To the best of my ability."

□

"Mph. Gou Ren, you lout, *off*."

Meiling woke to the sounds of and annoyed Yun Ren, Gou Ren having rolled over onto him in the night. A common enough occurrence. Gou Ren was a grabby sleeper, and a deep one. His brother, however, was an expert in removing him, shoving and prodding until he rolled over on his own. It was still the early hours of the morning, and the sky was dark, the sun just now starting to peek up over the hills. Meiling sat up and yawned, stretching to get the kinks out of her back, but—

There were none.

In fact, she felt *great*, despite the work she had done. Her muscles were still sore, yet there was none of the outright *pain* that she'd been expecting. Even her raw fingers felt mostly fine, the swelling having gone down a lot from yesterday. Jin was still asleep beside her, as was Gou Ren, but Yun Ren was already sitting up, looking annoyed at his brother.

Meiling whispered a good morning to him and got a muttered greeting in return.

"Start the fire, and I'll get the eggs?" she asked, and Yun Ren nodded, stretching his muscles.

He paused and then stretched his arm farther back. He seemed a bit surprised as he tested the range of motion, but pleased. He hopped up and didn't even stagger as he went to grab the wood while Meiling went to the coops. On the way out of the house, she noticed Bi De, the Spirit Beast, on one of the fence posts. He turned to her, in the light of the pre-dawn, and bowed.

Meiling returned the greeting. The chicken nodded, satisfied, then to her surprise, hopped onto her shoulder with a light step, like he did with Jin. He was lighter than she expected. Her hand came up, and she stroked his magnificent chest feathers. She got approving clucking sounds in return, and a gentle beak started preening through her still bedraggled hair.

Gathering the eggs was easy. Bi De simply squawked, and the hens moved aside. There were a lot of eggs. More than the village chickens laid, at least, and a bit bigger too. They looked like the same breed though. That would be a question for later. Yun Ren had the fire started when she got back, the wood spluttering alight as the first light of dawn creased the horizon. Bi De leapt from Meiling's shoulder, back onto the fence posts. He eyed the sun critically, waiting, and filled his chest with a deep breath.

Bi De greeted the morning, his voice echoing out over the hills and waking their host.

Jin thanked them both as they cooked breakfast, and then he went off to start loading his cart for the trip back to Hong Yaowu.

For breakfast, they had eggs and leftover rice, shared in good company.

→

Meiling held on for dear life as the cart careened down the road. Beside her, Yun Ren prayed.

"Honoured ancestors, preserve your unworthy son, for he is a fool of great proportions . . ."

Gou Ren, naturally, was howling with laughter at their predicament.

After breakfast, they had loaded the cart with a full forty bags of rice and strapped them down. The cart was most certainly overloaded, the frame bending but not breaking under the immense weight. Gou Ren had praised the craftsmanship, but Meiling noticed the truth.

It had Jin's Qi in it. Without it, it would have surely shattered into pieces, and even with it, it was a bit suspect looking.

They were ready to go back home. Jin had bid goodbye to his Spirit Beast, who bowed low to him in supplication and took up his vigil on the farm's fence.

The Xong brothers had looked worried about the load and had been gauging how they could help push it, when Jin lifted the front of the cart with ease. Then, without a hint of effort, began to walk with it like he wasn't carrying anything at all.

They had looked at each other and shrugged. The pace they'd taken had been pleasant and the weather mild as they set off, travelling until it was almost noon.

"Tomorrow evening I'd reckon," Gou Ren had said, looking up at the sky. "Maybe a bit longer. My legs are still sore."

Meiling had agreed. The pain was coming back, though it still wasn't that bad.

Jin had gestured to the cart. "Hop on, I'll get us there by tonight."

It was quite rude to sit and have Jin cart them around like he was their lesser, but he was insistent.

So, they had gotten onto the cart, on top of the bags, and Jin bid them to "hold on tight!"

And then he started *running*.

Not just running, but what felt like *sprinting*.

Which brought them to this point. Hanging on to a cart of rice for dear life while Jin ran as fast as a horse.

"Brother Jin, can you go any faster?" Gou Ren asked excitedly.

"DON'T YOU *DARE*, JIN!" Meiling screeched, too preoccupied with holding on to slap the idiot for his idea.

Yun Ren just kept praying.

Jin was right. They reached Hong Yaowu by nightfall.

Meiling and Yun Ren were pale, while Gou Ren wanted to hook up the hogs to a wagon to re-create the experience.

□

One of the scout-searchers had returned, slink-slinking into the nest-warren. It stunk-smelled of joy musk, the scent permeating through the gathered bodies.

"Yes-yes. We have scent-smelled it. The fine-good Qi, and tasty-delicious food." the scout-searcher squeaked. Its eyes were alight with the Lord-Master's power, enabling it to give its report.

Lord-Master was intrigued. These lands were bad-poor. They had been defeated-crushed and driven out of their first-original nest-warrens, in the lands of much-plenty. Many-many of their number-count had perished, and they were all that were left-remained.

To find-locate a new place of Qi? They would need it to grow-restore their numbers.

"Good-good. Find-locate the Land's guardian and seek-know its might-strength."

"Yes, yes, Lord-Master. I hear and obey!" The servant scurried off, its eyes dulling slightly as it left the Lord-Master's presence.

The Lord-Master nodded and turned to one of its other servants.

"Wake-rouse the nest-warren. We go-move tonight."

CHAPTER 11

THE NEWCOMERS

It was the Third Day since his Great Master's departure.

Bi De sat upon the Great Pillars of the Fa Ram in the light of the rising sun, his eyes closed. His contemplations centered on the state of Great Fa Ram and the harvest. The air was becoming colder. The leaves of the trees were changing. They were turning from bright and vibrant green to fiery oranges and dull browns, save for the trees with needles. Those stayed a verdant green. How curious.

He examined the energies of the land closely, finding them undiminished. They were difficult to set his senses on, scattered and ever-changing as they were, but he found it through familiarity and diligence, for the Land and his Great Master were nearly one and the same.

It was a vibrant and healthy energy, although it seemed to be preparing for something.

Like his Great Master, was the land too preparing for "winter"?

The preparations were subtle, and he could not comprehend the land's intent, but he observed anyway, searching for clues or patterns. The land shifted and recognized him. Upon feeling its intent upon him, he bowed his head and parted with some of his Qi, offering it up as a sacrifice. He could not feed it as his Master did, but he hoped the small measure of his power he could offer would be well received.

The land received it and consumed it. The feeling of being watched faded.

We give to the land, and the land gives back. As always, his Great Master's profound wisdom was peerless. Bi De was in awe every time he contemplated it. The Great Master offered sacrifices to the land often. All the waste of his toils was carefully catalogued, and that which could be returned to the Earth was given back.

He stared at where the bones of several interlopers had been interred and found the grass there of a higher quality than that of its surroundings. It was rich in the power of the Earth. The grass was fed upon by the insects. The insects were fed upon by his kin and the interlopers. And in turn, the grass would feed upon their bones.

It was a cycle.

This whole world was full of them. The phases of the moon, the night and the day, these were cycles. Such things were essential. Although he had not witnessed it, he knew in his bones that once this "winter" was over, there too would be a cycle, coming back to the time of his birth, with colder air, when the trees had but flowers and buds.

All things came and went.

This was the order of the world.

He felt a shift inside of his breast. He inhaled deeply of the land's air, exulting in it. Pride swelled at comprehending his Master's profound wisdom.

He rose from his position and went about his duties. Through his observations of his Lord, he knew what needed to be done. The chicks, his sons and daughters, were to be fed from his Great Master's largesse. It would hopefully make them strong and enable them to do their duties. They too would guard Fa Ram and slay the interlopers upon the Heavenly Herbs.

He went to the rice storage, where there was a bag of rice left for him. Bi De could eat as much as he pleased such was his Great Master's generosity. After taking his fill, he once more commenced his duties. The floor was swept. The storage areas were inspected. He knew not what the rice storage was inspected *for*, but he assumed interlopers would attempt to steal this too from his Great Master.

He would, naturally, slay any such creature that dared to touch what was his Lord's, and kept an eye searching constantly for interloper presences. Finding none, he left satisfied.

Finally, he went about the most distasteful part of his duties. The Great Master had left him as Master in his absence, and he would endeavour to never disappoint his Lord.

Chun Ke and Pi Pa required *direction*. They were stupid beasts that tried his patience, not understanding their place in the hierarchy. His

Great Master was affectionate to them, but Bi De felt no such niceties, especially not when they had the gall to dirty his plumage with mud. He had nearly slain them both on the spot, but such acts of rage were unbecoming. His Lord willed that they live, so they would, no matter Bi De's thoughts on the matter.

His Great Master cared little about becoming dirty, so Bi De strove to feel the same. No matter how the rage bubbled, or how long it took to restore his feathers to a pristine state.

Instead, he had merely toppled both of them with a flick of his wings. Now, they were more respectful, though they still dared to test him, squealing and snorting and defecating everywhere.

He opened the gate for them, and they trundled out, their ugly, beady eyes upon him. He leapt onto Chun Ke's back, and they wandered towards the forest, where they could root their noses through the dirt, consuming roots and tubers. Swift smacks of his wings directed both of the great beasts, when they sought to run from their pens. He had no desire to herd them across all of Fa Ram. They would stay within his sight and return when commanded.

Luckily, today they were cooperative, keeping their incessant noises to a minimum and returning after a mere hour, having eaten their fill. The pen was shut, and Bi De breathed a sigh of relief, then washed his feet and wings to rid himself of their smells.

At this point in the day, he would normally attempt to once more give his essence to the crops. He needed to carefully infuse his Qi into their structures. But the crops were all gone. Harvested, save for the Heavenly Herbs, which had been moved to a more sheltered area.

So instead, he sat upon the Great Pillars and turned to his contemplation. He was just settling in to properly cultivate, when he felt it. Eyes upon him.

He had been feeling flashes of interlopers. At first, he'd assumed they had fled, scared of his strength, but now he felt a horde.

He sounded the alarm, and his females ran back inside the coops. He glared at the invisible eyes watching him from the forest. The Interlopers would meet their doom!

The scouts were already fleeing when he turned back to hunt for them, so he followed their trail.

Across the hills, over the rivers, and through the trees he went, marching inexorably towards the interlopers. He laid his eyes upon them when he arrived in a small clearing. There were many, nearly twenty in total. Most of them were small things, even smaller than himself, with hairless tails and beady eyes, all gathered around an edifice of wood and metal.

He felt his wrath beginning to stir. Bi De considered himself of mild temperament, but even he could not stop the ugly bubbling in his gut. These interlopers dared, not just to intrude upon his Great Master's land, but they'd had the sheer wrenched gall to raise a structure on these sacred lands?

He glared at the scaffold and the cauldron. He would chase them off, or else slay them for this insult!

His feathers puffed up with wrath, and he leapt from his tree, descending upon them like he had once descended upon Basi Bu Shi. Yet this time, he did not slink or strike in silence. He was his Great Master's favoured warrior, and he would not hide away!

He landed in the clearing, announcing his presence to them, his mighty cry sending the small ones skittering away in fright and terror. The sound echoed through the hills, his rage resounding through his Great Master's entire domain. Bi De stalked towards the little beasts; his stride was unflinching.

His blades of moonlight formed upon his spurs. All could see their doom approaching.

"Peace-peace, guardian-protector," he heard a squeaky voice call. Bi De was taken aback at how clear the voice was, sounding like the speech of humans. From near the cauldron's scaffold, one of the interlopers appeared. It was larger than the rest, nearly as big as he was, it walked on two legs, hunched over and wringing its hands. "We plead-beseech you, stay your blades."

It bowed and snivelled in supplication to him. Bi De observed the prostrating creature. It was clearly of no threat. He let his blades dissipate, though he continued gazing imperiously upon them. The interloper took that as a sign to continue.

"This Chow Ji and his clan-family are but humble-pitiful refugees. We can feel the great-mighty power of this place and have come to beg-grovel its masters to grant us respite! We are starved-dying, mighty guardian-protector. Take pity upon us!"

At that, the black-furred creature threw itself to the ground at his feet. The rest of them cowered before Bi De, some nursing wounds. All squeaked piteously, begging for his mercy.

Bi De felt his anger dissipate. They truly were pathetic. Perhaps they were merely lost guests instead of true interlopers? They had not arrived at the front gate, as a guest should, but he could find it in his heart to forgive them this trespass.

Bi De made a decision. Guests were to be given hospitality.

He drew upon as much of his regal bearing as possible and gave these poor wretches some face, lowering his head and welcoming them.

The creatures cheered at his benevolence as he accepted them onto his Great Master's lands. As they should, for they were about to enter paradise.

□

"That's not even fully half of it?" Hong Xian asked incredulously.

"Yes, Elder Hong, eighty-three bags was the final total," Yun Ren confirmed.

"Astounding. And . . . how was he towards you?"

"Brother Jin is Brother Jin. He is as he was." Yun Ren continued, sounding mildly reproachful, "He builds a house as big as yours for your daughter, he is enamoured with her, as she is him. He gave us his home without restraint and fed us from his table until we were full."

Yao Che snorted from beside him; the bull of a man had his arms crossed and was frowning as well. "The boy's virtue was clear, Xian. He has spared not a single lustful glance at my flower Meihua, and even now promises to escort her safely with us to her intended. I shall hear no more of any doubts upon his character."

Xian frowned. "It is shameful of me to doubt such a man, this is true, but a father worries. I seem to remember you threatening Tingfeng with an axe, Che." He shook his head, while Yao Che had the grace to look embarrassed. "Still, today is a good day. I see your quick excursion has made you and your brother some wealth, Yun Ren."

At that, Yun Ren smiled softly. "Brother Jin insisted we all take a portion of the harvest as thanks. We tried to refuse him, but he would have none of it. I'm honoured to call him Brother Jin and have his friendship."

Finally, Hong Xian nodded his head. "And this settles the matter. I'm sorry to have had to ask you to check, Yun Ren. Now, off with you, and no more of this business. He is Brother Jin. Let no door in Hong Yaowu be closed to him."

Hong Xian sighed as Xong Yun Ren and Yao Che left his quarters. He walked to his window and looked out onto the fields, where Jin toiled, helping them with the last preparations to see Meihua off to Verdant Hill.

His daughter, so much the image of her mother, brought the man some water with a smile, and they stopped to talk and laugh.

His Meiling looked so happy. Xian couldn't help but smile at his precious daughter's joy. A good, productive farm and a good, productive man. He could wish for nothing better for his daughter.

The last of his doubts drained away. "Ah, my dear departed, I wish you could see them one last time," he murmured wistfully.

CHAPTER 12

THE MID-AUTUMN FESTIVAL

Drums thundered. Instruments clanged. Firecrackers popped and banged. The scent of food filled the air. It was barely controlled mayhem as people hollered and shouted, creating a massive cacophony for such a small village.

A dragon hopped and skipped throughout the village, the great puppet moving in time with the beat. The children attending the festival gleefully chased its tail while people talked and relaxed after finishing the harvest.

I cheered along with the crowd. Man, the village elders could move. They were making that dragon puppet *bop*.

I always appreciated the hard work that went into these things. I had seen a mid-autumn festival once in the Before, and honestly, this blew it out of the water. The sheer coordination alone was impressive as they began jumping in time, sending the dragon slithering up and down like it was flying. I was transfixed as it spiraled and whirled, completely absorbed by the performance.

The dragon got faster and faster. Slithering, jumping, and whirling around poles with increasing speed as the drums thundered towards the finale. And what a finale it was, as they ran up a wall and jumped off backwards, leading the dragon into a spiralling backflip. The crowd went nuts.

I went nuts with them. That was amazing!

"Brother Jin!" Yun Ren called out to me with a grin, and I held out my cup again. It was filled with rice wine to the brim, and I downed it in a single gulp so I could keep cheering. Yun Ren was dressed up like everybody else in the village, and so was I. The vibrant red clothes looked nice, even if this set wasn't mine.

I had planned to buy more clothes from town for Meihua's wedding, but I'd ended up borrowing some of her father—Yao Che's—clothes instead because we were roughly the same build. It was a red sort of tunic and black pants. With it, I looked like I belonged, like one of the villagers, instead of my usual outfit of old martial arts gis.

I was seated at the biggest table that had been brought out beside Xian, Meiling's father. His seat was currently empty, as he was with Yao Che and Xong Ten Ren, Yun Ren's father, inside the dragon puppet. The dragon was leaping and skipping off, which let the older men finally have a break, their performance finished.

This . . . this was great. I was relaxing in my chair, at a festival, with a good drink and the promise of better food later. I filled up Yun Ren's cup this time, and we drank again together. I sat back and just soaked in the atmosphere. Everybody was in a good mood, with wide, happy grins on their faces. From the kids playing around, to the people drinking and cavorting, even the people making the food. It was wonderful. I sighed with contentment and looked up at the sky; the twilight sun felt warm and gentle on my skin.

"This is fantastic!" I declared to my companion, grinning at the village.

"The village does have its charms, doesn't it?" Yun Ren said. "Our Hong Yaowu tries its best."

"*Try* our best?! Yun Ren, you scamp, we *succeed* with our best!" Yao Che thundered, red-faced and sweaty from the dragon dance, though he had a giant grin on his face. His beard and hair stuck out wildly, freed from the bandanna he normally wore to keep the sweat out of his eyes. He was the quintessential blacksmith. Big, wide, and strong-looking, with rough features. Yun Ren just rolled his eyes at the chastisement.

Meiling's father staggered into his seat beside me, puffing and panting. "That gets harder every year," he muttered, looking a little faint. He gave me a nod and a quick smile and then thumped down into a seat to rub at his legs.

"Your dance was fantastic, Elder Yao, Elder Hong. Let me pour you a drink!" I said, then grabbed the bottle.

Both of them looked a little surprised, and Elder Yao's grin widened further as he let out a booming laugh. "Look at how much face our honoured guest gives us!" he exclaimed as I poured both of them cups. "Call me Brother Che, Brother Jin! There is no need for formalities when you saved my precious flower from those wicked, vile men! Were she not intended for another, I would be happy to give you her hand!" His voice was as loud as his laugh—Yao Che had one volume, and that was booming.

My smile got a little strained. It was a bit awkward, that he was that loud with his opinion. But he seemed to disdain the scholarly sorts who weren't named Xian.

"I'm honoured you think so highly of me, Brother Che," I said as sincerely as I could. Yeah, awkward, seeing how his daughter was intended for another. And this was basically doubling as a party for her wedding as well.

At this, he took another bottle from the table and poured me another drink. He held out his arm, and Rou's memories told me to hook my arm around his. We drank our cups in a single mouthful.

Meiling's father was next, pouring me another cup. That went down the hatch too, along with the . . . twenty? I'd had previously. Well, as a cultivator, I was a lot more tolerant than your average person, but even I had a limit. But that limit was measured in bottles rather than cups.

Oh, man, I'm going to be so drunk later, I thought, kind of looking forward to it. This place was really relaxing, and if I got drunk, things *should* be fine.

Soon enough, the food came out. Roast ducks, dumplings, and moon cakes. The smell was heavenly. The tables started to fill with more and more people. It was like those big, summer barbecues back in the before, and man, I was all for it.

"The ones I made are on the left," Meimei whispered to me as she set down a platter before she whirled away, to get more things out for people.

My eyes lit up. *Hell yeah, Meimei's are the best, accept no substitutes!*

Hong Xian led a toast, thanking everybody for their hard work this year, and then the feast began.

We all tucked into our meal to music and pleasant conversation. We talked, we laughed, I held hands with Meimei under the table and praised her cooking until her face went crimson.

What a wonderful day.

→

I followed Xian back to his house, my stomach full to bursting and my head swimming pleasantly. He had asked me politely to follow him after the feast and judging by the look on his face, I had a bit of a feeling that I knew where this was going. Me and Mei hadn't exactly been *subtle* with our glances.

He sat on a cushion and gestured for me to sit before him. Xian's hair was the same green-tinted shade Meimei and little Xian had, and he had a small beard. He looked pretty dignified and was probably what most people in this world would consider attractive. He was about five foot five, so a full half-foot shorter than I was, but then again, the only man who I'd met so far that matched my height was Yao Che.

We sat for a moment, just staring at each other, and then Xian finally spoke.

"Rou Jin . . ." he said in a stern voice before drawing in a deep breath. "You are courting my daughter without my permission." I winced. I hadn't asked, and that was a *big* no-no, but he didn't seem too upset. Hong Xian continued, apparently satisfied at my show of contrition. "I will allow this, but only if you answer one question for me. When were you going to ask me for my daughter's hand in marriage?"

It was a loaded question. A question that I had spent some time pondering.

"When I had enough food to feed her, enough fabric to clothe her, and a house worthy of her," I replied without hesitation. What had started as an idle thought of "getting married" had rapidly overtaken my mind as I spent time with Meiling. It was fast. It was nearly Las Vegas fast, but . . . when in Rome. I had already met her three times, and to a lot of people here, that was good enough. Some people didn't meet the woman they were going to marry until the day it happened.

But . . . did I really want to make this commitment?

I *did* like her. She was cute, hardworking, and knew when to throw off the no-nonsense attitude to have some fun. There would be time after the betrothal to get to know each other. Like I thought before, this will end in tears or happiness.

I'd try my hardest for happiness. So, I cast my hand.

Hong Xian considered my words, and his stern visage melted off his face, revealing a smile, "I accept your proposal," he stated simply. "This spring, after the snows melt, I shall give my daughter to your house." Xian bowed his head. "Take good care of my Meiling."

I blinked. My stomach churned. This was *real*. Yeah, I had been planning for it, but planning and "this is happening" are two different things.

Getting married. It was a more mundane problem than I'd been anticipating when I first woke up in a world of battles and cultivation, but hell, it was better than my other problems.

I bowed back, not trusting my voice.

"Now, share a drink with me once more, for you shall be my son."

I got a bit misty-eyed at that. Family was *important* to both Rou and me. I felt a twinge from his memories of his parents and Gramps.

I grabbed the wine Xian offered me and took a deep drink.

Please, please *let this work.*

↔

Meiling wondered what her father's announcement was about. He stood on a platform with a lit paper lantern, the members of the village below him.

"My friends, on this holy night after our toils, on the eve of one wedding, it is with great pleasure that this Hong Xian announces another."

There were happy gasps and intrigued whispers all through the village.

She idly thought about who the wedding could be for. Maybe Yun Ren or Gou Ren to somebody? Probably not them, since she hadn't heard their mother or father say anything. Who could it be?

"When the snows melt in spring, the House of Hong will unite itself with the House of Rou. Hong Xian's daughter, Hong Meiling, will be wed to Rou Jin."

There was silence.

Huh? Meiling thought.

Meihua gasped happily beside her, pulling her into a hug.

Slowly, Meiling turned to her betrothed. He was watching her, both anxious and nervous.

This was really happening. Yes, she had daydreamed, and yes, it was something she had thought about . . . but he wanted *her*.

Slowly, she felt a smile form. When Jin saw the happy, near exultant look on her face, a relieved smile crossed his, too.

The paper lanterns rose into the sky.

The people of Hong Yaowu hooted and hollered as Meiling ran and jumped into Jin's arms.

The wine flowed throughout the night as people stuffed bottle after bottle down Jin's throat. Enough that she started to worry about him. He'd drank enough to kill a man already, draining bottle after bottle, and remaining surprisingly coherent, while others passed out. She had taken a glance at the stocks, and they barely had any wine left at all. But even Jin seemed to have his limits.

She was pressed up against his side, and he retained enough presence of mind not to start trying to kiss her in front of everybody, but every time he looked at her, he smiled. It was big and stupid, and it made her heart skip a beat.

But even that had to come to an end. They *did* need to leave in the morning.

Jin was staggering as Meiling led him back to the guest room. Honestly, she was surprised he was still capable of moving under his own power. He had to have drunk nearly twenty whole bottles of wine, as people kept on demanding to have drinks with him. Yao Che had long since passed out and required three people to carry him to a room.

Everyone who was to see Meihua off the next day would be half-dead in the morning. That included Meihua herself, who had kept toasting to Meiling's good fortune.

She would have to make plenty of hangover cures in the morning. It was *also* why she had wanted to postpone the festival, but Meihua had wanted to celebrate with them one last time before she would likely be spending her autumns in the town with her new husband. The thought . . . hurt. it was the one blemish to an otherwise perfect night.

She finally got Jin to the bed, and he tipped over, dragging her with him. He happily nuzzled into her neck and planted a sloppy kiss there.

She sighed fondly while she ran her fingers through his hair, cradled in his strong arms. Soon, this would be *every* night, and she looked forward to it.

But for now . . . she slipped out of his arms, and he frowned. She gently ran her fingers through his hair once more, and his frown disappeared.

She had some elixirs to make.

→

I smiled at Yun Ren as he glared at me through bloodshot eyes. "Brother Jin, your body is unfair. Trade it with me," he half-heartedly demanded.

Our pace was more of a funeral march than a wedding procession. Meiling's hangover cures had gotten everybody moving, and they were stumbling forwards instead of groaning messes unable to move from their bedrolls. They still looked dead on their feet as they trudged along the path like zombies. Even Meihua on her horse, who was still as pretty as ever with not a hair out of place, was slumped forward and swaying.

I leered at the stink-eye Yun Ren was giving me. "Come on, Brother Yun Ren!" I called in a loud voice, and half the people around me winced. "It's a beautiful day!"

The rest of the procession turned to give me a *look.*

I revelled in their spite.

CHAPTER 13

THE SPIRIT FURNACE

Bi De gathered the black-furs across the river, upon the edges of the Great Pillars of the Fa Ram. The little black-furs carried their cauldron with them, following in his wake with the hunched and robed Chow Ji sitting on top of it. The creature had a shuffling walk, like its leg was injured, and oddly Great-Master-like forelimbs. It barely moved as the smaller black-furs toiled for it, floating the cauldron along on its scaffold while they pushed it from behind.

They marched, squeaking and grunting, with Bi De at their head, leading them towards the area where guests were to be quartered. But all of them were dirty and tired, so some things had to be done first.

Bi De paused at the gate and bid them wait. He had to prepare, and there were a great many starving guests.

From the storage, he collected a bag of rice and a basket, taking three measures from it using the Great Master's tools. From the coops, he selected several eggs— although they were filled with Qi, they contained no life within them. And finally, from the Pots of Growth, he collected the Heavenly Herbs. All were arranged. *All* would be the envy of any who beheld them, their unsurpassed quality evident even to the blind.

Thus, he bought the offerings to his guests.

Their eyes went wide at the sight of the herbs and the rice. They shone with abject awe at the fruits of the Great Master's labours. Chow Ji, Lord of the black-furs, clambered down from his cauldron and fell to his knees once more. The rest of the black-furs swarmed forwards, prostrating themselves.

"Guardian-Protector, Great-Magnificent Bi De! Your generosity-virtue is beyond that of the highest heavens! Praise-praise him, Clan-kin!

Praise-praise him!" Chow Ji chittered. Chow Ji's face was twisted into a smile. It was an ugly thing, but Bi De forgave him for it. He was weak and disgusting, but that was why Bi De was there, to make up for these deficiencies.

He stood, proudly and regally, and allowed them to lavish their attention upon him for a moment longer. It was only right that he was praised and held up as a shining beacon of virtue, second only to his Lord.

He then gave them leave to eat.

The guests' food was set upon with gusto—but when the black-furs attempted to sup upon the herbs and eggs, Chow Ji snapped and snarled at them.

Bi De's eyes narrowed, and he let his displeasure be known with his mighty voice, his crow sending the beasts scurrying back. How dare he command them, when Bi De had given permission. The eggs and rice were for all. Chow Ji and the black-furs recoiled from him, and once more Chow Ji simpered.

"Great-Magnificent Bi De! We implore-beg you, stay your rage-wrath! These mighty-powerful reagents must be correctly-properly used-refined!"

'*So, he wishes to cook them in his cauldron?*' Bi De asked. The Great Master cooked all of his meals, so that must be it.

Chow Ji's eyes widened, and once more his *smile* covered his face. Bi De was unimpressed.

"Great-Magnificent Bi De, you do not know-notice what this is?" he asked in his chittering voice. "Come-come, let Chow Ji show you his great-powerful *Spirit Furnace*."

'*Furnace?*' Bi De gazed curiously at the vessel. It did not cook things? What use was it, then?

Chow Ji barked orders to his lesser black-furs, and they snapped into motion. The "Spirit Furnace" was swiftly erected upon a different configuration of its scaffolding. Chow Ji clambered up to the top and sat upon it.

Then he started chanting. The black-furs squealed in time with his rising and falling voice, and more of the little ones climbed as well, placing their paws upon it.

Bi De felt their Qi, and the Spirit Furnace began to *glow*. The Heavenly Herbs and the eggs were gathered by the black-furs, their voices making a discordant song, and raised up with reverence to Chow Ji and his cauldron.

And then, the herbs and eggs were placed within. On the top of the furnace, Chow Ji began making strange arcane gestures as the Qi became visible, directing and controlling it.

The cauldron swirled with prismatic colours, smoke occasionally belching out from the sides. Bi De could feel the Qi roiling and pulsing, changing and burning. He was transfixed by the sight.

Even Chun Ke and Pi Pa had ceased their annoying sounds, gazing upon what was occurring in from their pen.

For an hour, the black-furs toiled, the lesser ones becoming more and more exhausted, with some even staggering away from the cauldron and collapsing when their paltry Qi was exhausted. Yet for each one that fell, they were replaced by another of their kin. It was a baffling sight, as the flames got hotter, and the Qi swirled more intently, in time with the chants and squeaks. Suddenly, Chow Ji's eyes opened, and he began barking orders, his Qi clamped down and kept the glow stable.

And then, it was over. The furnace burst open, spewing multi-coloured fumes out into the air, along with an acrid, burning tang. Chow Ji laughed with glee as he reached his paws in and retreated, raising what was within the cauldron to the sky. Grasped in his hands were two round seed-like objects. They were yellow, with green swirls over them. Slowly, reverently, Chow Ji descended his scaffolding.

"Great-Magnificent Bi De, I gift-present this Spirit Pill to you!" Chow Ji exclaimed, holding one of them out for him.

Only two? Bi De thought to himself, raising an eyebrow.

Bi De was unimpressed. These small things would not fill a belly. And though they felt potent with Qi, to use so many of the Heavenly Herbs and eggs for this was . . . well, it seemed wasteful to his eyes.

Chow Ji's eyes widened. "Great-Magnificent Bi De, you have attained your great might-power without ingesting-refining a single pill? Truly, you are strong-powerful!" He once more fell to his knees in acknowledgement of Bi De's might. "But this will make you even more-more mighty-powerful. Refine it within your body, Bi De, and know-understand the difference."

Power. He wanted power. Power to defend Great Fa Ram. Power to make his master proud. Power to comprehend the world around him.

Power. Would this make him more powerful, more worthy of his Great Master's benevolence?

Bi De once again examined the pill held out to him. They were guests, trying to repay him. He supposed it was only polite to partake of their toils, like Great Master's servants cooking for him a meal and working his fields on his behalf.

"Be cautioned-warned, Great-Magnificent Bi De. Its power is mighty-great. It will not be content-happy to be consumed. It is power refined to its utmost-pinnacle . . . you must master-tame it."

Bi De hesitantly took the pill in his beak and looked to Chow Ji, who was watching him intently. The creature smiled again, in its twisted way, and nodded.

Bi De swallowed.

It was as if there was a fire shoved into his core. Bi De recoiled, as his Qi shuddered and jolted. The pill began to rampage within his belly, throwing off streamers of uncontrolled Qi. He grabbed with the sudden surge within him, struggling to hold onto the Qi as to prevent it from doing damage, but the black-fur was right. This was potent. He swiftly leapt onto the Great Pillars of the Fa Ram, taking his rightful perch, and began to sort through the disturbance in his Qi. His eyes closed as he directed all his focus within.

The Qi swirled and coiled as he refined the pill within him, and he examined it closely. It was similar to the feeling that the Heavenly Herbs normally gave off but was magnified greatly in violence and intensity. He had to tame it or be hurt by it.

He moved his Qi with the streamers of power. Guiding, directing. Consuming. *Refining*. Comprehending the flow, and the power that was now within him.

The once raging power quieted. Bi De mastered it, controlled it, and added it to his own. But there were parts of it that felt . . . *off*. The pill was imperfect, and there were some sort of impurities now within his body.

He considered them. They were small, almost unnoticeable. The tiny things would do no damage, bare specks, to one as great as he. He would examine those later, but he expected little to come from them.

He examined his Qi as well, and his sudden surge of might.

Bi De contemplated his new power and rose to his feet, beginning to perform his training. His leg snapped out in a kick. The air *cracked* with the new speed of his strikes.

Bi De smiled.

↔

Chow Ji watched Bi De from back atop the Spirit Furnace. His Clan-kin brought him more rice, and he took a few moments to consider the rooster's movements and his Qi.

His lips had quirked as he'd found what he'd been looking for, and then he returned to his own refinement.

The pill had been more powerful than he'd been expecting. Even he, who had eaten many pills before, was pleased by its quality. The Qi was bright and full of energy. Compared to their last home, the difference in quality was staggering. How lucky, to be forced out of one home, only to find one far superior?

There were many good reagents here. Their numbers would swell, and he would be able to operate his Spirit Furnace for longer periods of time as more and more of his lessers could add their souls to the cause.

"Yes-yes," Chow Ji muttered, staring out over the land and rubbing his hands together. His eyes landed on the Spirit Herbs and the chicken coops. "There are many, *many* fine-good reagents here."

The guardian of this place . . . the Rooster wished for power. Chow Ji would grant it.

But all power came at a cost.

Chow Ji chuckled to himself. Yes-yes, things were going far-far better than he planned-anticipated.

↔

The day turned to night, and Bi De once more patrolled. He had new charges to protect and new power to test. His spirit surged as he leapt from tree to tree, searching far and wide across Fa Ram for any threats.

Yes, letting in the black-furs had been the right decision. He guarded the pitiful creatures as they slept; it was the sleep of the unworried, secure under his unceasing vigil.

The cheer they gave and the prostrations they performed as he fed them the next morning swelled his pride. They greeted him as saviour and protector. Naturally, he would defend them. They were guests until they could be safely sent on their way, and the rights of hospitality were sacred.

Chow Ji also bowed, thanking him for his generosity.

Bi De went to work, his feathers puffed out and his step purposeful and confident. He hoped his Great Master would be proud of his benevolence.

CHAPTER 14

SOMETHING UN-BEAR-ABLE

We had made terrible time. With the hangovers it was expected, really, and Meimei's cures only did so much. I didn't mind. With the harvest in, I was in no rush, and this relaxed pace was nice too. I got to spend my time talking to Meimei about medicine. It was a subject I wasn't well versed in, but it was nice listening to her enthusiastic explanations.

It was actually one of the things the people here were strangely advanced in. Hell, she knew what germs were, and *that* had thrown me for a loop. Apparently, some cultivator messing around with a technique called *The Thousand-Li View* had discovered you could use it like a microscope, revealing germs and bacteria to him. *And then he actually shared the discovery.*

It still wasn't particularly *common* knowledge, but a bunch of Rou's memories did have him being told to wash his hands, at the very least.

Of course, most cultivators used the knowledge to make better poisons and bioweapons, but hey, that first dude?

Respect.

And then Meimei combined it with an explanation about the Four Essences. I vaguely remembered something like that from Traditional Chinese Medicine, and this place took a lot of cues from Chinese culture, even if it wasn't quite one to one. Back in the Before, lots of people considered such hocus pocus explanations bunk . . . but they were probably actually a thing here, so I would be deferring to her experience. They probably interacted with cultivation as well, not that I really cared about that part.

You know what? I'm going to see if I can buy some medical scrolls. Rou hadn't been interested in this kind of stuff, but I was.

As the day continued, everybody eventually got some more pep in their step, but I was 100 percent expecting *some* form of retaliation for speaking so loudly all day. Yun Ren and Gou Ren had been giving me nonstop stink eye and muttering to each other.

But now, we were camped out near a set of familiar hills, and I was sitting on a rock.

I like this rock. It's a very nice rock. It's got a lovely view through the trees, is actually pretty comfortable . . . and it's where I first kissed Meiling . . . Or she kissed me. That part of the night is a little bit fuzzy.

The point is, it's a nice, solid rock, with a great view, and I've got a beautiful woman sitting in my lap.

What's not to love?

"Jin, are you paying attention?" Meimei asked me, turning around so she could look at me with her nose scrunched up in annoyance. Her freckled face was inches from my own. She had my pipa held the proper way and was trying to teach me how to play as well. Granted, by her own admission, she wasn't particularly good either. But she'd been enthusiastic when I'd asked her to teach me.

I leaned down and kissed her. Her lovely violet eyes went wide, shocked into inaction for a moment, before she closed them and leaned into the kiss.

I slipped my hand into her robe and placed it against her warm, bare stomach. There was a sharp intake of breath, and then her hand came to rest on my own, and she pushed into my lips all the harder.

I pulled back, and she kept her eyes closed for a moment.

"Sorry. I was distracted by the beautiful view."

Her lips twitched into a slightly crooked smile.

"You're the only person besides my father to say that."

I grinned. "I am superior to all other men!" I declared pompously. "It is no wonder I have a superior eye for beauty as well!!"

She giggled and turned back around, laying against my chest.

"Are there other cultivators as strange as you?" she asked me.

I remembered all the stories about revenge, about extermination, and about even the heroes lying, cheating, and poisoning their way to the top, uncaring about the trail of bodies they left in their wake.

"I like to think I'm the normal one," I told her honestly.

↔

While yesterday had been a bit of a wash, everybody was bright and chipper today and in full "tradition" mode. We marched instead of trudged; Meiling's dad had borrowed my pipa and was playing it properly. Everyone else had the lanterns out, though they were currently unlit.

Yao Che led us onwards while I was positioned to the right of the bride's horse. I was in a position of great honour as the "guard" position, considering I was supposed to be the one to deal with any threats to the bride. Such a place would normally be occupied by Yun Ren, as the only other person who actually knew how to use a sword, but I had been asked, so I did it.

I had even been given a blade. From what I could tell, Yao Che had made a masterpiece. A blade that he had poured his soul into, and even I could tell that. The detailing, the engraving, the balance.. Everything about it felt perfect. It was wasted on me. I knew three things to do with a sword. Stick 'em with the pointy end, grab it by the blade, and use the cross guard as a bludgeon, or unscrew the pommel and throw it at the person. Then *End Them Rightly*. Rou's Gramps hadn't taught him anything about swords either, constantly repeating he wasn't ready for it when asked.

In other words, disregard the sword and get to punching. I at least knew how to throw those, and enhanced by Qi, they'd pack one hell of a wallop.

It was midday when Meimei suddenly called me, hurrying to my side.

"There's a mass of Qi in the woods moving towards us," she whispered. "It smells . . . *sharp* and fiery."

I nodded. *Well, shit.* "I'll go check it out," I promised. Meihua looked at me worriedly, but I just smiled in reassurance. *I hope it's not anything big. Or worse, skilled.*

But I had a job to do, and I certainly wasn't about to run off and leave everyone to fend for themselves. In any case, that was why I was here, in the weakest area in the continent. I would be able to handle anything that came at me.

I hope.

Still my confidence reassured her. She relaxed and bowed her head in my direction.

I marched off. There was a steep hill that I slid down into the forest, heading in the direction Meimei had given me. There were a couple of cheers as people watched me depart.

Off the beaten path, the land quickly became wild and untamed. There were giant trees, probably twenty feet in diameter. *Redwood*-sized, with height to match, towering into the sky. I had a few of them on my property, in the back. They were true giants that touched the sky, like particularly massive redwoods. They were just extremely beautiful trees that took my breath away every time I looked at one. There was also a light smattering of undergrowth. The light leaking in from the canopy illuminated it with little dots. Otherwise, it was pretty dark.

There was an odd rumbling, and I changed direction, heading towards it. The uneven terrain did little to hinder my stride.

There, I found my quarry.

It was definitely a Spirit Beast. Most looked a lot like normal animals. Just huge, or with spikes and stuff sticking off them. It was some kind of bear, but red and grey. A Blaze Bear, I think? They were endemic to the Azure Hills. For a bear, it looked pretty normal. Not too many spikes sticking off of it, and though it was big, it was still a height that was believable, instead of the mind-boggling bulk of the Earth-Crushing Devil Serpent I had run from when I was travelling to the Azure Hills. That thing was as thick around as the bear was long.

It saw me, and its eyes narrowed. The beast rose up onto its hind legs, rearing to its twelve-foot height, and roared to the heavens, spewing flame out of its mouth and igniting its fur. It brandished its massive sword-like claws and took a step forward, its eyes narrowing with challenge.

My heart began to thunder in my chest as the monstrous hell-beast took a step towards me. Sweat beaded on my forehead, and my mouth became dry. And this thing was a weak monster. Nothing from the Before could even come close to it.

I swallowed. Okay, time to prove my worth. It was my first real fight in nearly a year—that weak cultivator, the mangy wolf, and the foxes didn't count.

I took a deep breath and drew on my Qi, reinforcing my limbs and wrapping it around my body in a protective shell.

With a sharp exhale, I got into a stance, the one Rou had practised the most. The one I still did out of habit in the mornings, to wake myself up for the day. My Qi echoed out from where I stomped my foot. The ground seemed to shake as I gathered my resolve. I got ready to move into action, glaring at my foe. My Qi rose from me, a burning warmth in my chest and all around me—

The bear's eyes bugged out and it toppled over its own feet suddenly trying to reverse, its flames extinguishing. It rolled backwards awkwardly and came back up onto its knees, with its forehead pushed against the ground.

Huh?

I stared at the bear as its head went up and down, hitting the dirt.

". . . the hell?"

Is . . . is it doing dogeza? Or I guess it's kowtowing here . . .

Smack smack smack went the bear's head. I stayed briefly in my stance before slowly dropping my fist.

"Hey," I eventually said. "Can you understand me?"

The bear stopped slamming its head into the ground and nodded frantically.

Well, *this* was awkward. But . . . at least I could reason with it?

"Uh . . . stay away from people and the road, okay? It's dangerous."

The bear frantically nodded again.

I stared at it for a moment longer, the bear becoming visibly more uncomfortable. ". . . good talk. You can go now." I shooed the bear away.

The creature stared at me in shock and confusion.

"Go on," I urged it.

The bear got up and fled deeper into the forests, glancing over its shoulder to make sure I wasn't following.

"Bye?"

The bear kept running.

That . . . didn't make *any* sense. Was it young? I was shit at sensing Qi—I knew that much. This *was* the Azure Hills, the weakest place on the continent. But there was no way I should have enough power to just send it packing like that. Just from getting *ready* to fight.

I guess Meimei hadn't told me *how* weak it was. I'd have to ask her about it later.

I grimaced as a smell hit me and looked at the . . . *soiled* patch on the forest floor.

"Did . . . *did it crap itself*?" I shook my head, letting out a bark of laughter, and pushed through the dense underbrush back towards our caravan. It was quite a bit thicker here, but it *was* a clearing, so it made sense: more light, more plants.

In no time at all, I was back on the path and beside Meihua. Everyone looked at me expectantly.

"Just a Blaze Bear. Don't worry, I don't think it will bother anybody else," I reassured them, and the rest of them cheered.

The entire party seemed to want to slap me on the back or pound my shoulder, roaring that it was a huge accomplishment. Meiling just smiled at me, looking relieved.

"Ha-ha! That's our Brother Jin!" Yao Che shouted.

→

The gates of Verdant Hill finally came into view in the dim twilight.

Our paper lanterns lit the way as we walked on either side of Meihua's horse. The light caught her glossy black hair and red robe, producing an odd, ethereal effect. In that illumination, she was *enchantingly* beautiful. I had to force myself to stop staring.

I wondered how Meimei would look like when it was our turn. This procession was *very* nice-looking. I wish I had a camera to preserve this moment. Or a recording crystal.

Recording crystals were *expensive,* though. Like, enough to buy another set of my land at least. And while I *kind of* knew how cameras worked, there was no possible way I would be able to recreate one.

Maybe . . . I can ask for a few odd jobs during the winter in town. Or I'll go find some more foxes and sell them to those Heavenly Furs guys.

The gates, normally closed at night, were opened for us. The guards had known we were coming, and it wasn't too late.

People on either side of the street cheered at the spectacle as we wound through town until we came to a small compound—it was bigger than most houses, and the people within were definitely well off.

Zhuge Tingfeng and his parents greeted us at the entrance, as well as two servants.

"My friends! Please partake of my hospitality!" Tingfeng's father called. "I know your journey has been long, and I bid you rest and recover, for the houses of Zhuge and Yao shall be joined tomorrow!"

There was some soup with dumplings served to us as we entered the little walled compound. While Meihua would get an actual room, the houses weren't quite big enough to accommodate everybody. So, the rest of us were camping again.

"Hey . . . Meimei?" I asked, as we got ready for bed.

"Yes?"

"How strong was that Blaze Bear, anyway?"

She shrugged. "No idea. I can't give specifics, but it was a lot weaker than you. Yours is like the fresh smell of the harvest. The Blaze Bear's was like ash on the wind, a fire in the distance."

I frowned, as I got out my bedroll. *A* lot *weaker, huh?*

The thought swirled in my head as I laid down to sleep. Big day tomorrow. I've been to a few weddings before, but Rou hadn't. I wondered what they were like in this world . . .

CHAPTER 15

SIDE QUEST

I wasn't getting to sleep.

I tossed and turned on my bedroll, ill thoughts swirling through my mind.

That incident with the bear *bothered* me.

Rou hadn't been very strong. At least, he didn't *think* he was very strong, and he'd got beaten up so badly he died. Strong enough to drive off weak Spirit Beasts, yeah, but it still should have been a *fight*. It was "weak," but even weak Spirit Beasts were supposed to be tough as hell and hard to kill. If this was a story, it should have been a hard-fought victory. I'd eventually defeat the Blaze Bear with guile, or my technique, and then eat its Spirit Core and get the Blazing Bear scripture, something only I understood the value to, that I would then cultivate into a power that shook the heavens!

Or something.

I would've settled for Meimei fussing over some injuries—though, it would more realistically be her dad, since he was better with medicine, or so she said.

Instead, a Spirit Beast that I *should've* had a hard time with had literally shit itself when I called on my Qi and then begged for its life. Even if it was young, it shouldn't have done that.

Not unless I was so far beyond the bear, it couldn't comprehend beating me.

But . . . *I wasn't cultivating*. Okay, I was cultivating, but I wasn't *cultivating*. I hadn't been sitting around circling my Qi—I'm a *farmer*. I used my Qi like a tool, and by the end of most days, I was completely empty. There were no breakthroughs I noticed, no bottlenecks . . . and I hadn't even *tried* to gauge my own power.

I can feel the scent of flowers on the breeze. The suddenly thick underbrush around my legs— I rolled onto my side and called some of my Qi into my hand, pushing it into the granite tiles around my bedroll.

Nothing happened.

The stones got a little reinforced, I guess, but when I put my Qi into my plants, nothing else happened either.

If plants grow too fast, they deplete nutrients from the soil.

We give to the land, and the land gives back.

Was I unconsciously holding back? Every time I put my Qi into my crops, it was deliberate. I wanted to reinforce and nurture. To make them *better*, instead of making them grow faster because I didn't want to damage the soil.

What would happen if I just let go?

I closed my eyes and started to pull. It felt like I was tugging on a mountain. But slowly, ever so slowly, it started to move. My Qi churned and started to accelerate forward, like an avalanche, unstoppable in its might, ready to bear down on—

Nope.

I slammed on the brakes. I pressed back against the tide, and for a moment, it seemed like it would continue forwards anyway. Then it stilled, solidifying. I was breathing heavily as I clenched my hand into a fist. Sweat dripped on the ground. I bit my knuckle and rolled onto my back.

I'm afraid of what I'll see.

My mind flashed through memories, some fresher than others. Memories of losing my temper, starting a fight on a whim because I could, satisfaction that I would win. *My* memories. It wasn't just Rou that had issues. There were little flashes of irritation that threatened to escalate. The fur trader and his blabbing mouth. The people in the cities and the towns, pushing and shoving. The only thing that had stopped me from acting were the consequences. The consequences of the Before.

But what if there *were* no consequences? What if you could fight off the guards, fight off the army? Cultivators could do whatever they wanted.

It was a tempting thought. To truly be free. To do as you pleased, with nothing, nobody able to tell you otherwise.

To live out all the power fantasies I'd ever had.

All those powerful cultivators, killing and destroying without a care in the world. Crushing villages as collateral damage. Seeking out others with power, just to fight them.

Trees, strangling entire cities. The mountains venting their terrible wrath. The very earth, rising up and going to war.

An icy finger of dread crawled up my spine.

Me—in the middle of a field of carnage—and staring greedily at the heavens. The grim satisfaction I feel as everybody who had ever wronged me was bowed and broken at my feet.

If I had that strength . . . Then what could possibly stop me?

"Jin?" Meimei asked with a sleepy voice, rubbing at her eye. "Is something wrong? Your Qi smells like . . ." At this, her nose wrinkled. "Overboiled rice and peat."

The woman who would be my wife was concerned. She was concerned for my well-being, curious and ready to help.

A thousand villages like Hong Yaowu, shattered like so much kindling. An argument. Harsh words . . . and unrestrained power. Something fragile breaking.

The world of cultivation. The rat race for the heavens, coming for this sleepy little province.

I let out a nervous laugh, even as bile flooded the back of my throat at the horrid thought.

"Yeah, sorry, just a bad dream," I replied, waving her off. "Go back to bed, Meimei."

She squinted at me, considering my words, and then marched forwards.

She keeled over and thumped beside me onto my bedroll.

"Mei—"

Her arms wrapped around my head, and she pulled me into her chest. I could hear the steady *thump-thump* of her heart.

She smelled like an herb garden.

"Sleep," she grunted at me.

I let out a breath, and some of the tension drained out of my shoulders.

Underneath, my Qi burbled unpleasantly.

→

Meimei's warmth was gone when I woke up. I had obviously slept in a bit.

But there was something else in my bed. Something hairy, and it smelled like a warm animal.

I heard muffled giggling.

I opened my eyes, and a goat stared back at me, chewing its cud. It looked *spectacularly* bored with this situation.

You know, I'm not even mad. I'm impressed. How the hell did they slip this into my arms without me waking up? The goat looked at me and continued chewing.

"Have a good rest, my darling?" I asked it, and somebody choked, trying to hold in their laughter.

I stood and picked up the goat around its middle, holding it under one arm. The rest of the people from Hong Yaowu were staring at me, trying to hold back laughter.

"To breakfast, my dear. And speak not of our tryst to Meiling!" I declared dramatically.

The dam broke. Gou Ren fell onto his back howling with laughter.

My betrothed came out of the main house to find out what the fuss was about, and she raised an eyebrow at me as soon as she saw the spectacle unfolding.

"Oh no, she found us! We must away!" I started in a faux panic.

Her hand met her face, but she was clearly amused.

"Jin . . ." She sighed. "Wash your face well."

Ah, they drew stuff on me too, huh?

I just shook my head with a smile. They got me.

I pushed some of the lingering thoughts I had from the night to the back of my mind. There was stuff to do.

"Whose goat is this, anyway?" I asked.

→

Gou Ren didn't actually know whose goat it was. He thought it was the Zhuge's, due to him finding it in their compound, but they insisted it wasn't theirs.

So, after I finished washing the dicks off my face—people were the same everywhere—I set off to find the owner. I didn't have to do anything for the wedding yet either and had been shooed off from helping in the kitchen.

So here I was. A goat under my arm, placidly chewing some cud, and Meimei's little brother on my shoulders, asking around town if anybody had lost a goat.

Gonna be honest here, that wasn't how I expected my day to go. I thought I was here for a wedding, not a side-quest.

But again, I was in no rush. It was kinda fun.

I handed a skewer of meat up to Xian Jr. He had said that they smelled really good, so what the hell.

"Thank you, Senior Brother!" the eight-year-old cheered, biting into the glazed chicken and mushrooms.

I found a place to sit and deposited our goat. I handed the goat a carrot, and she took it with the same placid expression.

Xian Jr. slid from my shoulders to my lap, kicking his legs as he ate. I absently wiped some of the sauce on his cheek away with my thumb.

"Ho there!" a man that looked a bit twitchy called. "I see you found my goat!"

"Probably. What's its brand look like?" I asked. The goat didn't actually have a brand. *I'm just bullshitting, but he doesn't know I am.*

Mister Twitchy froze, sweat breaking out on his forehead.

"Maybe . . . it's not my goat, after all. I'll just be going!" he said as he turned around and quite nearly fled in the other direction.

Yeah, I thought so, buddy. Well, we've got about an hour left until we have to be back for the ceremony.

I lifted Xian Jr. back up to my shoulders and turned to the goat.

"Well, let's keep looking." The goat got up and shook itself. We set off down the street.

After half an hour of more wandering, we came to a little shack at the edge of town. The goat—which had been content to walk behind me—set off with its hooves clopping.

"Ah! Lan Fan, you devil! I was wondering where you had gone off to!" I heard an elderly voice shout. An old woman stalked out of her shack, waving a broom threateningly at the goat.

Lan Fan looked unimpressed. The old grey-haired and hunched woman harrumphed before turning to us. One of her eyes was cloudy and blind, the other an odd shade of grey. Both of them narrowed at us.

"And do I have this young gentlemen to thank for bringing this vile beast back to me?"

I made the appropriate gesture of respect with my hands. "Yes, Grandmother, she had wandered into the Zhuge compound, and I sought to return her to her rightful place."

The old woman frowned and grabbed my hand, squinting up at my face. Her good eye rolled around crazily for a second, and then she focused on me again.

She harrumphed, again.

"You, boy, stay here," she demanded, then wandered into her shack.

A little bit awkward, but I shrugged and waited.

She swiftly returned with a kitten, which she shoved into my arms.

"Take good care of it," she demanded. "A good farmer should have a cat."

And then she left.

I stared blankly at the stripy orange kitten. A kitten for a goat. *This . . . is a very strange side quest. I wonder what I trade the kitten for. A +3 sword?*

CHAPTER 16

COMMANDMENT

Meiling looked on as the wine was exchanged, trying to keep her eyes dry. Tingfeng and Meihua's heads bowed three times towards the west, right when the sun started to set.

Yao Che and Tingfeng's father and grandfather bowed to each other.

And then it was done.

It had been several months in the making, this wedding. And now, Meiling's best friend would be a two-day journey away instead of right next door.

Their parting would hurt, but Meiling would endure it. She was happy that her friend had married someone she actually liked. Tingfeng was a good man, and he would take care of her.

She tried not to cry as Meihua caught her gaze, unshed tears gathering at the corner of her eyes. In the absence of her deceased mother, it was Meiling who had done the traditional dressing of the bride. She was the one who had helped to hand her away.

Meihua's smile towards her was radiant. It was like the sun moved on a whim to perfectly illuminate her face, and the decorations around her took on a vibrant new life. Her red dress blazed with the sun.

Meiling guessed that it was just her emotions getting the better of her.

But for now, their participation was at its end. The young couple departed to their rooms, and the feast began.

Meiling's heart was full of joy, though there was a dark spot in the proceedings that had come out of nowhere. Meiling had expected this to be a joyous day—a time for thanksgiving and a time to enjoy herself after the union was done.

And yet, something had happened the previous night. Jin's once warm and refreshing scent had churned and boiled like an untended cauldron. He smelled *wrong*. It made her a bit nauseous, being so close. Last night, his face had been pale, and his mannerisms were off.

She knew something must have really disturbed him since he'd told her to leave instead of making even a token effort of getting her to sleep beside him. Because of that, she had braved the smell and held him tightly, no matter how much her stomach roiled.

Her presence seemed to have been a balm, and most of the ugly churning had died down. When she had slipped out of his embrace in the morning, he was almost completely scentless.

But then Jin started . . . *leaking*, for the lack of a better word. The smell was slightly too sweet—like overripe fruit. It was minute, but it was there—an undercurrent to his normal scent.

Oh, sure, he had acted like his usual self for most of the day. He took Gou Ren's prank with his normal good humour and brought her little brother out for a walk to return the goat, coming back with a kitten from the grateful owner. Jin had seemed bemused by the entire thing, and now the cat was sleeping in his carriage.

But his smiles were slightly off, and his brow was clenched with worry, even as he laughed with other guests and enjoyed the festivities.

Eventually, he had seemed to tire of even this and wandered away to go and sit in the carts.

Meiling smiled at her father and begged off some of the festivities. She picked up a pitcher of rice wine and a platter of dumplings and went to find him. They wouldn't be missed, and things were starting to get rowdy.

There would be many hangovers the next day, that she was sure of. And nothing left to dull the edge.

She found Jin sitting on his cart, absentmindedly stroking his kitten.

"What should I name you, little girl? *Pu Shi*?" His lips quirked slightly into a smile. "Nah, that's just rude. You're going to be a good girl. And though you may be a girl, this one is a powerful name, from a powerful, wonderful tiger . . . *Tigu'er* sounds good, right?"

The kitten yowled, snuggling into him.

Meiling said nothing as she clambered into the carriage beside him, setting down the plate and the bottle. Jin looked slightly surprised, but he smiled at her.

"You're too good to me, you know that?" his crooked grin softened slightly as he looked at her. "Keep spoiling me so much, and I'll become a useless man."

"Then I'll just have to set you straight again if that happens," she declared.

Jin laughed, took a dumpling, and downed a swig from the pitcher.

They lapsed into silence for a while, listening to the shouts and the laughter of people having a good time. Jin's face was set into a frown. Something was obviously still bothering him. The bear? Meiling didn't know, but she did know the best way to get to that topic was by talking.

"Jin?" she asked, and he flinched slightly, turning to look at her.

"Yeah?"

"You've said you're from Raging Waterfall Gorge before, but what kind of place did you grow up in?"

He paused, and his brow furrowed.

"I've never told you what city I was from?" He seemed surprised that it had slipped his mind. His eyes defocused again as he reminisced. "Crimson Crucible City, out above Demon's Grave Ravine. It's . . . well, it's a city. Most cities are the same everywhere you go. Noisy, crowded. Lots of people looking to make it big, and the gutters are filled with those that didn't." He frowned. "Never liked the city. Or *any* city, really. I'll go to one if I have to, but I much prefer it out there." He gestured in the vague direction of her village and his farm.

He handed her the wine, and she took a swig.

"That's far away. Dangerous, too. The things that live near Demon's Grave Ravine make the Spirit Beasts here look like normal animals." She leaned closer to him. "Is it true that the city gets attacked by demons?" she whispered.

Jin nodded. "I saw it once. Well, kind of. You don't really see much through the defensive formations. Most people just keep on doing what they're doing. If the formation falls, everybody's dead anyway, so no sense in worrying about it."

Meiling could scarcely imagine it. To just go about your life while demons battered at the gates? She had seen drawings in scrolls of them before, but somehow they seemed more fantastical than cultivators. They were all devilish bodies and corrosive Qi.

She handed the pitcher back.

"Who taught you how to cultivate?" she asked.

"Gramps. My grandfather. Well, he wasn't *really* my grandfather. He picked me up off the street after my parents died of the *Demon's Black Hate*. Watching somebody vomit up their entire stomach is . . . well, it was pretty gross, I'll be honest."

Jin grimaced, obviously replaying the memory. Meiling shuddered too. The reagents to cure it were expensive enough to buy the entirety of Verdant Hill twice over.

"He got me off the street and started training me. He was an old drunk, but he never seemed to run out of money. I never did advance as fast as he wanted me to. 'You're not done yet!?' he'd shout, then I'd call him an old bastard, we'd fight, and then we'd have dinner. But . . . he cared for me. He fed me. He took care of me. He was the only person I had." Jin's eyes went a bit misty as he reminisced. He took a moment and then shook his head, dispelling the memory. "After . . . after a couple of years, Gramps said I was strong enough and that he had to leave. Seemed pretty upset about it. Told me I should join a Sect."

Jin traded her the pitcher again.

"Did you?" she assumed he must not have and instead travelled to the Azure Hills. Likely to get away from all the demons. She took a swig from the pitcher.

"Yeah, the Cloudy Sword Sect."

Meiling spat out her drink and started coughing.

Cloudy Sword?! she thought, her mouth dropping open. *That was one of the most powerful Sects out there! The Indomitable Cloudy Sword Sect! Bane of Demons! Masters of the Raging Cloudy Sword Formation!* He left that*?!*

Jin shrugged. "I basically did what I do now, just with more Spirit Herbs. Lots of menial labour and fixing things. I was *barely* an outer Sect disciple. So, I did the laundry, the maintenance, and grew the Spirit Herbs. Fifth Stage of the Initiate's Realm isn't much out there."

Jin's grin was rueful. Still, even if he had barely been a disciple at the Cloudy Sword Sect, the Fifth Stage of the Initiate's Realm? That was nearly into the Profound Realm. The Azure Hills' strongest Sects had *core* disciples that were barely into the *Third* Stage of the Initiate's Realm. Even the pebbles of Cloudy Sword were the mountains of the Azure Hills!

She shook her head.

"Jin . . . why did you leave?" She felt thankful that he left and came to their village . . . but she had to know *why*.

He took the pitcher back from her and had a big swig. He stared at the moon with a frown on his face.

Eventually, he answered her after the silence started to drag.

"I . . . got into a fight. It was a stupid fight. One of the Inner Sect disciples was looking for somebody to 'trade pointers' with, and I didn't get out of the way in time. He kicked the shit out of me—I don't even remember his name. But I had broken ribs, a shattered arm . . . the works. He nearly killed me—well, I guess he *did* kill me . . . my heart stopped, at least."

Meiling felt ill at the confession. Her mouth went dry as Jin cataloged his injuries. He took another swig.

"The people who dragged me back to my room decided that they deserved a 'reward' for being so kind to me, and ransacked it because there wasn't anything I could do to stop them. As I was lying there, bleeding and broken, I thought, *What the hell is the point of all of this?*

"All the fighting. All the stealing. The obsessively hoarding power. The race to get ahead and ascend . . . I realised that I didn't care about it. That ascension, that power . . . it wasn't something that I wanted to pursue if I had to keep company with those people"—he looked back at her, his eyes full of conviction—"if men like these rule the heavens, then I want nothing to do with them. I'll make my own slice of paradise right here." The hardness in his eyes faded. Jin shrugged again.

"So, I left. Maybe I'm trying to justify my own cowardice. Maybe I could have mustered some noble reason to continue like, 'I'll get strong and protect everybody!' but at the end of the day, I *chose* to be a farmer," He paused again, looking at her, and his eyes turned sad. "Although . . . maybe I didn't leave that stuff behind as much as I thought." He stared at his hand and took a breath.

For a brief moment, it felt like Meiling was drowning, so heady was the scent of the harvest. It was like loamy soil clogging her nose. From his hand swirled green light, Qi so thick it roiled through the air like a liquid.

"I'm afraid," he whispered. "I'm afraid of what I'll do. This kind of power . . . what If I do something horrible with it? What if . . . what if I become just like them?"

His normal smile had been replaced with a grimace of distress. His warm eyes were full of fear.

Meiling replied, without thinking. "The answer is simple. Don't."

The green light cut out. He looked like she had just hit him over the head with a shovel. "Just don't?"

Meiling swallowed, casting around to try and salvage the conversation. "Correct. In fact, you're not *allowed* to become like them. You have a home to look after. You're not allowed to go gallivanting around the countryside, getting in fights. Your wife forbids it." She crossed her arms and stuck her nose up into the air imperiously, while she screamed internally.

There was silence. Meiling idly wondered what she was doing, commanding a cultivator. Jin burst out laughing. The kitten on his lap yowled in anger and leapt off him, glaring as it settled in her lap instead.

He laughed so hard he dropped the jug of wine, clutching his stomach. It didn't shatter, but it fell on its side, spilling the last dregs of it into the cobblestone.

She flushed. Was he making fun of her? What did she know of cultivation? Maybe that was dumb—

The sickly sweet smell went away. Jin grinned at her with his *stupid* grin.

"Just don't? I think I can do that. Thanks, Meimei." The brightness returned to his eyes, and his shoulders stopped slumping. He let out a breath, then ran his hand along the side of the carriage, snapping off some of the twigs that had grown there.

"It's good you became a farmer," she said quietly. "Any good man would want to rid himself of such company." The tales of murderous, raping cultivators sprang to her mind. "And . . . I don't think you're a coward, either. Cowards don't fight to stop girls they barely know from getting taken by scum."

Jin sighed, like a weight had been taken from his shoulders. His smile was still a bit crooked . . . but he seemed back to his normal self.

"Yeah. Yeah, I think you're right" he declared, with increasing conviction.

She smacked him on the shoulder. "Now stop moping. *Honestly*, today is supposed to be a joyous one, and you've been out here worrying. Now come, you have a party to attend!"

"You got it, Meimei," he replied, then chuckled again. He hopped out of the carriage and held his arm out to escort her. Meiling smiled at him and gently set the kitten off to the side onto a blanket.

They began to make their way back to the party, stepping over cracks filled with grass.

"Just don't, huh?" he muttered as she dragged him into a dance.

CHAPTER 17

COUNTING THE DAYS

It had been four days since the Great Master had left.

Bi De once more rose from his nightly vigil, for he had numerous charges this day. The black-furs had slept in shifts over the night. Some were awake and tending to the Spirit Furnace, and some were asleep. Some were also digging shallow tunnels around the scaffolding. Their little heads poked out and sniffed the air before retreating back into hiding.

Bi De once more swept off the Great Pillars and once more provided for his guests a meal of rice. This was supplemented by some of the normal herbs from the Great Master's garden, those that looked dying and withered, for even his Lord was sure to have limits, if he came back to find all of his food gone.

The little black-furs sang their praises of him, and he easily accepted their supplication, walking among them with his head held tall and proud. It was only natural that others submitted themselves to him.

Thus, he embarked upon his daily chores. The coops were mucked, the floor was swept, the garden was weeded. The little black-furs followed him, observing his mighty form as he completed the tasks his Great Master had left to him.

Surely, they were in awe of his superior skill. Even Chun Ke and Pi Pa were handled with grace, though they were even more ornery than usual, snorting and snarling at the black-furs.

They were dreadful beasts. But he still had to take care of them, as charged by his Great Master. So, they were released from their pens, as his Great Master released them, so that they could root in the forest. Luckily, this drained some of their aggression, the base creatures digging in the dirt with abandon. It was nearly time to herd them back when there was a commotion out in the fields.

The black-furs were sounding an alarm, pointing at the clouds and squeaking with terror. They ran every which way in a near-blind panic. Even Chow Ji had hunkered down, observing the skies, but the crippled one stayed near his furnace.

Bi De directed his eyes upwards and saw the source of their terror. Rage overtook him. One of the wicked feathers soared in the air, its gaze locked upon his charges.

At least Basi Bu Shi had had a body that was as wicked as his heart, his sharp teeth and cruel eyes proof of his depravity. The wicked feathers, however, dared to take Bi De's noble and righteous form. Their beaks were not straight and true, but hooked and cruel. Their talons were similarly bloodthirsty and could only grasp to destroy.

The Heavens had created Bi De superior, separating his weapons. His claws could be used for manipulation, to tenderly care, while his spurs were for violence. Both were equal to the task ahead, to care for his guests, and slay the wicked.

The wicked beast swooped into a dive, targeting one of the smaller black-furs, who had wandered outside the Great Pillars. It was frozen, staring at its oncoming doom.

This would *not* stand.

Bi De leapt into action, his powerful legs propelling him to meet with the foul creature. Aided by the draw of the world, the wicked feather's dive was fast. Its body was streamlined, its gaze intent, moving in for the kill on a little black-fur.

Bi De easily surpassed the wicked feather's savage dive. He noticed the small improvement in his speed as his Qi circled around him and the blades of holy moonlight formed upon his spurs. Bi De rose to the heavens, challenging that which dared threaten his charges.

The interception was swift and brutal. The wicked feather, for all of its speed and cruelty, was no Basi Bu Shi. With a single stroke of his spurs, it was slain, its corpse falling at the feet of the little black-fur.

Bi De landed atop it. With the sun at his back, he gazed down upon the little creature. It stared back, awe in its eyes, struck dumb by his power and majesty.

It kowtowed before him.

"Many-many thanks, Great-Mighty Lord," it whispered, its voice the highest pitch he had heard from the black-furs, but the most comprehensible after Chow Ji. "This one will serve its mighty-great Lord until it die-perishes."

He knew not what service such a small creature could provide, but he would not spit upon its pride by refusing. He inclined his head, generously accepting the little one into his service.

The little one got up and followed behind him as he walked back to the Great Pillars, and a tide of black-furs came out to meet him, Chow Ji at its head. He spread out his arms at the sight, bowing low.

"Great-Magnificent Bi De, you are truly a great-powerful and generous Lord," Chow Ji declared. "Please, allow this Chow Ji to add to your power and craft more-more wondrous pills for you! Let the little ones work-toil for you so that your strength may grow-ascend!"

Bi De nodded, accepting the tribute. It was only right that the weak venerate the strong.

And so, another pill was crafted from the Heavenly Herbs.

→

It had been five days since the Great Master had left.

In five days, he had learned much about his new guests.

Bi De contemplated the black-furs. Their tiny, squeaky voices chattered in terror when the shadows of the wicked feathers darkened the land, or when they shouted the alarm of a scaled slitherer or small, long, black-furred creature that could dart easily into tunnels. They hid under their scaffold or in the tunnels they had carved underneath it and begged for him to save them.

Naturally, he did. He struck down the threats to those under his care with steely eyes and no remorse. All who threatened the sanctity of Fa Ram were defeated. The little ones rejoiced in his victories and consumed the bodies of the fallen. Under his protection, they redoubled their efforts to take care of Fa Ram.

And indeed, the black-furs and Chow Ji were industrious folk. They constantly worked with that Spirit Furnace of theirs, the little ones holding their paws against it and filling it with their Qi, while Chow Ji directed it. When they were not doing that, they scurried about on his orders, doing some of the more menial farm tasks.

Teams of black-furs weeded the gardens, swept the floors, and ran around the perimeter, checking the Great Pillars. They mucked the coops and even braved the pen that held Chun Ke and Pi Pa, who took exception to their presence, voicing their displeasure with angry squeals. They even dared to attempt to stomp and bite some of the guests, and he had to send them onto their rumps with the power of his wings. They glared mutinously at him for that, but they accepted his decree.

Some teams went to the forests, picking up mushrooms and seeds. Some were tasked with ranging farther and found more small herbs with Qi in them to add to the pile for his or Chow Ji's approval.

They worked themselves hard for his sake, so he could dedicate more time to becoming stronger. They took a minute amount, less than he or his Great Master would take, and they ate heartily.

This left Bi De more time to look upon the world, more time to grow his Qi, and more time to hone his kicks and sharpen his spurs.

The second pill had been just as effective as the first, the Qi rampaging into his system until it was subdued and refined, adding its strength to his own.

Bi De concentrated within himself, feeling the flow of his newfound power. His Qi swelled, and he knew he would be able to take on a hundred, no, a *thousand* of Basi Bu Shi's ilk in single combat. His breath was better. His eyes were sharper. His spurs were even more deadly.

These pills were *most* efficacious. Indeed, his Great Master would see their worth. He was pleased he had followed his Great Master's example and given these guests hospitality. Give and receive, as is the nature of the world. Once his Great Master returned, he too could partake of the fruits of the guest's labours and concentrate upon his own strength as the black-furs toiled for them both.

One of the black-furs, the little one that had pledged her loyalty, squeaked to get his attention, holding out to him one of Chow Ji's newest concoctions, another pill. Ah, she was already serving. Eager to prove her worth, how admirable!

He accepted it with regal grace and turned his attention to circulating his Qi, refining the newest pill and adding its power to his own.

↔

That night, after he had finished refining the pill, he was approached.

"Great-Magnificent Bi De, this Chow Ji humbly beg-implores you!" the black-fur asked, bowing low. "Chow Ji needs-requires some more of the Heavenly Herbs, as so to perfect-refine his recipe! Greater-better pills will follow!"

Bi De, being a generous host, approved of his aims. Striving to improve oneself was the essence of life. The stock of Heavenly Herbs was high, and when his Great Master returned, there would be no doubt that they would be effectively limitless, nurtured by this Lord's Power.

It would be best to use them in this way.

"You are smart-wise to see the value of Chow-Ji's work, Great-Magnificent Bi De! I shall strive to make us ever more mighty-powerful!"

Bi De nodded magnanimously and returned to his meditation. Tomorrow was the most perfect form of the crescent moon, and he would need to be ready to once more contemplate it, hopefully furthering his understanding of it and his blades.

He commanded the black-furs to set up a night watch to fully invest himself, and they obeyed, promising him their utmost efforts.

→

It had been six days since the Great Master had left.

Now, Bi De stood with Chow Ji over the Spirit Furnace, adding his own might to the process. Many Spirit Herbs had been collected. Odd nuts and mushrooms and eggs had been procured by the toils of the little ones.

They were ready to proceed with the newest pill, but Chow Ji seemed nervous about his next request. "Great Magnificent Bi De, This Chow Ji would request something that may be insulting to the Lord of this land." He bowed his head and wrung his Great-Master-like hands. "For this recipe to reach its full strength-power, we will need blood."

Bi De turned his full attention upon the rodent.

Chow Ji cringed at Bi De's sudden sharp gaze, but Bi De gestured for him to continue.

"This would not slay-kill any of the females, but their blood is thick-rich with Qi; we can use it to stabilize this component and bring us greater power-might. With your leave-permission, we shall drain-harvest some blood."

Bi De thought on it. It could be like what the Great Master did. His Qi went back to him. Bi De was, however, loath to take what was his Master's.

But . . . he felt close to some kind of strength increase. As he contemplated the moon and circulated his Qi, he could feel his power knocking on some sort of wall, trying to find a way to break through it. Surely, the Great Master would not begrudge him?

The rooster turned to Chow Ji and gave his permission. A wide smile spread across his face, and his body nearly vibrated with joy.

Some blood was harvested from the hens. They clucked angrily as little teeth made incisions in their legs, but it did not seem to be too much pain. The industrious creatures harvested some blood from each hen, then returned once more for the ritual, the flames soaring as the blood was added. This one . . . this one was different. Bi De's head started to pound when the black-furs began to chant. Their voices rose and fell as the Spirit Furnace shuddered. Strange power filled the clearing, bathing everything in red light. It was a difficult refinement. The longest yet, with many smaller black-furs falling unconscious; their comrades left them slumped over, so intent upon their toils were they. Bi De himself joined the ritual, lending a bit of his own power to make sure the refinement was completed.

The Furnace popped open, revealing two blood-red pills. They were filled with Qi. Roiling, potent, and ready to be used. Bi De stared at them greedily, side by side with Chow Ji.

The black-fur leader reached in, examining them with an air of reverence. Then he turned and bowed to Bi De, presenting the potent medicine. It was the most powerful pill yet, thick with rich energy. He knew that he could only take one. A second would be too much for his system.

Bi De accepted his tribute and returned to the Great Pillars to contemplate and refine. Everything else was immaterial as he tuned out the rest of the world.

↔

Chow Ji smiled as the rooster consumed the pill. It was time to weave his spell. His Qi, along with the pill, entered the bird's body. It circulated within him and . . . *pushed.* Gently, almost unnoticeably. His Qi wriggled forward.

[Impure Earthly Desires]

It was a subtle thing, for it had to be. Bi De was terrifyingly strong for these lands. But with this, it didn't matter how strong Bi De was. Slow, constant pressure was all Chow Ji needed.

The rooster would have strength, as promised. But his strength would be Chow Ji's. This "Fa Ram" would be his. Just a little more.

He turned to his servants, to the dead forms of his Clan-kin, their very lives invested in the pill, drained of all their Qi and vital spirit. "Eat-dispose of the corpses," he commanded, and the little ones hastened to obey, setting upon their fallen kin. Soon, the numbers would be replaced.

But he did not notice the horror of the smallest of them, as she turned down her head and acted like she was obeying.

In her mind, her own thoughts whirled.

CHAPTER 18

CRACKED MOON

It was the fourth day since he had met Brother Chow Ji.

Wait. That was incorrect. Bi De paused in his thoughts and recentered himself. Why did he think that? Brother Chow Ji was indeed important, but to think of him before the Great Master? He was a disloyal disciple for that. He would need to perform some sort of penance for this.

After he was finished in this stage of his cultivation, of course.

It was the seventh day since the Great Master had left.

Brother Chow Ji's pills had increased his power greatly. He could see the Great Pillars of this stage of his cultivation, the barriers between this stage and the next. Soon, he would break past them and truly ascend. He would be the mightiest cock in the realm. The thought was heady. It had him driven to obsession, to gather his strength, to make himself mighty for his Great Master.

He needed more power. He needed to cultivate *more*.

The black-furs would take care of the menial labour. That was what they were there for. Fa Ram did not *need* his attention. He would serve it better from his current position. He had to cycle his Qi.

He *had* to cycle his Qi.

All day, he sat upon the Great Pillars. He did not move to eat. Food was brought to him by teams of his servants, who gathered for him his normal meal, even including some of the interlopers from the Heavenly Herbs. When the black-fur came to give him his pill, he ate it without thinking, totally focused upon his task.

Brother Chow Ji had his best interests at heart, and he had to keep cultivating. *He had to get stronger.*

□

She had no name. She was small and weak, but she *knew*. She knew the great one was in danger. Wicked Chow Ji had deceived the mighty and righteous bird with his pills and foul magicks.

Chow Ji was twisting and corrupting the great bird, but she had no idea how to help. The great one was so consumed with his cultivation that he had wholly disregarded her when she tried to speak with him. To warn him. He would hear nothing of her pitiful squeaks, and she knew she could not oppose Chow Ji directly.

She kept her act like she was like the others of her kin, but she knew the old one was smart. He would see through her eventually, and then . . . he would take her. She would be the mother of the next generation, the mother of Chow Ji's brood. Ones that knew were *rare*. While the rest of her kin could follow orders, they had no true spark to call their own. They simply acted out the knowing one's actions. They were like the ones that held the same form as the Great Bi De, filled with energy that could be used, but dumb.

And Chow Ji had been waiting for a female to use ever since his mate died in the great purge that had destroyed their colony.

And so, the little one fretted. She could not oppose Chow Ji physically or with her tiny amount of Qi. That was doomed to failure. So instead, she watched him and took note of his spells. How their energy moved, and how she could neutralize it.

Hopefully.

Now, she sat in the pen near the giants, behind a bucket and hidden from view. The smell was intense. Her kin were reluctant to come near this place, for the giants bellowed rage and hatred, and attempted to stomp and crush any interloper.

Here, she practised with her minuscule Qi, and in her mind's eye she wove and unwove Chow Ji's magicks. She didn't know if she could do such a thing while he was actively resisting her, but she had to try. Try, for the gallant and mighty warrior who had saved her . . . who had *cared*. Who would not just use her like Chow Ji used the others.

She was so consumed with her own thoughts that she didn't notice the giants until they had snuck up on her. There were no stomping feet to alert her. No enraged squeals.

A great gust of wind from their nostrils assaulted her, and the two giants beheld her tiny form. Their eyes were narrowed with wrath and hate. The larger of the two opened his mouth, revealing the beginnings of large tusks, ready to tear and rend.

She froze and felt despair. They would surely slay her, as they had tried to slay all others. She was not fast enough to run. Not powerful enough to fight. And if she could not help her saviour . . . then her life truly was worthless.

The giants' noses approached her. She closed her eyes and waited for the end.

□

It was the fifth day since he had met Brother Chow Ji.

His breakthrough was so, so close. He needed just that little bit more. Something that was even more potent, to push him beyond.

He cast his senses around Fa Ram, trying to find anything he could use for that final push.

He noticed the energy of the land and followed the twisting power into the ground.

We give to the land, and the land gives back.

Bi De, as was proper, took a portion of his energy and offered it to the land. He did so unthinkingly—while another voice derided such an action as useless. One does not *give* to take. They *took*. But someone important had said this to him, so he obeyed the voice that asked he give.

The land reached out for his energy—

And *recoiled*. The land fled from his Qi.

He was stunned.

And then, he was enraged. How dare the land reject his gift? He took care of it! He nurtured it! It should be thankful that he even considered it worth his thoughts!

We give to the land, and the land gives back. his Great Master's gentle voice instructed.

Bi De paused.

Something was wrong here. But what? What had changed? What was happening?

"Brother Bi De," Chow Ji's voice cut through his confusion. Brother Chow Ji would know what to do, for he was wise. "We are ready to make the most great-powerful pill yet. Come-come, you must see-witness this."

Bi De obeyed, journeying with Brother Chow Ji to the Spirit Furnace. It was upon its scaffold, and all of the small black-furs were gathered around it.

As well as the hens and the chicks—the entirety of his flock. Their legs were tied, and they were cooing worriedly.

Bi De hesitated. What was the meaning of this?

"This is the way-method of the world, Brother Bi De," Chow Ji said. His grin spread across his entire face. "The strong take-steal what they need. *Whatever* they need. These are good-fine reagents. Their lives exist for us to use-take as we please. In eating-consuming these, you will truly be strong."

Yes, they are full of power, aren't they? He absently remembered something eating a hen, and it being good, just like the Heavenly Herbs. His eyes turned to the pots of growth, how many should he use, in addition to these *worthless* lives—

What he saw rattled him to his core. The pots that should have been brimming with vibrant green life were nearly empty. The small forest of green shoots that should have been there were devastated and harvested, far in excess of what they would be able to grow back from. A few sprigs of Heavenly Herbs were all that were left—chewed on and desecrated, surrounded by black-fur droppings.

The land recoiled from his Qi.

The Heavenly Herbs had been ransacked. There was a bag of rice overturned, its contents consumed and soiled. Bi De's eyes whipped around. There was filth. There was devastation. The grass around the Spirit Furnace was *wilting*.

We give to the land, and the land gives back.

This . . . this was *wrong*. He felt horror in his gut as *something* brushed up against his Qi. Something small and helpful, demanding that he truly see.

It was like the scales were torn from his eyes. The gentle nudges. The strange thoughts that corrupted him. The foreign Qi in his body.

Wrath burned like a star in his breast.

How *dare* this disgusting little creature soil the land so?! It courted death! No, if there was a fate worse than death, the creature welcomed it with open arms.

The black-fur had desecrated blessed Fa Ram. It had perverted it. Twisted it. Taken advantage of his kindness.

His head snapped around to the wicked Chow Ji, whose eyes narrowed. His heavenly blades sprung from his legs, and to his dismay the once pure moonlight was riddled with streaks of red energy and cracks of black. It bled into the air around him, its edge snapping and sizzling instead of being proper, perfectly formed crescents.

It was proof of deception most foul. The holy light was tainted. His very soul had been stained by this beast's acts.

He turned to strike this *interloper*, this kin of Basi Bu Shi, for that was only what Chow Ji could be. His leg raised high, ready to purge the wicked, who dared, dared to abuse the sacred rights of hospitality—!

"How very disappointing."

[Internal Impurity Tremor]

The tiny black flecks in Bi De's body, so small that he had ignored them, spasmed as Chow Ji's Qi touched them. They expanded and grew like weeds, tearing outwards with sharp spines. They drove into his muscles, innards, and Qi, shredding and corrupting whatever they encountered.

Bi De *screamed.* His holy blades guttered and died. He stumbled, flailing. The agony was all-consuming. Blood poured out of his mouth as the malevolent technique took hold, ravaging his body like the black-furs had ravaged the land.

Bi De fell to his knees, nearly kowtowing before Chow Ji. He glared hatefully up at the interloper, attempting to kill him, or at least curse him, with merely the rage in his gaze.

Chow Ji simply chuckled, but his eyes were curious.

"How did you break-escape my technique? Impure Earthly Desires is something I have perfected-refined over the decades." Chow Ji asked, placing his Great-Master-like paw upon him. The black flecks spasmed again, drawing a fresh wail from Bi De. A fog started to cloud his mind, as *Brother* Chow Ji began to work his foul Qi. "It is no matter, soon-soon it shall be complete—"

There were two triumphant squeals. Chun Ke and Pi Pa's home broke open, the gate nearly flying off its hinges, and the howling beasts thundered out. Their eyes were wide and wild. Their trotters tore up the earth as they made their charge, aiming directly for their hated foe. The rest of the black-furs squeaked in terror at the rampaging beasts.

The Qi acting in Bi De paused, and the rat snorted.

"Very-very well. Chow Ji shall play-toy with you." Chow Ji's ire was clear. He stood from the defeated form of Bi De. There was a sickening snap as his once hunched back straightened, raising up to his full height. He threw off his cloak. Bi De was disgusted by what he saw.

His form *dared* to take after the Great Master, but it was twisted. A *perversion*. Some of his fur was receding off his chest, revealing smooth flesh filled with sculpted muscle. His skin was pallid and was crisscrossed with twisting veins. He had *hands*, not paws. His legs looked wrong, like they were in the middle of transitioning from a normal rat's leg to something . . . human. Chow Ji flexed, his balance unsteady from these changes, and he was only kept upright by his worm-like tail.

It was a blasphemy against the way of the world. Only through corruption could such a thing be done. Bi De was disgusted. Revolted. Yet he could only watch, unable to move.

"Restrain-restrict Bi De. I shall be done-finished shortly," Chow Ji commanded, and the black-furs hastened to obey.

The black-fur Lord *moved*. He was slower than Bi De, when the rooster was at his prime, but it was enough—he met Chun Ke's charge with one of his own. The great porcine beast tried to trample him, snarling with wrath, but even unbalanced and old, Chow Ji's strikes were too powerful. He struck Chun Ke in the leg, his odd, almost fingers curled into a claw, and the great squealing beast bowled over, rolling to a stop. There was a three-lined gash across his shin, a painful blow, but Chun Ke swiftly returned to his feet, snarling and snorting. He winced at the pain, then pawed at the ground, resuming his charge, tearing after the speeding form of the corrupted creature assaulting his home.

The other black-furs approached with ropes of grass. They needn't have bothered, so weak was he. His insides were on fire, both from agony and shame.

How could he have been deceived so easily? How could he have let such damage come to the Great Master's home? He pressed his forehead into the ground. He apologised to the earth. He apologised to the hens. He apologised even to Chun Ke and Pi Pa, for subjecting them to this.

Finally, he apologised to his Lord, for being such an unworthy beast.

He could not, however, apologise to himself. This was a deserved fate. And now, he would either die or be enslaved.

Chow Ji struck, dancing around stomping trotters and snapping tusks. Pi Pa was slammed onto her side, throwing her bulk into the grass. He whirled with unnatural grace and struck Chun Ke a second time, directly in the head. His curled fingers carved three massive rents in Chun Ke's face, revealing the white of bone beneath. Blood sprayed into the air from the horrific wound, but this was not the true blow. Before Chun Ke could even squeal, Chow Ji's Qi *pulsed*, driving itself into the fresh wound. It was wrong. It was disgusting, as it slithered in and burrowed deep. Chun Ke may have been able to weather merely physical blows, but this was too much. Bi De's heart seized at the scream of agony and terror that ripped from Chun Ke, the pig's eyes rolling back into his head as he collapsed, twitching and seizing.

At least Bi De took solace in the fact that the Great Master would be there soon, and this horror would be over. There would be a reckoning for these creatures. The black-furs would be defeated like Bi De defeated the creatures that ate the plants, by his Lord's might and majesty.

Ah, how he wished to see his Master's true power, laying low the wicked.

He hoped his energy would be returned to the Great Master, if he was worthy of such an honour. More likely, his corpse would be discarded and burned, for not even the land could find anything within such a worthless creature.

Bi De closed his eyes and awaited the end.

Two little paws landed on his back. Some of the agony disappeared.

'Please, Great One, you must get up.'

The little black-fur stared at him with both hope and concern. It was the one he had saved. The one who had sworn her service.

We give to the land, and the land gives back. The little one who he had saved, now returning the favour.

No. This was not for his Great Master to see. Not for the Great Master to solve. Bi De had caused this problem with his naïveté, and so he would fix it. When his Lord returned, he would find his home once more pristine.

The blades of cracked moonlight formed. Bi De staggered and rose as the vicious little creatures leapt at him, spurred by their master's command.

[Wheel of the Crescent Moon]

The surging black-furs, intent on restraining him, perished. They were torn in half by the whirling kick as a ring of burning silver energy formed around him. They were torn, and not cut perfectly, as his Qi hissed angrily. The blades were larger than he was used to, sparking and snapping, filling the air with energy. Ragged things, rather than perfect crescents. The little one looked at him, her dark eyes wide.

Bi De lowered his head.

'*Please. I need your aid*,' he whispered, lowering himself, and gesturing to his back. She obeyed, and once more there was blessed relief as her Qi circled around the impurities in his body.

He swayed, unsteady on his feet, but he was still standing. He was weak, but he persevered.

Chun Ke was laid out on the ground, unconscious and bleeding heavily. Pi Pa fought with reckless abandon, her eyes bloodshot and her squeals thunderously piercing. Her fury and grief mixed together into a sound of haunting madness. With one last strike, Pi Pa fell too, onto her side and panting.

"Ah, you shall be tasty-tasty. A fine good pill," Chow Ji said. His breath was heavy with exertion. His strange half-human legs wobbled. He was tiring but he still looked able to fight. "Ah, the years have taken their toll. Soon-soon, though, I shall once more break through."

He turned to Bi De, amused. "Good, good, mighty-strong indeed you are, to stand. Now, be good-obedient and sit; this Chow Ji shall be with you soon."

Slowly, arrogantly, he pointed his fingers at Bi De, like his victory was already assured.

[Internal Impurity Tremor]

The shards of black wrenched, but the little black-fur's Qi did its work, protecting and shielding him from being affected. This time, there was no pain. No scream. His Qi mingled with another's, and both were stronger for it. They were stronger together.

Bi De took a step forward, and Chow Ji's eyes widened. His face twisted with incredulity as his Qi surged again, trying to take hold.

Bi De struck. His legs wobbled, but his cracked Lunar Blades searched for his foe, screaming with coursing energy and streaming off into the air. Each movement was agony, the impurity, even coated in soothing energy, ripping and tearing with every step. But he fought through the pain. Chow Ji had to be defeated, here and now.

They clashed. Chow Ji was old and skilled. His arms and body flashed as he aimed for the gaps in the blade's coverage, blocking, deflecting, and dodging, trying his hardest to return a blow.

Bi De had sharpened his spurs upon the wicked Basi Bu Shi. He was no stranger to a battle where a single mistake meant death, and he wove around Chow Ji's own strikes. The little one had buried beneath his vest as to not be thrown off, all while protecting him from the internal tremors of the interloper's foul Qi.

Within three exchanges, Chow Ji was panicking. His eyes were wide and wild as Bi De started to move faster, an incomplete dodge drawing blood off the wicked beast's side.

"You worthless creature-thing! You dare use this power against me?! I, who have given you this strength? I have *freed* you! Freed you from serving your 'Great Master,' the Qi-less wretch. He is a squatter on land too good for him! You could have been mighty! You could have been *Lord* of this place!"

Bi De nearly laughed at the fool. Chow Ji had eyes, but he could not see Mount Tai. How could he not feel the Great Master's might? *It was all around them.* Bi De could have taunted Chow Ji. He could have laughed at the sheer ignorance the beast displayed.

Instead, he let his spurs speak. Slashes appeared on Chow Ji's limbs as Bi De struck with grace beyond the old villain. He danced around the clumsy and desperate return strikes. Chow Ji's eyes were wide and wild. He screamed and he ranted, spittle flying from his mouth.

Fool.

[The Rising of the Crescent Moon]

Bi De's blades burned as he rose in the sky, as surely as the moon, His spurs caught under Chow Ji's rib cage, tore him open, and exposed his heart, which pumped feebly into the air.

Bi De landed and shook the gore from his legs, gazing contemptuously at the defeated interloper.

Chow Ji hacked and gagged, gasping feebly for air as his life drained into the ground around him. Bi De allowed it. His suffering was good and just.

"I-I curse-curse *you*!" Chow Ji gagged. His Qi gathered as he managed to stand, his entrails hanging out.

The rooster held his ground, watching and ready to dodge. He would not be underestimating this particular foe.

"I curse this *land*! May it be covered-consumed in a tide of vermin!" Chow Ji screamed, his Qi and blood mingling in the air. Darkness gathered in his palms, blood leaked from his mouth, and the air around the monstrous creature writhed with malice.

[Curse of Vermin]

Bi De's eyes widened as Chow Ji drove his hatred and Qi into the ground around him, poisonous tendrils driving deep. He screamed in hate and pain, howling his hatred to the heavens—until Bi De's blades took his head.

The valiant defender collapsed to his knees. Then, the *pulse* hit. The little one squeaked in alarm as she felt something brush against her Qi, but her proximity to the Qi of the moon let her shake off the feeling. Though her body twitched and shook, and Bi De could feel the pulse of her heat through his feathers.

The rest of the black-furs *howled.* Their eyes rolled, and their mouths frothed. They started biting and clawing at the land around them, half-mad from whatever happened. Some of them fled. Some of them died outright, suddenly seizing. And some launched themselves at Bi De, intent on consuming him. The horde squealed, hate and madness driving their every action.

Bi De struggled to stand. He could not fall to such weak creatures! He could not be defeated so easily, even spent as he was!

He rose, ready to do battle.

The great trotter of Sister Pi Pa landed on one of them, and her great bulk crushed two more. She thrashed and stomped, though her body was battered and bruised, as she struck down the remainder of the enemies.

When her bloody work was completed, she turned and glared at the rooster, snarling in chastisement.

Bi De bowed his head, humbled, and staggered to his feet. There was much work to be done before the Great Master returned. The little one scampered out of his vest, to aid in Sister Pi Pa fussing over the fallen form of Chun Ke. He was breathing, but . . .

Bi De grimaced. He was absolutely exhausted, yet he was alive.

□

A half-blind old woman stared at the carving of a rooster. It had a massive crack that had started spreading over its back, growing every day. Today, if the growth followed the same pace, the rooster would have split in half.

Instead, the wood hung on, cracked but unbroken.

The old woman harrumphed and put it back on the shelf before glancing around the room and frowning.

"Lan Fan! Lan Fan, you devil goat, where are you?!" she demanded, stomping outside.

□

It was late in the day when Bi De felt the land breathe a sigh of relief. The grass stood taller, the air seemed sweeter, and the taint in the ground felt like it shuddered.

The Great Master was approaching.

They had dismantled the scaffolding, buried the corpses, and cleaned as much of the droppings as they could.

Brother Chun Ke had even woken back up, though he simply lay there, groaning and whining in piteous pain. His eyes seemed duller, and Bi De was concerned.

Now, Bi De looked upon the Spirit Furnace. The wretched thing that offered its tainted power. His master would surely not want it.

His blades of moonlight—his tainted blades, and the price for his foolishness—bit into the furnace and destroyed it.

Bi De limped to the entrance to Fa Ram and awaited his Great Master's arrival and judgement.

CHAPTER 19

R.O.U.S.

Unlike the rest of the people at the wedding, I didn't have anybody besides Big D to take care of my house. I had known a dog back in the Before that knew how to feed the other animals, and Big D was just about as intelligent—and probably hopped up on Qi. But he definitely wasn't foolproof or a permanent solution.

While everybody else would be hanging out in Verdant Hill for the rest of the week, generally getting drunk and having a good time, I had to go back home.

So, first thing in the morning, I went to the Exchange.

There were government-mandated rice prices, but as befitting a xianxia world, there were different prices for different grades, all strictly codified. This stuff was taken extremely seriously, and there were a bunch of stern-faced Imperial Clerks and soldiers who would examine the rice and make sure you weren't trying any funny business.

Most farmers had "green-grade" rice, which made up the vast bulk of the rice sold. It was good, solid rice that everybody liked. Grey-grade was mainly considered trash and for only the poorest sections of society or animal feed. The "blue-grade" was the prime stuff that would go to nobles and other wealthy people.

I fully expected my rice to be "blue" rice. Hey, it was damn good rice. I did have *some* pride, and my rice was obviously superior in quality and size to the other rice that was here.

I mean, sure, I'd cheated a bit with Qi, but hard work had still gone into it!

So, I waited the hour or so until the next clerk could see me, and I let the guards and clerk examine my bags. A bit of rice was taken from one randomly selected, and the clerk poured several grains into his hands.

"This is spectacular rice, farmer," the clerk said appreciatively. "Your hardship and toils have been rewarded this year. This is the best blue-grade rice this humble clerk has ever laid eyes upon!"

I smiled at him. "It took a while to clear, but the land is good."

The clerk nodded his head. "How many bags do you have for sale this year?" he asked.

After everything I had given away, as gifts and payment—

"Twenty bags of white rice," I said. "I've got a bit more at home. This was all the cart could take."

"The clerks and scribes of the Imperial Court here shall purchase all of the currently available rice you have to sell," the clerk declared. "Should you bring more of it, I would ask that you think of the Imperial Clerks here first. We would welcome the fruits of your labour."

Huh. That was easy.

We bowed to each other, and I got a receipt. The other clerks, when they looked at my rice, seemed just as agreeable as the first guy.

Now I just had to take these hawk feathers over to this guy, and I would be set!

→

My feet thudded as I set out a light jog back home. I had gotten quite a reasonable price for my rice and hawk feathers, so I had bought some good, solid jars for pickling, as well as a bunch of salt for preserving fish. I wasn't the biggest fan of *funazushi*. Salt-fermented fish was an acquired taste, and it would take a couple of years to become "real" funazushi, but it was good to start soon, right?

Everybody had been understanding about my needing to leave early, though Meimei had been a little bit pouty about it.

So, I asked her to help me with something around the back then kissed the hell out of her when we were alone. The way her red face perfectly highlighted her freckles was always great, and bashful Meimei was fun to see. The way she looked up at me and bit her lip—

Meimei was cute.

After that I'd started on my way. They would probably be fine on the return trip, and they had made that trip hundreds of times before without running into any Spirit Beasts, so all seemed good.

Tigger was curled up in the cart and managing to sleep. It was quite a smooth ride, if I do say so myself. I absentmindedly pushed a bit of Qi into the road as I ran. Hopefully, that would help with potholes, but it was mostly a dirt road. I wondered if I could make it better in the future, pave it or something? I certainly had the stamina and strength. *Or I could pay people to do it, improve the local economy a bit?*

More thoughts for the future.

When I'd first gotten to the area, I'd kind of had plans to go full hermit and do most of the things myself. That . . . well, that was a stupid-ass idea, really. I had been a moron, too eager to run. Then I'd gone and made friends and got a fiancée. Turned out most people I'd met so far were pretty normal. Save for the cultivators of course. But there was a small problem. The distance between my property and the village was pretty big.

If I had known what the future might hold, I *might* have set up shop in Hong Yaowu instead of what I did, but now, I wasn't about to trade my property for anything.

This was mine. And I was gonna make it the best goddamn farm in the world.

My feet kept thudding, traversing the empty road.

I eventually decided to stop for the night. Even at my pace, it was still more than a day's trip back home, at my current pace. Sure, I could have pushed it and ran as I had with the rice—but meh, it wasn't worth it.

Besides, this was my favourite spot and my favourite rock. I briefly entertained the idea of taking the rock with me. Meimei's "what the hell, Jin" face was hilarious, and bringing "our rock" back to my house would provoke another round of baffled amusement.

I decided to leave it for now. I didn't have any room in my wagon, anyways.

I went to sleep thinking about our house, and all the other things I needed. It was going to have medicine storage—*I should ask Meimei about it later, so I can build it properly . . .*

□

Do you know that sinking gut feeling you get from time to time? It started while I was eating lunch in the village, making sure to tell the people who'd had to stay all about the wedding. It felt like the bottom dropped out of my stomach.

At first, I hadn't thought much about it, but as I finished my meal and I neared my house, the feeling became stronger. It was a kind of nauseous feeling. Like something had gone really, *really* wrong.

I started to get worried as I neared the gates. Had I been gone too long? Big D was a scrapper, but had a Spirit Beast ransacked my house? Had some disaster befallen it?

Big D and Peppa were waiting for me at the gates.

They both looked like the animal equivalent of having gone twelve rounds with Mike Tyson. Big D had blood all over his feathers. His once vibrant plumage was dull and stringy-looking, and he seemed dead on his feet. It was all he could do to get into his customary bow, but I saw him twitch in pain as he did.

Peppa was better off, but only barely. She had massive bruises all over her body and dried blood on her nose. She too dipped her head.

A feeling of horror overtook me. My Qi unconsciously bubbled, and both of my animals took a step back and gulped at the expression on my face.

↔

When Bi De felt the Great Master's overpowering Qi, he thought his Lord's rage had finally been roused, and his life was forfeit. The little one squeaked in both horror and awe from her perch on his back. She nearly fell off of his body, such was her shock.

Even he felt fear. The Great Master never used his unknowable power for violence. It was always a calm, nurturing stream that dispersed into the air and ground. Even when facing the wicked beasts, it was still and serene, unbothered by them.

This was nothing so kind. The land responded to his wrath, bubbling and churning like a storm. His power rose, and the energy in the land rose with it, vast and overpowering. Terror seized Bi De's heart, but he stepped forward anyway, intent on shouldering all the dishonour upon himself. *He* was to blame. He should be the sole target of his Lord's judgement.

But instead of his Great Master smiting him for failure and dishonour, both himself and Sister Pi Pa were scooped into his strong arms and checked over for injuries. His Lord paused when he saw the cowering form of the little black-fur, his eyes narrowing, but she too was spared from his wrath.

They were taken swiftly to the coop of their Lord, where he made even more noises of distress and concern when he saw the damage done to Brother Chun Ke, still asleep on his side. The gashes had been tended to as best as they were able, and they had to hope that it was enough.

The Lord disregarded the pots of Heavenly Herbs, not paying them any attention as he tended to their wounds.

Bi De was once more humbled by his Great Master. He cared more for his disciples than the treasures of his coop.

Even with his gross failure, he was still afforded a place within this blessed land. His eyes closed, and he finally allowed himself to succumb to exhaustion.

↔

I was not happy.

Let me rephrase that. I was rip-shit *pissed.*

Big D and Peppa were bad enough, but poor Chunky had nearly lost an eye to whatever tore up his face. The poor boy had woken up and oinked pitifully before once more going back to sleep, his eyes clouded with pain. I used up nearly all the medicine I had, tending to him. At least I'd had the foresight to buy it earlier, just in case something went wrong with my chickens, but pigs were a lot bigger than birds and needed more of it.

I glared at the new addition to the house—as did Tigger. The little stripy kitten was staring greedily at the rat that had been riding on Big D.

"What happened here?" I asked, not really expecting an answer from the animals.

To my surprise, the little rat bowed its head and pointed outside.

Well, shit, I thought.

I got a little tour from the scurrying rodent, accompanied by a bunch of squeaks and words that I could *almost* understand. Peppa trotted along beside us, adding her own squeals and oinks where appropriate.

It started with a broken pill furnace. The short, squat, almost pot-like device with vents on the side had been torn open, exposing an inside caked in black tar.

A mass grave, some pills, and an absolutely *hideous* R.O.U.S., Rodent of Unusual Size, followed.

I glared at the Master-Splinter-looking motherfucker of a mutated rat. It was absolutely disgusting, halfway between human and rat, and despite the creature's stomach I could see the six-pack and pecs he sported, like some kind of demented rat bodybuilder.

The image of a fight nearly formed in my mind's eye. There were feelings of foulness, desperation, and deceit. I snarled, but there was nothing I could do now, besides trying to fix up my house and hoping that Chunky was all right.

I was in a foul mood the rest of the day as I stalked around the property, cataloguing everything. There was damage, but it wasn't too bad. Five bags of rice had been contaminated, chewed into, and soiled. Which, compared to the amount left, was a light loss.

The things that had taken the most damage were the Lowly Spiritual Herbs. Most of them were gone, with only one pot left. I had some seeds, and they could be grown in winter with enough care, but I was still upset. They were the only things that made my normally bland food bearable!

The weird root I was keeping was fine, though. Still hiding in its pot, its Qi signature unrecognisable until it was pulled from the ground. I honestly didn't know what to do with the root, and there was nothing about it in the Archive, so I just put it back into the pot.

I smashed the pills, mixing each of them with a bunch of water to dilute them. They looked a bit off, so they were probably toxic, and I didn't want them contaminating my farm.

After that, I ripped apart the Spirit Furnace. The metal could be used for something, but I didn't care about the rest of it. It was a gross thing, all caked with black tar on the inside, and it *stunk*. Fucking pills. *Of course it comes back to that.*

While I worked, I thought. The rat had confirmed a somewhat uncomfortable truth, with her direct answers to my question. Big D just kind of did as he was told most of the time, and the other time, he acted like a normal rooster. Now, I knew Big D was smart, but he was apparently nearly or as smart as a human? Same with Peppa and the rat?

I grimaced. I had no intention of eating Big D, but if Spirit Beasts weren't rare, that meant Peppa and Chunky, who I *was* planning on eating eventually, were off the table too. I had no intention of eating anything sapient. That was just . . . *ugh*.

Wait, I had eaten a chicken while Meimei and the boys were over. Had she been—?

I felt a bit sick to my stomach as I contemplated the horror of what I might have done.

All right, cognitive tests for everybody.

But only after I burned Master Splinter, because god *damn*, that guy was *nasty*.

I looked to the little rat, waiting by my feet, her head bowed.

"Helpful. Friend," something told me.

I smiled at the little girl, and scritched her head with a single finger. The rat shied away from my finger, still looking sad and lost. I sighed. The rest of the animals seemed to like her, and from what I gathered, she had helped fight against the other rats.

"All right, you can stay," I told her. "You need a name too, for helping out. How about . . . ?"

CHAPTER 20

AN AUTUMN LEAF

Bi De felt as if he had been trampled by a herd of pigs. Even after the Great Master's ministrations, his body protested every movement. He could not even perform his daily tasks, but the Great Master's benevolence was limitless. He was bid to rest and recover and was also praised for his defence of Fa Ram.

Even though it was his fault that Great Fa Ram had been in danger in the first place. He had been taken in by Chow Ji's lies, and he was now shamed.

He sat upon the Great Pillars, but today it was not to cultivate strength. Today, it was to rid himself of it. The Qi that had been added to his soul was tainted, and there were impurities throughout his body. So, he expelled his Qi. He carefully released it into the air as to not infect the land with his own folly. He carefully examined his Qi, each and every portion, and stripped out the parts that he could not be entirely sure were pure.

It would be the work of weeks, if not months, to carefully remove every piece of tainted energy without destroying himself completely and having to start over. A delicate task. Until that time, he could not bear to look upon his cracked and scarred blades of moonlight.

The physical impurities, the ones lodged within his body, were another problem, one that he needed assistance with. Sister Ri Zu, his master's smallest disciple, used her Qi to coat them, and working together, they broke them down.

He knew his Great Master was righteous beyond compare and able to sense good in the hearts of others. Even though her kin were wicked, Ri

Zu's spirit was just, and she had been given a name of power and a place upon Great Fa Ram.

Sister Ri Zu spent her time with his humble self or with Brother Chun Ke, tending to his wounds. His brother disciple could finally stand again, but he was . . . lesser. Diminished. The spark that was in the rest of them seemed to flicker and fade within Chun Ke's eyes, barely hanging on. He had nightmares some nights, squealing and whimpering. Bi De flagellated himself in his mind for his ill thoughts on both of his Master's disciples. They had proved themselves far better judges of character than he, and he feared that Brother Chun Ke had paid a terrible price for it. His brother disciple was perhaps crippled for life. His mind had dulled and had perhaps returned to an unthinking one. Bi De knew only shame. The bitter taste in the back of his beak intensified. Truly, in this world, there was no medicine for regret. He would clean the pigpens in penance and kowtow a hundred times before the Land's Spirit, and Brother Chun Ke.

The burn of shame in his beak was accompanied by a burn in his chest. He winced as his concentration faltered, and his Qi recoiled, the energy within harming him. He nodded his thanks to Sister Ri Zu, as she too fell back, panting slightly from aiding him.

She bowed her head to him and clambered up to her usual spot upon his back. Sister Ri Zu made sure she was accompanied by one of the other disciples at all times, for the Great Master had brought along one more to add to their number.

Bi De greeted Tigu respectfully as she ambled past, and she turned her nose up at him. No anger swelled within his breast, for her derision and contempt were well earned.

He knew not *what* to make of Tigu. She had a wicked form, with sharp teeth and claws, almost as Basi Bu Shi. Yet if the Great Master trusted her, she must have a noble heart. Still, she was aloof and arrogant. She ignored the other disciples of the Great Master and insisted on going alone about her business. She slept in the Great Master's bed often, and he was very affectionate towards her. Yet she was of a carnivorous bent and eyed Sister Ri Zu most disagreeably.

But she was powerful. And her power was needed. The curse that stained the land called wicked members of Chow Ji's kin.

Tigu slew them mercilessly. She stalked them with a grace that Basi Bu Shi would have envied, and her claws were the death of all that stood before her.

Her arrogance was off-putting, but she contributed to Great Fa Ram while he was weak.

For reasons unknown to him, the Great Master had left the taint Chow Ji embedded in the soil. The Great Master likely intended to use it as training and food for Tigu. Perhaps, when she was mighty enough, he would remove the taint. The previous week had made clear the need for multiple defenders of this Blessed Land.

Bi De returned to the coops and rested his body. He would need all his strength for tomorrow, to continue to strip the taint from his body.

↔

My property passed me by as I trudged through it, working in a rough grid. My mind was wandering as I thought. I seemed to be getting into the habit of giving female animals male names—first Tigger, and now Rizzo.

Although the little one was probably *significantly* braver than my favourite muppet, considering she'd gone against evil Splinter. That little bastard had done a number on both my seasonings and my animals. Big D was no longer as energetic these days, which was a shame; I liked seeing him hop all over my fence. When I asked him if he was okay, he just bowed his head and, after a while, nodded.

Man, it's so weird that they're people. It was something I was still wrapping my head around.

Peppa was constantly around Chunky and tried to goad him to play, but my poor little boy was still hurting. He was uncoordinated at the best of times, and nearly catatonic at the worst. I spent a lot of time with him, letting him lean against me, and making sure he didn't get any worse.

Rizzo was helping too, and the pigs seemed to like her. Everyone seemed to be getting along well . . . except Tigger, who was most certainly a cat. I had some suspicions about her too, seeing as she mostly ignored Rizzo while brutalizing the rest of the rat population. She lined the corpses of the ones she didn't eat up for inspection outside my wall, which was kind of gross, but she was doing her job. The rats went into the fire. Rou's memories relayed the times he had to eat rats to me, which churned my stomach something fierce. I got the mental feeling of detachment. To him meat was meat . . . but after getting actual food again, he would rather not, and I agreed with him. "Rats are gross"—except for

Rizzo, she's a good girl—was entirely too ingrained into my psyche. *Only if I'm starving.*

Still, even with this incident, life went on. Fish were salted and smoked, vegetables pickled, and the house started to come along nicely, If I did say so myself. I'd based it a bit on a Japanese design, the Satoyama. Basically, the house had part of the river inside it, and you used the running water to wash dishes and had carp to eat some of your scraps.

The only problem was . . . I had never built a house quite like this before, so there was a *lot* of trial and error going on. I had done houses and barns in the Before, but this close to water, flooding was a major concern.

Still, there was a nice wood interior, and I was planning to have some windows. I would need to sell some more rice, but glass here was cheaper than I'd been expecting it to be. It was still bloody expensive, but a price I could manage. Some lacquer for the floorboards would be required, but nothing could really be done until the frame was up.

It also would need some nice fireplaces. Sure, the winter wasn't as bad as I was used to, but there was no excuse to slack and not have the creature comforts I desired. Rou had had some experience on the streets, and I respected him for surviving it; I had pretty much been roughing it for a while, as well.

The thought of a nice warm house appealed greatly to me.

That, and you could cheat a little, as it was xianxia land. Light crystals were a bit pricey, but probably worth it in the long run, and If I could find a fire crystal, I could get a self-heating bath.

Or a sauna. *Hell, yeah, a sauna sounds* awesome.

I'd been bathing in the river every day, but that would be pretty hard in the winter. It'd be cold as hell man.

I yawned as I continued my wandering. I had been a bit lax in exploring my property. I had followed the river and found the boundaries, but for the most part I had been too busy working to have a real, in-depth exploration.

So that was the plan today. I hadn't really found anything too special yet, just beautiful trees, turning into their fall colours. It was such a nice view, and it almost reminded me of Algonquin.

I should invite some people to have a nice lunch and do a fall colours viewing. I always loved doing that in the Before, but the timing was super awkward. *Probably* not going to happen this year, but something to think about. The leaves were falling whenever there was a breeze, drifting down round me.

Smiling, I reached up to grab a falling leaf out of the air. It was a lovely red colour and perfectly formed.

I froze.

It was also a *very* familiar shape.

A spiky leaf, with five lobes, the bane of every child trying to draw the flag. Little key-shaped seed pods littered the ground around it.

I thought Xianxia land was supposed to be *China*. The culture, the food, most of it seemed like it had come from around there. But this? *This* was something from my home. Something of the Before.

A massive grin formed on my face as I walked into a brilliant red grove. It smelled so familiar. It felt so right. For the first time in a long time, I *remembered.* The laughter and voices of my mother and father. The simple joy of a walk with my family.

The gaping hole it had left when it was gone.

A single tear rolled down my cheek as I just stayed there for a while, soaking in the smell of leaves and the crisp air.

CHAPTER 21

THE FIRST FLAKES

The needles clacked together along with the red yarn.

I hadn't seen anybody for a month. Now, that was pretty normal, I hadn't seen anybody for six months when I first got here, and at that time, the lack of communication didn't bother me one bit.

Now that I'd gotten the taste for human interaction again, though, it was a little more challenging. But I persevered! The outer walls went up, as did the roof. Things go fast when you could drive in a nail with a single stroke. Even the roof was pretty easy, and I remember *hating* having to do roofs.

It was going to be a change. The "living room" alone was the size of six of my shacks. It was also going to be the only insulated room this year. I didn't have enough rice straw and cedar fiber to get every room I was planning. As for the size, I hoped to have space for my potential future kids and places for guests. So, things needed to be a bit bigger.

I grunted and undid the row I had been working on. The tension was too tight.

The sugar maple leaf I'd gotten from the tree was carefully pressed and preserved, and I had added a second sign, next to my "Beware of Chicken" one, a simple carved maple leaf. The kind that only grew in North America.

I may not be there any longer, but that place had made me who I was.

I'd like to think that my parents would be proud of me. They *definitely* would have liked Meiling.

It was a little melancholy, thinking about these things, but all it did was drive me harder to make something that would be worthy of those memories. Of both sets of memories. Rou also remembered his family fondly.

Life was hard and full of work, but it was good. All I had to do was make this better.

And just don't be an asshole, like Meimei said. Easy-peasy.

I kept the company of my animals. Chunky's injuries were healing well, constantly tended by both myself and Rizzo, but the scars across his face were still raw and angry-looking. While my little porkers had started pink and hairless, they were getting in a set of rust-red fur—combined with Chunky's tusks and black mane, he looked quite fierce.

Looks were deceiving, though. He was like a fat golden retriever, always bouncy and happy to follow you around. He also loved belly rubs. Peppa was more reserved, but when Big D was back in his coop and Tigger was off doing what she did, Peppa would gleefully roll over and get her own scritches.

As for Big D . . . well, he was getting better. I'd caught him practising his kicks earlier, but he was still pretty mopey. Man, I'd never thought I would have to deal with an angsty chicken.

The other chickens, though, weren't smart. They were the same as they had been, just chickens, which was a relief.

A winter without chicken soup was a bad winter.

I continued my knitting. I wasn't very good, mind you, and I was slow, but I *could* knit. Just don't ask me for any designs . . . yet.

It was a hat—a nice red toque. Toques need to be red, you see. Just like red barns, they're just something that *is*.

Tigger strolled up and hopped into my lap, making herself comfortable without a care for what I was doing. Chuckling, I set down my knitting and let myself rest for a while, and lavished affection on the little stripey beast. She mewled in contentment, and soon enough, she was asleep in my lap.

I sighed in contentment and leaned back against my wall.

→

And so, life went on. I never did manage to get anybody around for a proper autumn colour viewing— I just had too much work to do. The preparations were never-ending, and If I wasn't a cultivator, there was no possible way I could have done it alone.

It was just difficult, instead of flat-out impossible.

A cold cellar was dug and lined with my knock-off concrete to keep some of the dampness out.

I also invented a technique! A truly frightening fire-based attack that I used to surpass the will of the heavens!

And by that, I mean I used it to defeat rain and dry things out. By injecting Qi into things and heating them up, I basically had a drying machine. It works really well for seasoning wood and to keep things from moulding. Behold, gaps in my knowledge and skills were surpassed by my mystic wisdom! Truly, I am beyond all other men!

I also spent a lot of time clearing leaves from places I didn't want them, and with the beginnings of the fall rainstorms, the rivers had to be cleared of fallen branches, so they didn't make an unintentional dam. I kept a careful watch on the river and kept an eye on the banks to see if my house would flood if it rose, but it seemed it would be fine, barring some truly catastrophic circumstances.

I also wasn't entirely alone, either. The clerks had sent a merchant to pick up some more rice, so I'd sold five more bags of white rice. I might be being paranoid about keeping so much at home, but it was my first winter, so better safe than sorry.

My second visitor was Yun Ren, who just dropped by to see if I was okay.

It was rather touching that people were concerned about my well-being, and he came with some medicine from Meimei as a "just in case."

It was a shame that she couldn't come around, but she was busy too.

Still, I appreciated everything they did for me. Sadly, after marvelling at my house for a while, Yun Ren had to go too.

I got back to work. If my reckoning was right, the first snows would hit us soon.

□

It was a particularly cold day. Bi De could see his breath as he sat upon the Great Pillars, and Sister Ri Zu was curled up in his feathers to ward off the chill.

Bi De's blades of moonlight carefully formed. They were still not as pure as when he first earned them, but it was a vast improvement over the ugly cracks that ran through them a few months ago. Soon, they would be holy again and not tainted filth.

It was strange, he thought, that though this "autumn" was a time of ending, it was a time of renewal in other senses.

For the land seemed to be dying. The leaves fell from the trees, creatures burrowed deep and slept, and the air turned increasingly bitter.

But he could still feel the land and its comforting presence. The earth beneath him was just tired. It would sleep, and then awake refreshed. He was sure of it.

As for renewal, new sprigs of Heavenly Herbs poked out through the ground inside the Great Master's new coop, protected from the cold and rain.

His Master's female was a sage of power, with knowledge far beyond him. She had gifted medicine to the Great Master, and with its potent power, Brother Chun Ke was beginning to exhibit once more flashes of thought. His eyes were brighter on most days, and he was more active, trundling around the pen happily.

Sister Pi Pa was beside herself with joy, though she was still frightfully cross with Bi De. He bore her barbs with stoicism, and they became less and less frequent with each day that Brother Chun Ke improved.

Yes, a renewal in a time of ending. That was what this was.

Bi De turned his attention once more towards the spirit of the land. He bowed his head and presented his Qi to it.

The land gazed upon him and mulled over his tribute.

Bi De waited patiently, holding himself still and ready for rejection.

Slowly, almost haltingly, the land accepted his Qi, pulling it into itself. That was its last act of the season. He could feel it, the soft sigh, as the land finally closed its metaphorical eyes and fell into a deep slumber.

Bi De's eyes opened.

From the sky, great flakes of white began to fall, like the heavens coming down towards the earth.

CHAPTER 22

MEANWHILE, BACK AT THE TOWN

Zhuge Tingfeng sighed with contentment and continued eating his lunch. He was greatly enjoying his married life. His wonderful bride was as enthusiastic about their marriage as he was, and he'd become the envy of all of his colleagues. To have such a beautiful and caring flower coming to visit had earned him many dirty looks, though most were in good humour or jest.

Those that weren't understood attempting something was foolhardy and likely suicidal. Everyone knew that a cultivator had once before brutally chastised a man for daring to express uncouth interest in his Meihua.

They didn't know that Jin had attended his wedding and given him a gift that even now the other clerks *desperately* wished to have. No silks or fashions, but rice.

Rice that he got to eat every day, and for every meal, if he so desired.

But Tingfeng was a canny man. To gloat about having a powerful friend would be terribly disrespectful, and Brother Jin seemed to desire a simple life. So, he endeavoured to do his utmost to keep his peace and Brother Jin's privacy. Most simply knew him as a "wandering cultivator" who, for some reason, had decided to make the area his haunt.

Most didn't know what to make of cultivators. They were either the greatest of heroes or the most wicked of villains, but any man who would defend a woman's virtue without thinking of repayment was indeed a righteous man.

He took another bite of his rice. Some had thought he angered his father to be eating brown rice instead of polished grains, an inferior product, but the truth was far more straightforward. Brother Jin had been adamant about consuming brown rice, claiming that it cleaned the bowels of harmful impurities and, when eaten regularly, made one resistant to the Quivering Death.

Naturally, he and his family deferred to this wisdom.

It also helped that his brown rice tasted better than most white rice he had eaten. Brother Jin's wedding gift of rice was humble on its first appearance, but like the man himself, its depths were unfathomably vast. He would bet his entire salary that His Imperial Majesty would be pleased with brown rice if *this* is what had shown up on his table.

Work was fulfilling, his superiors looked kindly upon him, and his grandfather and father were proud of him. He had good friends and a good reputation.

Life was good.

↔

For the Lord Magistrate of Verdant Hill, life was *not good.* His stomach churned, and his face settled into a frozen mask as he tried to stay calm.

"They *what*?!" he demanded.

"They sent a merchant, Lord Magistrate," one of his guards confirmed. The captain that had been investigating the new "commodity" of extremely high-quality rice nodded with him.

"They sent a *merchant* to the cultivator's farm. After they bought his rice for *blue-grade prices*, drastically less than what the rice is actually worth."

"Yes, Lord Magistrate." the man replied evenly.

"And what happened to this merchant? I presume the cultivator was angry about this?" he questioned.

"No, Lord Magistrate, he sold him the rice at blue-grade prices. Invited him in for tea and made him lunch, too."

The Lord Magistrate felt a migraine coming on. He waved his hand, dismissing the guards.

At first, when the polite young man had bought some land, he'd thought he was some sort of cripple who wished to live his life out in peace. The Lord Magistrate agreed with the sentiment. The Azure Hills were peaceful, beautiful, and *safe*. Sure, it was a bit of a dead-end posting, with no room for advancement, but he was happy here. The Sects didn't bother him, and he got to be involved in the community. Sure, it was mostly to stroke his own ego, but having the populace genuinely like him did wonders for his self-esteem. They treated him like their stern and just patriarch, and that appealed greatly to his sensibilities.

It was a small pond, but it was *his* pond.

And then the . . . *incident* happened. Jin had easily defeated a cultivator in the Profound Realm and had gone so far as to say he was so weak he was an *imposter*.

The man hadn't been an imposter, despite the assurances of the Expert that had come to get him.

It had been a genuine member of the Shrouded Mountain Sect, the Lord Magistrate was sure of it, but he certainly wasn't going to advertise *that* piece of information. The suppression seals every town was equipped with as a precaution had barely held, taking every single one that they had, just to contain the man's power. It was lucky he seemed to be suffering some sort of control loss from the hit Rou Jin had given him.

He shuddered to think of what could have happened if they had broken, or if the Shrouded Mountain Elder had taken longer than he had to arrive.

Again, luck had prevailed where he hung at the knife's edge. The old monster had wished to save face and accepted one of their members gift-wrapped. As far as the Shrouded Mountain knew, it was simply a wandering cultivator who defeated the boy, and he hadn't heard about them searching the province for the man, so it was likely a ruse that was holding.

When cultivators warred, mortals suffered.

He was glad things ended there, or so he thought . . . And then his men had mistaken the rice's classification. He couldn't *entirely* blame them for it. None of them had the frame of reference, and few even knew that rice went beyond blue grade into silver, gold, and jade. It just didn't *happen* in the Azure Hills. Maybe in some of the cultivator compounds, but they didn't sell that sort of thing out *here*.

Honestly, he was just waiting for some sort of retribution. He still remembered the verdant grass and sweet-smelling blossoms. Houses growing branches out of previously dead wood. He stared at his lovely oak desk and imagined spines ripping free from the surface. He shivered.

He pressed his fingers to the bridge of his nose as he turned to his friend.

"What do you make of this, First Archivist?" he demanded.

First Archivist Bao stroked his chin in thought before answering, "I have met this man, 'Rou Jin' as he is in his documents, and I believe I have taken a measure of his personality. That he decided to accept the price in the first place means he either did not know the value of his goods . . . or he did this *intentionally.*"

The Lord Magistrate paused. " 'Intentionally' ?"

"I would gather that he knows of your . . . interdiction on his behalf and wishes to provide some manner of recompense."

The Lord Magistrate mulled it over.

"So . . . he wishes to reward us for services rendered?" he asked, some measure of hope filling him.

"And if that was not his intention, he did not strike me as a vengeful man. I heard that he was searching for a recording crystal in the Exchange. Perhaps we could accelerate this search?"

The Lord Magistrate sighed. *Why does this one have to be so strange?*

"Make it so. But . . . do it discreetly. Are you *sure* he won't destroy Verdant Hill?" A cultivator who thought they had been cheated would surely be vengeful, and there was no way they could fight a man who in a single strike had defeated another cultivator who needed thirty suppression seals to contain.

Thinking on it, he'd need to order more of those.

"I believe it would take far more than this for him to become enraged enough to begin to destroy our town. Though I would advise to avoid trying his patience. Perhaps he shall only be visited by merchants who know their place and not men who only see a farmer with good land?"

Some of the roiling in the Lord Magistrate's stomach ceased. "Yes. Yes, and this may also be a good thing. It seems he will continue to visit Verdant Hill, so it shall be good to have friendly relations with him. Keep his privacy, and we shall only gain from his patronage."

"And it would be a shame to lose access to his rice," the rotund First Archivist said, nodding his head.

The Lord Magistrate nodded, some of the tension bleeding out of his shoulders. "A shame indeed," he muttered, remembering the taste on his tongue. He had eaten silver-grade rice once before, during his examinations, when a supremely wealthy merchant had thrown a party for his own son becoming a member of the court. "Very well, we shall accept the rice for what it is and speak no more of Rou Jin's generosity—only be grateful that it is there. Until he moves on, at least."

The First Archivist shrugged. "He will be here for decades at least, considering he is betrothed to Hong Meiling."

The tension came back, along with the Lord Magistrate's headache.

The First Archivist had the grace to look embarrassed. "I hadn't told you? They are to be wed this spring."

He slumped forwards onto his desk. Hopefully, things would be uneventful. Hopefully, a river had not just connected his pond to a lake—or worse, an *ocean*.

His stomach churned unpleasantly.

CHAPTER 23

THE YOUNG MISTRESS

She was power incarnate.

She was grace given form.

She was death made manifest.

Her legs propelled her through the forest after the fleeing prey. She bounced from branch to branch, never making a sound. Her quarry stank of panic and desperation as it dragged its maimed leg behind it.

The foolish thing had thought it managed to escape her when she had *let it run*.

A lady needed her entertainment, after all.

And this one was entertaining beautifully. It had been so full of arrogance when she had found it. So full of confidence in its skills.

She had stripped it of its false strength and shown it what *true* power really was. In a single blow, she'd shattered its pride, and its look of triumph turned to horror.

But now . . . she tired of the chase. It was a small distraction, and tracking this in this new, white blanketed world tested her skills.

Sounds were muffled, and the snow hid things from sight—a minor challenge, but a challenge all the same.

Her prey collapsed as its leg finally failed on it. It lay there, in pain, but relishing its escape.

She descended before it, her breathing unhurried. The look of pure terror upon the faces of the wicked were a balm to her soul.

The rat cowered.

The rat begged.

The rat pleaded.

'If the heavens wished for you to live, then you would have not met me.'

The rat died.

She strode away, her head held high. Another one of the wicked beasts that dared come into her territory was defeated.

And it was *her* territory. The chicken was not up to the task. It was cowardly and weak. The others said he was some great warrior, but she could not believe them. His slow, uncertain kicks were pitiful. He rose not to her provocations, and so she allowed him to exist within her presence. The pigs were large but ultimately dumb. The less said about the prey-rat . . . the better.

Only *she* was capable of protecting this place. Only she was capable of defending Fa Ram, and all her Master's possessions. They would come to realise this and praise her in due time. She preened. The others would respond to her like her Master! They would aid her and praise her.

Though . . . the Master could protect this place too. She *supposed.* Though it would be best that he remained . . . *unbothered.*

She shuddered at the memory. Of one of her first memories.

The Land did not even notice her. She was nothing before the boundless power directed at another. Her breath was being crushed out of her lungs by the weight of the world as *he* stood there, a mountain rising to the heavens.

The Master's wrath was something that should not be roused, so she dealt with annoyances for him. He had more important things to do, like tending to his home and scratching her back. *Yes! These are all worthy things for the Master to do.*

He could even spend his time making sure the other miserable creatures had the slightest bit of skill, so they wouldn't be complete burdens.

Like he was doing now.

"*Chunky boy, chunky boy, Chun-Keeee Boyyyyeeee!*" the Master shouted gleefully, crouched down in the snow with his arms held apart in a stance, ready to receive his disciple's blow. She knew he needed no stance to withstand Chun Ke's strike, but he was being kind to the dullard.

Chun Ke squealed happily and immediately tore off after the Master, ploughing through the snow. His charge shook the land, and the covering on the ground barely slowed him. If she had been hit by this mighty charge, she would not emerge unscathed. Although he wouldn't be able to hit her—she was too fast.

Probably.

She might need to increase her own training.

When Chun Ke struck the Master, however, he didn't so much as budge. The Master caught him by the tusks. They began to rock from side to side, and the Master easily bowled him onto his flank, laughing at his disciple's enthusiasm.

Chun Ke rolled to a stop and then eagerly righted himself, ready once more to receive the Master's personal instruction. He was weak, so it was only right. His recent recovery from his injuries meant that he needed more attention.

She would be monopolising the Master's bed tonight anyway. None of the others got that honour, so really, she spent the most time near the Master.

She bit down on the dead rat. *Ooh. This one is* tasty.

Once more, Chun Ke charged, and once more the Master took his mighty blow without care, rolling him onto his side and scratching his belly, showing him how an enemy would disembowel him. Then, he unleashed a series of slaps onto the pig's stomach, miming a devastating combination of strikes that would have surely slain the oaf had even a fraction of the Master's strength been in the blow.

Chun Ke went limp, as he should, until the Master let him up and began scratching his mane affectionately.

She turned her nose up at the display and left with a flick of her tail as the Master continued to wrestle with Chun Ke and roll him around in the snow. She stalked her domain, heading towards the Great Pillars.

The weak coward Bi De was upon them as always, silent and dwelling on whatever ailed him. The little prey was on his back as always. She could appreciate that the rat had some measure of intelligence, always keeping the other disciples around so that the two of them couldn't . . . *play*.

Bi De greeted her, but she ignored him and continued to stare at the rat, who was observing the Master's training session.

She is a disciple, isn't she? She ate the Master's food and lived on the Master's land, wasn't it time she learned to contribute?

She finished eating her meal while the little thing cowered at her attention and accusation. The rat was weak and needed to be strong to survive the world. Otherwise, she was just food. She was the Master's—which meant she couldn't be weak. She was not allowed to be. Ri Zu seemed to be trying to muster up her courage to confront her when they were interrupted.

Bi De shook his head and stood. He looked upon her and declared: '*If she needed a sparring partner to test herself against,* he *would oblige her.*'

She found this amusing. He had nearly been beaten by prey, of all things. That he thought himself able to match her was laughable.

Very well, this Young Mistress would teach him how the world worked. And then, after that, she would trade pointers with little Ri Zu.

They both stepped onto the ground, a section cleared of snow. She washed herself after her meal, unconcerned, and Bi De landed before her. The rooster bowed his head in respect.

Fool. Tigu pounced. Her form was impeccable, her sudden strike sure to defeat the cock instantly—

She missed.

No, Bi De *sidestepped.* She whirled with grace beyond measure and struck again, only to hit empty air.

Her eyes narrowed at Bi De. He tilted his head to the side, observing her, and then nodded his head.

'*Slow,*' he commented. '*Basi Bu Shi was much faster.*'

Fury overtook her. *This preening cock dared?! I will disembowel him for the insult!*

Her claw intent filled the air. Her mighty weapons unsheathed themselves.

Bi De stood unconcerned. His eyes were closed.

Her body moved with speed surpassing her previous movement. Her strikes could slaughter a hundred rats each, her claws extended past her own body. They tore into the snow and ground mercilessly.

But they did not tear into Bi De. He moved with her, not a single feather ruffled by her passing. The coward ran, hopping back onto the Great Pillars, and she followed, unable to let her prey elude her.

Over the Great Pillars, and through its mighty construction, they travelled as blurs of colour. Her claws bit deep, even into the Master's reinforced structure, proving her might. But she could just not hit this blasted thing!

Her Claw Qi sharpened. That he had forced her to use her technique . . . it was unbelievable. But her pride would not allow her to be made a fool of any longer.

She was the Master's blade. *She* was the most valuable disciple.

This worthless creature was courting death!

Her Claw Qi burst towards Bi De's form, sure to finally land a blow.

She did. Her blades met Bi De's skin and *stopped.* Her claws were defeated utterly by the rooster's power. The rooster who winced with every kick. The rooster who sat upon his pillars. He was this strong, even while wounded?

She gazed in incomprehension.

'*Acceptable,*' Bi De informed her.

He flicked his wings, and she went flying off the Pillars and into a snowdrift. She lay there, stunned.

How . . . how was he this strong? He was toying with her!

She burst out of the snowdrift, snarling at Bi De, her fur raised and eyes wild.

But he was already sitting back down, his eyes closed.

'*As the Great Master once said: Pride comes before the fall,*' he instructed her.

Wrath coursed through her body, but she forced down the feeling. '*You would know, wouldn't you?*' she sneered.

Bi De's eyes opened. There was pain and loss in those depths. Shame, humiliation . . . and *peace.*

'*Yes, I would. My hubris nearly bought Great Fa Ram to ruin, even with all of my might.*' Tigu sneered again at his words. She would surpass him. She would never be so foolish!

'*If this tale prevents you from making the same mistakes I have, I will be content.*'

Her rage was building again. How dare he act so unaffected—

"Hey! Bi De, Tigu'er, are you two fighting?" the Master asked sternly, picking her up out of the snowdrift.

Ah, Master's warm hands, she purred.

Bi De shook his head in her distraction. Her pride stung that the rooster was saving her from dishonour.

The Master sighed. "Good, good. No serious fighting, either of you." She was stuffed down her Master's shirt and pressed against his warm body, with only her head peeking out.

Bliss.

"Now, let's go! The General That Commands the Winter isn't going to build himself!" Bi De tried to protest, but the Master lifted both him and the rat, placing them on his shoulders. The rooster looked mortified.

He then started walking, calling Chun Ke and Pi Pa to him, gathering the snow in his hands into a ball.

"See? Just like old times," he said, smiling at the . . . Senior Disciple. This was not over, but she could not beat him yet. She would be his superior in time, though, her training and skill far surpassed his—all she needed was a bit more experience!

She would begin . . . tomorrow. This was just too nice.

Bi De seemed to relax more and more as the Master worked, with Chun Ke and Pi Pa helping him amass a great amount of snow. It was gathered into a giant ball as the Master toiled with energy and enthusiasm.

Slowly, the rooster began to hop from shoulder to shoulder, watching the ball intently while the pile of snow grew and grew.

Finally, Bi De could contain himself no longer and crowed mightily, his voice echoing out through all of Fa Ram.

It hurt her ears, the wretched beast.

However, the Master smiled.

"*You tell 'em, Bi De,*" he said happily in his arcane and profound tongue, the one Bi De could not understand yet, scratching the rooster's wattles.

→

The next day, Tigu *allowed* the Senior Disciple to have her attention as he kicked along the Great Pillars.

He noticed her attention and invited her up.

'*Come*,' he told her, '*there is no short path to power.*'

She scoffed but heeded his wisdom.

She blessed him with her presence—surely, it would only take a single night to see his secrets and decipher them!

She did not.

She was *very* sore that night.

CHAPTER 24

THE PRINCESS AND THE GENERAL

If there was one season Meiling absolutely loathed, it was winter. The cold cut right through to her bones, wracking her slim body with shivers. The snow piled up on the ground, necessitating the shovelling off of their houses, and it made travel a chore. But the worst part about it was that everybody got sick. The shaking fevers and phlegmy coughs always proliferated around this time, and it was her family's job to fix it.

It was hard, soul-draining work that sometimes ended in the deaths of the patients. That was always the hardest part, trying so hard to save somebody, only to have their life pass through her fingers.

Still, she would count her blessings this year. Sickness had largely avoided Hong Yaowu, and save for the occasional case of the sniffles, things were good. Even the cold didn't seem as bad, which was why they were even out here at all. Her father had asked her to deliver a letter to Jin from Uncle Bao. He *could* have just gotten another messenger, but he told her to spend some time with her betrothed.

Her betrothed. Meiling still couldn't quite believe it. Oh, she had been to the matchmaker's plenty of times. Her father had been rightfully concerned for her prospects— especially after she started getting a reputation. She hadn't always been that way, but after hearing the first boy, *who she had actually liked*, call her ugly and boney . . . well, she had been devastated and angry. She regretted lacing his drink with laxatives, but word had quickly gotten out about her "nature." The rest of the men who met her all knew her reputation and came to "tame the shrew." Which led to more retaliation. Which led to more men trying to take her in hand, more insults, more belligerence.

Honestly, there was a worry that she would *never* be wed—save perhaps to one of the Xong Brothers, which would have been awkward. She did love them, and they loved her like a sister . . . but the thought of being with either always made her feel a bit ill. According to them, the feeling was mutual.

And then, out of nowhere, Jin had shown up. The betrothal had been a surprise. She had thought at first that she was merely a passing distraction—that was all she could be to a cultivator. But he had been serious about it.

Part of her was still waiting for some deception. But . . . as she spent more time with him, the less that seemed likely. The one spot of dark energy had faded. He was as he showed himself to be, and she could feel the growing fondness for the man each time they met. And with her betrothal, she'd gotten special privileges—like her father's command to visit, accompanied "supervision" that would be more likely to encourage rash behaviour than condemn it.

Now, she was trudging through the snow towards Jin's house. The snowshoes made things easier, but it was still difficult work—especially for the two heavier boys. She was a little annoyed that her two "guards" were coming, especially Yun Ren. The narrow-eyed man had been even more fox-like than usual, grinning and constantly making references to her "beloved's palace" and calling her "the Princess of Hong Yaowu."

She'd spiked some of his clothes with itching powder for his cheek, but even that couldn't keep the insufferable smirk off his face, even as she scratched at his back.

The one good thing about the brothers being here was that she didn't have to forge her own path. Yun Ren or Gou Ren took the lead, switching off, and all she had to do was walk in their footsteps.

Gou Ren was in front more than Yun Ren; he was just as excited as she was to revisit Jin.

The night they had spent on the road was cold, but not unbearably so. The trees provided plenty of protection, and Gou Ren's body was a furnace compared to theirs. He complained mightily about the chilly feet and clammy hands pressing against his skin as they shared the bedroll, but he rarely made any real effort to shoo them away. Furnace duty got him out of tending to the fire and cooking.

They were getting so close she could feel it. Though instead of rice and harvest, a crisp scent of pines and cedar filled her nostrils—with a hint of something almost spicy. The scent changed with the seasons, it seemed, and she couldn't wait to see what spring brought.

They trudged for a while longer, and then, for the first time in Meiling's life, she was caught completely off guard by something with Qi.

A large, rust-red boar with a black mane seemed to spring up out of nowhere along the path. Three massive scars decorated its face, and tusks curled out from its lips.

It was a fearsome-looking creature, with razor-sharp tusks and beady eyes. Steam hissed from its nostrils as it beheld them.

Gou Ren flailed, staggering backwards. The scent of pines and cedar was thick on the boar and *entirely* too strong for it not to have Qi. Meiling froze.

"Hey, Chun Ke," Yun Ren greeted it, completely unconcerned, while Gou Ren tried to skitter backwards on his hands. Meiling let out a breath she had been holding. *Is that one of Jin's?*

The boar let out a happy squeal and approached them, moving aside the snow without a care in the world. Yun Ren grinned as he started scratching along the boar's mane. The porcine beast leaned into his touch, whuffing and snuffing with joy. The last time Meiling had seen him, he was hairless and pink, not . . . *this*. His shoulders already reached her waist. She could probably ride him.

Yun Ren gave him a dried persimmon, and the beast seemed to get even happier, nuzzling Yun Ren's legs.

It was a far cry from the regal rooster, who bowed and insisted on courtesy.

There was another pig watching them from the path. Probably *Pi Pa*, if she remembered Jin's strange names right. The female didn't approach but seemed satisfied with the affection Chun Ke was receiving.

Eventually, Chun Ke got tired of greeting them and oinked, turning around to trot along the path. The *clear* path. They didn't need their snowshoes anymore—it looked like a combination of a shovel and a boar's snout had done most of the work.

"Why didn't you tell us that Brother Jin's pig turned out like *that*?" Gou Ren snarled at his brother.

"Because it was funnier this way," Yun Ren answered cheerily as he walked and whistled.

Meiling and Gou Ren looked at each other. They nodded.

Meiling's foot smacked into the back of Yun Ren's knee, while both of Gou Ren's hands slammed into his shoulders.

Yun Ren went headfirst into a snowdrift.

He caught up to them a minute later, scowling and shaking snow out of his shirt.

They made excellent time along the path, with Jin's boar in the lead. The female had disappeared, likely gone ahead.

It was nearing noon when they finally arrived at Jin's property, and once more they stood outside the fence.

The "Beware of Chicken" sign now had a companion, a carved leaf.

Gou Ren squinted at it before shrugging. "A maple leaf of some kind? Looks spikier than I'm used to."

Meiling studied it a moment before recognising the shape.

"We've got a maple with leaves like that in the forest to the north. I *think* they're known as giant vermillion maples. Or at least that's what Father called them," she said before shrugging.

Yun Ren looked smug again. "Brother Jin said it was a *sugar* maple."

"What? A sugar maple?" Gou Ren sounded excited. "Is it like sugar cane? Do you cut it down and squeeze it?"

They reached the fence where the rooster sat.

They bowed to the rooster, who bowed back. This time he did not impede their way as they ascended the hill, instead staying on the fence. He smelled a little . . . off, this time, a little acrid, and had an underlying scent of medicinal herbs.

"I don't know. I didn't ask him how it worked. All I got was the name. I think he might have said something about—*what the hells?*" Yun Ren stopped and stared as he finished cresting the hill.

Gou Ren burst out laughing. Meiling's hand met her face.

Before them, on another hill, was a massive edifice of snow, taller than the Imperial Palace in Verdant Hill. Taller than the buildings in the city that Meiling remembered seeing. It had the crude form of a man. Ash and soot made up its eyes and buttons, entire tree branches made arms, and a bunch of carrots lashed together made a truly magnificent pointed nose. There was even a strange hat in construction near it. The hat was tall and cylindrical with a wide brim and made out of dried grass.

Jin stood atop its head, his hands on his hips, grinning like a madman. He wore a bright red hat and lumpy-looking mittens.

"BEHOLD!" he boomed, his voice carrying across the farm. "THE GENERAL THAT COMMANDS THE WINTER!"

Meiling was flabbergasted. She raised her hands in confusion as Yun Ren started cracking up beside her, struggling to comprehend. Just . . . *why*?

It was so dumb. That stupid smile, and he looked so *proud* of it.

Eventually, she gave up and started laughing too. It was just too absurd.

A snowball slapped into Gou Ren's chest.

"You dare insult the Great General That Commands the Winter?!" Jin yelled in mock outrage. He jumped down into a drift and then sprung up to his feet, another snowball hurtling out and pelting Yun Ren in the face, sending him spluttering.

They immediately started up a war, the brothers teaming up and striking back.

She sighed. *Boys and their games, they never grow up—*

A snowball struck her right in the forehead.

"I'm going to murder *you sons of a flea-bitten whore!"*

Meiling joined the fray.

→

It ended with them soaking wet from the snow and exhausted, two things that nobody wanted to be in winter—which could have been deadly, were it not for Jin's house.

And she had to admit, Yun Ren calling it a palace wasn't *entirely* without merit. It was big. Certainly bigger than her house back home, with two stories to the building.

Inside, the house was incredibly warm, with a merry fire going in the fireplace, crackling and snapping. There was also no draft, and when the door closed, it was as if the elements were cut off completely.

"All right, let's get warmed up!" Jin said, and they stripped out of their wet clothes.

Blankets, warmed by the fire, were wrapped around them. They leaned against thick cushions made out of leftover rice bags filled with cedar fibre.

Meiling's mind replaced Yun Ren and Gou Ren with two significantly younger children. One with Jin's green eyes and one with her violet, and both with their combined freckles. She shook her head and blushed, snuggling into the blanket.

Jin made them tea and bowls of fish soup, cooking in the large fireplace.

He collapsed onto the cushion next to Meiling and took a big spoonful of broth.

Gou Ren was looking around eagerly. "This place is great, Brother Jin! Yun Ren wasn't exaggerating things!"

Jin blushed. "Well, I might have gone a bit overboard with the size, but that just means that I can host more people. Brother Yun Ren, Brother Gou Ren, you two are welcome to stay whenever, so shamelessly take advantage of my hospitality. And . . . you can just call me Jin, ya know?"

Yun Ren laughed and raised his bowl of soup in salute. "Don't mind if I do!"

"Not that I'm complaining," Jin said as he adjusted his position, pressing up against Meiling, "but what brings everybody around?"

Gou Ren shrugged. "Boredom, mostly," he said with a grin. "Done most of the stuff that needed doing, and we were told to take a break. Oh! Also, Meimei has a letter."

Meiling jerked at the reminder. She had almost forgotten about it . . . but she would need to get up to actually grab it. She stared sadly at Yun Ren, pleading with him to get the letter with her eyes. He sighed and shook his head but got up all the same.

"In the pack, top left," she told him, snuggling closer to Jin.

Yun Ren tossed Jin the scroll, who opened it and began reading. He seemed a little confused and concerned—until he reached the end of the letter, and then he nodded his head. He looked down at her expectant face, considered for a moment, and then spoke.

"There was a little bit of a mix-up with the rice prices, but Uncle Bao sorted it out for me. He also said that there would be a merchant going to Verdant Hill with a recording crystal. I was asking around for one earlier."

Meiling cocked her head to the side. "A recording crystal? What did you want that for?" *Was he going to do some kind of strange cultivation art with it?*

He blushed, and his grip around her waist tightened a little. "So I could record our wedding."

Her jaw dropped, and red bloomed across her face.

"See! Princess Meiling!" Yun Ren shouted.

CHAPTER 25

THE STUDENTS

They finished eating, and Meiling helped Jin collect the dishes. After their lunch, they once more took the "grand tour," since the place had changed so much. Their clothes had dried fast, and they were freshly warm from the fire. Warmed up, they went tromping through the house. The room they had been in was nearly finished—the other rooms of the house were uninsulated, and their floors were bare. The walls were up and the roof on, but it still needed a lot of work. He had the beginnings of a kitchen, but he cooked in his "living room" and used the fireplace there. The rest of the house had the second floor blocked out, but it wasn't entirely installed yet.

It was an odd house, very unlike the normal manors and walled-in courtyards.

The most interesting room in the house was the one closest to the river, as part of the river was *inside* the house. It wasn't frozen over, for the walls of this room were heavily insulated, and it was very cold, but it wasn't as damp as they'd expected.

"This is mostly for the summer," Jin said, "but it's for easy access to the river. Keeps things cool in the summer—like milk, and if you need it, cheese. Just put it in a container and drop it into the water. And it's easy to wash the dishes." He smiled, obviously proud of the room, before pointing to the water. "We've already got an assistant. It's been hanging around for the last week."

And sure enough, a carp had risen to the top of the water, eager to get some of the leftovers from their soup bowls. It was a rather drab thing with brown scales and short whiskers. Jin rinsed the bowls out, and the fish eagerly ate what came off of them.

"Aren't you concerned with it flooding, Jin?" Yun Ren asked, studying the banks of the river.

"A little," Jin admitted. "But it would need to rise quite high. See this grate?" At their nods, he continued, "It's a pipe, and it goes under the house to the other river. If this rises so much it starts to spill over, it will take the water here back outside. Unless it's *completely* catastrophic, everything should be fine."

They nodded.

"I can't wait to see it when it's finished. If you need some extra hands, call upon us. We need everything ready for our *princess* here." Gou Ren said, grinning at Meiling.

Jin nodded. "I'll hold you to that," he replied with a joking smirk. "Speaking of extra hands, though, I'll need some help. Like how to build proper storage for medicinal herbs and the tools."

"Are you planning on making medicine, Jin?" Meiling asked. *He had been attentive when I spoke on it in the past.*

"I have an interest, but it's mostly for you." Her heart started pumping faster at the statement. "You said you liked studying medicine. There's going to be a bit of a library here too, once I can afford the scrolls and books—"

"Yun Ren, Gou Ren, *out*," Meiling ordered, cutting Jin off.

The boys took one look at her face and wisely fled. Jin looked a bit confused.

Meiling grabbed his shirt and pulled him down. There was no way that she could have budged him if he hadn't allowed it, but he obliged her.

Her kiss wasn't gentle—it was full of passion and fervour. She pushed, and Jin backed up until he hit the wall and then slid down, pulling her into his lap.

His hands reached up to her sides, and she held onto his neck with both arms, one hand pressing into the back of his head so that he couldn't escape, though she doubted he wanted to.

When they finally separated, flushed and panting, Meiling whispered to him. "If you spoil me this much, I might become a useless woman."

Jin laughed at his words thrown back at him, though he appeared a little dazed.

Meiling decided that the look was very cute on him.

→

Meiling hummed in contentment, laying in front of the fire. She would have drifted off to sleep long ago if the boys hadn't started getting rowdy again.

Her bath had been pleasant, relaxing, and just the thing she needed. Jin had a building outside that had a large tub—over what looked like the beginnings of a forge. With each pump of the bellows, the temperature increased, heating the water far swifter than she was used to. He had added dried herbs to it, leading to a fantastic-smelling, luxurious soak. If Yun Ren and Gou Ren hadn't been here, she could have maybe asked Jin to join her, even without them being married yet . . . but they *were* here, so after she finished, the three of them had crammed into the tub. It had been decadently spacious for her, but not so much for three nearly grown men.

This, of course, led to them starting to shove one another, which escalated into splashing.

And now they were running and jumping into the stream, into the ice-cold water, then running back into the tub while shouting and whooping.

She had gotten an eyeful of all three of them when she'd opened the door to check what the hell they were doing before wisely deciding to retreat. There were some battles she knew better than to fight.

She loved them all. She really did, but *heavens*, those boys were morons sometimes.

Still, Jin had good tea, the cushions were comfortable, and she had a medical scroll. It was one she had already read before, but it never hurt to refresh one's knowledge.

She was in the middle of reading the section on poultices when the door opened, coming along with the scent of the moon with a medicinal undercurrent.

She flinched and looked up. The rooster, Bi De, had opened the door and entered. He then closed the door with a flap of his wings.

He turned to her, bowing in greeting, and Meiling inclined her head. The rooster was satisfied and clucked. He turned his head and picked slightly at his vest, cooing something.

From out under his garment, a little head peeked, blinking worriedly at her. Slowly, nervously, a small rat clambered off the rooster's back. The smell of medicine and the smell of the moon separated.

The little rat bowed to her.

Meiling once more inclined her head, a little nonplussed. *Are there more Spirit Beasts on Jin's farm than actual animals?* she wondered.

The little creature got itself a tiny bowl—evidently *its* bowl—and served itself a small portion of the leftover rice. Hesitant, the little one approached her, sniffing at her.

It squeaked. '*Medicine*,' it almost sounded like to her ears. '*Healer-Friend*.'

"Ah . . . yes, I make medicine," she confirmed to the rat, and it brightened. *Somehow*.

'*Helped Brother Chun Ke!*' she once more "heard."

The rat bowed low, kowtowing before her. '*Great Master, teach Ri Zu!*'

Meiling had *no idea* how to respond to that.

↔

You know, sitting naked in a tub with two other dudes isn't something I'd ever done before. My memories of the Before told me that this should have been mortifying, but I crushed that feeling down. I had seen them naked before, when we'd bathed in the river.

Honestly, it was kinda nice chilling, literally, with the boys. I'd done a couple of polar dips before. They were bracing, but it wasn't too bad. And being able to get into what was essentially a hot tub right after, with a bottle of rice wine? Well, that just made it fun.

Especially when it wasn't your rice wine. Yun Ren had brought some nice stuff.

We sat around for a while, just soaking. Yun Ren had one of my bathing cloths over his eyes, his head leaned back, while Gou Ren appeared deep in thought. It was one of those nice silences—the ones where you just enjoy the other person's company.

Yun Ren held out his hand blindly, and I passed him back the bottle. He nodded and took a swig while his brother started to frown.

Gou Ren seemed to decide something and composed himself.

"Brother—er, *Jin*, I was wondering, this spring—" He sighed and composed himself. "I was wondering if you needed some help on a more . . . permanent basis."

I blinked, surprised at the offer, and scratched my head. "What about Hong Yaowu? Can they spare you?"

Gou Ren nodded. "If you don't need help, that's fine. You haven't needed help so far, but you're going to be married, and if you're planning on expanding . . ."

I considered his words. I probably would need help. I was strong, and I had a lot of stamina, but I couldn't be *everywhere*, and the harvest had shown me that even a little bit of help made things a lot easier. But I also had my animals, and they were willing to assist me. Did I need a permanent farmhand?

"I'll need to draw up a list of what I'm planning to do next year. I can't promise *permanent* employment right now, but there are definitely some things I'll need help with. And I'll have to work out what's proper compensation."

Gou Ren nodded at my words. "I wasn't expecting an answer today, anyway."

A thought struck me. "Actually, I have a better idea. I'll teach you how I do things here, and then you can teach the rest of Hong Yaowu." It would certainly be easier than me teaching everybody everything.

Gou Ren's eyes widened. "You would share that knowledge, Jin?"

"Of course. I'm going to have family and friends in Hong Yaowu, after all."

The brothers smiled at me.

"Well, then, I hope I am a worthy student for your teachings," Gou Ren said.

We stayed in a little longer before we decided we'd had enough. The tub was emptied, and we dried off.

We walked into the house and happened upon a strange scene.

Meimei was reading a medical scroll to Rizzo, pointing to each character and carefully enunciating each word. The little rat was sitting on her shoulder, nodding along and squeaking occasionally. With Meimei's soft smile and patient voice, she looked almost like a mother teaching her child.

She eventually noticed us staring at her.

"What?" she asked us. "She's a better student than my little brother."

CHAPTER 26

TWO-PIG OPEN SLEIGH

We had leftover fish soup for dinner. One thing I'd had to get used to was eating lots of the same stuff every day, but it wasn't too bad. Not to mention, that every year I stayed and farmed, the selection for meals would get bigger, so that was something to look forward to; instead of complaining about the present, I would instead use it to hope for a better future. This stuff was a bit bland because the Spirit Herbs were still growing, but the rice and veggies were good.

Man, I had really become reliant on the Spirit Herbs for seasoning. I needed to find some other stuff. There had been barely any left after the rats, and now I had far less than I would have liked. Well, that was something for later.

That evening, I was just kind of lazing around. The only one of my animals that was still unaccounted for was Tigger. Chunky and Peppa had come in to warm up. Peppa had laid down beside me, while Chunky had gone to mooch more scratches of the Xong brothers.

Meimei had finally reached her limit on teaching, getting up to stretch, then grabbing some of her sleeping attire out of her pack.

Gou Ren got up and stretched too. "I'll take care of cleaning up, Jin," he said, and went off to do just that.

It didn't take long for us to hear his giggling as he fed the carp. The thing was a damn vacuum with how swiftly it attacked the food on the plates, eagerly hoovering up anything you put in front of it.

Well, it looked like he would be a permanent addition to the house at this rate. *Like the garbage dino in* The Flintstones. *I wonder what I'll call him. Magikarp? Mr. Fish? Nemo? Eh, it's a thought for another time.*

Eventually, Yun Ren couldn't take the laughter anymore and went to go and play with the fish too.

Ha, my kids are probably going to love that fish. The heavens know I used to have a magnetic attraction to water. I was able to seek out and fall into the only puddle in the parking lot. Or get all my clothes wet in the first hour of our camping trips.

I'd have to keep a close eye on them.

"Jin, where did you get these, anyway?" Meimei asked, staring at my mittens with a bemused expression.

I opened my mouth to cheerfully proclaim them mine when she continued:

"Why did you even spend money on the mittens, whoever made these was *terrible*!"

Ouch. I know I wasn't good, but they worked!

I winced at the unintentional insult. "I made them. The hat, too."

Meiling looked up in surprise. "You have a loom?" she asked.

"Nah, I knitted them," I replied.

"Knit?" She looked like she was puzzling the word out.

"You know, like with needles?"

Meimei looked confused. "No, I don't. Could you show me?"

Wait, really? I wracked Rou's memories, and they came up blank for anything resembling knitting. Huh. That was one of the more surprising things I'd learned. Shrugging, I went and got my needles. I had made them out of wood and sanded them down until they were as smooth as metal. I took some of my leftover yarn and cast it on the stitch. The ball of yarn was thick and chunky, just the way I wanted it, and it had been cheap as an "inferior product." To be fair, it *was* a little itchy.

Meimei watched my fingers intently as the rows took form. I had been getting a little faster recently, but I was still pretty slow. Soon enough, there was the beginnings of a scarf.

"This . . . this is *great*. A loom is still better for finer detail and bigger pieces, but being able to make things while travelling is . . ." Meimei looked so eager and excited over something so mundane to me that I couldn't help myself—I kissed her on the nose. She flushed at how close our faces had been, and my surprise assault.

"Well, one more thing to teach, then. I dunno how good I'll be at this, and I'm *bad* at knitting. I can only really do straight lines and tubes, which is why my mittens look so bad."

Meiling nodded and kept looking at my rows. It looked like she still had some studying left in her.

Grinning, I patted my lap. Meimei got the message, smirking and settling in. She was a lot smaller than me, and even sitting in my lap I could rest my head on top of hers. She smelled *very* nice after her bath. She hummed and leaned back into my chest. "All right, so, to cast on . . ."

Our fingers worked together. Gou Ren and Yun Ren eventually stopped teasing the fish and started getting their own blankets out. Gou Ren opened the door at the sound of tapping, and Tigger ambled in, looking pleased with herself as always, while Big D bowed to us all and started up his night watch. Meimei had begun to get the hang of it, but it was getting late.

"Jin, do you have anything to divide the room?" Meimei whispered, glancing at the Xong brothers.

I nodded. I had a couple of wooden dividers that could be set up for privacy, or just to section off the room. I realised what she was getting at by her sly grin.

A couple were set up around my bed, as the "master of the house." The Xong brothers just rolled their eyes and bid us sweet dreams.

I normally slept in a shirt and short pants, while Meimei had a sleeping robe . . . but I had something I wanted to see her in. I handed one of my clean shirts to Meimei, who had stripped down to her dudou again. She raised an eyebrow at it, but she indulged me, sliding on the too-big garment.

We got into bed and under my covers. I have to say, the best thing about the new house was my new bed. It was a lot bigger than my old one, which had barely fit me, let alone the both of us. I still needed a down duvet, but for the moment . . . well, everything was perfect.

Our arms wrapped around each other. Her lips tasted of the pine paste we'd used to brush our teeth.

There was an irritated meow from beside us. Tigger hopped up onto the bed and squeezed between us petulantly. Meimei had frozen, and the cat sniffed her a couple of times. Tigger licked her nose and then flopped over.

Meimei snorted with amusement, breaking out into little giggles, and I started chuckling too. My arm settled around her waist, and our foreheads pressed together, Tigger sandwiched between us.

I slept the sleep of the content, curled up under a thick blanket, while the snow fell outside.

□

"Yeeeeeaaaahhhhh!" Gou Ren howled as Chun Ke dashed as fast as he could. He was riding on Jin's "Toba gan," lashed to the boar. Chun Ke had immediately gone wild, running around the property and jumping over small rivers while Gou Ren held on for dear life. He slalomed through the turns, barely managing to not get thrown off.

"Yee-haw, Gou, Yee-haw!" Jin shouted back at him, whooping as he continued to walk up the hill.

They had come here on a sleigh. It was bigger than his cart and had obviously been lovingly worked on. The runners were worked to look like tree branches, and there were eight-pointed stars carved into the sides. Jin evidently liked the colour red, because this was also supposed to be lacquered red and the stars painted yellow.

Jin had mumbled something about "San Ta" coming to town and got a big grin on his face.

That was how Meiling had gotten roped into finding out the favourite animal of every child in the village. She had no idea what he was planning on doing with the information, but he was obviously planning *something* amusing.

The front of the sleigh could either accommodate Jin or be hitched to an animal. Both of the Spirit Beasts seemed to greatly enjoy being hooked in, and they trotted off at a sedate pace through the silent forests and into the back of the property, where the biggest hill was located.

There, Jin had brought out a variety of devices to take advantage of the incline. Some of them were reminiscent of what Meiling remembered using not too long ago, or what her little brother was probably using right now. Jin's Toba Gan was just a fancy piece of wood, but Yun Ren had taken an interest in his "skis" and was currently falling over repeatedly while Jin tried to coach him on how to use them.

"Yeeee-haw!" Gou Ren shouted, and Chun Ke obligingly sped up. Jin's other pig was almost daintily using one of the longer planks to slide down the hill and then drag the board back up using the attached rope, only to go again.

They reached the top of the hill, and Jin sat down behind her.

"Let's do the jump this time!" he urged her, and she finally caved.

"Fine, we'll do the jump," she said with a sigh and braced herself.

She would have to take her little brother along the next time. He would never forgive her if she got to enjoy this and he didn't. A moment later the sled hit the mound of snow and catapulted them into the sky.

Sailing through the air was more enjoyable than she'd thought it would be.

↔

"Come on, you little shits, move faster! If one of them falls over, leave them!" a giant of a man snarled. His muscles bulged beneath a cut-up shirt, and his eyes were still wild with adrenaline. Blood had long since dried onto his face, making him look even more crazed than usual.

"Yes, Boss!" his underlings gasped as they continued their flight into the forest.

He snarled. The Whirling Demon Sword Gang was reduced to *this*. Those Verdant Blade Bastards! To think he, an Initiate of the Third Stage, would be forced to flee!

He would get his revenge! That Young Mistress of theirs would be warming his bed by this time next year! And he would sack a hundred more villages after that, just to prove a point!

"Boss, the boys can't take much more of this," His new second-in-command muttered in his ear. The promotion had been by virtue of survival, but he had been a loyal comrade for years and was proving his worth now.

He snarled again, as he remembered his brother, slain by that whore.

"Fine! Enough! We stop here for today! Ration the grub out! You and you, go scout ahead!" he commanded, pointing at his underlings, who hastened to obey.

"Yes, Boss!"

The camp was set quickly and their meagre food stores carefully rationed out.

The scouts came back several hours later with news, just as the sun was starting to set. A farmstead had sprung up not too far from their old hideout. The Boss of the Whirling Demon Sword Gang grinned.

Tonight, they were going to have some fun.

CHAPTER 27

THE MARCH

From his perch up in the trees, Bi De gazed upon those that took the noble form of the Great Master. They were humans, like the Great Healing Sage, but just as the hawks stole his form, they stole his Great Master's. They took no notice of him as he observed their movements.

He was tempted to fly down and offer them a greeting, but something stayed his wings. Experience, that harsh teacher, had taught him both the folly of trusting too easily and acting too rashly.

These beings did not act as they should. Their clothes were tattered. Their eyes were hard and full of foul intent. They slunk like the black-furs did . . . Like Chow Ji had.

Bi De could not make his decision yet, so he simply observed.

He watched them closely as they sniffed around what was the Great Master's domain.

↔

It had been another great day. Who *doesn't* enjoy going tobogganing with friends? Hell, it was better than the ski resort I'd been to. Mostly because I could just run up the hill faster than a lift. Eventually, Meimei and Yun Ren got so tired they didn't want to walk up anymore, so I just pulled them up.

I was training my dad-ing abilities, one hundred reps of "pull the kids to the top." Heh.

Our lunch that day had been some Japanese-styled fare, in the form of onigiri filled with fish. I didn't have any seaweed, so I'd ended up using the green part of a leek. It wasn't the right flavour, but it was still pretty good. They were grilled over a quick fire to char the rice a little bit and heat them up on the still cold day. Chunky and Peppa got their share of rice and veggies.

But all good things come to an end. It was starting to get late again, so we decided to pack up for the day, instead of doing more nighttime sledding.

Meimei and Yun Ren were pretty tuckered out. Gou Ren and Chunky, however, had to be coaxed back to the house. They were still bright-eyed and raring to go even after hours of running around, but I managed to corral them eventually, and we set off for home. My only regret was that there was no hot chocolate.

It was the one damper on the otherwise perfect day. I swear, though, I'll find a cocoa tree *somewhere*. Maple trees exist, so I assume I can probably find cocoa pods. Considering they were considered medicinal, and a bit of an aphrodisiac, the chances of finding them in xianxia land were pretty high.

And then, I shall have hot chocolate, I thought, a smile on my face.

Peppa and Chunky hooked themselves back into my sleigh, and we began the trek back home. My sleigh was coming along nicely. I definitely still needed some good jingle bells— and probably a horse, but Chunky and Peppa seemed to like the whole thing. Now all I needed was some antlers, and they'd be like Max from the Grinch. Soon, Santa would descend on Hong Yaowu-ville and bring gifts for all the good boys and girls!

Sure, none of the religious reasons existed, but I'd always held a sentimental attachment to what the holiday had come to mean. It was the same reasons people here celebrated: mostly family, friends, and an excuse to party.

I hoped this would be the kid's first taste of gingerbread too. China probably has something like it, but I couldn't tell ya.

I was still planning for my "Great Christmas Caper" when we got back to the house. There was nobody else around, with Big D and Tigger off somewhere. I fed my pigs their dinner, then started thinking about some other important questions, like, what was for *our* dinner?

"Any votes on what to eat tonight?" I asked.

The Xong brothers looked at each other and nodded.

"Let us make you food tonight, Jin," Yun Ren said with a smile.

I have to admit, it was pretty cool to see them make hand-pulled noodles. They were *fast*. Considering they also brought some chili oil and salted beef, I knew it was going to be a great dinner.

I eyed my small stockpile of Spirit Herbs. These would be the last until the shoots matured, in a month or two. But to hell with it. This was a meal that deserved the extra *oomph.*

They somehow found their way onto the cutting board. And into the noodles.

Dinner was delicious, if a bit more oily than I was used to. The extra zest was noticeable.

Gou Ren sighed contentedly after we finished eating. "Things always taste so much better when we're here," he mused out loud.

This got nods from Meimei and Yun Ren.

Huh, really?

I personally thought that the food at Hong Yaowu was delicious . . . but that may just be the fact that it was Meimei's cooking most of the time. She's good. *Real* good.

I collected the dishes and went to wash them up. Sure enough, the carp was ready and waiting for me. I was a little worried about how the oil would affect the fish, but he had eaten some to no ill effect before, so it was probably fine. If anything, he seemed to suck on the plates even harder.

Gluttonous little thing.

When I got back to the living room, Meimei had my pipa out.

"Could you play, like you played for me?" she asked with a hopeful smile.

That is how I knew Meimei was absolutely superior to all other women.

She liked John Denver.

↔

The man grinned as he heard the stomping feet and laughter coming from the farmhouse. Yes, these people were going to be ripe for the taking. Their guards were down, and judging by the house, they were absolutely loaded.

Rich enough to build that monstrosity made out of snow. He felt a surge of vindictive pleasure at the thought of tearing it down. These bastards were living large, while *he* had been running for his life.

And if he wasn't mistaken, he could hear a woman's laughter mixed with the men's. This was just too perfect. It had been so long since he had a woman.

He turned, going to report to the boss, but then paused. There was a rooster in the snow in front of him. It was quite the vibrant thing, and he could see its thick, surely juicy thighs. It cocked its head to the side and stared at him in the creepy way every chicken stared at people.

His stomach growled. He hadn't eaten much today. Nobody would notice the chicken disappearing. The damn bird had probably eaten better than he had recently. Grinning, he reached out for its neck to wring it. His fist closed around the rooster's throat and *squeezed.*

And squeezed some more. The rooster looked spectacularly unimpressed. The man was confused. He didn't seem to be doing anything to the bird. He went to pick it up. The chicken reached out with his beak and bit down on the offending arm.

Its head jerked.

And the man's arm was plucked from his body.

The man gaped stupidly at the stump where his arm once was. The pain hit. He opened his mouth to start scream—

↔

The man's head hit the snowy ground with a dull thud.

The rooster retracted his outstretched wing. No blood had stained him, and this filth had been unworthy of his spurs.

His suspicions were confirmed. Those that sent scouts ahead to slink in the shadows and offer no respect to the Great Master's Pillars were *interlopers.*

And interlopers had no place in Great Fa Ram.

He called the disciples.

From the trees, a stripy orange cat descended, walking behind and to his right. She prowled with unnatural grace, her footsteps not damaging a single snowflake and leaving no footprints behind her. She eyed the rooster with disdain, annoyed that he dared to command her, but she obeyed, nonetheless.

A large boar emerged from the gloom. His face was battle-scarred. In contrast to the cat, the snow parted as if fleeing before his unstoppable might. It vacated his presence, lest it be destroyed utterly.

From the left, a second pig emerged. She was smaller than the first and moved with precision, stepping gently through the snow. She paused a moment, sniffing at the corpse. And then with a single, dainty bite—

Consumed it whole.

She sneered with disgust, swallowing. Faint whips of Qi surrounded her mouth. '*The things I do for Fa Ram,*' she muttered, her voice prim and proper.

On her back, a nervous little rat sat. She wrung her paws and fidgeted, checking and rechecking her little satchels of herbs, ready to provide aid to her fellow disciples. But the little one's eyes were firm and focused. Her resolve was set. She would follow this path until the end.

The rooster gazed over their forms and was glad. He bowed in respect for the other's resolve. The cat sneered. The rat took a bracing breath. The pig raised an eyebrow. The boar oinked happily.

They were prepared. Bi De, the First Disciple of Great Fa Ram, turned his gaze to where the interlopers gathered.

With great dignity, the rooster began his march. Each stride was regal yet humble. His stature was kingly and yet not tyrannical. His presence was as bright as the moon, his intent, deep as the darkest night.

Behind him, the might of Fa Ram followed.

CHAPTER 28

STRENGTH AND SKILL

It was important to be well rested before a raid.

That was the one thing he always insisted on. You needed your energy to do what needed to be done. And being fresh meant that if there *was* a fight, then the boys would be raring to go instead of being tired and distracted.

Sure, it made them a little antsy and aggressive, but he liked them mean. Not too mean, because then they tended to burn, then try to pillage, and he couldn't have that.

It was going to go smooth. He and his boys could have a bit of a sponsored party—courtesy of the farmer, have some fun with the girl, kill the men, and then be gone. The people in the house were obviously rich and stupid.

He didn't expect much in the way of fighting. Three men and a girl, against thirty bandits? Three of whom were cultivators?

And what of he, Sun Ken, the Whirling Demon Sword himself?

He would've had a fourth cultivator if that whore of a Young Mistress hadn't killed him. He would mourn his brother later. Even just remembering that they'd had to flee from the Verdant Blade Sect stoked his rage. The bitch of a Young Mistress had been far, far too tenacious.

His fist clenched, and he growled. His boys might not get a turn if he stayed this angry. Mortal girls were so *fragile*.

Still, his boys were as rested as they could be, and they had some food in them.

It was a good night for raiding too, with clouds covering the moon. Darkness always made him feel at home.

"Gather up, you worthless bastards! Gather up!" he commanded, his voice booming through their camp.

There were some things one had to do as a leader to maintain order. These speeches were one of them, to hype the men up. He knew there had been grumbling about leaving the wounded behind, for even men like these disliked abandoning their comrades.

But soon, soon, everything would be in the back of their minds.

His boys staggered to their feet with hungry looks in their eyes. Oh yes, they were *definitely* ready.

"I know what you want, so I'll keep this short. We got a bunch of rich bastards an hour's walk that way. They have *generously* decided to add their wealth to the Whirling Demon Sword Gang."

At this, his men laughed. The mood was getting good.

"I know we've been through hell these last couple of days. Those Verdant Blade bastards thought they were hot shit, and we still managed to kill a bunch of 'em! But today is the turning point. Today, we get what we need and"—he paused to make sure everyone was paying attention—"what we're *owed.* A night beneath a good solid roof and all the grub you can eat!"

Some of his men started to cheer.

"This is what I promised all of you when you joined underneath my banner! A life to live, instead of just exist! A life without the Sects of the officials breathing down our necks! A life of *freedom*!"

The cheers got louder.

"Now, let's have a good night! A wild night! A Whirling, Demonic night!"

The men roared their approval when a voice cut through the night. Most of his men seemed deaf to it, but a small voice said to them:

'This is not a good-wise course of action, Interloper. You approach the border of Fa Ram.'

He froze at the voice that drifted in on the wind. "Who dares?! Who dares approach the camp of the Whirling Demon Sword Gang?" he demanded.

'We are of Great Fa Ram. Thy scouts have fallen-perished, for attempting to assault-kill its disciples and Interloping.'

His hackles rose at the statement, the voice a Qi-filled whisper. His men formed up around him; their swords drawn and ready. The rest of his gang inched closer together. That was stupid, when fighting cultivators, but they could not control the fear, or the feeling of being watched.

Sweat beaded on foreheads. Men, already antsy and remembering the attack of the Verdant Blade, looked close to breaking.

'Our Great Master is a kind-generous soul, and you are not yet upon his land, so the First Disciple instructs you thus:

'That you do not know the strength-power of Fa Ram is forgivable. Attempting to strike at it anyways is not. To continue upon this course-path is to end your lives.'

Sun Ken let some of his intent leak out. His men's resolve firmed as they felt his presence.

"Show yourself, you coward! Show yourself, and this daddy will kill you swiftly for daring to dictate terms to him!"

'You shall see the First Disciple, then, and Fa Ram shall instruct you . . .'

There was a burst of snow as something landed at the entrance of their camp. The men, confused by their leader's shouting, flinched back from the puff of white powder.

The men shifted nervously as footfalls echoed out, stepping assuredly through the snow.

Sun Ken's grip tightened on the hilt of his sword.

The snow was abruptly blown away, wind howling from the direction of the voice. Sun Ken's blade inched out of his sheath, ready to strike—

When he paused, incredulous at what had been revealed to him.

He blinked, just to make certain what he was seeing was true.

He started laughing. A rooster? With a vest on? Who dared to precipitate this absurd farce?

"You little shit!" one of his men barked at the rooster and stepped forwards to strike it with his blade.

And then Sun Ken felt it. The laughter died in his throat, and sweat beaded on his brow.

Spirit Beast.

"No! wait—" the Whirling Demon Sword tried to shout, but it was too late.

The man's body hurled through the air, his chest caved in by a mighty kick. He slammed into a tree with a sickening crack and dropped, dead before he hit the ground.

One could hear the hearts of the men, hammering away in their chests, but their breaths were silent. They dared not breathe at all.

The rooster cocked his head to the side and lowered his leg. He walked into the bandit camp, uncaring that he was surrounded.

The voice whispered again.

'The First Disciple wishes to tell-inform you that your disciples are very ill-disciplined, but he shall forgive you this time.'

The rooster gestured to him.

'You sniff-slink around the Great Master's land like rodents. The First Disciple demands to know why.'

This damn Spirit Beast. An up-jumped cock dared to threaten him? Calling itself "First Disciple?" Fury burned in his gut at the thought. His boys were no match for Spirit Beasts, but *he* had slain many.

This one would be no different. He would consume its core and put its flesh in his cooking pot!

Sun Ken drew his sword and pointed it at the outnumbered avian.

"I am the Whirling Demon Blade, Sun Ken! What I do is what I desire to do! I will take what I please from your Great Master! I shall slay his brothers and rape his wife! I will burn down his home, eat his flesh, drink his blood, and sleep in his skin for daring to mock me so! Sending a Spirit Beast, a chicken, against me instead of facing me himself?! A more worthless 'Great Master' I can't imagine!"

His aura erupted. Demonic red saturated the clearing as he drew upon his full might. Some of his men's eyes started to go blank, his aura infecting them with bloody-minded zeal. His blade began to whisper and gibber madly, demanding that he cut.

The rooster's eyes were wide in shock. Sun Ken grinned. The thing had probably never been truly challenged before.

'So, you have chosen . . . death.'

The little voice sounded both angry and slightly fearful.

The chicken screeched with fury. It was a shock wave of noise. Several men staggered backwards from the force of the rooster's cry, their ears leaking blood. One of the closest, directly in the line of fire, clutched his heart and slumped to the ground, frothing at the mouth.

Twin blades of moonlight sprung from the rooster's spurs, pure, bright silver, and the snow seemed to explode around him as he moved.

The Whirling Demon Blade rushed to meet him along with his lieutenants—and then all hell broke loose.

↔

From the right, an enormous boar that reached the bottom of some men's chests slammed into the encampment with a joyous squeal. Bones shattered. Organs ruptured. Skulls split. Its mighty tusks gored and savaged as it flung its head from side to side, intent on spearing and trampling everything before it. Where it strode, bare earth was revealed, trampled flat and coated with the blood of the wicked.

The beast's presence demanded attention, for his grunts of happiness and squeals of joy forced all eyes to him.

Men swung swords and thrust spears with strength fueled by terror, trying desperately to halt its advance, but the mundane weapons simply bounced off its skin as it forged ever deeper into their ranks.

From the left, a more measured threat came. Its trotters struck and kicked. Its bulk carefully crushed and smashed. Its maw opened and shut politely, relieving men of their limbs—before the offending objects were spat back out in disgust.

The pig, for all its mass, fought with purpose. While the boar accepted blows, uncaring and unheeding of them, the pig deftly dodged, or daintily pirouetted between strikes, and struck back with its own, never stopping its own thrust into the enemy's ranks.

A tiny rat was upon its back, and occasionally the little beast would throw pepper powder into eyes or leap off to bite into fingers before retreating back to safety.

These three were bad enough. But there was one more.

From the back came *death*.

Mere mortals could not perceive its passing.

Throats split open. Thighs were flayed through the arteries. Eyes were blinded in a blur of orange. Some were merely crippled, falling down and wailing in pain and terror, which only added to the sudden cacophony.

The mere men, assaulted and surprised from all sides, broke. Some tried to flee; some tried to hide, dragging the bodies of their slain comrades over themselves to use as shields; some simply collapsed, unable to take anymore. They were all easy pickings. But death's eyes were upon a more powerful prize. One of the Whirling Demon Sword's lieutenants leapt back from a mighty blow from the rooster, his sword nearly flying from his hand with the force of the strike, before death was upon him.

He nearly died in the first three exchanges.

He could not believe his eyes as his sword desperately parried Qi-infused claws. The beast *bounced*, springing off trees and the bodies of his men, claws scoring great furrows wherever it landed on flesh, leaving no trace upon the wood or earth.

The man could feel it—the sheer bloodlust and glee the beast had, the predatory grace and savage fury. It was like facing his boss, condensed into the form of a monster.

It was a tiger in the body of a cat.

Three more strikes were exchanged, and he threw the beast backwards, then entered into a stance. He ignored the scream of one of his brothers as an arm and blood arced through the air. He sharpened his intent and focused his breathing as the beast stalked towards him.

"Go!" he heard his leader yell, "take the boar, and return to me!"

One of the other cultivators split off, bleeding from a cut on his head, while another of their number fell, struck down by the rooster.

He moved into the first Step of the Whirling Demon Sword.

[Whirling Dance of Blood]

Bloody red energy collected around his blade, and his heart squeezed painfully in his chest as he forced out the incomplete technique. He had not yet learned enough of it, but it would be sufficient, even this lowly version. The beast's eyes widened.

What came forth was the mad dance of a demon; his sword flew into befuddling patterns as he struck with crazed abandon. Each blow chained into the next as he spun, leapt, and smashed. Each strike got closer and closer to ending the beast. He started laughing, red creeping into the edges of his vision. He embraced the power of the demon.

Orange fur drifted on the breeze. Tiny drops of red fell.

The cat landed and took a breath. Qi gathered around the little monster as he surged towards it.

[Claw Art: Fivefold Blades]

Blades of pure cutting force bit into the ground, extending as long as a sword. The cat's form blurred as it raised a paw, then brought down the technique. His blade whirled skywards in defence.

One blade was blocked.

Then two.

The third he dodged by a hair's breadth.

The fourth scraped along his ribs.

The fifth cut deep into his arm, but he was through the barrage of Qi, his sword thirsty for blood. He roared, barrelling down upon the tiny creature, a demon about to taste blood.

The cat's other paw rose from beneath.

Five more blades struck true, biting up into his gut. One ruptured his liver. One punctured his kidney. One burst his stomach. One penetrated his lungs. The last one tore through his spine.

Blood erupted from his mouth. His sword stopped, inches from striking the beast. He fell.

↔

The cat nearly collapsed but caught itself, panting.

Her eyes turned to the true fight.

She could intervene and slay the pathetic thing that dared to threaten the Master whenever she felt like it.

Her limbs shook.

Whenever she felt like it.

↔

Bi De chastised himself. His recklessness had *not* been fully tempered. He had dared to preach to Sister Tigu when he was still so lacking. It was shameful.

This wretched thing's words had driven him nearly to folly. It was bad enough that he was an interloper. He dared to threaten the Great Master's disciples, friends, and woman—the Great Healing Sage!

He knew in his heart that the Great Master could slay all of the interlopers with but a glance and a flick of his fingers, but the words most foul had driven him to wrath. To threaten his benevolent Great Master with such atrocities? This man did not just court death; he embraced it wholeheartedly.

Bi De had charged into four of those wicked men and barely survived the first few moments. It was not their strength that was nearly his undoing.

It was their *skill.* It was no wonder Chow Ji had sought to corrupt his form into one that resembled this. Their bodies were optimized for fighting and wielding spurs made of iron. His enemy's arrogance had prevented them from capitalizing on his mistake, however. They hadn't used any of their Qi-empowered techniques.

He had trained greatly. His holy Lunar Blades were nearly completely refreshed, with only a few minor blemishes. And the timely intervention of his fellow disciples had given him the ability to fight only the leader.

Tigu had slain her opponent, while the last one flailed, assaulted with Sister Ri Zu's concoctions, Brother Chun Ke's overpowering might, and Sister Pi Pa's fearsome—*beautiful* maw.

His intent was now completely focused. This Sun Ken's strikes were befuddling, a mad dance that he needed to use every inch of his ability to see through and comprehend. Sun Ken's sword whispered and gibbered every time it got close to hitting Bi De. If he had started the fight with such a technique, Bi De surely would have fallen.

Holy silver clashed with demonic red as they leapt off the trees. It was a dance in the air, a clash of light and darkness. The man was spewing bile and vitriol, but Bi De had centered himself now. The words were as rain upon his back.

But he was tiring. Sun Ken's blows were mighty, and his skill undeniable. Bi De would have to redouble his efforts. Small nicks accumulated on his form, and his spurs protested every time he directly clashed with the man. It only truly highlighted how far Bi De had to go.

He drove forwards, dodging a blow that would have decapitated him, and landed a kick to Sun Ken's ribs. The strike made something crack, and the man was thrown up into the air.

[Rising of the Crescent Moon!]

Bi De rose to meet him as surely as the moon rose at dusk. The man's iron spur intercepted the blow, demonic red clashing with holy silver.

Sun Ken roared with fury. His Qi thickened. His sword burned with unnatural light and screamed with wrath, the very metal seeming tortured, along with what sounded like a faint voice from *within* the blade itself.

[Whirling Demon Slash!]

Bi De's eyes widened. The spur struck three times in quick succession, hammering into his legs and sending him falling back down to earth.

Sun Ken appeared an instant later, his spur screaming for blood. The maddening screeching voice coming from the blade begged its master to cut. Bi De's wings flapped, and the wind howled, propelling him back out of the way.

Sun Ken glared around the silent clearing filled with corpses and started laughing.

"The great terror of the Azure Hills, Sun Ken the Whirling Demon Blade, defeated not by the Verdant Blade Sect, but by farm animals! How bad a joke this is!" The smile fell off the man's face. "Come then. One last blow, *First Disciple*."

Red surged around the man as he focused his intent.

Bi De panted. This was not working. The man gripped his blade with two hands, blood leaking out of his mouth. Madness and fury contorted his face into a demonic visage. His blade began to wail as the energy collected around it.

Bi De closed his eyes and took a deep breath. He was nearly spent.

Above him, the clouds parted. The half-moon hung above their heads, shedding its light upon the world.

The half-moon. It had its own lessons. Like the Taijitu, it was half-dark and half-light, but the separation was perfect unlike that symbol. No light stained the dark, and no dark stained the light.

His feathers drank in the holy light, armouring his body in the purest argent.

Yet Sun Ken struck first.

[Spiraling Demonic Whirlwind!]

Red roared out, forming a ravening twister of destruction. Like demonic teeth, it consumed everything in its path.

Bi De charged to meet it, racing into the jaws of death. The red, ravening energy slammed into his chest, and he howled in pain, but it was nothing compared to the pain Chow Ji had inflicted upon him.

He drove through it as Sun Ken spat blood, the mist flowing out and into the red wave, burning his vital energy in his last attack. The luminescent feathers faltered.

His pure armour began to fail. Little red cracks formed. Like the fangs of a demon, the whirlwind bit deep, offering no mercy. It ripped into silvery flesh and tore it to pieces.

Bi De screamed.

The silver light guttered out.

↔

Sun Ken stood, panting. He couldn't believe it. It was the strongest Spirit Beast he'd ever encountered. The strongest creature he had ever faced, which had nearly led him to death, was a chicken. Not a Blaze Bear, or a Wrecker Ball, or something from another province. A base rooster that could use Qi.

He opened his mouth to shout his victory, but no sound came out. Instead, blood poured down his chin splattering onto the ground.

"Sneaky little bastard," he said, almost impressed.

A black, nearly invisible spur was embedded in his heart. Red bled into black as Bi De revealed himself, his blackened feathers fading back to their red tones. His body had been the night itself, the shrouded face of the moon.

A second rooster formed for an instant, made out of silvery light. Two roosters stood in front of him as he toppled, breathing his last breath.

[Split Faces of the Half Moon]

CHAPTER 29

THE GREAT MASTER

I woke up slowly, still in a good mood from last night. I had a couple of weights on my body and a damp spot on my chest. I opened my eyes and looked down.

I was missing my shirt, and I saw a shock of green-tinted hair. Meimei was still asleep, face down on my chest and drooling, with a contented smile on her face.

I chuckled and rubbed her bare back but then paused. Her shirt was missing too. I absently pulled Gou Ren's leg off my throat where he had put it in his sleep. He was only wearing his loincloth and still snoring away. After that, I extracted *my* leg from Yun Ren's grip, who was at least clothed.

I smiled at the memory of our increasing rowdiness that eventually led to . . . *this*. I'll admit, I was just a little buzzed and not absolutely hammered like my friends had been after three bottles, but I went along for the ride anyway.

Including the part where I had a Xong brother on each shoulder, while Meimei sat on *their* shoulders, forming some kind of strange human . . . shape. Like a cheerleading performance—while Meimei double-fisted rice wine.

Drunk Meimei was hilarious. Her personality shifted completely as she turned into a dirty old man. She'd busted out a *spectacularly* vulgar drinking song about a brothel madam and a donkey, complete with pelvic thrusts. The Xong brothers had been in tears from her song, and I hadn't been much better because she started getting handsy halfway through.

I drew the line at her demanding me to pour what was left of our booze down my chest so she could lick it off.

. . . Okay, I hadn't drawn the line there. Don't judge me. *It was hot.*

Ah, good times. My hands circled around Meimei's back, and I lifted her up from our position on the floor.

Meimei was very light. I could hold her with one arm and not feel the weight. Gently, I carried her to my bed and put her under the covers. I gave her a kiss on the forehead, and she murmured happily.

I scratched my back.

The Xong brothers got some blankets and were transferred to bedrolls. To be fair, they were light to me too. There was no real effort involved in moving them, even when I was taking care not to wake them.

I stretched and left them to sleep for a while longer. If I had to guess the time, maybe five in the morning? I wish I could have slept a bit more too, but I was awake now, so I figured I might as well get some work done.

I looked around and frowned. I was a little surprised that none of the animals had come in last night, especially Tigger. Maybe we got a bit *too* wild?

I got dressed and headed out into the cold.

The farm is always silent this early in the morning, save for when Big D goes and sounds the alarm. There hasn't been as much of that lately, though. Tigger and Big D had been taking care of things without waking me up, and maybe they'd finally depleted the vermin population around here.

But nobody was around.

I frowned, considering for a moment. I looked at the snow trails and began to follow one of Chunky's. It meandered away from the house and across the river, into the "back left" of my property relative to the road. I followed it for a while, confused and concerned because the trail went way further out than they normally ventured. It looked like it went completely off my property.

I was about to break into a light jog when I saw them. Everybody was trotting back home, without a care in the world.

I breathed a sigh of relief and stopped my walk, just standing there with my arms crossed.

My animals noticed me and transformed from triumphant and proud-looking to suddenly looking like children who had been caught with their hands in the cookie jar.

Well, everybody except Chunky. He squealed happily at the sight of me and ran over, ramming into my legs and begging for scritches. I obliged him, scratching away. Peppa had something tied to her back. I couldn't quite make out what the bundle was from the angle I was at.

"So, where have you guys been?" I questioned, and— "Wait, what happened to you, Tigger?!"

I walked forwards and scooped my cat up. She was covered in little scratches, and her fur had been shaved down in places. She preened into my touch, rubbing her head against me.

'We have been slaying vermin, Great Master.'

I "heard" Rizzo say. *Ugh, more Spirit Beasts? Well, as long as everybody is okay.*

Big D stepped forwards and bowed, as did the rest of my animals. And then there was a clunking noise as a bunch of swords fell off Peppa's back . . .

Okay, *what the fuck kind of vermin carries* **swords.**

I turned back to Rizzo, feeling a bit light-headed.

This . . . might be a difficult day.

→

It was a tale straight out of a story. Five brave disciples who'd fended off the wicked bandits. Each one of them puffed up when it was their turn to be the center of attention, save Big D, who just stood silently, as if it was natural that he had led an assault against a bandit encampment without warning me first.

My fist clenched at what Rizzo said the bandit had wanted to do to my farm.

I got worried when they described the techniques used.

And I didn't know what to feel when they said they'd defeated the bandits and "cleaned up."

I was very concerned. I was very, very, *very* concerned.

Okay, all my animals becoming Spirit Beasts? I could handle that, or so I thought. The ugly mutant rat who attacked the farm was maybe a one-off. Defending the farm from pests? understandable.

Fighting a battle against cultivators and *winning?*

Maybe it was my fault for being lazy and letting them do whatever. Giving them so much responsibility and not really telling them what should happen.

Yeah, I didn't know how the fuck to deal with this. Honestly, I didn't know how to feel about them killing the bandits. A part of me recoiled and screamed that all human life was sacred. That they should have been detained and offered a fair trial . . . even if a fair trial meant summary execution or living out the rest of their lives as slave labour in the mines.

Some part of me wished that I could have talked to them. Gotten them to see the error of their ways, like some kind of saviour, and then we all lived happily ever after. But the bandit's words made it clear what he would have thought of that plan.

Another part felt visceral satisfaction at their deaths. They'd threatened to hurt Meiling and my friends. They'd threatened to tear down all I had built.

Trees strangled entire cities. The mountains rose up and vented their terrible wrath. The very earth rose up and went to war.

My fist clenched, as my Qi bubbled to the surface, unbidden.

Some part of me wished I had been there, right alongside my animals.

The last part was just annoyed. The fact that I had encountered the bastard in Verdant Hill, the super rat Spirit Beasts, and now this? Was the world *trying* to fuck with me?

I stared down at my animals, my face as impassive as I could make it. They waited for me to praise them.

They gazed at their trophies with pride.

How long will it be until they start going on more "adventures."

They had no guidance. I'd left them alone and treated them like pets. Even when I *knew* they weren't.

How long until they attract some cultivator's attention? Cultivators who want to eat them and won't take no for an answer. Cultivators who want what's here.

All they wanted to do was make me proud. All they wanted to do was live here.

They'll just keep causing problems.

They were offended on my behalf. On Meiling's behalf. On the Xong brothers' behalf. They went to war to defend us.

They're going to ruin things. That peaceful life you want so much.

Great Master, they called me. They thought me brave and wise, strong beyond measure. The kindest thing they had ever met. I was the man who nurtured them, even when he didn't have to.

Just end things. Try again with other animals, and this time, no Qi.

I took a breath and bent down, my hand landing on Big D's head.

It's simple, Meimei's voice whispered. *Wherever you feel that urge . . . don't.*

A small smile spread across my face as I started to scritch his wattles. "Thank you, everyone. Good job protecting the farm."

My animals preened, basking in my attention. I doled out scratches and praise, and they absorbed it like I was their own father.

Well, just think of it as training. They're pretty childish. Hey, if you can raise a rooster, you can raise a kid.

Fuck what I just thought. I'm ashamed it even entered my mind. What the hell are you trying to get me to do, me?! There will be no more violence and hate here—no Xianxia bullshit. Life WOULD be good.

I would *make* it good.

My own little slice of paradise, right here.

For a brief instant, I felt warm, like I was being hugged. Something at the edge of my awareness twinged, like a rat squeaking in shock before being pounced on by a cat.

The feeling faded.

I picked up the swords. "Come on, let's go get some breakfast," I told them. The disciples perked up—everyone except for Peppa, who looked vaguely ill.

CHAPTER 30

SOMETHING WORTH RECOGNITION

Meiling awoke to what felt like Gou Ren jumping up and down on her head. She was queasy and sore, and she had no idea what she'd done last night.

This was why she never drank heavily—this and the fact that everybody always looked at her strangely afterwards. Nobody said why. They would just start laughing.

She opened her eyes, expecting stabbing pain . . . but her eyes didn't protest too badly. In fact, most of her headache disappeared as she came to full wakefulness.

Along with the memories.

"The ol' spry whore, and the donkey that came in her back doOOOoor!"

"Chug, chug, chug, chug, chug!"

"Kyahahahahahaha! Shake it, darlin', shake it!"

"Come here often, cutie?"

"*Gimmme that butt!* Gimmme *that butt!*"

"Thirsty!" "Really, Meimei—"

"Do it!"

Her tongue running along solid muscles. Sweat mixed with wine tasted surprisingly good.

Her face turned crimson.

She grabbed Jin's pillow and screamed into it, kicking her legs under the sheet.

"You okay, Meimei?" Jin asked. She could hear the grin in his voice and the Xong brothers' own laughter.

She staggered out of bed and glared at the pack of idiots. And the animals.

"Last night didn't happen," she decreed.

Jin leered. "But what about the wine pouring? That was fun!"

"Didn't. *Happen*," she snarled, sitting down and snatching the bowl of rice and egg out of Jin's hand. She glared around, daring anybody to contradict her. The Xong brothers just smiled the smile of men who had blackmail.

She clicked her tongue and looked at the animals. At least they were—

"Jin, what happened to your cat?"

Jin's cat had some bandages covering her and several places where the fur was shorter.

Jin's smile became a little strained, but he still seemed quite happy.

"Funny story, that . . ."

□

Cai Xiulan was having a difficult day.

She threw herself out of the way of a blast of flame and leapt backwards from monstrous claws trying to rend her in two.

Well, it was more like a difficult week.

The Blaze Bear roared savagely, its entire body igniting. It stood on its hind legs and glared at her.

If she was honest, a difficult month.

Or three.

Her once pure white robe was stained with dirt, her hair was matted, and she had lost one of her hair ornaments. She had a massive gash in her side from Sun Ken that might already be infected. She was hungry; she was tired and hadn't had time to cultivate for three months.

She *hated* Sun Ken.

[Verdant Blade Sword Arts]

Two green blades whirled at Xiulan's command, cutting through the air. They stabbed downwards, penetrating beast flesh, but that just made the bear angrier.

A tree disintegrated under the force of the Blaze Bear's charge. Her side twinged as the wound nearly opened, and she called back her blades.

It had started with the Whirling Demon Sword Gang having the gall to attack Green Grass Valley. The 150-strong bandit gang had despoiled the town, slaughtered its inhabitants, and stolen a shipment of Spiritual Herbs meant for the Verdant Blade Sect.

They spat in her Sect's face directly and challenged them brazenly. It had been so distressing that her honourable father had coughed blood when he found the message carved into the flesh of the innocent, proclaiming him a coward and a cuckold.

Unfortunately, her honourable father had to attend the Martial Summit of the Azure Hills, a dialogue of all the top experts, and that was something he couldn't miss even for *this*.

So, she had been chosen. Since she was a match in power for the arch-bastard, she had gone with the forces of the Verdant Blade to slay the Whirling Demon Sword Gang and their leader, Sun Ken.

What followed was a brutal game of cat and mouse—as skirmishes broke out, their mortal troops were ambushed, and they ambushed in return. The months had been spent finding false trains and having to double back, searching every craggy hill and deep ravine, and stumbling onto burnt-out villages as they chased their quarry north.

She flipped over a gigantic paw, and her swords danced behind her, scoring more shallow cuts along the beast's limb.

After several months the final ambush had happened. Sun Ken had hit their flanks while his brother, Sun Rong, sought to slay her.

It was a battle, but her force of ten men had all ascended to the Initiate's Realm. Eleven members of Verdant Blade Sect and their mortal soldiers versus 150 bandits with the element of surprise. There should have been no contest.

It had turned even far too quickly.

She had slain Sun Rong, the Whirling Demon's brother laid low by the Verdant Blade Sword Arts and had then sought to cut the head off the snake. But Sun Ken was canny and knew the battle was lost. He had managed to withdraw by collapsing the ravine and slaying one more of the Outer Sect disciples.

It was an outrage that could not be borne. The rest were more heavily injured, so she had forced them to rest while she continued on alone. The pride of Verdant Blade was on the line. She had finally picked up his trail again and had been making good time when she ran face-first into a Blaze Bear.

A spectacularly angry Blaze Bear.

Regret was not becoming of a cultivator, but she wished that compassion hadn't made her reckless, forging ahead alone, to finally lay low the shattered remains of the bandits. Still, a tiny voice in her head urged her onwards. She could win. She just needed to find him.

Her twin swords whirled and cut at her command, proof of her mastery, slashing down at eyes and trying to split open its nose.

The bear shrieked with rage, and she grimaced. It was too much to hope that she would be able to defeat it without *truly* fighting.

She landed and took a breath, drawing on more of her Qi.

[Verdant Blade Sword Art: Eight Blades of Grass]

Her blades multiplied. Two became four, four became six, and six became eight, the Verdant Blades growing like the grass of her home.

She shot towards her enemy, her blades following around her, with three splitting off to strike from behind.

Each punch sent a sword forwards, and each sweep of her hand became a slash that raked and bit deep.

The Blaze Bear was caught in a whirlwind of green steel. It roared and raged, gouts of fire erupting off its body, but its fate was sealed.

She drew back her fist, and all of her blades returned to her, spiralling around her arm. She ducked under a last, desperate strike and thrust her weapon into the center of the beast's chest. Her swords struck true, penetrating to the hilt, even as the bear's fur burnt her knuckles.

[Verdant Blade Sword Art: Lotus Bud—]

It let out a whimper but raised its arms to grab her in a backbreaking hug. Its eyes were full of desperation as it sought one last spiteful blow.

[—Bloom!]

Her fist twisted. The blades tore out of the beast's body from where they had landed, cutting an eight-petaled flower into the Spirit Beast. It remained standing for a moment, a testament to its vitality, before finally falling.

Xiulan let out a gasping breath and collapsed to her knees, allowing herself a moment of respite. She touched her wound, and it came away slick with blood and little black flecks. When she touched it, her head pounded. She took a deep breath, and then she rose again. She would need to be careful. Scouting only today. She could not afford a battle right now. She swiftly removed the bear's core and resumed her search.

The trail was not overly hard to find. A thirty-strong band of mortals, no matter how sneaky, could not keep their path hidden, especially with how many wounded they had.

She followed their trail when her nose scented blood.

Approaching slowly, Xiulan was ready to hide should this be a trap. But it wasn't. One of the bandits was slumped against a tree, frozen in death. He was covered with wounds from what looked like claws, his eyes glassy and unseeing.

At first, she suspected the Blaze Bear, but his wounds had come from far smaller claws.

Cai Xiulan was wary. Her search continued slowly. She came across another dead man, whose eyes had been gouged out, and his face locked in terror.

Another had fallen on his sword.

And then she came into a clearing. The snow was trampled flat. Several trees were felled.

But there was no blood and no bodies nearby. The trail *ended.*

She didn't know what to do. She focused her Qi, feeling around the clearing—

Nothing. She felt nothing.

She groaned and continued her search, spiralling outwards. She found another bandit corpse, far from the clearing, this one too savaged by an animal.

Eventually, she broke through the trees and happened upon a peculiar sight: a giant golem made of snow and a farm.

She touched her hand to her side again, her fingers coming back slick with blood and yellow pus. She was starting to get light-headed. Her swords couldn't float behind her anymore, so she had to tie them to her back.

She would warn the mortals of the dangerous beast living nearby. Hopefully, they would have time to run.

↔

"Sun Ken," Meiling stated as she finished retying the bandages around Tigu—or was it *Tig-ger?* Jin slurred his words oddly sometimes. Ri Zu was watching her hands intently as she worked.

"Yeah."

"Sun Ken, the Whirling Demon Sword, leader of the Whirling Demon Sword Gang, wielder of the Crimson Demon Tooth. *That* Sun Ken?"

Jin reached behind him and deposited a large, two-handed sword in front of her. The supposedly demonic blade certainly didn't smell demonic—there was a faint afterthought of blood, but it mostly smelled clean and a little bit like pine.

But it looked the same as the drawings of it. Crimson Demon Tooth. Meiling studied it for a moment and then turned to the cat. Tigu nuzzled up to her, sweet as could be for a thing that had apparently been out killing people mere hours prior.

"You're such a good girl!" she praised, and the cat just looked smug. "Good job killing those nasty men!"

Jin looked surprised, and Meiling sighed. "Verdant Hill had to take care of the survivors of one of his raids, a few years ago. Nearly all of them were injured. Men missing eyes, arms, legs . . . *and the women* . . ."

She trailed off, remembering the haunted eyes.

The Xong brothers nodded their heads solemnly.

"It is a good thing that they died, Jin. They normally never come this far north. I daresay there will be parties across the entirety of the Azure Hills when Sun Ken's death is confirmed."

Jin grimaced at this. "I . . . don't really want the recognition for this," he finally said.

Gou Ren looked stunned.

"But . . . but you would be rewarded greatly! You could have wealth beyond . . ." Gou Ren trailed off at Jin's sad smile.

"It's for the best if he just disappears," Jin said. "After all, I didn't kill him. *They* did. And what happens when the cultivators come calling to see how a farmer and some animals slew the mighty Sun Ken?"

Gou Ren considered it for a moment and then paled, pausing in his scratching of Chun Ke. "They take what they want and make pork belly?"

Jin shrugged. "I'd do my best so that wouldn't happen . . . but no man can last alone forever."

Bi De, his rooster, looked incredibly affronted, but Jin's hand on his head calmed him down.

They lapsed into silence.

"Well, enough of this heavy talk. I'll make the sword into a plough or something. Meimei, could you help me with Ri Zu? I've been lax in their . . . *training*."

All of the animals perked up.

"Well, we'll have to go back to Hong Yaowu today, if she's okay with coming along?" She raised an eyebrow at the little rat, who nodded its head vigorously.

'Great Sage teaches Ri Zu!' the little beast confirmed.

"We should probably get going soon," Yun Ren said with a shrug. "There were no bandits killed last night, and Sun Ken's sword *certainly* won't be turning into a plow. It was always that way." His lips quirked into a smile.

Gou Ren still seemed a bit conflicted, but he nodded too.

"I'll give you a ride home on the sled. Takes at least half a day off the journey, and I need that list of the children's favourite animals from Meimei," Jin said.

They were in the middle of packing their bags when Jin started scratching his back, and Meiling started sniffing the air.

"Grass, flowers, and blade oil," she said conversationally. "And something *rotten*."

Jin sighed, sounding resigned.

"Well, I guess I'll go greet our guest, then."

↔

Xiulan was limping by the time a man opened the door. His face was carved out of stone, and he had a shovel in his hand. Things were starting to . . . *tilt* a little in her vision.

His eyes widened when he saw her.

"Greetings, farmer, this Cai Xiulan—"

The mortal cut her off, the impudent man, dropping his shovel. "Holy shit, lady, what chewed *you* up?" He sounded shocked and concerned. A woman poked her head out of the door and gasped.

Xiulan nearly struck him as he approached swiftly, laid his hands on her, and picked her up.

Had she been well, she would not have allowed this outrage. In her current state, she was just glad she didn't have to walk. The door seemed a bit far away.

"Dangerous beast . . . In the forest . . ." she slurred. "Be careful . . ."

She was brought into the warm house, and the farmer's wife began tending to her with surprisingly skilled hands. Two others were there, following orders to get hot water and helping to tend to her injuries.

It was very nice and warm . . . in . . . here.

CHAPTER 31

A GLORIFIED BATTERY

Jin. Put her on a bedroll. I need boiling water right now," Meimei declared, already rolling up her sleeves. "Yun Ren, I have some bandages in my pack." Rizzo hopped over beside her, clambering up onto her shoulder and waiting for instruction.

I put the cultivator woman down as gently as I could as Meimei continued barking orders.

Welp, I had a cultivator in my home.

It . . . well, it was a knee-jerk reaction that I'd just grabbed her and started helping. Somebody needed help, so you help them—even if they were a cultivator. I think she was trying to warn us about a dangerous beast as well. I wonder what that was? Did the Blaze Bear who'd run from me set up shop around here?

Regardless, she looked like she had gotten in a fight with a blender and lost. And a toaster, judging by the burns all over her body.

I shook my head, grabbing the bucket from Gou Ren. Meimei said hot water right now, so she'd be getting it right now. I had no idea if I could make this work, but hell, I'd go for it.

I shoved my hand in the bucket.

Qi was energy.

Energy meant *heat* . . . right?

I had been toying around with the idea for a while, but they were more idle thoughts than anything concrete. I didn't mind waiting for the stove to heat things. But right now, we didn't have time to wait.

I *pushed.* The water in the bucket immediately started boiling—with my hand still in it. I spasmed, jerking it out of the water . . . but it didn't hurt. My skin wasn't even red.

Huh. *Nifty.* I suppose I shouldn't be surprised. I didn't get a single sunburn despite being outside the whole summer, without any sunscreen or hat.

"Meimei!" I called, and she started washing her hands, surprised at my speed. She shot me a grateful smile.

Yun Ren deposited his bandages, and Gou Ren hovered worriedly.

"Yun, Gou. You two go take care of things outside for a while. Jin . . . help me get her clothes off," she demanded.

I nearly made a joke about her telling me to undress another woman, but it wasn't the time, nor the place.

The Xong brothers ventured outside, and we started. I was tempted just to tear the clothes off . . . but she might be pissed about that later, so they came off normally. As gently as I could, I revealed the full extent of the damage.

And Meimei went to work.

It was amazing watching her in her element, cataloguing wounds and treating burns like a nurse or surgeon from the Before. All with Rizzo on her shoulder and that focused look in her eyes. She looked like some kind of fantasy character. It was cute and cool at the same time.

Shut up, can't a man be distracted by his fiancée?

The cultivator was pretty screwed up. Hurt badly enough that if she wasn't a cultivator, she probably would be dead, instead of just dying. There were numerous cuts and scrapes, a few nasty bruises, and two significant cuts that would need stitches, along with burns up her arms. There was a big slash wound too, leaking nasty-looking pus.

"She doesn't have much Qi left, which is why she passed out," Meiling stated, then sniffed. She recoiled and gagged. "And I think one of these wounds has Demonic energy in it. I know how to get that out, but it needs Qi . . ." She trailed off for a second.

"You think you could give her some Qi? Is that possible?" she asked.

I rifled through Rou's memories, but they came up useless. A half-remembered conversation popped up, but that was even less than useful. *No, I'm not going to pork an unconscious girl. Seriously, man? That's the only way you know how? I could just try to do what I did with the plants . . .*

I shrugged. "I could try . . . It might hurt her though. Qi generally doesn't play nice, and I don't know any healing arts."

Meiling bit her lip. "Untested Qi infusion . . . or some of the Spirit Herbs," she said, looking apologetic.

Hey, it's what they were there for. That and seasoning. Mostly seasoning.

I nodded and got the Spirit Herbs. They were still young, and so were less potent, but they were still serviceable. I ground them into the correct consistency while Rizzo watched me work.

Meanwhile, Meiling got more "mundane" medicine, but the herbs used in them were super effective. They definitely worked better than the stuff I was used to, considering how fast they'd healed Chunky's face.

She applied these where she could and stitched up the ones she couldn't save for the nasty one on her side. For that, Meimei used some kind of mystical stuff involving a bit of copper wire and a bucket filled with what looked like Spirit Herbal tea. She had also drawn on my floor with chalk, referencing from what looked like her personal notebook.

"This is to draw out Qi," Meiling explained as she worked. "I've only done this once before, and that was with my father letting me siphon his Qi. He doesn't have enough to be a cultivator, but he does have *some*."

She let out a breath after examining the formation again. "The Demonic Qi is damaging her spirit and body. See how it's leaking some pus right here, and how the veins are going black?"

I nodded.

"So, we need to get it out, and I'll need your help. I know how to guide the energy, but . . . I don't have Qi to start it. The Spirit Herbs *should* be taking care of it, but this Qi is *thick*. Almost like tar."

She put her hands on either side of the wound.

My hand rested over top of hers. I smiled. "Whatever you need."

Rizzo eagerly added her hands.

Meimei smiled. "All right, on three. Just a little into my hands. One, two, three!"

I let my Qi flow.

Meimei gasped, her pupils dilated and contracted, her violet eyes focusing on the formation. Something small and weak brushed up against the Qi I put into Meimei. It felt like a bird guiding a bear to honey.

I could still feel my Qi. It latched on to something absolutely vile. A gibbering, ravenous thing that felt like rotting pus and diseased blood.

There was an odd thrumming down the wire, and black, infected-looking Qi spilled into the bucket. There was strength being siphoned off, and it writhed in the Spirit Herb liquid, twitching like it was dying.

"This is very easy to work with," she muttered. "The last time I did this, the Qi fought me, and it tried to find its own path. It was like trying to hold fog. But yours is so responsive and solid. Like working with a needle."

"It knows to keep its wife happy," I joked, trying to lighten the mood.

She rolled her eyes and continued her work, carefully siphoning off the Demonic Qi.

The grassy field got stronger, and the Demonic Qi got weaker.

Sweat beaded on her brow as she carefully extracted the impurities.

One of my hands was on hers, while the other was on her back. I became a glorified battery.

↔

She was losing the battle for her soul. The verdant grass that was her cultivation was wilting, turning brown from the corrosive Qi. It smelled of rot and death, the lush valley being corrupted into a charnel house.

The Demonic Qi was tricky. It had hidden itself well, pushing and prodding at her soul, tugging at her mind, and waiting until she was weak enough to pounce.

It was bad enough that her body was weakened, but her spirit was also under assault—the last vestiges of the Sun brothers striking and biting at her.

She thought it was her end. Yet she kept fighting regardless, trying to resist the foul and blighted energy for just a moment longer.

She threw her all into the attacks, and to her surprise, she started pushing the Demonic corruption back. She was elated she had accomplished such a feat—when she saw it. Little tendrils of green energy, defeating the Demonic Qi with as much stealth as it tried to take her.

She was blessed by the heavens. Either another cultivator had helped her . . . or the mortals knew healing arts. Both possibilities were luck beyond measure.

She redoubled her efforts, blades made of grass striking, stabbing, and pinning the Demonic Qi, and allowing her healers further help her.

The Demonic Qi screamed and cursed, but it was all for naught. The last vestiges of corruption were lifted from her soul, and comforting darkness embraced her.

□

Meiling was panting by the end. Her face was flushed, her brow was slick with sweat, and she had a triumphant grin on her face.

Gods, she is so beautiful.

Her face flushed, and she looked away. Ah, I had said that out loud.

"Gods, you're beautiful," I told her again.

I kissed her on the forehead, and she buried her head onto my neck, sighing with exhaustion and contentment.

The container of water was sludgy looking. I had no idea what to do with it, since it seemed pretty nasty. I'd have to dilute it again, and hopefully that would be enough. *Maybe throw some Qi into it to make it . . . less toxic?*

I carried the cultivator to my bed. She'd been put into one of my shirts, to preserve her modesty.

There was no disguising that one of her wounds was packed with Lowly Spiritual Herbs, something that normally couldn't grow here, and obvious cultivation resources, but I couldn't bring myself to care.

It was something that may cause me problems in the future, but I would deal with them when they came.

The cultivator girl spent the rest of the day asleep.

My friends didn't end up going back home that day, but none of us minded.

CHAPTER 32

CHOICES

I had been procrastinating all day.

The cultivator had provided a distraction, as had the Xong brothers when they started making crude jokes about me undressing her.

I'll be honest, they were in pretty bad taste. Seriously, the cultivator had just got the shit kicked out of her. She *might* have been attractive under the black eye and split lips, but there was no point in gawping.

This was partially why I hadn't been bothered when Meimei asked me to get her undressed. There's nothing sexy about blood, bruises, and wounds starting to leak pus. Quite honestly, I'm glad Meimei was there, so I had something to focus on. I'm not particularly squeamish, but that was pretty hard to look at.

But now, as the sun started to set, I would need to address my . . . animals? Students? Unwitting children? I could put it off until tomorrow, but I needed to do this, and no time like the present.

"Big D, could you get the rest of the . . . *Disciples.* Gather them at the old house?" I asked him.

My—well, were any of them really *mine* anymore? Animals were possessions. But they were people.

The rooster snapped to attention and hastened to follow my orders.

This wasn't a conversation I could say I was looking forward to.

But it was one that needed to happen. It was a story I had avoided thinking about. Avoided telling.

I wondered how they would react?

↔

Bi De sat with the other disciples at the Great Master's old coop. The Master had bid them to gather here, away from his new coop, so that he could speak with them in private.

He was concerned about the interloper who had acted like Chow Ji, feigning weakness. But the Great Master was the Great Master. His insight was beyond Bi De's comprehension. This person would surely be worthy of the benevolence the Great Master graced her with!

Once she awoke, that is. She was being tended to by the Great Sage of Healing, so her recovery was assured.

Perhaps she was also to become his female? The Great Master would need many females, if only to make sure his offspring inherited his spark. Bi De was growing worried about his females and his own abilities. Those he had fathered displayed none of his own ability. He would think it restricted to the male half, but the young cock he had sired also displayed nothing. Nothing but annoyance at Bi De's mastery of the flock.

At least it had *some* intelligence: He knew it was folly to challenge Bi De.

Still, it was not all a waste. Their Qi would be returned to the Great Master, who would continue to grow and nurture them all.

He had guided them all greatly, and yet the Great Master considered himself *lax* in their training.

Truly, his Lord's depths were incomprehensible. And now they sat in front of their Lord, awaiting his instruction. He observed them with an impenetrable gaze, his eyes roving over their forms. He sat down with them, lowering himself to their level.

The disciples gasped as he bowed his head to them.

"Firstly, I wish to thank you. I would like to thank you for all you have done. You have taken up tasks of your own accord. You have defended this *Fa Ram* from predators. You have taken up arms in its defence against vile men."

The Disciples were struck dumb. Thanks from the Master? He gave them great respect by thanking them for merely doing their duties! How benevolent was he? They bowed their own heads, kowtowing before their Great Master.

All they had done was attempt to repay his benevolence. The Heavenly Herbs, medicine, protecting them until they could protect themselves, forgiving their mistakes—especially *Bi De*'s mistakes—he need not thank them. He was their Lord and Master. Their loyalty was only right.

"No. I *must* thank you. To give thanks for deeds others have done for you, is only right. If you don't give acknowledgement to somebody, then you show you do not value them." He paused, making eye contact with each disciple sitting before him.

"And I have not been valuing you as I should have." He sighed, running a hand through his hair. He seemed to be contemplating what to say. "What do you want out of life?" he asked them.

The disciples replied as one: '*To defend Great Fa Ram, and see it grow.*'

The Great Master looked to Ri Zu, the only one who could properly give him their declaration. He nodded his head and smiled at them.

"That is a good goal. A noble goal, to defend your home and see it prosper. I'm glad that you think that our *Fa Ram* is worth protecting. I want to see it grow too." He paused again, considering another question. "Why do you want to cultivate strength?"

'*To defend Fa Ram*,' was once more the reply.

"Oh? Most human cultivators say that it is to defy the will of heaven—to ascend past your limits, and become immortal, a ruler of the world. It is what I once desired, after all."

The disciples listened raptly. They knew nothing of their Great Master before his life in Fa Ram. Bi De knew they were about to receive some profound wisdom.

"Let's talk about choices. *Everything* begins with a choice. Every individual must choose what it is they want to do in their lives. What they desire, and what they wish to do to obtain those desires. These aren't things I can dictate to you."

"They are for you to decide freely. Sometimes we may feel like we have no choice, that only one option is available to us. But it is always there. If you wish to walk away from this place, I will not stop you. If you wish to stay, you will always have a place here." Again, the Great Master gazed upon each disciple, ensuring the weight of his words were understood.

Leave Great Fa Ram?! It was unthinkable to Bi De.

"While we are free to choose, remember the choices you make will always have consequences. Saving somebody may backfire, or it may not. Killing somebody may bring you great power, but it may also spell your doom. Our choices guide us. They forge us. We may make our choices, but in the end . . . *our choices make us.*"

Bi De was silent, drinking in his master's profound words.

"Let me tell you the story of Jin. And the choice he made."

"Let me tell you why this *Fa Ram* exists."

→

Bi De needed to meditate. They all did. They needed time to digest their Great Master's story. The tale of cultivators, and their power. Of the many ways to cultivate. And most shocking of all—

That their Great Master was one of the *least* of them.

It was a night of revelations.

The race to the heavens. It sounded both absurd and right at the same time. To walk the path of the warrior, never flinching and driving one's enemies before them. Something in it appealed to him greatly. To venture forth and claim the world.

But his Great Master had seemed so sad when talking about it. So . . . *disappointed.*

Bi De remembered Chow Ji. He remembered the feeling of lusting for power. Of how he'd considered slaying his own children for Chow Ji's cursed power, too young to have the spark. Of consuming the hens and leaving nothing left. His mind conjured an image of total desolation, of rampant slaughter. Of taking from the earth without *giving.*

He remembered the days spent with his Great Master. Tending to the fields, playing in the river, helping him keep watch at night. Of learning from his Great Master, as his Lord helped and nurtured them all, even though they were not human.

His Master cared not for their flesh or their cores.

He wanted them to live. He wanted to guide them.

He wanted them to have good lives.

Bi De was once more humbled by his Great Master's benevolence. The rooster knew that he had jumped at power when it was offered to him. He'd seized that power and faced the consequences. The consequences that lasted to this day.

His Lord had said it was better to be kind and be hurt than to live your life as a monster. That it was better than living a life of cruelty and wrath, taking and taking without caring for others.

Indeed, if he had been cruel to Chow Ji, he never would have been hurt. His spurs would have never been marred. He would not have grown. He would still be as he was, arrogant and prideful.

But if he had been cruel, Bi De would never have earned the friendship of Sister Ri Zu. He never would have gained an appreciation for Chun Ke and Pi Pa.

Compassion and kindness had hurt him.

But they had also been his salvation. It was the reason why he could stand tall and proclaim himself a great First Disciple.

He gazed upon the moon, that wonderful celestial object. There were some that wanted to tear it from the sky. There were some who could not see its glory.

There were men who were so focused on achieving power for their future ambition that they could not see the present.

His Great Master was correct, Bi De decided.

To covet power was not the path forwards. To race for the heavens to claim them was folly.

Like his Great Master said: Why claim the heavens when you could make your own?

He offered his supplication to the earth. The dormant energy took what he offered without hesitation and seemed to sigh in contentment.

Something broke inside him, like the ice on the river being broken. His eyes saw more clearly. His breath was more perfect—his plumage, radiant. He had grown greatly in power from this revelation, and yet—

He disregarded his breakthrough.

He had a moon to observe, and its soft and soothing light was much more important.

CHAPTER 33

A BLADE OF GRASS

Cai Xiulan awoke to the sound of voices.

"When do you think she'll wake up?" a male voice asked.

"Dunno. Could be days, could be weeks. She's pretty messed up," another returned.

She was warm and comfortable. Her body ached, but it did not hurt.

This was a *lovely* bed. It was warm and soothing and comfortable, unlike the cots or the dirt she had slept on, when she slept at all. She nearly fell back asleep, but she knew she shouldn't, so she persevered, shaking off the last clinging grasps of sleep.

"I'll stay here if she's still asleep for a few days. Or we could transport her back home?" a female voice said.

She kept her eyes closed and took stock of her body, focusing first on the wound in her side. The Demonic Qi had been driven out, and there was nothing left of the taint. Defeated completely and utterly by whatever had helped her last night. With the most pressing concern dealt with, she continued, focusing further. Her Qi flowed through her body, rather more than she had expected to have. It felt full of vitality and verdant. As the name of her Sect, it was energetic and wanted to grow. The wounds she had were scabbed over, and she was well on her way to healing.

She examined the poultices that had been applied to her wounds, touching them with her senses—

The poultices had Qi in them. They had used Spiritual Herbs on her. She knew not what kind, but they were incredibly potent, more potent than she had ever felt before. These would command a prince's ransom if they were sold to her Sect elders. To think they had been used on her, even if she was the Young Mistress of the Verdant Blade—

No, the only thing she could be was thankful. They had spent their pearls upon her. All she had to do was prove worthy of such gifts.

She extended her senses, but she detected no more Qi. So then, it *was* a farmer who had found her. Mortals, who could have been rich in selling these herbs . . . had spent them on her without truly knowing who she was.

It was a humbling thought. The mortal soldiers of the Sect always seemed to have so little— she winced, then she cut the thought off. Memories of the horrific battle in the valley circled. The roars of men drugged with some potent elixir, fighting like demons. Falling rocks and a valley full of screams of her allies. Her heart started to beat faster as the screams got louder and louder in her head. The sounds of death and monsters—

Her eyes snapped open as she remembered the Spirit Beast—the one that had made Sun Ken disappear. Her heart seized in her chest before she calmed. It had not come to claim their lives yet, so it would do her no good to panic them.

She took a deep breath, circulating her Qi and concentrating on her recovery. She would need her full strength to even think of protecting these people from the beast that had slain Sun Ken.

They would be defended until her last breath for the kindness they had shown her.

The Qi in the Spiritual Herbs responded. The energy flowed into her body, swirling around her wounds.

Qi surged, flooding her wounds. Cuts sealed shut and bruises stopped aching. Her broken bones melded together, and her battered organs were refreshed instantly.

She gasped, and her eyes flew open in shock.

She pulled down the rough shirt she was clad in and stared down at her chest. All that was left was smooth and unblemished skin. She tugged at the shirt but didn't see her normal garb. Her face flushed. Had the man undressed her? Or had his wife done that? She hoped dearly it was his wife who had seen her shameful state, but it was a forlorn hope. Her wounds were all over her body, and the bandages and poultices covered all of them.

Her modesty, though, was secondary to gratitude. Should he have seen her body, it was in the process of saving her life.

She sat up and looked around, taking in the room. The bed was cordoned off with a wooden divider, giving her some amount of privacy.

"I'll go check on her," the female voice said again. "Make sure nothing has changed and see if I can get some water into her. Or . . . clean her up, if she needs it. If she's unconscious for much longer . . . Well! The body still produces waste."

Soft footsteps padded around the divider.

The woman was small—in all respects, really, bony and angular, with sharp, violet eyes. Unfortunate freckles formed a bridge across her face, from cheek to cheek, and across her nose.

Still, she wasn't *ugly* by any means. A bit severe-looking. Or like an angry cat.

Her eyes widened in surprise, when she saw Xiulan sitting up.

"Ah!" she gasped. "Don't move; your wounds are still—" She paused, taking a closer look at her. "You're . . . healed?" she asked, sounding curious.

Most likely her wood-aligned Qi had been particularly compatible with the herbs, if the woman sounded amazed, they had worked that fast.

More footsteps pounded across the floor as the rest of the house came to look at her.

Two of the men gaped at her, their faces flushing. One looked like a monkey and the other a scheming fox. They both had the physiques of farmers, well-muscled and slightly rough-looking.

"Even prettier than Meihua," she heard the fox-one mutter. Their eyes were awestruck . . . until the woman elbowed both of them, glaring. Xiulan appreciated her intervention. Men undressing her with their eyes was a common occurrence, and she couldn't chastise the family of her saviours.

The third man was just calm. He was wearing one of the same shirts as she was, and evidently the master of the house, by his bearing and the way the two boys moved around him to give him space.

He was large and well-muscled, one of the tallest men Xiulan had ever met. His body was rugged and solid-looking, like a rock or a bull. His skin had a light tan, even in the depths of winter, and a light dusting of freckles stained his cheeks.

He didn't stare. His eyes ghosted over her once, observing her for damage, before returning to her face. He just looked happy at her recovery.

"Hey, that was fast. You've only been out for a day," he said conversationally.

Xiulan opened her mouth to respond, but the little woman beat her to it, turning around and glaring at the two men. "Clear off, you two, she needs some space, and I need to check her injuries."

"I'll go get your clothes. They've got some holes in them—I didn't have the silk to repair them," the master of the house said as he left.

The woman turned back to Xiulan as the men left.

"Come on, shirt off, I need to check on things. Make sure my medicine did its job properly."

Xiulan was surprised.

"You were the one who made the medicine and used the healing arts upon me?" She was utterly stunned. This woman was a peasant, with no detectable Qi, and yet she had been taught such things. It was hard enough at times having her skills questioned even as the Sect's Young Mistress. As a peasant woman? Things must have been worse.

Xiulan was not an easy woman to impress, but she felt a surge of respect for the woman frowning at her stomach.

"Yes. My husba—*betrothed* was the one who provided the herbs, but it was I who drew out that Demonic Qi," the woman explained, pressing an ear to her chest. "Now, breathe in for me."

Xiulan did as she was told. Healers and miracle workers were to be obeyed. Her mind was whirling at these revelations.

"Meimei, her clothes are here," she heard the man say. And her dress was placed over the top of the divider.

"Well, everything looks fine. Pulse is normal, breathing is fine, and everything is gone. Not even a scar," her saviour declared. "Now get dressed, and we can get some food into you."

And then the woman was gone.

Xiulan carefully removed the shirt, grasping for her dress. There was no blood or pus or filth staining it, having been meticulously cleaned. It was warm and emanated a soothing heat, like it had been resting beside the fire. It even smelled good. There was a nasty slash in the side, but it exposed little. Her swords, the Jade Grass Blades, were leaning beside the bed. They leapt at her command and floated behind her.

She took a moment to calm herself, thinking on what to say to her saviours then nodded decisively.

She stepped out from behind the divider, ready to present herself and hopefully make up for her atrocious first impression. She hadn't even gotten her saviour's *names*. For her to make such a mistake was nearly unforgivable.

The Master of the house, and his wife—no, the woman had said she was his betrothed. It was a bit odd, to be in the home of her intended before they were wed, but she would not dare cast any accusations about their conduct.

As far as she was concerned, their conduct was pure and intentions honourable. If there were any who would dare suggest otherwise, they would be ended by her blades.

In any case, the members of the household turned to face her. The two boys started staring again as she gracefully fell to her knees and pressed her forehead to the floor. It was shameful to kowtow before a mortal, but it was a thousand times *more* shameful to keep her head high after they had done so much for her.

"This one is Cai Xiulan, Daughter of Cai Xi Kong, Young Mistress of the Verdant Blade Sect. Cultivator of the Third Stage of the Initiate's Realm," she declared, and she heard the fox and the monkey take sharp breaths.

"Without your intervention—and your medicine—this Cai Xiulan surely would have perished. This Cai Xiulan swears to you, this debt will be repaid, or my life will be forfeit."

"Please, raise your head," the large man said. "It was never my intention to extract promises—or reparations from you. You were in need of aid. You were aided. That is the extent of what our thoughts on the matter were."

She kept her forehead against the floor, even as she heard the woman make noises of agreement.

"That is of no matter. To not repay you would shame both myself and the entirety of the Verdant Blade Sect. This debt will be repaid a hundredfold!"

The man sighed. "Very well, it's nice to meet you, Xiulan," he said. His address was overly familiar, but she raised no objection. "My name is Rou Jin."

He gestured at the rest of his household for them to introduce themselves. "Hong Meiling" was the woman, "Xong Yun Ren" was the fox boy, and "Xong Gou Ren" was the monkey.

"Now, let's get some food in you."

→

"Why did you come here, anyway?" Jin asked her, as he served her rice. "You were muttering about a dangerous beast? Was it a Blaze Bear or something?"

She took a breath. "Please, do not be alarmed. I was on the trail of Sun Ken, the Whirling Demon Blade." There was a look of interest and recognition on their faces. "I was tasked with slaying him, to bring an end to his wicked life. Our Verdant Blade Sect had defeated him in battle and driven him off, that worthless coward. I was tracking him, to finish him when the trail suddenly ended. There were few corpses left, only men who had managed to flee, savaged by some terrible beast," she explained. They did not seem worried, which was strange.

"Fear not, though, I shall track down this dangerous beast. I require proof of Sun Ken's death, and I shall drive the beast away as well, so that it may leave you in peace."

There were no gasps of shock, nor any overt display of recognition of the threat . . . simply acceptance. The monkey even seemed *amused.*

This . . . this is not right. Something is going on here.

Her eyes flicked around the room. The room was large—denoting wealth. It was skillfully crafted in a style unfamiliar to her.

But the most interesting thing were several large basins containing Spiritual Herbs. *Shoots* of Spiritual Herbs. Shoots that had more Qi than the most high-level Spiritual Grass she had ever laid eyes upon.

They faded in and out of her senses, like the sun hiding behind thick clouds. She suspected the only reason she could feel them at all was because of the herbs that had been packed into her wounds. If they had not been added to her Qi, she was sure that they would be invisible to her senses.

Xiulan focused her senses again, trying to see beyond her nose. There was nothing. What she was looking for was unimportant. The more she tried to see, the less she saw. She pushed yet achieved nothing. She paused and stopped trying to force her vision.

This was her saviour's home. It was rude of her to try to force anything, but . . . she was curious. She was having doubts that this man was a mere farmer now, with his lack of reaction to Sun Ken.

From herself to the Spiritual Herbs. From the Spiritual Herbs to the world.

And the mountain, shrouded in mist, was revealed to her. The energy that had been invisible to her was brought to her attention. How she could be staring at a mountain and not have realized it was shocking.

There was the energy of a Profound-level cultivator outside. Four more Initiates were with it, ranging from the Third Stage to the Second, and in the house, there was another Initiate of the First Stage.

The monkey, the fox, and Meiling were nearing the power of Initiates, connected lightly to a web that threaded through the house, while Jin himself . . .

It was like looking into a lake and never seeing the bottom. Like looking at a mountain and not knowing how much of it was hidden by clouds.

This was no farmer. This was a *Hidden Master.*

As swiftly as it was revealed to her, the feelings faded. Master Jin stared at her, his eyes considering.

She flushed under his intense gaze. He had surely noticed her intrusion but had yet to chastise her. She hoped he would stay his mighty wrath.

"Well, it's good that you found us," Meili—no—Senior Sister Meiling said, smiling at her. "It could have been bad, otherwise."

Though she was less powerful in cultivation, Xiulan guessed the woman utterly surpassed her in knowledge as the disciple and future wife of such a powerful expert. It was no wonder she could perform healing arts at her level of cultivation; her foundation must be something that took a long time to properly construct, and once constructed, would likely surpass her in moments.

"Thank you for the warning, Miss Cai," Master Jin said. "But I don't think there will be any problems with Spirit Beasts," he continued with a gentle smirk, like he cared nothing about what had slain Sun Ken.

He most likely didn't.

"As for proof of Sun Ken's death?" Master Jin asked, considering her further. He seemed to come to a decision. "I actually found the clearing earlier than you and came across some blades there. I believe this is Sun Ken's sword, if what you say is true."

He left the house for a moment, and when he returned, he did so, holding a blade Xiulan instantly recognised. Her hand unconsciously went to her side, as she remembered the feeling of the blade tearing through her flesh.

The Crimson Demon's Tooth. The blade that screamed of cutting. An unholy, demonic thing.

It was utterly silent.

"This is largely useless to me. I was planning on turning it into a plough, but if this is cause for people to celebrate, and for your own return to your Sect . . . then you should take it, as proof of his demise."

The Crimson Demon's Tooth as a *plough.* The very thought was absurd. And the reward for Sun Ken's death—it was apparently so worthless to him that he would rather turn the cursed blade into a gardening implement.

How truly frightening.

First, the Hidden Master had healed her. Now, he wished to have her take credit for Sun Ken's death. It was dishonourable to take credit for the work of others.

But it was a greater sin to refuse such a gift, a boon from a powerful Hidden Master. He had his own reasons, and if she was to be his instrument, she would obey without question.

She clasped her hands in front of her, and then she bowed deeply in thanks. "If that is your will, Master Jin."

↔

You know what, this was going pretty well. Xiulan was much more agreeable than most cultivators I'd met—polite, too.

I'd been rather shocked when she called herself a *Young Mistress*, which meant she was pretty high up in the Sect's power structure. She didn't *seem* particularly arrogant or icy, like the cliché of a Young Mistress was. They were always shown to be stone-cold and calculating, like some caricature of a woman. Sure, she gave Yun and Gou a bit of a stink eye when they wouldn't stop staring, but other than that, she seemed almost . . . normal?

Teach me to stereotype and profile. I was thinking in good guys and bad guys, but most guys were somewhere in between.

You'd also think that being around Meihua would make the Xong brothers a bit less inclined to stare. Yeah, I know, boys, the cultivator girl is superhot. Even I thought she was pretty attractive. *Shut up, Brain. Yes, she's* bouncy. *You can stop with the monkey noises.*

She seemed to be going along with my plan without protest and with excessive thanks. I guess she was the kind of woman to seize opportunity with both hands, which for a cultivator did make sense. It was a bit strange to hear her refer to me as "Master Jin." She had essentially declared that she had a life debt to both Meiling and me. So, I guess it was pretty natural that she would be respectful.

You never hear about the reasonable people. It's always the caricatures that get the screen time.

And it was absolutely hilarious to see her eyes bug out when she ate her first bit of rice. I remember the food at my Sect being pretty meh, so my food must taste like heaven.

Fool. This is only the first form of my cuisine! Teriyaki burgers will flow! Poutine will flourish! I will master the Dao of Cooking, and all will fear my might!

I think I just *foodgasmed* her, actually. She's making all of these little noises of pleasure and squirming around in her seat.

The Xong brothers were distracted by her movements . . . yeah, not gonna go there. I just turned to look at my fiancée and blotted out the salacious sounds coming from the cultivator.

Christ, lady, I appreciate the vote of confidence, but . . . it's a bit much.

"Well, you should stay here for another night anyway, just to make sure you're completely better before you head back to your Sect." I decided aloud.

Xiulan jumped at my voice, jolted out of her distraction with my food, her face flushing. "Thank you for your hospitality, Master Jin. Your food and home are of a quality unparalleled!"

Aw, shucks. It's nice to know my cooking is well received, though.

"After we eat, would you like to see the healing formation we used?" Meiling asked.

Honestly, the girl looked like she was about to cry when Meimei said that.

"Yes please, Senior Sister." Meimei went crimson at the term of respect, and then her chest puffed up with pride.

You know what? Things are going pretty good.

CHAPTER 34

THE GOALIE AND THE DISHWASHER

Healing. Rare reagents. Credit for slaying Sun Ken. The most delicious meal Xiulan had ever eaten. Now, Senior Sister was about to tell her how the technique that healed her worked. Somebody, not of her Sect, freely teaching her a technique, with the approval of Master Jin. How unexpected!

Truly, she was the luckiest of the Younger Generation in the Azure Hills. She just hoped that she could comprehend the profound wisdom she was about to receive. Xiulan had never studied the healing arts, focused entirely as she was on mastering the Jade Grass Blades and the Verdant Sword Arts. Oh, she knew how to set a bone and heal minor injuries, every cultivator did, but to be able to draw out and purify Demonic Qi with such speed and subtlety? That was beyond her.

Senior Sister had sat down beside the fire after rummaging through her pack and withdrawing a well-used notebook. *Her* personal *notes. Not a codified scroll.* Had she created her own formation?

Xiulan was beckoned over to a pair of cushions by Senior Sister as the men and Master Jin prepared oddly curved sticks, fishing poles, and an axe. Master Jin was quite excited about whatever was about to transpire.

"Ice fishing and *Ha Qi*. We don't have any *skates*, but it will work just fine," Master Jin explained to them. "If you want to come watch us, join in, or if you need us, we'll be down by the pond."

Xiulan bowed to the Hidden Master. "May your time be fruitful, Master Jin." She guessed *Ha Qi* was the monkey and the fox's training, some sort of art to improve their bodies. She held off a brief surge of desire to follow immediately and witness Master Jin's physical training. She had already committed to learning a healing art under Senior Sister. Also, he hadn't forbidden her from joining in, so she might get to see it later.

"Could you send in Ri Zu please, Jin?" Senior Sister asked, and Master Jin nodded. She was indeed a most cherished woman, to be able to ask such mundane tasks of a Hidden Master.

Xiulan wondered what they were like. Possibly an Outer Disciple, as they had been outside when they ate.

"Now, this is the technique that was used to draw out the Demonic Qi." The book opened, revealing the formation employed to save her life. Xiulan turned her full attention to Senior Sister, ready to put her mind completely into comprehending this formation.

She had not been expecting a squeak at her feet.

'Good-fine day, Young Miss.'

A rat was staring up at her.

'This one is Ri Zu. Ri Zu greets you and wishes you good health.'

She stared at the Spirit Beast as it bowed respectfully to her, the image of politeness. Behind the rat stood the most magnificent rooster she had ever laid eyes upon. Its plumage was radiant and its eyes full of profound wisdom.

She felt a brief flash of the rooster's power; it had ascended into the Profound Realm.

The rooster's eyes pierced her, and it too bowed in greeting.

She kept herself from screaming. There were no disciples outside—only Spirit Beasts. *Obedient* Spirit Beasts. No wonder Master Jin was unconcerned about monsters lurking about his land. The chicken was probably the most powerful Spirit Beast in the Azure Hills. Were these the ones who had slain Sun Ken?! It would be well within their capabilities.

She wavered under the rooster's piercing eyes. Then, she did something she'd never thought she would do. It was an injury to her pride, one she would have to swallow.

She bowed to an animal in greeting. The rooster was satisfied.

The rat scampered up onto Senior Sister's shoulder while the rooster settled onto the ground, seeming to meditate.

'Ah!' the little rat squeaked. *'What we used to save-cure Young Miss!'*

"Her name is Cai Xiulan, Ri Zu," Senior Sister said, seeming amused at the question on Xiulan's face. "And yes, Ri Zu aided in your recovery."

'Ri Zu was useful to Master!'

A Spirit Beast that not only was polite and docile but also studied the healing arts?! For what reason could Master Jin want them for? Was he growing them to consume their cores in an artificial development cycle? She could not comprehend his motives.

She took a calming breath and decided that it was just something that was. If she kept being shocked about every little thing in the Hidden Master's domain, she would start coughing blood, or suffer Qi deviation.

So. A Profound-level Spirit Beast that was a *chicken*. A medical rat. Would there next be pigs that could shake the earth?

There was a happy squeal from outside and the thunder of trotters, as the heavens decided to mock her.

Her eyebrow twitched.

She took another breath, as her father had told her. A deep breath in and out, to center one's self.

"You get used to it," Senior Sister said, her eyes lidded with amusement.

□

Oh, the good ol' hockey game is the best game you can name, and the best game you can name is the good ol' hockey game . . .

Yun Ren shoulder checked me, and I let myself go flying from the hit to skid across the ice. I could have just sat there, and he couldn't have budged me, but that would be a dick move. Completely unsportsmanlike.

Okay, it wasn't *really* hockey. We had no skates, our puck was made out of a piece of rock, and it was a free-for-all.

But it was close enough, eh? Nothing like a bit o' hockey with the boys.

Yun Ren glared as he approached the goal, and Chunky started blowing steam out of his nostrils. He had a stick clenched in his teeth, eager to defend the net once more—which was a fishing net and two poles.

Yun Ren slapped his stick from side to side, trying to confuse Chunky, while the massive pig bounced up and down with excitement. Yun Ren thought he saw an opening and reared back, firing off a praiseworthy slapshot and trying to overcome the defence with pure speed. Chunky's head twisted at the last second, and the puck bounced off his stick.

Yun Ren swore at the miss while Chunky squealed happily, prancing around his net.

Gou Ren laughed at his brother's misfortune while I hauled myself out of the snowbank.

Ah, I need to get some metal soon. This experience will be so much better with skates! Wait, I'm an idiot. Do I even need metal? Can't I just reinforce some wood with Qi?

Well, it was something to try, at least.

Gou Ren lined up at the net and tried his luck, snapping the puck up and over . . . only to hit Chunky's bulk as he moved, intercepting the pass.

Best goalie in the Empire. The Azure Hills Maple Leafs represent.

"Come on! He's not fair! He's too good, Jin!" Gou complained. "Let *Peppa* try!"

Peppa, who had been content to sit off to the side, got a calculating gleam in her eye at Gou Ren's words.

Oh, this poor soul.

Peppa trotted over, her steps light and dainty, as she carefully took the stick from Chunky. They nuzzled each other, and Chunky squealed encouragement as Peppa settled into the net.

Yun Ren and I sat back to watch the fireworks.

Gou Ren lined up his shot—and got tackled by the goalie. He folded in half over the strike, and Peppa squealed with triumph.

Let me tell you, watching somebody get circles run around them by a pig was the funniest shit.

The score ended 12–nil, with Peppa in the lead and Gou Ren's pride just as bruised as his tailbone.

Eventually, we got bored of discount hockey and did my activity of choice number two during winter: ice fishing.

The pond was a bit small, but there were plenty of fish to catch for our dinner tonight.

I cast my line into the hole in the ice. We were using bits of leftover scrambled egg as bait.

There was a lake a bit farther down that would be better for this . . . but I wanted to stay a bit closer to the house, just in case.

I wasn't expecting any trouble from Xiulan. She seemed like a pretty good person, and people tended to take life debts seriously here. Even though I wasn't *expecting* any trouble from her . . .

Trust, but verify. That was why Big D was being a good lad and waiting with Meimei. I had a feeling that if something did go wrong, Big D would be able to take care of things—

Something hit my line.

Something *strong* hit my line. Hard enough that my fishing pole was nearly torn from my hands . . . I instinctively reinforced it with Qi and pulled back. The line cut into the ice as whatever it was tried to drag the egg away, and I wasn't having any of it.

I took a deep breath and *pulled.* Somehow, whatever was under the water resisted, pulling as hard as it could. It felt like I was trying to dredge up a fridge.

I snarled, then pulled on my Qi. Like hell whatever on the other end was getting away!

With a mighty heave, a rather large carp burst from the hole, his body wriggling in the air. He had brown scales and long whiskers.

Son of a—

"Washy, you greedy shit!"

My dishwasher flopped onto the ice and stared at me with piteous eyes. He flopped around for a bit, playing up his helplessness. I had half a mind to eat him for that stunt, but . . . Sighing, I got the hook out of him.

"Hey. You get food at home, all right, buddy? Biting onto fishing lines is dangerous."

Washy flopped into what looked like a nod.

"Go on. *Get,*" I commanded sternly.

He flopped his way into the hole and swam away with all due haste.

I had figured out Washy last night when I had jokingly asked him what food he liked best and got a piece of egg eagerly shown to me.

I'd nearly fallen into the river. What was I, some kind of Spirit Beast magnet? . . . or it's *probably* the food. *I hope I don't have an entire ecosystem that's sentient. I want to eat meat, damn it.*

I swear, if my rice starts talking to me, I'm going to have a very, very sad time. I sighed, internally grumbling, and tossed my line back in.

We returned to silence. What should we have for dinner tonight to go with the fish though? I had to make more for Xiulan . . .

Gou Ren shouted in outrage as his line snapped.

Seriously? I just told you not to do that—

Yun Ren yelped as his fishing pole was pulled into the hole.

"Okay, that's it! *Come here, you little trash compactor—*"

CHAPTER 35

CONNECTIONS

"And that's how this last part fits into it. Tell me if you don't get anything, okay?" Senior Sister said as she finished drawing out the diagram for Xiulan. She took the note, staring at it intently.

Senior Sister Meiling was an odd teacher. Good, but . . . *strange*. While her own teachers would explain in exacting detail how she needed to move her body and the proper stances she was expected to follow, book education was more . . . free form. She was assigned texts to study, then given a test. That which she did not comprehend was set as revision, and she was expected to figure it out herself. Or she was just told to research things on her own time. It was the way most cultivators did things. You either comprehended something, or you didn't.

Many masters had no time for those who could not figure things out swiftly.

Senior Sister had asked about her experience with medical techniques, and she had honestly answered "none." She supposed some would find this more . . . involved way of doing things to be weak and dim-witted. Like her martial instructors, every part of the formation was explained in exacting detail.

The beginning made her head spin a bit. There was . . . quite a lot of math involved. However, once she worked her way through that, along with a whole stick of chalk, they moved on.

From *why* it was an octagon that was used, to which characters were used, to the characters' placement within the octagon—all the way up to how to create the "energy differential" that would draw out Qi.

It was an involved process, but . . . it was dramatically more straightforward than she'd been expecting once Senior Sister explained it. The initial concepts were complex, but once one grasped those, it was relatively simple in execution. The process didn't actually need the powerful reagents used—that was just what they had on hand. Normal chalk, any plant with Qi, a copper wire, and clean water. The mortal instruments combined to form something exceeding the sum of their parts.

It was so easy that a mortal could use it if they had a good head for numbers and a steady hand. And yet, it had defeated Demonic Qi.

Most medical formations were supposed to be extremely complex, requiring months of careful study to comprehend even the basest portions of them. This one had taken a few hours to explain not just *how* it worked, but *why* it worked.

And now she had a copy of the formation in a gifted scroll.

"Senior Sister, where did you learn this, if you don't mind my asking?" Xiulan questioned. "Or did you craft this yourself?"

"Hm? Oh, in Pale Moon Lake City. The Grand Archives there has some interesting stuff. I didn't get to copy all of the book, but the formation was fascinating. I mean, it didn't work right at first. Father, Uncle, and I had to swap out most of the characters, but the concept alone was fascinating."

The capital of the Azure Hills? It is a quaint place, with few cultivators and no tournaments. Most of the true *business of the Azure Hills takes place on Azure Cloud Summit.*

"How did you gain access to the Grand Archives? Surely this book must have been well guarded?"

Xiulan didn't know how the "Grand Archives" worked. It was a mortal institution, for mortal information. To go to the Grand Archives would be a loss of face. It was simple information, not their profound secrets. To admit that their Sect couldn't figure it out on their own would be . . . unwise.

Besides, the archive system was barely three hundred years old. They couldn't have much good information, simply because of their youth.

"I walked in with my father, and while he was in a meeting, I found it on one of the carts. I asked one of the Junior Archivists if I could copy it, and he let me. The book was *on Formations, Mathematics, Their Applications in the Healing Arts, and Their Interaction with Qi.* Most of the scroll was designated on the theory, and I haven't had much chance to use it."

Ah, so she was a powerful noble mortal before this. That makes sense.

Senior Sister shrugged. "I'm more knowledgeable on plants and mushrooms and their effects than formations, though. Formations are interesting, in the more academic sense, but herbology is *much* more exciting."

Senior Sister got a disturbing gleam in her eye. "Did you know that you can make a tasteless laxative by combining yellow glass fungus and the juice from reed thistles?" Her face twisted into a smile. It was *extremely* vindictive, and Xiulan felt a chill rise up her spine.

Xiulan learned more about debilitating concoctions and mortal medicine in that hour than she probably should have.

It was almost a relief when Master Jin returned.

He looked absolutely serene as he entered the house—steam rising from his body from wet clothes and a large carp held by the tail in his hand. The fish dangled there, resigned to its fate.

The fox boy and the monkey boy walked in shortly after, fishes in their hands and looking incredibly amused.

"There's no more ice on the pond," the fox boy said cheerily. "We got some nice fish, though."

The Hidden Master walked into the back room and returned to the house with a clay jar filled with water.

The fish's head popped out of the jar, and it began slapping its pectoral fins on the edge of the vase, swinging from side to side happily.

Xiulan was silent, for the rest of the time was spent preparing dinner and taking deep breaths. It was not her place to question the Hidden Master.

Not even when her dinner companions were a fish, two pigs, a rooster, a cat, and a rat.

Not even when, after dinner, the fish launched itself out of its jar, and flopped itself across the house into the "river room," and started acting like it had been starved all day, begging for the dishes and scraps.

↔

Meiling felt some kinship with Xiulan. The poor girl looked utterly baffled as the carp got a bowl of food and began scarfing it down. With Wa Shi's addition at the dinner table, Jin's general weirdness had started to get to even her.

Well, as she said to Xiulan . . . you get used to it.

Hopefully.

Xiulan was the only cultivator other than Jin she had really interacted with, and the woman was . . . strange. Not Jin strange, but in a different way.

Her emotions seemed . . . *magnified.* With her guard down, everything showed on her face. The sheer joy she had at learning something new. The almost frightening anger at Yun and Gou when they were staring. The naked shock, like her entire worldview had just been shattered when Ri Zu walked in. The awe, like she saw a god walking the earth when she was staring at Jin.

The boys hadn't seen it. Yun Ren and Gou Ren were too busy trying not to stare at Xiulan's chest, and Jin was too preoccupied staring at Meiling herself.

Meiling appreciated that her intended had eyes for no other woman, but she wouldn't have minded. Even *she* had stared a bit at Xiulan's general *Xiulan-ness.* Really, this poor woman's back.

But . . . Meiling didn't think Xiulan was a bad person and not just because the girl was an eager student who called her "Senior Sister!" Xiulan even took notes when she was talking about herbology! Meiling's passion hadn't scared Xiulan off!

No, the first thing Xiulan had tried to do was warn them of danger, and the next was to assure them that she would die before she let anything hurt them.

The conviction with which she had made that oath . . . *She meant it.* Meiling would have to talk to Jin later. He seemed to be taking Xiulan's oath *lightly.* Like she *wouldn't* go and charge headfirst into certain doom if Jin asked her to.

And Meiling was confident that the girl had some . . . strange ideas about what was going on, with her calling Jin "Master Jin." Did she think he was some kind of "Hidden Master" from the stories? It was preposterous—Meiling paused and thought it over.

Actually, now that she thought about it, it was *true. Jin really is some kind of Hidden Master, isn't he? Powerful, with strong "disciples," and living as to not be disturbed?*

She looked over at her intended, and he perked up, giving her a big, goofy grin. Meiling grinned back, for an entirely different reason.

He would figure it out . . . or he wouldn't.

↔

The next day, Senior Sister and the two boys had to leave to return to Senior Sister's father. It was unfortunate, but the trio had been planning to leave when she had unexpectedly arrived and had already stayed longer than they'd anticipated.

Senior Sister smiled at her. "Stay safe, Xiulan," she said. "I would be happy to see you again."

Meiling was given a ride worthy of a princess: A sleigh, pulled by a Spirit Beast called Pi Pa, with little Ri Zu on her shoulder. The monkey boy, Gou Ren, began his endurance training as he was lashed to the boar and sent careening around the trail.

These were undoubtedly strange beings. No Spirit Beast would allow itself to be yoked so easily and eagerly, but these creatures seemed to enjoy the treatment, eager to carry out Master Jin's will.

Are they not to be food, then? Is he trying to make them ascend to human form?

Xiulan was healed, so she should be going back home as well . . . but something compelled her to stay. She was curious about the Hidden Master.

Master Jin stared at her as if he was wondering why she was still here. She swiftly made up an answer.

"May . . . may I see *Ha Qi*? I did not get to yesterday, since Senior Sister was teaching me." The worst he could say was no.

Master Jin grinned. He went into his house, then returned with the strangely shaped sticks . . . and two sets of broken swords.

"You're a bit higher level than the Xong brothers, so you should be able to handle this," he declared. Xiulan steeled herself for harsh training.

She was taken downstream, past a pond with ice chunks strewn about it, and onto a frozen lake.

She first had to learn how to stick the blades to her shoes' soles with Qi alone. It took nearly an hour, with Master Jin's gentle coaching. When she finally managed to stand up, he gave her a short moment to gain her balance.

Master Jin's eyes turned predatory the moment she completed a lap around the lake without falling over.

Then her real training began.

He was grace and ferocity incarnate upon the ice. The blades on his feet propelled him at speed, even when he used barely a fraction of his might. He never struck her directly, but instead tweaked her balance, forcing her to correct or be sent into a humiliating sprawl.

Perception.

Endurance.

Balance.

Timing.

Ha Qi was a multi-layered art. The blades on her feet tried their hardest to throw her to the ice. The speeding stone puck forced her to dodge or block with the stick.

She was hunted relentlessly, always pushed to the edge and forced to stay there. There was no mortal peril to this—yet being hounded by a more powerful cultivator was still thrilling. He had found her limits, like all Great Masters did, and then proceeded to *push*.

"Come!" he demanded. "Stop *trying* to hit me and *hit me*!"

And then he forced her to go on the offensive. He danced around her blows, sprays of ice slashing out from their bladed feet. He blocked every shot at the "goal."

Xiulan tried her hardest to hit Master Jin, throwing herself again and again at him, and each time, he dodged, until she finally, *finally* managed to strike him with her stick.

It was like slamming into a steel wall. He didn't slide at all from his position, even on the skates. He merely nodded, smiled, and retook the initiative. Each tap nearly sent her sprawling. Each correction was firm but not harmful. Each goal slipped past her guard with ease.

Finally, she could take no more and begged respite.

Master Jin had a great smile upon his face. "Ah, that was great fun, wasn't it?" he asked, looking cheerful.

Fun? She . . . supposed it was. She put on a tentative smile, and he helped her to her feet. They took a slow path back to the house. It was stunningly beautiful here.

"I'll go draw a bath so you can clean up. We'll have some more fun after." His grin was sly as he stared at her.

Ah. She felt her smile turn brittle. Well, such a thing was within his rights, and his betrothed was not here to comfort him.

"Yeah, we're gonna play answer-go!" he chirped. "Winner gets to ask the loser one question! Dare you challenge me?"

She paused. *Wait, what?*

"You are . . . not . . . ?"

"Not what?" he asked, tilting his head to the side.

Xiulan smiled tentatively. "Nothing, Master Jin. Forgive this Cai Xiulan, but she will be challenging your might."

The Hidden Master drew her a bath. It was strange, so strange, to be served by one so much more powerful than her, but Master Jin did not seem to care. She was his guest, and so she would be served. The bath was fragrant with herbs and wonderfully warm. It was heavenly to sore muscles.

But some small part of her still doubted. Still thought that what he'd said was a euphemism. It pained her to have such doubts, but this world was not kind to women who trusted. She would do as he asked, but . . .

"Master Jin, I am finished," she said, her body wrapped in a towel. She stood before him and waited. Waited for him to change his mind. Waited for hands to take her towel off.

He perked up, then nodded to her as she stood waiting. "You're done? Awesome. My turn. Come on, *Bi De*, let's get cleaned up!"

He brushed past her, along with the rooster, before pausing and turning around.

"Your clothes are by the fire," he told her and entered the bathhouse.

Xiulan stood alone in the house, save for the Spirit Beast cat that was glaring at her. Indeed, her clothes were by the fire. She picked them up; they were warm and clean. She looked at the table. There was a go board on it, the pieces arranged to play.

There was no touching. No grasping hands, or lust-filled eyes. She was safe.

Xiulan hugged her clothes to her chest and laughed until she started crying.

↔

I sighed, and my eyes roved over the board, one hand scratching Tigger's back. She really didn't like Xiulan for some reason, and I didn't know why. Constantly glaring and turning her nose up at her.

I looked up at the girl. Well, she wasn't *really* a girl. She was older than I was, at twenty-one, but she looked a bit younger than me . . . maybe. Her face had a kind of ageless quality to it. My first ever victory in a game of go yielded that piece of information.

I'm pretty sure she threw the first match, because she promptly kicked my ass the second time, looking confused.

"All right, ask away." I threw the ball in her court, wondering what she wanted to know.

She pondered her question, and finally, she answered.

"Master Jin, do you have any wisdom that you think is essential?"

"Always remember a clean pair of socks," I responded firmly. She pouted at me. I laughed and shook my head.

Well, that was a broad question, wasn't it? But she is a cultivator, so she probably wants something profound. I dunno If I could do profound.

"Remember that everything is connected," I finally settled on. "The water we drink, the air we breathe, the food we eat. Everything has some part of it that leads into each other. Disrupting one thing can disrupt many others. Fixing one thing can fix many others."

↔

"Master Jin?" Xiulan asked as they were getting ready for bed.

"Yes, Xiulan?"

"If it is not too presumptuous of me to ask, is there a place that I could meditate this night?"

He considered the question for a moment.

"The roof might be best," he eventually told her, and she bowed her head in thanks.

She travelled to the roof of the house, where she could be out in the bracing cold. She turned her attention to the strange snow golem briefly before deciding that it was some sort of Qi construct. A brief flash of insight revealed that a web of power circulated through it like the web that circulated through this entire domain. The land here was shy. It was unwilling to reveal itself, and she could only conclude that it was by design.

This Hidden Master was the strangest and most eccentric cultivator she had ever heard of. His methods were utterly alien to her, but what power she could sense was undeniable. His gifts to her were unparalleled.

His future wife was strange too. Strange, but kind in her own way, terrifying concoctions aside. She had been . . . fun to talk to and a wealth of information.

Xiulan closed her eyes.

She circulated her Qi *properly* for the first time in three months. Three months on the road, chasing Sun Ken, without any rest. Her body was tense as she focused.

It was a balm to feel her energy moving throughout her body once more. She would soon be able to return home—return home with Sun Ken's sword and a new technique. Return home *victorious* . . . when she had done nothing. She frowned as she thought about it.

"Xiulan."

She nearly jumped out of her skin at Master Jin's voice.

He handed her a cup of tea. Her beating heart calmed. "Here. Drink this. It will ward away the cold," he instructed her.

The tea was warm—it was fragrant and herbal—and tasted delicious.

She relaxed.

She gazed out over the land. It was beautiful, even covered in snow. The air was fresh and pure, the freshest and purest she had ever smelled, even more so than the air of her own Sect in the grassy hill on which they lived.

She let the peace of this place fill her soul.

It was beautiful.

She closed her eyes once more, feeling the threads of energy, protecting and invigorating.

It was all connected.

When she opened them again under the dawn light, she was at the Fourth Stage of the Initiate's Realm, the lingering taste of the herbal tea on her lips.

→

It was time for her to leave. Xiulan was a dutiful daughter, and so would finish her mission to report Sun Ken's death.

No matter how much she currently wished to get on her hands and knees and beg Master Jin to take her as a disciple. The Fourth Stage. The Fourth Stage! It had long eluded her, and in a single night, even after being grievously injured, she had managed it.

She was prepared to do anything he asked of her. What were his orders? Surely, he would have some task that she would do after she reported Sun Ken's death. Would it be to gather some herb or powerful cultivation ingredient? Would it be to strike down his enemies?

"Now, we like our privacy here, so I'd appreciate it if you didn't spread the word," said Master Jin as he handed her a bag of rice.

She clasped her hands and bowed. "On my life and honour, none shall disturb you, Master Jin."

He smiled at her and nodded, accepting her words.

"Other than that? Don't be a stranger. It's always nice to have someone to talk to. Our wedding is after the first snows melt, if you feel like coming."

She nodded. She would not miss it, even if the heavens tried to prevent her from coming!

Master Jin gave her a small bow of respect, his hands clasped.

"Then, good luck on your journey, Cai Xiulan. May fate favour you."

That was it. No orders of repayment, no demands for her.

He'd given her a gift and a blessing. Tears sprang to her eyes.

"This Cai Xiulan will never forget the kindness you have done her." Xiulan's face was parallel with the ground as she showed the Hidden Master great respect.

She forced herself upright and began her march out of his "Fa Ram" and headed back towards her home.

She paused outside the gate and turned.

"Beware of Chicken," the sign beside the maple leaf said. The rooster watched her from on top of the posts, the profound Spirit Beast's gaze intense.

He bowed.

This time, she bowed back without reservation.

CHAPTER 36

HOMECOMING

There were many ways Hong Xian expected his day to go. Reading medical scrolls, taking care of his son, harvesting winter-caps, or looking to the horizon for his daughter.

He was not expecting . . . *this*.

His knuckles were white as he held onto the edge of the *Toba Gan*, the boar careening through the snowed-over fields and up hills, squealing with delight. He had *no idea* what the children and Gou Ren saw in this. It was all he could do to hang on and *not* go flying off the piece of wood and into a snowdrift.

It had started out innocently enough, with a sleigh delivering his daughter back to him. She was in a great mood—they all were. He'd expected them a day earlier, but they were still young. It was in their nature to tarry.

And then Gou Ren had come up from behind them, howling with mad glee, pulled along by an enormous boar. The boar ploughed through a drift, while Gou Ren took it on the side, and he sailed through the air, slamming back down to the ground and whooping as the boar once more accelerated.

Naturally, this had drawn the children, who all wanted to have a good time on the speeding pig.

All the while, his daughter was carried into town at a more sedate pace . . . also, by a pig . . . a pig who was a Spirit Beast . . . with a rat—another Spirit Beast—sitting on her shoulder, transmitting her voice to everyone and calling Meiling "Master."

It was one of *those* days. The same type of day where he'd met his wife, and the type of day where he and Bao had become sworn brothers: a type of day where it was getting just a little bit too *interesting* for his heart to handle. Xian wasn't getting any younger.

But unlike those interesting days, nothing was trying to poison or disembowel him. Or get him executed. Instead, the strange, befuddling creatures of the world played with children and asked politely to learn medicine from him.

If he was honest, he much preferred this. Even with the loss of money, the loss of position . . . he did not regret being filial and returning to Hong Yaowu. Things were lively in a good way.

So, he'd joined in. What harm was there in having some fun?

Or so he had thought. This was *entirely* too fast for him. His heart was hammering in his chest, but just as his grip was about to fail, the tremendous porcine beast slowed his stride, allowing him to recover and not smack into a tree. His grip loosened, and Chun Ke wandered back to the children, happy as could be.

His son eagerly took over his position, and the boar was off again, kicking up a ruckus.

He shook his head and traveled back to his house, panting with exertion and exhilaration the whole way. The sow, Pi Pa, nodded her head in respect from where she watched the children play. There was a small pile of dried persimmons beside her, and she daintily took one in her mouth and ate it, the very picture of table manners and politeness.

Inside, his daughter had ransacked half the medical scrolls and had them spread out, Ri Zu glued to her side as she explained the theories and plants contained within. It was cute to see his daughter so enthusiastic, gesturing authoritatively. But the little rat nodding along beside her was still rather strange. He shook his head and put it out of his mind.

The Xong brothers were lazing around as they always did when they finished work, ready to get their "payment" for escorting his daughter. It was what they were always paid when they did odd jobs for him.

A free meal was a low price for his daughter having *some* protection. Yun Ren's skill with his sword was passable enough to ward off normal animals, and Gou Ren would simply pick his daughter up and run if things got too out of hand. They would never let his daughter come to any true harm.

They were good boys. Loyal and strong, and Hong Yaowu was the better for their presence . . . when they weren't doing something idiotic, like jumping out of a tree into the river, or trying to catch each other in their hunting snares.

"So, did anything interesting happen this time?" he asked them, getting down a cup.

"Meimei got drunk and started singing about the whore and the donkey," Yun Ren said, scratching his behind. Yun Ren had struck with speed and grace, his skill as a hunter shining through admirably as he pounced on his daughter's weaknesses.

His daughter's head snapped up, her face flushing red.

"Oh? She did, did she?" Xian asked, his lips curling into a smile.

"Yun, if you keep talking, I'm going to turn your skin blue!" his Meimei hissed, but Yun Ren had spotted weakness and went for the throat.

"Then she told Jin to take off his shirt so she could lick wine off his chest." Yun Ren's vulpine grin spread across his face as he mercilessly drove for the kill, revealing the depths of his daughter's wayward ways.

Some fathers would be upset at their daughter's impropriety. All Xian could think was, *Just like her mother*. Those were fond memories. And really, he would have gone himself if he wanted to stop youthful indiscretion. The Xong brothers would never let her come to harm . . . but they would *certainly* never stop anything they thought was funny.

But she needed to sweat a little. It was a father's duty to poke his entirely too headstrong daughter.

"Oh? Daughter, you dared?" he joked. "Is your purity intact, after you performed those actions?"

Meiling started stuttering, her eyes jumping to him and then to the floor, caught between rage and embarrassment while she made vague strangling movements in Yun Ren's direction. She was too unbalanced to notice the mirth in his voice.

Yun Ren shoved a digit into his nose, looking entirely bored with the proceedings, and a languid smirk spread across his face at the destruction he had wreaked. It was a rare day that he managed to defeat Meiling so utterly. Xian's daughter was absolutely fuming and eventually just gave up to hide her face in her hands.

Xian filled his cup as Meiling made whimpering noises, her face as red as a wedding dress. He drank. His daughter really was too cute when she was flustered. Almost as cute as her mother.

It was then Yun Ren pounced, his sly eyes turning to him. "Also, Jin's chicken killed Sun Ken, and we met the Young Mistress of the Verdant Blade Sect."

The water went down the wrong way. He choked, coughed, and spluttered as the hunter claimed his second kill. "What?!" he finally got out, after he had managed to catch his breath.

→

Dinner was an interesting affair. His son was sitting upon the back of Chun Ke, feeding him off the plate. It was an amusing scene and one he could imagine Meiling's own children doing in the future. It was sad that they were to live that far away and over such a rough road. He would like to visit often.

The other two were more reserved, with Ri Zu using a little pair of chopsticks and Pi Pa somehow managing to eat without getting food anywhere.

It was very surreal.

Still, more strange events had happened in the year since Jin had come than had happened in decades prior. The Wicked Blade, a Blaze Bear, that scum who tried to put his hands on Meihua, and now Sun Ken?

Was it fate? Was Jin causing these things to appear . . . or were they destined to appear anyways, and Jin's presence was a shield?

It was something to consider. Cultivators were either the greatest of heroes, or the vilest of villains.

Xian looked to his children's happiness. His son, playing with Chun Ke. Meiling, still patiently teaching Ri Zu.

He would be an optimist, he decided. Jin's appearance was a great fortune, not the precursor to calamity. That is what it was, and that is what it would be. His daughter would be happy. His grandchildren would be well cared for.

He smiled at the only unengaged Spirit Beast. She seemed to be content to simply watch, but he would be a poor host if he did not entertain his guests.

"Miss Pi Pa, would you like to learn about some of the more specific mushrooms we grow?"

The sow perked up, looking shocked. She turned to Xian, Gou Ren, and Chun Ke, who were all falling asleep together. He saw an almost motherly smile cut across her face.

The sow nodded, content that her charges were too tired to cause trouble.

"Very well, then, come with me. I will show you the knowledge of Hong Yaowu."

Hong Xian the Elder began to teach a pig.

She was a surprisingly good student.

→

The two pigs left the next morning to carry a list and a letter to their master. One note would be the children's favourite animals, the other contained news that the merchants would be at Verdant Hill in three days, along with their recording crystals if Jin wished to get anything specific.

They hitched themselves to the sleigh and bowed in respect to those that would see them off.

Xian smiled, waving them goodbye.

Meiling said that the village would be seeing them again soon enough, for Jin had some kind of grand plan for the solstice.

He faced the future with a smile..

□

Cai Xiulan strode, her head held high, through the gates of her Sect. Disciples and mortals gathered around her as she walked, at the head of her small band. The survivors of the battle against Sun Ken all hailed when she returned to them. The people lining the streets gaped at the Crimson Demon's Tooth. They shouted her name, and they praised the might of the Verdant Blade Sect, who had laid the wicked low. Her comrades had all been amazed at her feat, and they walked beside her with their own heads held high, an honour guard for their Mistress.

The battle had not been without losses, even though they had returned victorious. She would lay flowers at the graves of the fallen and those that could be recovered.

In addition, the mortal soldiers would receive their compensation. They had fought bravely and had taken heavy losses to the ambushes, but their families would not be left paupers by their sacrifices. They had done their duty, and that was honour for their family.

Even so, many children would be without their fathers. It was a sobering thought, and one that plagued her heart. But none of the adoring crowds saw that.

Her robes were pristine white. Her hair was immaculate. It was like she had fought the Whirling Demon Sword Gang and sustained not a scratch.

This was pomp and circumstance. Word had been sent ahead of her arrival. Fresh clothes had been provided for her, as well as medics, to see that she had no scars or blemishes. They found none, for Senior Sister's healing was perfect. Her appearance showed that the Verdant Blade Sect was powerful. That their Young Mistress was untouchable.

The Sect leader, the Elders, and the disciples had been gathered. They stood with stern faces and proud bearing in the main courtyard, elevated above the mortals.

They reached the correct distance, and as one, her party dropped to their knees, clasping their fists, and bowing their heads.

"Sect Leader of the Verdant Blade! Honoured Elders! This Cai Xiulan returns from her mission, successful! The Whirling Demon Blade Sun Ken, and the Whirling Demon Blade Gang lie vanquished! Their bones are shattered, and their lifeblood now nurtures the earth! No longer shall the wicked plague the world!"

She reached to her back and presented the sword.

"I present to you, honoured Elders, the Crimson Demon's Tooth, as proof of Sun Ken's demise!"

They made the appropriate noises of approval as the crowd roared and cheered her name.

"Rise, Daughter of the Verdant Blade Sect," her honourable father called. She could see the pride in his eyes. "You shall be rewarded for your triumph." He looked to Elder Yi, the second most powerful man in the Verdant Blade Sect. His face was inscrutable and cold, as he assessed her victory, yet he nodded at her honourable father.

"Go!" Elder Yi commanded, "Take the news to all corners of the Azure Hill! All must know of Sun Ken's defeat at the hands of our Verdant Blade Sect!"

The crowd roared in approval.

Though it was her duty to present things like this, the praise tasted like ashes.

→

"Its demon is suppressed, and I dare say leashed—remarkable! Daughter, how did you accomplish this feat?"

Her honorable father's gaze turned to her from the Crimson Demon's tooth. Slowly, the joy faded as he beheld her.

"My daughter, what troubles you?" he asked, quenching his excitement. The crowds had long since been left behind, as she gave her report privately. His eyes were concerned as he stared at her conflicted face.

"May . . . we have some privacy?" Xiulan asked.

He nodded his head, and with a flick of his hand, the others that were in his room exited, though Elder Yi seemed a bit suspicious. The silencing formation was put up, and her father's eyes softened.

"Now, tell your father what ails you, little orchid," he commanded quietly.

Xiulan considered the question. Master Jin wished for his privacy, yet she could not lie to her father. The two instincts battled as guilt mixed with shame. She would not tell her father Master Jin's whereabouts. But she needed at least *one* person to know the truth.

"It was not I who slew Sun Ken," she stated, hoping to speed through the worst of it. Her father's eyebrows disappeared into his hair. "I was on death's door, crippled by Demonic Qi. When I finally retrieved the blade of Sun Ken, he was already dead."

"Then, how did this occur? How did you survive?"

She bowed her head. "I had a fortuitous encounter. I was taken in by a Hidden Master and I was healed. Then I was gifted with profound techniques and new training, presented with Sun Ken's blade, and told to take the credit. With his assistance and his wisdom, I have reached the Fourth Stage."

Her father's jaw dropped. "He . . . assisted you so greatly?! And raised you so high in mere days? Is there a way he could be convinced to join our Sect?"

She shook her head. "No. He wishes not be disturbed. I will not betray this single task he has set before me. I beg your forgiveness for this, Father, but I must honour his request."

Her father pondered her words. "How powerful was he?"

"I could not see his depths."

Her father nodded and stroked his beard. "We shall abide by his demands. Thank you for telling me, Daughter. To insult a Hidden Master who has done you such a kindness is the height of dishonour."

"He also gifted me this and requested that I attend his wedding with Senior Sister."

Cai Xi Kong opened the bag of rice. It was the finest silver-grade rice he had ever laid eyes on, nearing gold-grade.

And it was absolutely *stuffed* with Qi. Sweat beaded on his brow.

"Then we must prepare a suitable gift for him, Daughter. Can you consider anything that he would desire?"

Xiulan considered. Her gaze turned to the Crimson Demon's Tooth. Her lips quirked into a smile.

"He mentioned wanting a plough."

Her father stared at the blade as well and began laughing. "The wicked whoreson's blade as a *farming implement*?! I can think of no better insult!"

CHAPTER 37

REWARDED

The Lord Magistrate checked over the prices one last time as he paced around his office. It was sure to be enough to placate the cultivator.

At least he hoped it was. He may need to make a request from the man, and if Rou Jin was not satisfied or sufficiently compensated, he might refuse.

Reports had come in of Sun Ken—the Whirling Demon Blade and his ilk had come north.

Reports that were days late. Really, is it so hard to use a transmission stone?!

According to the scattered reports, the roving band of scum had been bled, but most of their cultivators had survived. The Lord Magistrate's men were scouring the countryside, searching for them. He had authorized the use of minor transmission stones as well, just in case his men found anything. The stones were rare—and expensive—but he wanted to have as accurate information as possible.

The Lord Magistrate hoped to find the bastard before any more villages were destroyed. They were his tax base!

Damn the Verdant Blade, couldn't they have taken them out?! He didn't want to have to deal with cultivators! He might even have to personally visit the places of devastation. He hated the smell of blood. He always had to take that disgusting concoction to calm his stomach before he went anywhere near the substance, lest he void his stomach! What sort of Lord Magistrate vomited at the sight of a little blood?

It was even worse because Sun Ken would occasionally hide after attacks and ambush the relief parties. There was one thing the Lord

Magistrate hated more than blood, and it was danger. He always ended up freezing in the moment. He wanted to *run*, heavens damn it, not stand there like some unflinching, stoic fool.

The Patriarch of Verdant Hill was stern and unflappable, after all. The men and women under his aegis couldn't see weakness. They wouldn't think so highly of him then.

Damn cultivators, damn Sun Ken, and damn Rou Jin. Damn all of them. Why did they have to come here*?!*

His stomach was killing him.

"Lord Magistrate, any more of this and you'll wear a hole in the floor," First Archivist Bao chided around a mouthful of dumpling. "I see no reason to be worried. He is a calm man. I'm sure he will hear you out, especially after he learns what kind of vile demon is lurking about his home." He ate another bite of his lunch.

His *second* lunch.

How dare Bao chide me about nervous habits, when the man eats whenever he's upset?

But it had the desired effect. The Lord Magistrate's pace stopped just as a guard came in and bowed. "Lord Magistrate, sir, Rou Jin has arrived, as requested."

"Excellent, excellent, what about his demeanour?" he asked.

"He seems to be pleased with the recording crystal, Lord Magistrate," the guard replied. "He also obtained candied orange peels, cinnamon, sugar, and several other spices, along with red lacquer, rabbit fur, red glass bottles, bells, and the antlers of deer."

He considered the strange purchases . . . and decided he had no idea what the cultivator would use them for. Some kind of pills, formation, or ritual?

Feh. *Cultivators*.

He turned to Bao, and the other man nodded. "Good, good, thank you, Ren Ji," He told the guard, who puffed up with pride. He always had been good with names. It cost him nothing to remember them, and his men were all the more loyal for it. "Now, if you could fetch him? He and I must speak business."

"At once, Lord Magistrate."

It did not take long for the cultivator to arrive. Rou Jin hadn't changed much since he had last laid eyes on him, nearly a year ago now. If one didn't know better, he could be mistaken for any other farm boy, if a slightly taller specimen than typical.

He had a large, happy grin on his face as he entered.

"Lord Magistrate, First Archivist, I hope you are in good health," the cultivator said, clasping his hands in the proper courtesy.

The Lord Magistrate was certain the boy was mocking him. No, he was *not* in good health! His stomach felt like there was molten lead inside it, and he longed to throw the inkwell at the cultivator but stayed his hands. To do such a thing was courting death.

"I am well, Rou Jin," he said, trying to sound as stately as he could. "Has our Verdant Hill treated you well?"

Rou Jin nodded. "Yeah, thanks for telling me about the rice, First Archivist."

The Lord Magistrate's eyes shot over to Bao. He had *thought* they had agreed not to question the cultivator about the matter and then bring it up next time! That was what they had agreed on! He started sweating. "And I . . . trust things have been resolved satisfactorily?" he asked, hoping that the cultivator would be pleased.

"Better than satisfactory, really. Thank you for finding the recording crystal for me. I really needed this. And don't worry about the rice. It was an honest mistake, and I don't mind selling it at that price if you can't afford the higher one. We could do a trade like this again, if that's what you want. I do have certain things I need."

Well! Well, that was good, at least. The cultivator was happy with his service and was willing to work with them in the future. Honesty was apparently a good policy. He wasn't angry at all!

But now came the hard part. Rou Jin was happy, and now the Magistrate would potentially make him angry.

"Well, it is good that all parties were satisfied. I would ask you something, however. Have you heard the news of Sun Ken?" he asked leadingly.

Rou Jin nodded. "That he's dead?"

His face froze. *Sun Ken is dead?*

The cultivator was calm and absolutely serious. Well, there went the plan to ask Rou Jin to kill the barbarian.

The Lord Magistrate's gut churned . . .

His mind raced . . .

He made a choice.

"Ah . . . yes, that joyous news, yes," he managed to get out. "Ah, well, I just wished to inform you of his demise, if you hadn't heard already!"

Rou Jin nodded. "Well, thank you for informing me. Did you need anything else?"

"Oh no, no, I just wanted to make sure everything was fine after our little mix-up. You know how things are!"

The cultivator smiled brightly. "Then if that is all, I need to get back home. I'll be leaving today. I hope that the heavens favour you, Lord Magistrate."

"And you as well, Rou Jin . . ." he replied.

Rou Jin bowed, displaying proper courtly manners, before he turned on his heel and left.

The Lord Magistrate whipped his head around to the First Archivist. The man only shrugged, looking just as perplexed.

One of his scribes rushed in.

"Lord Archivist, priority message from the Verdant Blade Sect! Sun Ken, the Whirling Demon Blade, was slain by Cai Xiulan, the Young Mistress of the Sect!"

"Was he now . . . ?" the Lord Magistrate asked.

"Yes, Lord Magistrate!"

"Well, that is good news. I will make an announcement in . . . one hour. You're free to go, Fang Hei. and close the door behind you."

"Yes, Lord Magistrate!"

The scribe left. The Lord Magistrate slumped onto his desk and groaned. "This is . . . good news," the Lord Magistrate decided.

"Indeed," the first Archivist said, putting down his food for the first time since they had found out Sun Ken had come north. "But . . . how did he know that Sun Ken was dead if we just got the news?"

"*I don't care*. Sun Ken is dead. The cultivator is happy. Recall the men."

It was good news! It was a good day!

Now, if only his stomach would *cease its incessant roiling*.

At least his wife listened to his woes, patting his back and murmuring to him with amused kindness.

□

You know, I finally realized why everybody liked the Magistrate now. The man was *really* nice. Calling somebody up just to apologize for the rice mix-up? He should have had *people* for that, but he'd done it himself.

No wonder he was "The Patriarch of the Verdant Hills"!

I smiled. I'd have to do something nice for the guy.

The recording crystal was mine. Like most "profound" things, the only problem was it didn't really come with an instruction manual. I'd be futzing around with this thing for a while to make sure it recorded the way I wanted.

The spices and orange peel I'd bought were for my family gingerbread recipe, red lacquer for my sleigh, and antlers for my pigs. I got glass to decorate a tree. Rabbit fur, for the white trim. Yes, I know the "traditional" garb of jolly Saint Nick was invented by a certain corporation. But it was iconic and had stuck around for a reason.

In any case, this was the shortest I'd ever been in Verdant Hill since this time, I was in a rush. As soon as Peppa and Chunky had gotten back with the kids' "Christmas List," I had started running. Turns out you can make the trip in a day if you *really* push it.

It was nearly to the solstice.

Hopefully, the village would like my additions even if they weren't traditional.

Ho, ho, ho, boyos.

Jin-ta Claus is coming to town.

CHAPTER 38

PREPARING FOR THE NIGHT

Pi Pa observed the Master. Ever since they had returned with the letter from Hong Yaowu, he had been a flurry of activity: painting things red, "knitting" small caricatures of animals, or mixing some kind of dough.

Today, though, there was an absolutely wonderful smell permeating the house. It was spicy and tantalizing, and it came from what the Master called an oven. Oh, she could just eat it all up!

These things intrigued her. The dough smelled absolutely *divine*. She wondered what the occasion was.

Bi De *thought* he knew what was happening but had said that he needed more time to confirm his thoughts. She had left him to his musings. The arrogant cock who had gotten her dear Chun Ke hurt was no more. He had shown proper remorse, and so she would treat him as a gentleman, and a gentleman was allowed time to properly convey themselves.

Indeed, she was quite pleased with his transformation and repentance. He was *almost* enjoyable to be around now, instead of a morose boor.

Tigu didn't know either but acted like she did. Really, that kitten fooled no one. She was the most rattled by the Master's revelation and story, yet pretended she was fine. Such a child, that one. A nasty, rude, and arrogant child, but a child all the same.

Her dear Chun Ke had been at peace with the story, just as happy before the Master's revelation. He just loved life, and this place let him live as he pleased. He received the training he wanted, the food he wanted, and the play he wanted, and so he was content—a simple, happy soul, her dear, even after the horrors visited upon him.

As for herself, she didn't mind much either way. It was a lady's duty to take care of the household, however large that it may be. She didn't exactly know how she knew that, but it seemed right. Her dear lived here, and the Master lived here, so she would remain.

Even if she would occasionally have to perform some unladylike actions. The most recent interlopers had been disgusting—so disgusting, she was still getting bellyaches a week after they had been dealt with, and the pains had only started to subside after the Master had given her some of Miss Meiling's stomach medicine.

But now, she was curious about the event that was occurring. The Master seemed to sense their curiosity and had bid them gather in the main room. Even Wa Shi, the glutton, was collected. The slimy thing had the gall to call them similar. Nay, he was a nasty little bottom feeder, messy and gross, a beggar who wanted to get fat.

She was a lady. Her bites were precisely as big as they were meant to be, and her appetite within all reasonable realms.

Everyone knew that.

The Master paused in his work as they all entered, Wa Shi, dangling from her mouth. She placed him gently against the floor.

He made a rather sharp report as he slapped onto the floor, then began to whine piteously.

She laid him down a second time, for good measure, just so that he could properly know he was at their destination.

She ignored his blabbering and sat primly before the Master.

The Master looked greatly amused by the arrival of Wa Shi. "I'm guessing you want to know what's going on?" the Master asked.

She nodded with great dignity.

He put down his needles and picked up Wa Shi. The slanderous glutton was put into his jar, and the Master sat once more. "Well, I'll first ask you a question. Have you noticed the nights getting longer?"

Bi De's eyes lit up, and the rooster nodded.

She *supposed* they had been. The days had been much longer when she was a piglet, hadn't they?

"Well, soon it will be the longest night of the year. After then, the nights will start becoming shorter, the days longer, until the snow starts to melt, and spring returns to us."

Ah, was that what Bi De meant as a cycle?

Bi De stood tall and vindicated, nodding his head.

How interesting. They would have to have a discussion over tea about these cycles later.

"On that night, there is a celebration. It is a time to be with family and friends, as we stay together during the Longest Night. I would also like to ask for your cooperation. There is something that I would like to do. It reminds me of my home, and it shouldn't be disrespectful to the festival they already have. Where I am from, we—family and friends—give gifts to one another as a reaffirmation of friendship and our bonds. Particularly to children. I wish to give these to the children of Hong Yaowu, because I received gifts when I was a child. Something fun, on the deepest night of the year. I will need help from all of you—" He paused and looked at Wa Shi. "Well, *almost* all of you."

The glutton slapped his fins upon the edge of the jar, looking upset.

The Master sighed. "This would not be fun for you. You'd be in the jar all night."

Wa Shi considered the Master's words and slapped his fins again.

"Well, if you think you can handle it, then you may come. No one should be left out of the proceedings."

They all nodded their heads. This seemed reasonable. Tigu, however, looked angry—likely angry that the children got presents, and not her.

"Of course, I have gifts for all of you, as well," the Master said, and Tigu's foul mood vanished as if it'd never been.

Dear Chun Ke chuffed with excitement.

Even she was quite excited. *Oh my, I was not expecting this!*

"You have to wait until the Longest Night, though, which is what is normally called the solstice."

Her curiosity was satisfied, but she could tell that Tigu would be scouring the house later, trying to find her own present. Wa Shi looked similarly excited, bubbling happily.

The Master sniffed the air and considered, before getting up and going to the oven. He removed the sheet of metal with his bare hands and placed it upon the table. The smell intensified, and drool nearly escaped her lips.

No, I am a lady, and ladies didn't drool! No matter how much she wanted to *gobble them all up*.

The glutton was not so refined. His beady eyes locked onto the dough. The Master turned around to place another sheet into the oven when he struck. His body coiled, and he launched himself from the jar towards the Master's food.

He was caught from the air without the Master even looking.

"Naughty boys and girls, however, *get nothing,*" the Master said sternly, and the glutton slumped in his hand, pathetically begging and grovelling for the Master's mercy.

"You will be on your best behaviour, or you will not be coming along," he continued, the decision was swift and brutal.

Wa Shi nodded frantically.

The Master smiled at all of them. "You can help me decorate some of the cookies. We'll save one for Ri Zu to decorate when she gets back."

Indeed, when the "cookies" were cooled, the Master ground some sugar until it was but powder, then mixed it with water and an equally powdered piece of dried lemon peel.

The Master brought out a crystal. "Now, let's see how this thing works," he muttered. After a few moments, as the Master concentrated, the crystal began floating in the air. He nodded in satisfaction and then took the icing and spread it over the cookies. He arranged the cookies before a selection of dried fruits, nuts, and larger lumps of sugar.

In front of all of them were crude representations of themselves. Even the Master had two cookies in the shape of men.

Pi Pa daintily took each ingredient in her mouth, placing it against the frosting and sticking it fast. It was a passable rendition of herself.

Dear Chun Ke was distressed. He lacked the fine control to properly decorate the cookie, grunting softly as he tried to grab one of the pieces of colourful decoration but only knocked over the container. But the Master aided him, allowing himself to be her dear's hands. He let dear Chun Ke pick out the nuts he wanted and placed them accordingly, much to his enjoyment.

Tigu, of course, swiftly reconstructed herself in near perfection, her claws cutting and dicing the toppings to the proper size. She puffed up with pride when the Master praised her skill, looking smugly down at thcm.

Bi De was humble. His rooster took on few decorations, only enough to add some colour.

Wa Shi, the glutton, had actually managed to restrain himself and gotten the Master to help him as well. Although, his carp cookie looked more like an obese dragon and was covered with as many nuts as it would fit.

The Master acted as Bi De did. His creations were humble but understandable—one of himself and one of his lady.

The Master took the crystal out of the air and studied it intently. He focused again, and an image came to life, projecting itself onto the wall.

It was an image of them as they had been, the tray of cookies in front of them, sitting together. A moment captured in time.

"I'm glad this worked," the Master mused. "A record of our first solstice together, may many more follow," he said, smiling at the vision.

The elegant pig stared, enraptured by the vision. *'Ah! Dear is even more handsome from this angle!'*

"Now, let us see how they taste—and *Wa Shi* is already done." The Master appeared amused by the crunching noises coming from the fish.

Pi Pa daintily placed the cookie in her mouth. Indeed, it was delicious.

□

"Zang Li," a voice called, and he opened his eyes. "The Patriarch has lifted some of your restrictions in light of your progress. You may leave the inner courtyard, but you are still confined to be within fifty li of the mountain."

Zang Li's head bowed in acknowledgement. Inside, Lu Ban was content. Truly, he was a dragon amongst men. Even confined and suppressed, he had risen another stage, enough for the Shrouded Mountain to finally begin to put resources into him. The imprisonment was an irritating setback to his plan, but not insurmountable.

The first few months had been hell. His "father" had slapped him across the face thirty times for the disgrace he brought to the Shrouded Mountain. The Patriarch had been so incensed that the old man had confined him to the inner courtyard, in ripped and tattered robes, so that he could be adequately shamed by the other disciples. They knew not what he had done, but they laughed anyway.

The joke was on them. Lu Ban had endured far worse than the stuck-up disciples could spew at him, and those that tried violence were swiftly suppressed by his superior combat skill. It was enough that the shame of being defeated in the Azure Hills, of all places, was beginning to fade. Lu Ban had heard the whispers. The Elders had begun to think of his defeat as a wandering powerful cultivator, instead of him having lost to a weakling.

Slowly, the Elders had stopped sneering, and his "father" had, in private, apologized for striking him so many times. He had said that it was just bad luck that he was caught by some powerful wanderer.

For now, he rose. He would continue to rise. He would take everything that the world owed him. When the restrictions ended, he would be powerful. When the restrictions ended, he would have the full might of the Shrouded Mountain.

When the restrictions ended, he would find the man named Jin and slay him. Lu Ban would be so mighty the other man would break himself on Lu Ban's chest.

He clenched his hand into a fist as he imagined it.

He rose from where he was seated, having finished his cultivation for the day.

He stared up at the sky, and a genuine smile overcame his lips.

The Longest Night was upon them. How he loved the darkness it cast the world in.

CHAPTER 39

JIN-GLE BELLS

"Come on now, Xian'er, stay still for me, okay?" Meiling asked her little brother as she tied the red sash around his waist. As all little boys did at this age, he was fidgeting, eager to go out and play.

"Everybody else is outside already, Meimei!" her little brother grumbled, upset that he had to get dressed up more than any of his friends.

"Yes, they are. However, those little ones aren't going to be the next leader of Hong Yaowu. There is a time for play, Little Brother, and there is a time for duty."

He pouted fiercely but accepted her judgement.

"Besides, if you went out earlier, you'd be falling asleep before the night was half done. Didn't you say you'd stay up with the rest of us to be able to see the sun this year?"

Xian flushed at her words. He had nearly made it last year, after boasting for months that he would be able to stay up all night with the rest of the adults. And then he'd ended up passing out on her shoulder, snoring away as the sun rose. It was cute, but her arms were sore by the end of it, especially after carrying him on her back for hours.

He was starting to get heavy. She used to be able to hold him up without any strain at all.

Ah, how time has changed things.

"I'll make it this year," he muttered stubbornly, refusing to look at her. "And next year, Dad is teaching me the Sun Dance," he said with a fair amount of pride.

Meiling smiled at him. "And then you get to dance all night. You're right. Maybe I should let you out to play. You need to build up your endurance."

Xian went silent as he realized that playing a lot meant that he would have trouble staying awake. Finally, Meiling could work uninterrupted by him moving or saying something. She just had this last piece, and then they would be done. He obligingly lifted his feet for her, and she helped him get on his hide boots, tightening the laces so they wouldn't come off.

She finished tying the knot and stood up to examine her handiwork. Xian's warm robe and jacket looked like the colours of dawn, reds and oranges symbolizing the fires that would burn through the Longest Night.

"Well, there's the Little Headman. *So handsome*!" Meiling teased and pressed a sloppy kiss to his cheek.

"Meimei!" Xian yowled, disgusted by the spit smeared on his face. He glared at her and leaned forward as if going for some retaliation. She leaned back, dodging. Instead, he leapt from the stool he was on and raced out of her grasp, turning around once to stick his tongue out at her.

"Stupid head!" he called, rubbing his arm against his face to get the worst of her attack off.

Meiling, as the mature older sister, stuck her tongue out in return. He giggled and fled the house.

She smiled fondly at his exit. He really had grown up so fast. Ten years of difference between them, yet sometimes, she felt like she was already a mother. She had certainly raised him for long enough. Seven years already since their mother's passing . . .

Meiling sighed and went to check on her father. He was in his office, stripped down to his waist, and in deep meditation. In front of him, a candle was burning, and smoke filled the room. He always looked troubled when he was meditating, his brow scrunched up and his face in a slight frown.

But he needed this moment of peaceful respite. He had a long, long night ahead of him, for tonight's dance was even more taxing than the Dragon Dance. It was one of the founding rituals of their village, practised for millennia, if the texts were right. He had already been preparing himself for a full week, conditioning his body and focusing the tiny scraps of Qi he had.

His eyes opened as she entered, but his breathing remained the same.

"Daughter," her father greeted as some of the worry lines disappeared from his face.

"Just wanted to see if you needed anything, Father," she whispered, unwilling to disturb the quiet of the room.

He shook his head. "I need nothing else." He deflated. "Nothing but these last moments."

She nodded her head at her father's request to be left alone and exited the room. She had to get ready too.

Her own robes were dark red, with a few lighter orange highlights, and they were to be hidden by a dark shawl with white fur around the collar. Now, it was time to start helping out. Most of the preparations were done, but everybody always appreciated another hand in the kitchens.

She exited her house and went out into the cold air.

The village was bedecked in colour. Like the Mid-Autumn Festival, red paper lanterns hung from the houses, and red cloths were strung between the roofs. The smell of cooking and food permeated the villages, the scent of glutinous rice balls and soup. It was a good smell, with fond memories. Meiling had always loved sitting in her mother's lap and watching the sunrise.

The others in the large, communal kitchen greeted her as she approached, tossing her an apron so she could start working as well. Hu Li, the Xong brother's mother, grinned at her and passed her some meat that she had to butcher. She slotted herself into the assembly line with ease, as the ladies of the village talked away.

The day was short, and there was lots of work to do.

□

Meiling yawned as she took a small break, sitting on a cold bench and watching over the children. She idly wondered when Jin would show up as he'd said he would. She turned her eyes up to the clouds above.

The sky was overcast and drab.

The snowfall and the mist limited visibility.

But music was coming from the swirling mist.

The steady ringing and *ching ching ching* of bells sounded throughout the streets.

The puffing of animals.

As soon as the children heard it, they turned from their games and looked towards the noise, curious and excited. The adults simply watched on, already having a good idea of who was visiting them. Only one man came from that direction.

Deep, joyous laughter sounded out. It boomed out over the village, carrying cheer with it.

From the mist, something emerged.

It started as a silhouette.

A strange, puffing beast, with tusks and an antler upon its head.

Another, with her nose painted red.

Together, they pulled a magnificent sleigh. It was adorned with pine branches, and the wood was lacquered in shining scarlet, along with silver and gold stars running down its side. A man stood upon it, his arms crossed, and one of his legs placed up on the front of the sled.

Jin wore a bright red robe and a fur-lined jacket, mostly similar to what the rest of the village was wearing. The only thing strange about it was the pointed and fur-lined hat, with a pom-pom on the end.

He was with a rooster, who also had a red hat. The Spirit Beast was perched primly on his shoulder, and a cat who laid upon a truly massive bag attached to the back of the sleigh, a ball in her mouth.

It was an amusing sight.

"Jin!" the children cried happily, and he laughed again.

"Ho-ho-ho! Hey, everybody!" the broad man shouted as the sleigh came to a stop. He slung the massive sack over his shoulder and picked up a jar before hopping off the sleigh. "Good tidings on the solstice!"

"Good tidings on the solstice!" the children echoed back.

The children crowded around as he began his march to the center of the town. They eyed his over-large sack with excitement or began scratching the boar that they all remembered, who had pulled them around the fields for hours. He huffed happily at the attention, shoving his nose into faces and sniffing excitedly. The single antler, which had been tied to his head, made him look even more friendly and comical than normal.

Jin greeted the rest of the adults, some simply nodding in his direction while others clasped his arm in a more informal greeting.

Meiling poked her head out from the kitchen, then rolled her eyes at the sight of the advancing man. Jin came to a stop just outside her own house and sat down on one of the chairs.

"Now," he began, "I have one question to ask you all. Have you been good children this year and listened to your parents?"

The children nodded eagerly.

Jin stroked his chin in consideration. "Oh? Will your parents say the same?" he asked, and several of the eager children suddenly appeared worried.

It was the parents' turn to chuckle as their children squirmed under Jin's mock scrutiny.

"Now, then, let's see what I have in my bag . . ." He made a great show of rummaging around in it.

"I believe I have something here for Maomao . . ." The little girl's eyes widened as she was handed a smaller sack, which she eagerly opened. She gasped at the small toy and cookies.

She grabbed her necklace and held it up beside the small stuffed butterfly. "It matches what Father made for me!" she cheered.

It only spurred on the growing excitement.

Each child got a small sack that contained two cookies and a toy. The cookies were devoured, and they ran off to play, Chun Ke in tow, leaving Jin in his chair and watching them fondly. Jin smiled at Meiling as she approached.

"Not too disruptive, I hope?" he asked her quietly, and she shook her head.

"Joy helps bring back the sun. Joy, colour, fire. Little sparks that the sun can see, even when it's so deep in its slumber," Meiling replied simply. She didn't resist as an arm hooked around her waist, pulling her into Jin's lap. "What possessed you to put a horn on Chun Ke though?"

"It was funny," Jin said honestly. She rolled her eyes, then shook her head in bemusement.

"You are so strange," she told him fondly.

Jin grinned and reached into his bag again, bringing out a large cookie and a small stuffed cat.

She raised an eyebrow at the cookie. It was well done, though she thought her smile didn't get quite *that* wide. "Me? Am I supposed to eat myself? It seems a bit morbid."

Jin shrugged. "I could always eat you up, if you want," he mused, his tone turning husky. Meiling flushed, smacked him on the chest, and took a bite of the cookie.

Her eyes widened at the sweet, spicy taste. "This is really good."

"I've got enough so that everybody should be able to have some, not just the kids." Several of the parents crowded around as Jin opened his bag wider and handed out a jar filled with the treats. Noises of appreciation sounded out while his gifts were devoured. Somebody handed him a honey candy, and he popped it in his mouth.

The sleigh moved past at a sedate rate, crowded with children as they cheered on mighty Chun Ke, to the sound of jingling bells.

"We'll come back every year," Jin said to her. "Or whenever you want to. Doesn't have to be a special occasion. Family is important."

Smiling, Meiling closed her eyes and leaned back into her soon-to-be husband. That sounded . . . nice.

□

"Really?" I asked skeptically. We were all sitting at a table, waiting for the feast to begin, and Yun Ren was telling a rather tall tale, made more outlandish by the strange blue tint to his skin. I dunno what had caused it, but nobody seemed too worried.

"I swear, it had antlers *this big*," Yun Ren said, stretching out his arms as wide as he could make them. His movements caused the knitted snake he was using as a scarf to bounce around.

"*Sure* it did," his brother harrumphed, as he stuffed another cookie into his mouth. "And I'm the Magistrate." His other hand played with the stuffed dog I had given him. He had complained mightily about how he wasn't a child when I gave it to him . . . but he had yet to put it down.

Ah, "the ones that got away" stories. Those were always good, but I'm actually kind of sure Yun Ren is telling the truth this time. It is xianxia land after all. Maybe it was a Spirit Deer?

"Yun Ren lies as naturally as he breathes," Meimei heckled him, and his face flushed. She was currently wearing my Santa hat and had the knitted cat stuffed in the front of her shirt.

It was cute. I'd have to make her a hat too.

"I'm not lying! I swear, it was out past the creek!"

→

It was steadily darkening, and we had been served dinner. I'll admit, the glutinous rice balls that were traditionally served weren't my favourite, but they were traditional. I looked back through Rou's memories and smirked. He hadn't liked them much either.

There were a lot of snacks and sweets, which agreed with my taste buds a lot better. The village version of gingerbread was super spicy, and *delicious*. Honestly, I thought it was nearly a match for my own family recipe. It was like getting punched in the face with pepper and ginger, and it was glorious. There was also honey candy and dried fruits, which rounded things out.

Things were winding down a bit as everybody sat around and digested. The kids, however, had eventually gotten bored of riding around on the sleigh and had found another source of fun.

Namely, throwing pieces of food over Washy's jar and watching him leap up to snap them out of the sky. The little glutton was in heaven, eagerly popping his head out of the water to slap his fins on the edge and demand more food. Even some adults had joined in, trying to get the little bits of nuts past the all-consuming fish-shaped void.

Chunky was being used as a backrest, and Peppa was nearby, simply watching over the children. Big D was on Meiling's roof, Rizzo on his back, as he examined the town.

Tigger was playing with her new toy out in the forest. My disciples had gotten their gifts a bit early. Tigger's was a reinforced hacky sack. I'd probably need to do a lot of maintenance on it, because Qi reinforcement only lasted so long. However, it was something that could take her hits for a while, and she had been extremely pleased with the present. Big D got a new perch that had been installed on the top of the house. Chunky had gotten a new hockey stick, Peppa a selection of dried fruits and nuts—which she had enjoyed immensely—Rizzo had gotten a new bag, and Washy received a new basin for him to sit in at dinner. The rest of my disciples had kept their gifts back home. Tigger was the only one that refused to put hers down.

There was an angry splash, and a person started shouting with fear. Somebody had decided to be a smartass and had tried to use a rock instead of a piece of food.

Washy had taken an issue with that.

One of the older boys was yelping and howling as he ran away from an irate fish. Washy's bounces were impressively high, and he could move fast enough to keep up with the guy trying to lose him.

I was going to intervene, but . . . the rest of the village found it funny, so I let it go.

It *was* pretty damn funny.

I turned back to my future family and continued listening to Yun Ren's story about the buck that had escaped him.

Finally, I asked what had been on my mind for the entire time I had been here.

"Yun Ren, why is your skin tinted blue?"

He flinched and then scowled at his brother and Meimei. They both looked *entirely* too innocent.

"Some people don't know how to take a joke," he said flatly.

CHAPTER 40

DAWN

And that was how the Great Sage San Ta defeated the wicked Kram Pas and banished the child-stealer from the world. His talisman-gifts protecting the virtuous children from the evil beasts," Jin explained. Meiling raised an eyebrow at the fanciful story.

They were walking to the shrine, as the sun disappeared behind the hills and twilight came. But the village was not plunged into darkness. Paper lanterns cast red shadows, and giant fires blazed as the village gathered.

Little Xian gasped from his perch on Chun Ke's back, eyeing the stuffed dragon he had received. "So, this is a protective talisman that can ward off evil?" little Xian asked.

Jin shook his head. "That's what they started out as, but . . ." Jin pointed to the trinket Little Xian held. "That's just a toy. Nothing protective about it."

The boy pouted but didn't seem too upset. He was obviously thinking about San Ta chasing the demon all over the world on his trusty horned steed. He grinned and settled on the great boar's back, peering beside the horn tied to the pig's head.

"My eyes see all the wicked and all the righteous!" little Xian cheered to himself. "Ya! Charge, Chun Ke, let's jump over an ocean in a single leap!"

The boar obligingly trotted forwards, chuffing with amusement, until he was interrupted.

"Chun Ke, to the shrine, please, not on an adventure," Meiling said reproachfully. The boar stopped in his tracks and turned to the woman. Somehow, he managed to pout.

Meiling was having none of it.

"Shrine," she stated simply, and both boar and boy slumped.

"All right . . . *Kram Pas*," little Xian muttered.

"*What was that?*"

"Nothing!" Xian yelped, then under his breath said, "Demon sister."

Meiling eyed his back. "He's getting entirely too cheeky." She sighed.

Jin shrugged. "You can always put on some horns and haunt the end of his bed. Kram Pas liked naughty children the most." His tone made it clear he was joking.

Meiling's eyes, on the other hand, gleamed with the kind of gleeful malice only an elder sibling could possess.

That boy was going to get the wakeup of a lifetime.

Jin sighed and wrapped an arm around her. "So, what's happening at the shrine? I know most people pray for a good year, but I get the feeling this is more than that."

Meiling smiled. "You'll see very shortly. A lot of the villages around here do this."

They had all gathered at the shrine when, suddenly, a hush swept over the crowd.

Hong Xian the Elder strode from his home. His robes were the colours of the dawn: reds, oranges, hints of pinks, and purples spread out like the sunrise. On his face he wore a mask, a stylized depiction of the sun. He carried a staff with loose rings on it.

Jin's eyes widened at his measured steps and his almost trance-like breathing. The crowd parted for him as he strode into the ring of braziers that had been constructed, burning low with barely noticeable flames.

From the other side of the village came Yao Che, his robes dark shades of blacks and deep purples, the mask of the moon on his face. He took up position outside the ring, before a massive drum.

They both stood, absolutely silent, as they waited.

A gong sounded.

The last of the twilight faded away, overtaken by the Longest Night.

The drums began to pound. Slowly at first, and then with increasing ferocity. An ancient beat that had burned its way into Meiling's memories.

Hong Xian danced. His body moved through old forms, passed down from father to son for generations. A tradition that had endured the trials of centuries. His bright robe whirled. His feet stomped. The staff jangled and chimed as it went through the motions that had remained unchanged since their inception.

For nearly ten minutes, the dance continued, Xian's body never stopping its movements, his breath just as perfectly steady as it had been at the start.

The gong sounded again.

The drums pounded.

The dance continued, repeating its first movements.

Some villagers broke off at the sound of the gong—those with children too young to even attempt to stay up all night. But most stayed, standing together in front of the shrine.

Some had their heads bowed in prayer.

Some simply stood with their family.

Others started to dance as well, leading their children through old steps.

"He's going to go all night, isn't he?" Jin whispered to Meiling. She looked up at her betrothed. His eyes were locked on her father's form, genuine respect shining in them.

"Until the sun rises again," she confirmed.

"Is there anything I can do to help?" Jin asked.

"The fires are to get higher throughout the night—we put on more wood and stoke the fires higher—a beacon to call back the sun. You can help by adding to those if you really want to. They'll start stoking the fire in three more repetitions and then every ten after that."

Jin nodded, still entranced by her father's dance.

"Until that time . . . come here." She grabbed his hand and dragged him off to the side, where the rest of the people danced.

"These are the steps for *this* one," she said, looking around at the couples.

Jin's eyes lit up with happiness as she shared her village's traditions with him.

↔

Bi De's night was extremely pleasant. He now understood why the Great Healing Sage wished to visit their Great Master as often as she did. The time spent without Sister Ri Zu had been a trying one. Her company was a balm upon his soul, her presence a calming draught, and her weight on his back a welcome pressure.

It was even more welcome to hear of her time spent in this place, apprenticing under the Great Healing Sage. She spoke with great enthusiasm of medicines and concoctions, and though he comprehended a bare fraction of what she said, he enjoyed hearing about what she had learned.

The Great Master was right, as always. Spending time with one's friends and family upon the solstice was only fitting—even if they were here, instead of on their blessed Fa Ram. His fellow disciples had been received with great enthusiasm by the mortals, especially Brother Chun Ke, who basked in their attention. Bi De kept himself largely apart. Most pointed covetously at his hat, a gift from the Great Master, so he had retreated to the rooftops lest they pester him enough to draw his ire.

Brother Chun Ke was already a fixture, beloved by the children. Bi De's kindly brother let them clamber all over his body without reservations, and in doing so he received much of their affection. Bi De could not imagine what he liked in their screams; they were most annoying.

But to each their own.

The only other who remained aloof was Sister Tigu, who was consumed with the training aid the Great Master had gifted to her. She had not put it down since she had received it, and even now was asleep in the sleigh, curled around the gift.

Bi De sighed in contentment as the instruments below clanged. The mortal's dance was mildly entertaining, but his movements were slow. On the third repetition, he turned his gaze away from their dance and onto the heavens. To the moon. The moon, which had been obscured by the clouds, was revealed.

The full moon.

It was auspicious that the longest night of the year was also the night with the brightest moon. It took over for the sun, shining its light upon the world.

He gazed upon the celestial body, pondering upon this cycle. If there was the longest night, there was also the longest day. His awareness back then had been . . . limited, so he could not remember seeing this longest day.

He pondered, not for the first time, on the moon's counterpart. Though it was his duty to herald its coming, he could not bring himself to love the sun like he did the moon. He could not observe it directly. Its light gave life, but it was also harsh and unforgiving, gazing sternly down upon the world. He knew he would have to spend more time pondering the predicament in order to be able to truly comprehend the cycles. Still, he had decided to complete his contemplations upon the lunar glory first.

He gazed upon the moon as it travelled across the sky, waiting for the sun to reclaim its rightful place. He noticed there was a brighter glow coming from beneath, and he turned his attention to it.

Bi De chastised himself: he had been arrogant again, believing that because they were mortal it meant they were naturally inferior. The mortal was still dancing. The other, still drumming. The snow had melted entirely around his legs, and the flames around the dancer surged with passion and energy.

What had started humbly was now a mesmerizing sight. The mort—nay the man, still danced with skill, his breath as perfect as Bi De's own despite having so little Qi he might as well have none.

The Qi that was around the dancer seemed to be invigorated by the Great Master's own energy. It danced through the air, pulsing in time to the dancer and the drummer, yet not touching them. It was a formation of fire, and yet it did not seem to be really doing anything. He observed the Qi carefully and the way it moved. It was gathering and dancing, swirling and twisting.

It spiralled.

It cycled.

The day into night, the night into day.

He watched the dance, watching the dancer's breathing, his movement and his kicks.

He paused, examining the performance more closely. As thin as could be, there was a thread trailing from the formation and into the distance.

'*Hold on please, Sister Ri Zu,*' he requested, and at her acknowledgement, he leapt into the air. His ability to fly was limited—his legs were more powerful than his wings.

Still, just this once, he offered an apology to the heavens, ascending high into the sky. So high he reached the clouds and then surpassed them. So high it was hard to breathe. He turned around to gaze upon the world.

The tiny thread of flame that circled around the dancers went off into the distance. Bi De saw, from this highest perch, another spot of fire. It was not as grand as the fire tended to by the Great Master, though the tiny thread was trying to invigorate this one as well.

He saw the tiny spots of flame, and in his mind's eye he saw some sort of formation, stretching out across the landscape. A web that went farther than he could see, even from all the way up here. A formation that, unless he missed his mark, covered a hundred thousand Fa Rams in distance.

But there were empty spaces in this grand web—dark spots, in a formation of fire.

Something stirred at the back of his mind, yet it did not coalesce. *What is this?* he thought curiously. *What is this formation of fire?*

He and Sister Ri Zu fell back down to the earth, alighting upon the roof of the house again.

He pondered deeply what he had seen . . . and yet he stayed upon the ground. It was a massive formation as far as he could tell. A curiosity was struck. What was it? What was it for?

The question ate at him. Just what was the great formation fading into the distance. What could require something so mind-bogglingly huge?

He shook his head.

He need not break that code tonight. He watched the man diligently instead, as the moon crossed the sky and light began to return to the world. The swirling bands of Qi dispersed.

The sun broke the horizon, the Great Lord of the heavens peeking out almost shyly from behind the hill. The world seemed to sigh contentedly as the celestial body revealed itself.

And in its deep, deep slumber, the earth stirred once more.

Bi De shouted his greeting as the warm rays touched his body. The humans below and his fellow disciples all added their voices; even Tigu yowled from where she was on the sleigh, and Wa Shi splashed happily.

It was nothing more, and nothing less, than a beautiful view.

↔

Hong Xian staggered to a stop as the sun crested the horizon.

Those who were still awake cheered as the first light of dawn hit them, including his own son, who he could hear shouting with glee that he had madc it.

It got more challenging every year; his body was steadily wearing down. There would soon come a year when he couldn't perform this dance at all.

And yet this year . . . Xian's body felt as though it was on fire. His breath had finally failed him, and he nearly fell to his knees. Yet instead of bone-deep exhaustion . . .

He felt so *alive.*

A hand on his back steadied him before he could fall.

"Are you all right, Father?" a male voice asked.

It was still strange to hear those words out of Jin's mouth. They were not family yet, but . . . his eyes were full of genuine concern. Jin's hand was gently pressed against his back, and yet it felt like the entire world was supporting his exhausted body.

His breathing evened out, and his shaking legs steadied—just in time for his actual son to collide with his middle. If Jin's hand hadn't been there, he would have been thrown onto his back.

His son grinned toothily up at him. "I did it!" he cheered again, through the bags under his eyes.

His hand rested on his son's head. "I'm proud of you." he rasped, his throat terribly parched. His legs wobbled again. "Jin . . . help me sit."

The man nodded at his request. Out of the corner of his eye, he saw the Xong brothers helping Brother Che. The poor man was without any family of his own this year, with Meihua unable to make it back home, but he would still be well cared for.

Jin helped him walk out of the circle of snow. It was a light touch, so soft that he felt like he was walking of his own power—unlike last year where they'd had to carry him back to his home. He was escorted to the shrine, where he was gently sat down. His daughter came with water and helped him drink when his hands shook too badly.

He gazed out over the world, the sun rising up from its slumber. In contrast his youngest was in his lap, having finally succumbed to his slumber. His daughter supported him on one side. On the other, was his soon-to-be son.

The shakes stilled.

A daughter on the left, a new son on the right. The sun illuminated their faces as they sat with him, allowing him to truly enjoy the rising sun for the first time in years.

He closed his eyes in contentment, settling his breathing, as golden light warmed his face.

CHAPTER 41

TICK TOCK GOES THE CLOCK

Yun Ren stalked through the forest, his footfalls as quiet as he could make them. He wasn't the best hunter in Hong Yaowu, but he was second place. In first place was his father. His father supplied most of the wild game—fat juicy boars, deer, and bears in winter—the village ate, and he also provided the hides that went to the city. Most of Yun Ren's game ended up being rabbits and other small creatures, which got him relentlessly teased about how even his hunting habits were fox-like.

He honestly didn't mind that much. His eyes were the same as his mother's, and all of the qualities ascribed to him were positive, as far as he was concerned. Foxes were devious and cunning. That just meant he was smart.

And his traps were excellent. He caught his rabbits and the occasional one of his "kin" with them, though the foxes were the rarer of the two. He didn't really have to do much stalking at all. That gave him more time to train with his sword—not that he had ever actually had to use it in anger, but it was cool. Sure, it got him put on guard duty or tasked with escorting people, but that just meant he got to travel a bit, and people paid for his food.

But today, he was going after larger game: the deer with the giant horns. His own brother had cast doubt on his story! Yun Ren hadn't lied to him—this week at least. It was perfectly trustworthy information!

At least Jin had believed him. He had told Yun Ren to be careful, though, before he left. Such a thing may be a Spirit Beast. Yun Ren doubted it, though. It was just a big deer, no more, no less.

He was hours into the hunt and on a fresh trail. Soon, he would find his quarry, and soon, he would bring it down. He would have deer with Jin's rice. And it would be *delicious.*

There was a snap as a deer broke a twig. Yun Ren froze and redoubled his efforts at stealth. He crept forwards, inch by inch, until he saw it.

The buck. Its antlers were massive, spreading out like the branches of a tree. It was unaware of his presence.

Yun Ren focused, steadying his breathing, just like Elder Hong and his father had taught him. Deep and measured.

His vision sharpened.

The world fell away.

Just him, and his target.

He could see every hair on the buck's body, every bit of moisture glistening on its nose; he could count the beats of its heart as its lifeblood pulsed beneath its skin.

He pulled back just a little more, drawing to full length, ready to take his prize—

There was an ugly *cracking* sound as his weapon splinted where he was grabbing it. His bow snapped in two.

The buck's head shot up at the noise and bolted, fleeing deep into the forest.

Yun Ren gaped. *How the hells did my bow break?! I take good care of it, damn it!*

He slumped. He had been so close. So close! And it had evaded him. *Stupid, worthless bow, and stupid, worthless lousy luck!*

Frustrated, he kicked a large rock and was surprised when the part he kicked cracked, flipping off into the forest. He stared blankly at the chunk.

Had it been weakened by the frosts?

He shook his head and began his meandering route back home in a foul mood.

□

"A joyous New Year to you, Lord Magistrate!"

"Yes, Happy New Year, Lord Magistrate!"

"It's good to see you again, Lady Wu!"

"A toast to our illustrious leader's health! May his life be long and prosperous!"

The Lord Magistrate was in his element. He waved to the crowds, and his wife had a small smile on her face as she greeted the well-wishers, their arms linked together. This . . . this was what he lived for. The common folk came up to him, gave him small gifts, poured drinks for him, and toasted to his health. His guards in the barracks shouted his praises for their New Year's bonuses. His clerks spoke in whispers of his foresight over the festivities.

He *greatly* enjoyed listening in when they thought he wasn't around. This truly was the apex of life: to have men sing your praises and kiss the hem of your robe because they *wanted* to. Because they genuinely admired you.

He could have more power and influence in a city. He was certain his administration skills were more than capable of handling two hundred thousand souls, nay, *five* hundred thousand! But in those cities, could he walk around without guards, without any kind of escort, secure in the knowledge that none would even *think* of harming him? That those that would dare would risk the wrath of all their peers, for this simple, common-born man who had achieved greatness on his own?

Still, he did have some people. In addition to his wife, he had one of his junior guards along to carry the excess gifts he was given. They waved appropriately at the people and were greeted in turn.

Yes, this was the life.

Their pace was slow and leisurely as they strode through his domain, out of respect for his wife's condition. She had been quite well recently, and he was glad to have her this night.

There was a slight tremor in her hand, and he stopped, under the guise of watching the bursts of colour in the air. The fireworks were marvelous this year. The Lord Magistrate would have to personally pay his compliments to their makers. The New Year festivities were much more exciting than the Sun Dance. He absently rubbed his thumb across the back of his wife's hand, trying to soothe some of the shakes.

Yes, yes, it was tradition, but staying up all night was so *boring*. The old men of the older families were impressive. Especially in how they could continue to dance for so long . . . But it was absolute hell standing there for nearly twelve hours, ringing the gong occasionally and watching over their performance. He would have to learn how to fall asleep with his eyes open and delegate the gong to someone else. At least his padded mat he had started sneaking to where he had to stand took the worst of the pain off his back.

He had stayed up all night enough when he was studying for the civil service exams! He should be able to rest now, damn it.

The tremors ceased. None had noticed, just as his lady willed it. They began their walk again.

He nodded imperiously at the gaggle of venerable grandmothers as they strode past them, even the one that was absolutely insane and lived in the hovel. The others seemed to like the crazy old woman. They giggled at his passing and made japes about how handsome he was. He just smiled charmingly at the old ladies—they were experts at making tea, and he did enjoy their offers to sit down with them during the colder months.

His tour of his town was going splendidly. He graciously rejected the food he didn't like and accepted what he did. He would be calling on every family of interest to check up on them, though mostly to receive their hospitality.

He was in a good mood as he wandered into the Zhuge compound.

"Lord Magistrate!" the Patriarch of the Zhuge clan greeted him along with his family. He was one of the old families, and his son did good work. Tingfeng was a credit to his clan.

And to his office, when he brought his wife around. The other men *loved* to stare. The woman was absolutely stunning. His heart pounded whenever he looked at her. He had nearly asked her to accompany him to his quarters!

Only his better judgement prevailed. To break all of his hard-earned reputation for simply a pretty face? *Unthinkable*. Letting power go to your head was how a not insignificant number of Magistrates got lynched.

Besides, he doubted the girl would enjoy the kinds of things he and his wife did. Ropes were an . . . acquired taste.

So, he ignored her as much as he could. He nodded his head and took in the pleasantries. His wife giggled at the appropriate moments and complimented the girl on her pregnancy.

Simple, safe topics. A fine visit, with the Zhuge Patriarch, once more affirming that he was at the Lord Magistrate's command and that his son would serve however he decided.

He was about to leave, but then another voice called out.

"Lord Magistrate!" His smile froze on his face at the voice. "It's great to see you, sir!"

"Ah, yes. It is . . . good to see you too," he managed, his body freezing under the cultivator's grin. Hong Meiling stood with him, and the youngest of the Hong family was on his shoulders.

"Here, I wanted to give these to you, as thanks for everything you do." The man gave him a sealed box that smelled a bit medicinal and spicy as well as a bow. The cultivator smiled warmly at his wife, and the Lord Magistrate felt a surge of irritation. His arms managed to move and take the box.

"Let us hope this year is as productive as the last," Rou Jin said, grinning without a care in the world.

The Lord Magistrate nodded his head, but his gut had started to churn again. He felt his wife lift a hand to wave pleasantly at them.

"May our relationship continue," he managed to get out, and the cultivator nodded as Hong Meiling started to gush over Yao Meihua.

His night . . . Well, thankfully it wasn't ruined after the visit from the cultivator. Rou Jin had given him a gift and then left him alone. Even so, he kept the box on him and only opened it when he was once more safely in his office.

He stared blankly at the Seven Fragrance Jewel Herbs. They had come with *cooking instructions.*

He was *so confused.*

□

"Thank you for your pointers, Senior Sister!" Li said, bowing respectfully. He was exhausted and sweating, his green hair slick with sweat, and had some light bruises but was otherwise uninjured.

"Footwork is key, remember this," Xiulan instructed him, "you live and die by your positioning. Could the next come for instruction?"

"Yes, Senior Sister! This An Ran humbly requests to trade pointers with Senior Sister!" The next disciple entered the ring up, bouncing with enthusiasm.

They bowed, as was custom, and began their bout. The girl was enthusiastic, but her defence was full of openings. Xiulan maneuvered her blade with ease, gently chastising the girl with a swift rap to the forehead.

The girl fell back with a cry, nearly hitting the ground, but managed to remain standing.

"Aggression and enthusiasm are good, but do not forgo your defence. A more measured approach is necessary. Now, again."

The girl nodded, struck again, and took her lesson to heart. They traded a few more blows, with Xiulan looking for things to correct. Feet were smacked into the right position. Arms were guided gently. And the girl's blade was struck from her hands when she let her grip loosen.

"Adequate for now, but you need more experience. Train diligently, disciple."

"Thank you for your pointers, Senior Sister!" the lightly bruised girl panted, bowing in respect.

Xiulan nodded her head. "This will be all for today, disciples. This year is the Dueling Peak Summit, the tournament for our generation. The best of you will be chosen to come along and observe the proceedings. Continue to polish your technique and cultivate your strength."

"Thank you for your instruction, Senior Sister!" the voices shouted, and Xiulan departed.

She strode swiftly through the compound and managed to reach her room without any more interruption.

She entered her room and performed the most important action of the day.

Eating lunch.

She let out a sigh, as she was finally alone. Training others was so taxing. She knew why the other teachers had no time for fools. Still, sometimes the clumsy movements of the students did provide valuable insight. And it was good to have "the Demon-Slaying Orchid" inspiring the disciples to greater heights.

She loathed the name but bore it without flinching—even as the guilt ate at her. Even as everybody else forgot those who had died in the search. "A great victory!" they proclaimed, even as her sleep was disturbed by nightmares.

The praises lavished on her had been high. Cultivation materials and more instruction had been spent like water on her. Yet . . . they had not improved her cultivation nearly as much a simple meal and a revelation from a master. Her number of blades had grown from eight to twelve, but that was her musings on the nature of connections, more than the spiritual pills.

While the eyes of the Elders brought great rewards, it also brought tremendous pressure. She was to win the Tournament at the Dueling Peaks—not just bring glory to the Sect, as there was middling in power for the Azure Hills, but she was commanded to win it outright.

She had even been given a leave of absence so she could go out into the world and train, coinciding with the spring melt. Her honourable father was as good as his word, and the Crimson Demon's Tooth was now a plough.

Still, she would be taking a roundabout route to Master Jin's farm to try to lose any pursuers. The heavens knew even more men had come out of the woodwork since she had returned. Her suitors were weak, and they were arrogant. Completely and utterly unsuitable.

Just thinking about it made her bite down a bit harder than necessary.

She served herself another bowl of rice.

How quickly the bag of rice disappeared. The Sect Elders had taken their due and left her with half of it, which was frustrating in the extreme. She suppressed her negative emotions. She would soon be able to meet the hidden Master again, and hopefully her stay would be measured in months, rather than mere days.

Soon, she would be able to see Master Jin and Senior Sister again.

Soon, she would be able to feel at peace again.

CHAPTER 42

A LULL

It was that odd moment, at the end of the year and the beginning of another. There were always so many events crammed into these months and then, all of a sudden, there was a drought of activities until the spring. It was a kind of lull in the world, as most people just seemed to be waiting for spring.

The New Year was a time for reflection. Reflecting on my choices over the last year, I can safely say that I didn't regret a single one—especially the decision to leave the Sect. Hell, transport me back in time, and I'd do it all over again.

Things had been good to me here. Mainly the people and what we'd done together.

I had always been a fan of festivals, even the mostly overpriced crap they were back Before.

Wandering around with a pack of friends, shooting the shit, and having a good time? Sign me up.

While the Solstice was held in the village, as many people as could be spared had gone to Verdant Hill for the actual New Year. Hong Yaowu could certainly put on a party—but it was *nothing* compared to what had happened at Verdant Hill.

Fireworks and an entire town-wide party had been an interesting experience. Almost as interesting as the amount of stupid shit the drunks got up to.

You know, I never really liked New Year's celebrations before I had gone to one here. The ones back in the Before had been so boring to me. Sit around—normally we'd be at home because it was so goddamn cold—and watch the ball drop. Sure, there were some parties and stuff, but it never really felt like as much of an *event* as the Lunar New Year was.

Or maybe I just hadn't gone to the right parties. I certainly liked the Lunar New Year more than anything I had done Before.

Most of our time in Verdant Hill had been spent in a buzzed haze or eating something. Elder Xian eventually got so sloshed that he started singing the same song about the whore that Meiling had, his arm wrapped around Bao's shoulders. Meimei had left out of embarrassment, dragging me along with her, as the town got increasingly rowdy.

We had visited Tingfeng and Meihua, the latter of whom was beginning to show pregnancy. It would still be a couple of months, and she was due in the spring.

I had also finalized some deals and checked on the progress of some glass merchants. The house needed proper windows. I currently didn't have any, as I was too worried about heat loss during the winter, and I could just open the door if I wanted to air everything out.

Now, though, with spring on the way and the days already starting to get a bit warmer after the Lunar New Year, it was time to complete everything I needed to get done.

There was paradoxically less—and more—work in the winter. It was a bit surreal to be teaching this stuff to animals, but they took to it rather well. These were the standard repairs, as well as feeding the animals, though there was nothing to grow and tend to besides the Spirit Herbs. But where there was a lack of labour, there was a massive increase in planning, now that I actually had some time.

Fields needed to be plotted, seed considered, and logistics codified. It was a lot of work deciding everything. I had been keeping track of my food consumption—and that of my disciples—to see how much I could sell the next year and roughly how much I could grow. I was also thinking of things that I would need in the future.

It was boring work, frustrating work, drawing on half-remembered logistics lessons that I had never really had to use. It was stressful, especially now that I was guaranteed to have another mouth to feed with Meiling. I never wanted her to go hungry.

If I wasn't constantly reviewing my numbers, I was working on other things.

Like making good on my promise to my disciples.

□

"Now, that's all the questions. Everybody ready?" Bi De's Great Master stood before them at the head of the room, his arms behind his back. They had received a test that day—not of the body, but of the mind. Bi De would endeavour to do his best. They all would.

His Great Master had spoken true: He had an enormous amount of things to teach them. From reading the characters that conveyed knowledge, to "math" and "science." It was all, according to the Master, "basic."

But it was difficult. The Great Master was a calm and patient teacher. He would explain it as many times as was needed. Though they still had difficulty communicating without Sister Ri Zu, he could tell if they were confused or not understanding the material.

Unfortunately, there was a great lack of understanding on Brother Chun Ke's part. It was vexing that he lagged behind so greatly, but Bi De spoke not a word of rebuke to his brother. His head wound still caused him difficulty some days, and thus he was slower in learning. His boundless physical energy coursed through his body, and when forced to sit for long periods, he began to fidget.

His self-control was lacking, but if he had not been rebuked by the Master, how was it Bi De's place to do the same? They cultivated different styles. Brother Chun Ke required much exercise and play to reach his potential and seemed to gain limited value from meditating—not that Brother Chun Ke's style allowed him to sit still for too long. It was so overwhelming for Chun Ke at times that the Master had to send him outside to run laps before coming back in.

Bi De put it out of his mind and focused on the numbers he had been given. Something, deep in his soul, told him that the characters he was using were wrong. That one was supposed to be a line that was horizontal with the ground, wasn't it? This one was straight up and down. And the number two should be two lines, and not this strange, swooping shape? He didn't know *how* he knew this, but it was a little itch in the back of his head.

He ignored it. This was the Great Master's profound wisdom. It was naturally superior to any gut instinct Bi De could have, because it came directly from his Lord.

Though that same gut instinct did seem to concede that this was an easier way to do the problems he had been given, especially when arranged in one of the Math Formations.

He held the piece of chalk in his beak as he swiftly completed the problems set before him. While his slate was small, Brother Chun Ke had an entire slab of stone in order to practise, and a large brush. Sister Pi Pa had the fine dexterity that she would be able to have a small slate; she too had been given a larger one, so that Brother Chun Ke did not feel like he was different.

There was a splash, and Wa Shi slapped his fins on the water, looking smug. This new trough allowed him a great amount of maneuverability and allowed him to partake of the lesson as well. At first, the fish had cared little for the Great Master's teachings, content with his lot in life. Then, the Great Master had said he would give him a small parcel of food for every correct answer.

Now, Wa Shi was his most dedicated and skilled student. The Master nodded at the fish and went to look over the answers to his questions. Bi De redoubled his efforts.

After Bi De completed his task, he let out a call to inform the Great Master and waited. He received a nod, and the Great Master went to look over his answers.

In the end, it was a perfect score.

"Good job, *Bi De*," his Master complimented quietly, as he fed Wa Shi his promised reward. The glutton eagerly ate his fill.

The next to finish was Sister Tigu, who got but a single question wrong. Though he assumed that this might have been on purpose. She was picked up and placed in the Master's lap, so that they could review what she had done wrong. A mere miscarrying of a number, something easily fixed. But she remained in her place, purring contentedly after she was done.

Finally, it was time for Chun Ke and Pi Pa. The boar was nervous, shuffling his trotters, while Sister Pi Pa was calm, awaiting judgement.

The Master gazed upon them, his face pulled into a slight frown.

"*Pi Pa*, you got the same answers wrong as *Chun Ke*," he stated, and the sow raised her head primly. The Master's gaze held no recrimination.

"It's fine to be loyal, *Pi Pa*, but harming yourself and holding yourself back serves no place here. Everybody learns at their own pace, and I'll spend as much time as I need to with him."

Pi Pa frowned and looked at the floor, embarrassed that her plot had been discovered. "Now, I'm going to ask that you do this again, while I go over things with Chun Ke. I know you can do better than this."

The sow nodded.

The Master then sat with his slowest disciple, affectionately rubbing the top of his head.

"All right, you did a good job here. You *tried.* I can see that you were showing your work, which is good. It helps us to figure out where you went wrong . . ."

Bi De followed his Master and sat down beside him, to better see how he was making corrections.

As the Great Master had once said:

'Sometimes we learn more from failure than success.'

He would endeavour to put this saying into practise.

CHAPTER 43

BROTH AND ICE

Bi De was meditating upon his Math Formations when the disciples were called by the Great Master. His voice was as strong as always, but today it had an undercurrent of tension.

He, being a loyal disciple, swiftly rose and accompanied his Master outside. It was a black day. The clouds were ominous, and the wind was like daggers hurled through the air. Something terrible was brewing on the horizon.

He wondered what the matter was. Had something vexed his Great Master? The thing that dared would be swiftly destroyed by his spurs!

The Great Master gestured for him to sit, and he gracefully did, then waited for the rest of the disciples to arrive. The Great Master sat still and appeared to be meditating. His fellow disciples assembled and prepared to receive his wisdom.

"I . . . will be eating one of the chickens," his Great Master stated.

Bi De froze at the statement and bowed his head. He'd known this day would once more come. One of the hens had stopped laying eggs. She was plump, and full of Qi, and yet . . . she had no spark still. Even after receiving a Name of Power, *Bun Te* was just as she had been.

The rest of the disciples . . . Well, Wa Shi looked eager, the piscine glutton just happy for food. Tigu snorted contemptuously and gave him a nasty smirk. One of his kin was to be consumed. It was a petty gesture. Pi Pa nodded her head.

Of them all, only Brother Chun Ke looked worried and nosed at the Great Master. He smiled sadly at the large one.

"If she . . . was like you are, then she would not be eaten. People who can *think* are not food," his Great Master reassured them, but Bi De was unconcerned. He had long ago deduced that.

Still, it was good to hear it from the Great Master's own mouth.

Chun Ke oinked sadly, gazing up with piteous eyes. "Death is not always a bad thing, *Chun Ke*. She will feed us and make us strong. Just like the rabbits and the deer, and the other fish. This is the same as that, okay?"

Chun Ke whined but allowed his Great Master to rise.

The axe was retrieved, and Bun Te was taken. Bi De watched, unflinching, as her life went on to nourish the Great Master.

With a single blow, the deed was done. He bowed his head in respect, to the one who had given both her life and Qi back to the Lord.

Brother Chun Ke wailed.

↔

There was a storm outside. One of winter's last hurrahs. The wind was howling like a demon, the snow was flying so fast and thick it made the world white. You couldn't see your hand in front of your face, and anybody caught outside would be in for a bad time. It was one of the storms that *defined* winter.

I was, naturally, enjoying it immensely from inside my house. The fire was crackling merrily away, and the house was warm and dry. I had finally gotten my chicken soup. I'd been a bit leery about killing the hen . . . but she showed no signs of intelligence beyond what chickens should show, so I made the decision. It always hits a bit different when it's an animal you own, rather than an already slain chicken in a market. You took care of them. You raised them from a chick. And then . . .you took everything away from them.

It was too much for some people. Some farmers responded by hardening their hearts and caring little for their animals. Me? Well, I just wouldn't take my food for granted. I don't think I have it in me to go vegetarian, either. I'd give them the best life I could, so that when they did go, they had actually had a bit of a life.

I took another spoonful of broth. It was gods-damn *fantastic* chicken soup. Best I've ever had, even from the Before. Thanks, Bunty. I held out a bit of chicken for Tigger, and the cat eagerly ate, cleaning off my fingers with her tongue. Out of all of them, she was the most enthusiastic about this meal—even more than Washy.

I sighed and reached down beside me again, rubbing my Chunky boy's head. He snuffled sadly. Peppa was leaned up on the other side of him, also refusing to eat any of the chicken. I sighed. Chunky did not look good sad. How a two-hundred-pound boar could look so much like a kicked puppy was beyond me.

"You don't have to eat it if you don't want to," I said simply. "I understand. But this *is* what she died for." Chunky gave a sad oink and shook his head. "That's all right. Do you want to have any meat in the future, or just no more meat from the farm?"

He tapped his chin twice on the ground, indicating the second part of my question, and shook his head again.

I nodded and scratched his head affectionately. Peppa was staring at the meat but shook her head when she caught me looking at her.

Chunky nudged her, and she somehow managed to blush at getting caught. She wanted it but wasn't eating any because Chunky didn't want any. She daintily took the offering, nodding her head at the taste.

The other animal who did not partake was Big D. But I have to admit, I would have been pretty concerned if he did. When I had explained why I was killing the hen . . . Big D just accepted it. And not just accept, but he seemed to *approve*.

I still remember as he looked on, unflinching. I had made it as quick as I could—a clean death.

He'd simply bowed his head and then returned to the house. That he had already rationalized it was both a relief, and a bit concerning. But . . . Big D seemed to think that they were almost a separate species. He mated with the females and joined in on the cognitive tests I gave them, watching for any sign of intelligence . . . but after they all turned up failures, even the other rooster, he'd lost interest in them. He seemed disappointed.

I'm going to be honest. I don't really know how to deal with his problems. It was something I certainly had no experience in. All I could do was be there if he wanted to talk, I guess.

I finished my soup, then turned back to my thoughts on where to go from here. Plans changed all the time in light of new information, but I should at least have a plan.

I mean, take the bath for example. First, I'd wanted a fire crystal and a water crystal, to produce water and heat. But when you could literally lift the entire tub up, dunk it in the river to fill it with water, and then flash-heat it with Qi? Well, you don't really *need* those things, do you? Necessity was the mother of invention, after all, and if you don't need something, you tend to leave it.

Or at least, it gets put on the back burner. I still did want them, if only for convenience when Meimei got here. I had built an entire setup to heat the water faster, with bellows and a chimney . . . and then I ended up not really using it. Trees and wood were important resources, and I didn't want to start clear-cutting my land to fuel everything.

It was good it was still cold enough for me to freeze the broth. I could have it for a while longer. One of the biggest things I had to contend with was preservation. I already had a pseudo-refrigerator in the river room, where the colder water ran over my food, but I needed the ice to last.

There was always the pit method, which people here already used. I could just dig a big hole, cover it, and hope the ice didn't melt. It would take a while, but that would still only last a couple of months. I knew that because Meimei had shown me Hong Yaowu's storage area, and there wasn't any ice left.

I frowned as I tried to come up with something. Could I just cheat again? Qi reinforcement made things more durable. Could I just use it on ice, and have it last longer?

I absently picked up two pieces of wood. One, I reinforced with Qi; the other I didn't. I placed both ends in the fire and waited.

The unreinforced one caught before the reinforced one, but it was a near thing. There's only so much Qi something can hold, after all. Only so much stronger it can get. Push too much into it, and it will break, or even explode. I talk about how I'm just kind of "shoving Qi at things," but . . . well, it is a *bit* more delicate than that. Normally, it does require quite a bit of concentration to fill something new up with your essence and make everything perfect, but this was one of the few things I was good at.

The shoots of plants were very delicate, after all. One had to have a light touch. That was probably why the new initiates of Cloudy Sword Sect were put on plant duty. To improve Qi control. Or . . . maybe it was just because we were expendable labour.

Probably the latter.

In any case, I had another experiment to run. I walked out into the cold, howling blizzard, and got some more ice from the river.

Honestly, the improvement wasn't much. It took about twenty seconds longer for it to start melting. But it was movement in the right direction.

Well, no time like the present to teach the scientific method.

→

The thing about science is that we always think of the cool shit. The giant spaceships, the cars, the guns. What most people gloss over is that most of the time, unless you're super passionate, science is super god-damn boring.

I was *literally* watching ice melt, so I could see if Qi could make it melt *less*, helping it last longer and making it so I wouldn't need a complicated storage area.

Most of my experiments were duds. I had several groups near the fire and then leading outwards towards the river room. There was just a set amount of Qi that ice could take before it shattered. And it was mundane ice, not the stuff Young Mistresses magicked up, so it wasn't harder than steel and twice as deadly.

Now I had a bunch of ice all over my house, arranged into two groups.

"Washy, mark down twenty seconds again." The fish nodded happily. "Seconds" being the intervals that I was tapping my leg at. They were all pretty even, so it was good enough for taking time. Honestly, he was the most interested in this—but only after I'd told him it was for food preservation, of course. The rest of my disciples had gotten bored with the repetitive nature of what we were doing. Big D still checked in occasionally, but the rest of them had gone off to play or hunt.

Like I said, watching ice melt was *boring*, even if it could be important.

I sighed as I tried to reinforce the ice again. Maybe if I put it in a different way? I carefully began constructing a horizontal lattice—

It shattered. Nope, not *that* way. Maybe it was a mass thing?

I stared around at the wet spots on my floor.

"You know what, let's call it a day. I'm going out to find Chunky," I decided. "You get back to the river room, okay, Washy?"

The fish nodded his head, slapping his fins in frustration. *Yeah, I know little buddy. Maybe we'll have better luck tomorrow.*

CHAPTER 44

A FOX AND A "DEER"

Tigu stalked along the property of her Master, inspecting it for any traces of interlopers. It was a thankless task, but one infinitely more exciting than whatever the Master was currently working on. Really, watching ice melt? It was surely for some profound reason, and she would praise him and allow him to pet her when he figured it out, but such things were beneath her.

She had a patrol to maintain. She had to train her body. She consented to learning the strange numbers the Master taught, but sitting there was boring. She was a creature of action! She would find her Master's enemies and slay them!

But today there were no enemies. What had once been a near-constant skirmish against a tide of verminous filth had died down dramatically ever since she had slain the bandits. Bi De had said that a curse had been cleansed from the land after they defeated Sun Ken. The Master destroying it was a sign that he considered her powerful enough for her to not need the swarm of training aids, but now . . . there was nothing.

There was nothing to hunt. There was nothing to prey upon. She wasn't allowed to eat the glutton. She could peel back his armored and surprisingly thick scales anytime she liked, but the Master had forbidden her from eating those with the spark.

None of the others would trade pointers with her. Bi De was . . . well, he was. A powerful existence that currently surpassed her. She would beat him eventually, but constantly running her face into a wall was stupid. Ri Zu fled from her and was unavailable. Wa Shi would sit in his river and spit water at her, the gluttonous bastard. Chun Ke just thought it was a game, cheerily charging after her. That was enjoyable enough, but she had tried to truly trade pointers and turn it into a proper spar, once.

Once. The fight had stopped as soon as it started when she brought out her Five-Fold Blades. Sister Pi Pa's wrath had been magnificent. She was truly a most powerful brute—*Lady.* Pi Pa was a lady. Tigu would respect her and call her that. Being swallowed was a decidedly unpleasant experience, even if she had managed to fight her way out.

It had been quite a good workout, until the preening cock had put a stop to her fun. Now Pi Pa spent her time glaring and avoiding Tigu while the Master was away. A pity, that they were so intimidated by her might.

It's not like she wanted to play with them, or anything.

Tigu sighed with boredom. She didn't even have the Master's training aid! Her claws had finally defeated it two days ago, and though the Master had promised her another, it was not ready for her yet.

She wished she still had it. She wished for *strength.* Growing in strength was only right! Eating meat was only proper, no matter how much Chun Ke wailed and blubbered, the oaf.

She frowned as she thought about the Master's story again. His tale of why he came here. Ah, why did the Master content himself with this? He could rule this world with ease; she was sure of it. His strength was beyond every other man! Contenting himself with only the land around him, it was just so strange!

You may go, if you wish. But you will always have a place here.

She could go off on an adventure. She could just step out for a few days. Find some beast and slay it. Go on one of these "adventures."

She shook her head and pushed those thoughts from her mind. No, she could not. She could not do that—the Master needed her here. She was the most reliable. She was the most comforting. She was the one who understood him the most!

Even if she didn't understand why he said he had given up power. It was surely a ruse, wasn't it?

She stared at the boundary between the land and the outside. She shook her head, then turned around. Maybe . . . maybe next time. Maybe she would expand the Master's territory! Yes, next time she went out, she would go and conquer in his name.

She turned and began to head back to the Master. She would allow him to pat her again, for deciding to expand his land. Yes, that was what she would do.

Though she wondered what that thundering sound was. She approached swiftly, only to see the Master assaulting the frozen ground furiously while Wa Shi looked on and slapped his fins on the bank of the river.

That . . . that was a big hole he was digging. Chun Ke had climbed in after him, and was using his tusks and nose to aid the Master's quest.

Was it some sort of training? She supposed cutting through the hardened soil might prove some challenge. And it was better than working on the infernal numbers.

Tigu hopped into the hole. The earth could not withstand the might of her blades!

□

When I'd first left for the Azure Hills, I had planned to be a hermit. I had planned to do everything myself and visit the least amount of people possible. If I *hadn't* been a cultivator, that plan likely would have killed me. But then again, if I hadn't been a cultivator, I probably wouldn't have decided to go full pioneer in the first place. There were too many things that could go wrong.

But to hell with that mindset. This may have been xianxia land, but that didn't mean everybody was a shithead, going for the backstabs and the betrayal like in my old sect. I had friends. I had a soon-to-be family. Even Xiulan was pretty cool, and she was a cultivator. The point was, I had people who would *help*. And that made everything worth it.

I needed to get a move on if I wanted to have the house done in time for Meimei's arrival. The days were getting warmer. I had spent a lot of precious time digging a giant pit to store ice. Like . . . a *lot* of ice. The frozen ground didn't do much to stop me from digging out a nice big underground storage area. Honestly, it was mostly borne out of frustration with the fact that my ice experiments weren't going that well. The several tons of ice now sitting pretty in their bunker was me finally snapping.

In other words, I had been procrastinating on finishing up my house, because I had my attention captured by a dumb project—one I had borked up. By the time I realised how much work I had put into it, I had stripped an entire small lake of its ice. It was good stress relief though. Tigger was *really* good at cutting it into perfect blocks.

And making ice sculptures, once I showed her how. Though I didn't really know how to feel about the life-sized replica of me, standing triumphantly atop a pile of defeated enemies.

They all had their quirks, I suppose. And really, it was a *fantastic* sculpture. She had even managed to make it look like I had beads of sweat rolling down my bare chest. I . . . I guess I should probably encourage it. It was art! She had a hobby!

My feet plodded along the melty path back home from Verdant Hill. The Magistrate had sent me a letter, telling me my glass had arrived, just in time for me to be able to finish my house before the wedding. This was the last step. The Xong brothers had offered their help, and I would be taking them up on it.

I could probably do it all myself, but the question was: Why? Having help would cost me a bit of food, and I got some extra hands and some company. It was always a pain in the ass installing windows and sanding floors. That stuff was boring as hell. Even when you could do it as fast as I could. Many hands make light work, after all.

The brothers were out in the woods when I called on them, so their mother invited me in to wait. They still lived with their parents—most people here did, with multiple generations living in the same house. Honestly, it was pretty nice. I was never a fan of the "out at eighteen" mindset a lot of people had in the Before.

The matriarch of the Xong family, Nezin Hu Li, was appropriately named—*Huli* being the word for fox. I could tell where Yun Ren got his looks from. She had the same fox-like eyes as her son, surrounded by laugh lines.

"Please, make yourself at home, Master Jin," she said demurely as she brewed us some tea. "You've aided this Hu Li's sons greatly, and she would like to thank you for it."

"Please, just Jin. I'm good friends with Yun Ren and Gou Ren. There's no need for you to be so formal with me," I told her, and took a sip of tea.

"Well, if that's whatcha want, then it's all good, yeah?" I nearly spat out my tea at the swap from "formal, demure host," to whatever the *hell* her accent was. She sounded almost like she was from *Brooklyn*. Let me tell you, that coming out from a little Asian lady was *hilarious*.

Her grin was so wide it split her face in two as she saw my amused look.

"Where's *that* from?" I asked.

"A remnant of my tribe," she said without the accent. "A week's journey north, through the forest." She swapped back. "So, you're grabbin' one of my brats fo' tha summah?"

I chuckled. "Yeah. Gou Ren is going to be helping me and learning about how to grow rice like I do it. Should improve yields here by a lot, but it's also quite a bit more work."

She nodded. "My boy likes to complain, but he always does good work. Take care of him, ya hear?"

I nodded. "Gou's a good friend. And you're welcome to come visit whenever you want."

She smiled again. "I might just take you up on that. Little Mei will need a woman to talk to, in any case. There are some things men just can't handle," she said authoritatively.

I nodded. She *would* be better at handling the "womanly issues" Meimei might need help with. If Meiling wanted to include me in that kind of stuff, I was absolutely fine with helping, but if she wasn't, that was her choice.

She seemed a little shocked at my easy surrender, her vulpine eyes opening completely. They were a lovely amber colour, the same as both her sons.

As quickly as the shock had come, it left. "So, how did you and your husband meet, anyways?" I asked.

"Oh? Ten Ren got hurt in the forest, and I found him. He thought I was some kind of fox spirit at first, and I thought he was some kind of ascended monkey. He shaves them off now, but back then—his sideburns! Well, I nursed him back to health, and he ended up challenging my father to a hunting contest to win my hand—"

I listened to the rather funny story of Ten Ren's increasingly mad ploys to win the hand of a tribal girl.

Finally, he just snuck in in the middle of the night and *kidnapped* her. Which was apparently what both she and her father had been *waiting* for, judging by the fond sighs and blush she got when relaying *that* piece of information.

All right, that's a piece of culture shock, but judging by the story it was consensual, so I'm not gonna judge.

"And then my uncle looked *right* at him. Ten Ren always says he got away cleanly, but don't believe a word," she told me conspiratorially.

"—I swear the wood is faulty. It split right down the middle, *again*," I heard Yun Ren's raised voice exclaim from outside.

"*My bow wasn't faulty*. Say that again, and I'll beat your teeth into the back of your skull. It's something else. That thing is cursed, I tell you, cursed!"

The brothers entered, looking quite upset, while Hu Li narrowed her eyes.

"And what are you two grumbling about now? Yun Ren's mystery deer?" she demanded.

Both boys jumped. "Mother!" Yun Ren yelped.

"Jin?" Gou Ren called.

Hu Li glared at her sons. "It wasn't even an hour from the village!" Yun Ren protested. "It had torn up a bunch of snow to get at a patch of still-green grass. I tried to get it, and Gou's bow broke."

Gou Ren grumbled.

Hu Li frowned and raised an eyebrow at Gou Ren. "So, it's real, then, and not a tall story?"

Her younger son nodded. "I don't think it's a Spirit Beast. It looks too dumb. Here, let me show you. Yun Ren can't draw worth a damn, and you told me to get what it looked like."

"I can draw just fine . . ." his brother muttered while Gou Ren got a piece of charcoal and started drawing on the table.

My first thought when the drawing was done was, *Gou Ren is really good at making things look cute.*

The second was, *That's a goddamn* moose.

Well, if there are sugar maple trees . . .

Hu Li looked a bit confused. "A thunder-hoof? This far south?"

"Hey, that's kinda cute. Nice drawing, Gou," I said, looking at the little picture. *Look at those doe eyes!* He blushed. *How could you mistake a moose for a deer, Yun Ren?!*

"Yeah, the babies are cute. You won't be saying that when it grows up bigger than the headman's *house*," Hu Li shot back.

Okay, *what*?

"And they're *not* Spirit Beasts?" I asked incredulously.

"Some of 'em are. Mostly, they're just *big*. They live up in the northern wastes, out in the Sea of Snow. This one is real lost to be this far south."

What the hell, xianxia land.

"Do you . . . want me to chase it off?" I finally asked.

She shook her head. "It'll clear off on its own. And it won't hurt us none, as long as we *don't poke it with arrows*," she snarled, glaring at her sons. They had the grace to look embarrassed. "They're good fortune, anyways. It'll stay for a while, then head back to the wastes."

She shook her head.

"Now! You came here for my boys! Take them, before they cause any more trouble!" she demanded, shooing us out of their house.

Both of her sons started whining about needing a change of clothes, and she relented. She leaned against the wall of their house as we packed up.

". . . you know, sometimes the tribe's hunters are around the area where you live. I'll pass the word on that you're open for business, if you want some things from further up."

"Just tell them to enter through the gate. Big D and Tigger don't take kindly to trespassers," I warned. *Especially if those trespassers were carrying weapons.*

"I'll tell 'em, don't you worry. I'd tell you to take good care of little Mei . . . but I don't think you need to be *told* to do that."

I nodded.

"Well, take care now, and don't be afraid to tan their hides if they muck up," Hu Li said with a wave. "*Really*, trying to hunt a thunderhoof," she muttered.

I resisted the urge to go running off and find the baby moose. I had a job to do. The house had to get done. *Maybe I can see if I can find it after I finish?*

Anyways, we hadn't spent long packing up before we were approached by Meimei, Yao Che, and Xian the Elder.

"What are you boys up to?" Che asked leadingly.

"They're going to help me with my house. Gotta get the windows in and the floors done, so I asked for a hand."

"Oh, glasswork?" Che remarked, not sounding surprised at all. "Don't leave it to these two miscreants, if you want a fine touch. I've little to do right now, and I want to see what these brats have been squawking about!"

Hong Xian nodded. "I would see your home as well," he asked politely.

Well, the more the merrier.

I shrugged. "Hop in," I said, banging the side of my cart. "We'll be there in a couple hours at my pace. Meimei, you coming too?"

Meiling looked like she wanted to but had a silent conversation with her father. He shook his head slightly, and she nodded.

"I'll stay here this time," she decided. "Let some things be a surprise."

Well, it wasn't too long till we were married . . .

I scratched Rizzo's head and nodded at Meimei.

"Well . . . I'll see you soon, then." The rest of the men seemed to be busy with the cart, so I darted in and kissed her on the forehead.

She giggled and swatted me away.

There was a bit of a nervous flutter in my stomach, as I would be showing my father-in-law around my house for the first time. He would like it. I *knew* he would like it.

I picked up the cart once they were all settled in and started running.

CHAPTER 45

STATUES AND A HOUSE

There was less rocking than Xian had expected. They were travelling forwards at a terrifying pace, the wind in his hair . . . and yet the cart was nearly completely stable. Not a single piece of glass rattled against another while Jin's stride utterly consumed the ground in front of him.

If there was one thing Xian never thought would happen, it was to be carted around by a cultivator. But ever since Jin had shown up, the improbable seemed to become rather more likely to happen.

He had travelled this fast only once before, under decidedly more dire circumstances, in a vastly more uncomfortable ride. There had been horses screaming, soldiers shouting, and arrows *thunk*-ing into wood.

Instead of a freckled maid shouting obscenities, an Archivist screaming in a *much* higher pitch than said maid, and himself praying to whatever gods would listen, Brother Che was looking mostly bored, while Yun and Gou argued about what meat tasted the best. Jin occasionally interjected over his shoulder.

Yun Ren had championed rabbit, Gou Ren beef, and Jin chicken.

"Chicken?! But it tastes so bland!" Gou Ren scoffed.

"Bland?! It has a lovely subtle flavour! And it takes seasonings so well!" Jin shot back. "And fried—fried chicken is the ultimate dish!"

"All of you youngsters are wrong! Pork is best!" Brother Che derided them. "Sausage and dumplings are what a man needs to grow big and strong!" He flexed his muscles, bulging from a lifetime at the forge. Both the Xong brothers went quiet at the declaration but glared mutinously. Jin just laughed. Even into his forties, Che's muscles rivaled Jin's in size—and Che *wasn't* a cultivator.

Xian liked deer himself. Both his late wife and daughter made *excellent* roast venison. He absently watched the passing trees, remembering the speeding carriage. No evidence needed to get to the court the next day, else their heads would roll. The lack of urgency was letting him enjoy the speeding ride.

Court intrigue was hazardous to one's health. Doubly so when you got involved by accident.

He shook his head to rid himself of the memories. Even the years couldn't make him think fondly on those terrifying days, though the times that came after had more than made up for them.

The journey to Jin's house, which was nearly the same distance away from their village as Hong Yaowu was from Verdant Hill, took mere hours instead of days. And Jin wasn't even winded. He looked a little nervous, shooting glances repeatedly at Xian, but it was understandable. What man wasn't nervous about showing his future father-in-law his home?

The gate to his land was large and sturdy, with a maple leaf and the amusing "Beware of Chicken" sign displayed prominently. The Xong brothers and his own daughter had thought the sign was hilarious.

And there too was the aforementioned chicken. He had seen it before at his village, briefly, shrouded in dusk on the rooftop.

In the bright light of the day, his true colouration was revealed. His plumage was more vibrant than any painting Xian had seen, including in the Palace of the Pale Moon Lake City. His red neck and breast looked like fire captured in plumage. The blues were like the most perfect of sapphires. The green on his tail, pristine jade. His talons and spurs shone like silvery metal, and his comb was a deeper red than what the noble ladies wore on their lips. The fox-fur vest he wore paled in comparison to his magnificence.

The rooster's gaze was stern but not judgmental. A proud guardian. The rooster bowed to them, as Jin and the cart passed the threshold, welcoming them into Jin's "Fa Ram."

The Xong brothers bowed back, as much as they could sitting down. Che started to bow, and then his eyes caught on something else.

"What the hells?!" he gaped.

"We didn't tell you about the General That Commands the Winter?" Yun Ren asked cheekily.

Xian started laughing. Meiling had told him, but it was one thing to hear about the massive golem made out of snow, and another to see it. It was a happy-looking fellow, with a dumb grin and a giant hat coloured black with ashes. It was a creation that would have taken their entire village a week, and Jin had apparently built it in a day for the fun of it.

Jin continued his walk, bypassing a small shack and continuing down the hill to a small river—until Jin suddenly started to slow, his mouth open in shock and a bright blush forming all over his freckled cheeks.

"Tigu'er . . ." What came out of Jin's mouth was almost a whine. Gou Ren and Yun Ren burst out laughing, and Che sounded like he was choking on something. Xian turned from "The General" and looked forward.

There was a little cat, still a kitten really, sitting in between a bunch of ice sculptures and looking like it had just managed to slay a thousand mice. It bowed to Jin.

A bunch of ice sculptures depicted Jin, nude, in various martial poses. Trampling on a giant rat. Staring boldly forwards, his hands on his hips. One even had him in a one-handed handstand, flipping over a boar.

Xian was honestly impressed by that one. How had the Spirit Beast managed to balance it? And the detail was *incredibly* fine in some areas while others were a bit off. Amateurish, compared to the sculptures he had seen in the Palace, and some of the anatomy was questionable. Some parts were too big, and on other sculptures they were too small. But it was all honestly impressive, considering they were made by a cat.

"These . . . these are *very nice*, Tigu'er . . ." Jin managed to get out, ignoring the cackles behind him. The kitten preened at the praise, rubbing up against Jin's legs. "But . . . how about you . . . *diversify* your sculptures. It'll make you better, to have other things to practise."

The kitten considered and then nodded. She hopped up onto his shoulders and lay atop his head. The Xong brothers were gasping for air, and Che had begun crying. The kitten glared at them.

"I'm sure they're just overcome with emotion at your beautiful sculptures," Jin said, his eye twitching, and his face crimson. "Now, how about I put these in the ice room, so they don't melt?"

The kitten slid its way into the front of his shirt and yowled happily.

"Is the *weapon* accurate?" Che managed to choke out, tears streaming from his eyes. He pointed at the sculpture's . . . *bits*. One of the parts that Xian had a feeling was *not* correct.

The kitten looked confused by the question, looking to where Che was pointing and then to the *actual* sword that sculpture was holding. It nodded its head.

Jin's face screwed up, and actual steam started to billow off the mortified boy's shoulders. Che *howled*, doubling over. "Looks like Meimei is going to have her work cut out for her!" Gou Ren, caught in his mirth, leaned back so far he fell out of the cart, thumping onto his back and continuing to gasp for breath.

For a moment, Xian was worried that even Jin's patience would have limits, especially with such a topic. Jin was clearly embarrassed . . . But he seemed to find the whole thing at least a little funny. He took the laughter in stride, without retaliation. An even temper. Xian approved.

"Well, make yourselves at home—I gotta . . . yeah," Jin managed, sighing at the sculptures. His hands spasmed briefly, like he wanted to do away with the embarrassment. The moment passed. He quickly, but *carefully,* collected the sculptures and began carting them off.

Xian took a good look at the front of the house. The style was unfamiliar to him. Yun Ren had originally said that the house was bigger than Xian's own, and he had been impressed. His home was the largest in Hong Yaowu, though a good portion of it was storage for the medicine his family created. The actual livable section was a bit more modest, but it was no hovel.

This, however, was a veritable *manor.* There were more foundations roughly marked with stakes outside. The other completed buildings were an outhouse, what Xian assumed to be a bathhouse, and a large stone oven. It was not a walled compound. Instead, there was what looked like a veranda surrounding the entire house, with the tiled roof extending past the outer walls.

"I think he might be compensating for something." Gou Ren snickered, gesturing towards Jin's lower half. Yun and Che laughed along with him, while Jin rolled his eyes.

They bundled the glass into the house, the rest of their party having stopped laughing for long enough to actually do some work. They were greeted at the door by Pi Pa, the sow brightening up and bowing politely when she saw Xian. The entrance was on a slightly lower level than the rest of the house and covered with easy-to-clean slabs of stone. The Xong brothers took off their wet shoes at the entrance, and he did the same, stepping onto the lacquered and waxed hardwood floors.

They were so smooth they were almost slippery. He shuffled his feet, and not a single splinter threatened his socks. They were also a lot warmer than Xian had been expecting. Gou Ren was allowed to set down his load

. . . and then he was promptly bowled over by Chun Ke, the boar excitedly nosing him.

Xian took the opportunity to look around the house. The main room was warm and inviting, with a divider and a bed, as well as a warm hearth. There were several large cushions around the fire and a table that had what looked like a blanket under its top, to warm the legs of those who sat under it.

Xian would have to steal the idea. It looked comfortable. There were several half-finished projects as well. One was what looked like some gears from a waterwheel, each of them with a different number of teeth, and one that had been snapped in half. Strange-looking stone that seemed to be almost *poured* into its shape. A box filled with empty frames that could be slid in and out.

If this had been the entirety of the house, Xian would have been satisfied. But there was also a large kitchen, another storage room, and an entire second floor—as well as the famous "river room," complete with a gluttonous carp. It eyed them excitedly as they entered . . . and then realised that they didn't have any food. It made a noise that sounded suspiciously like "feh!" and went back to sleep.

Yao Che nodded in appreciation as he looked around the house. "Well, *I* certainly approve. It will be a lot of work, but I see no reason why we can't get this done by the time the snows melt. A week or two to finish? Jin is cutting it close."

"A week or two?" Jin's voice called out as he entered. "I was thinking a day or two. Less if we hustle. All the flooring is cut, it just needs to be put in. And we should be able to get through all the windows today."

Yao Che raised an eyebrow and then seemed to remember he was dealing with a cultivator.

"Well, if you say so. I want to see this when it's finished! Xong brats! Get to work!"

CHAPTER 46

VENGEANCE AND HIVES

"Carefully, now, carefully!" Che demanded, rather unnecessarily. Jin was exceedingly careful with his windows. It was the most expensive part of the house, after all. Four large glass windows—three for the front, one for the back—four smaller windows, and the rest would be made of treated paper and have large shutters. The panes themselves were two layers of glass, which according to Jin would help keep the cold out.

It turned out that Jin's assessment on time would likely be accurate. The walls of the house were made of sturdy hardwood, the kind of trees that blunted axes and saws alike. They were as paper before Jin's sawblade. It tore through the planks with a harsh, almost buzzing sound, carefully arranged to exactly the size he would need for the windows.

While Jin was cutting, Che was inspecting the glasswork, taking measurements, and examining hinges. After he did that, Jin would lift them into place, while Che made sure everything joined correctly and that the glass wouldn't shatter due to any twists or warps.

The Xong brothers, meanwhile, were put to work on the floors. Gou Ren took the ground floor, while Yun Ren handled the second floor. True to Jin's words, the planks were already cut and premeasured. All that was left was to hammer them in, in the order that they were shown.

Xian observed them as they worked. The Xong brothers were moving far faster than he'd expected them to, even while seeming spectacularly bored and almost *vacant* throughout the process. Gou hefted an entire stack of twenty planks and began tossing them up to his brother—who easily caught the heavy floorboards and put them aside with a world of thanks. Their hammers drove down nails in but two strikes, as they followed the floor plan Jin had set out. Their breathing was deep and steady. Almost like his own breathing was when he had to perform the rituals of Hong Yaowu.

They noticed Jin watching their progress too. The young man was watching their progress with an unreadable expression on his face. Gou Ren made another crack about the size of the statue's parts. Jin shook his head and got back to work.

It was not backbreaking labour, but it was intensive. They toiled for hours, and the sun was starting to set, but they did indeed, finish putting in all the windows in a single day—even the one on the second story. The Xong brothers finished putting in the planks—they would be sanded, lacquered, and waxed tomorrow. Xian *expected* them to be tired from the ordeal. He certainly needed a break. Instead—

"Let's go, Chun Ke!" Gou Ren shouted, grabbing an oddly shaped stick and a disc made out of stone. His brother raced after him onto the ice, where they began a game of tackles and shoves.

"How the hells do those brats have so much energy?!" Che demanded, sitting on a stump. Xian's old friend was rubbing his back and squinting at the two youths. He winced as they collided with a bone-jarring crunch—only for both of them to start laughing and continuing on with their shoving match.

"Elder Hong, Elder Yao, it's ready," Jin said as he came back around the front of the bathhouse.

"Brother Che, Jin, *Brother*," Che scolded him. "Honestly, you're too polite for your own good!" Jin looked a bit sheepish at the reprimand, scratching the back of his head. Xian smiled at him.

"You've already called me father once. Continue that, Jin," Xian said, clapping him on the shoulder.

Jin's smile got cheeky. "Sorry, Pops, I'll keep that in mind," Jin said, putting on an inner-city accent. The kind of speech pattern that the guttersnipes, gangs and his wife used. Xian rolled his eyes at the irreverence and reached up to cuff Jin's ear. The boy dodged deftly, his smile growing wider.

There was a yelp, and an *oof* as Gou Ren flopped into view, spun end over end by Chun Ke's tackle. He groaned in pain, but didn't seem seriously hurt, despite being folded in half by the boar's charge. He popped back up, ready to go.

Jin scratched thoughtfully at his chin, but he left them to their games until he declared that the bath was ready.

↔

I splashed more water on the rock and then returned my hands to Brother Che's back, the older man sighing in contentment.

I had replaced the normal pool of water with a slab of rock, and that was being heated instead of the water. It was sauna time after a hard day of work. Che had been grimacing and pressing his hand against his back, so I decided on a bit of steam relaxation. Or "Naked with the Boys 2, Electric Boogaloo."

In any case, there had been a crack about my dangly bits from Gou Ren. Tigger's statues hadn't been anatomically correct, as she hadn't really seen me naked before. But I held my peace, even as the guys' mocking laughter filled my ears. Vengeance was a dish best served cold, after all. Though in this case, it would be hot, because we're in a steam bath . . . and I've lost control of this metaphor.

I wasn't spectacular at massages, but I knew enough not to hurt someone. And Qi makes everything easier, once you know how to use it. I remembered my father from Before, who'd had his own back pain.

"Gods damn it, why couldn't you have been born here," Che muttered. "I could have an apprentice, and my flower would still be at home, instead of all the way off in Verdant Hill. You like blacksmithing, don't you? Every man should!" he declared, then continued grumbling under his breath.

He was lamenting that Meihua wasn't married to me instead of Tingfeng. *Again*. I didn't say anything and finished working the knot out of his back. Honestly, if it wasn't for how I'd helped her out, I don't think Meihua would have liked me much. I had seen her grimaces on the way to Verdant Hill the first time. I was a bit too boisterous for her. Tingfeng was a quiet, scholarly sort. She fit the town life better too. While she had a bit of muscle, as no one was allowed to sit on their asses in Hong Yaowu, I got the feeling that she didn't like working too much. And Tingfeng's family had a couple of servants to take care of the heavier physical labour.

I kind of wondered about what Pops would think of the remark, but his eyes were simply closed, and he was at peace enjoying the steam bath. I certainly wouldn't want another man making noises about poaching my daughter's husband for his daughter.

My soon-to-be father had a build that I really should have expected but caught me by surprise anyway. He was a bit thin and wiry, but he looked strong, with well-defined muscles, and a rather nasty-looking scar on his arm. I had been expecting a bit less, but it was xianxia land.

"This is *very* nice," Xian finally declared. He looked at peace with the world, and like he was genuinely happy to be here.

I grinned back, all of my teeth showing, and slapped Che on the back. "You're done. Now we cool ourselves down . . . and start the medicinal treatment," I declared.

We all walked outside into the snow, Che stretching and grinning at his range of motion. We simply drank in the fruits of our labour: the exterior of my house looking finally like a proper home. The exterior was *very* Japanese with the engawa, or veranda that enclosed the building, even going out over the water of the river as a pseudo dock. The back river was deep enough to jump into and fish in, though fishing that close to Washy's lair was a fool's errand.

We took a couple of minutes to cool down, and then we all got back into the sauna for the second steam.

It was time for my revenge.

"Now, lay down here. This will improve the circulation of blood and allows you to sweat out even more impurities."

Gou Ren eagerly laid down. Grinning, I brought out the bundle of branches. The venik, or bundle of oak leaves and branches, would be my *instrument of death*. I mean, I was telling the truth, it did help improve circulation. But I had added a few more branches to it, thicker ones that would certainly smart when they hit.

Make dick jokes about me all day, would you? You're courting death!

Gou Ren shrieked as I slapped down the branches with a little more force than was probably necessary, onto his ass. I held him down and smiled at him.

"Jin?!" he yelped out.

"It's medicinal. It's *supposed* to feel like this." I hit him again.

"What—Elder Hong, there's no way this can be"—*smack*—"*son of a whore, Jin!*"

Xian stroked his beard, considering for a moment. Hitting somebody obviously wasn't medicinal.

We had our first father-son bonding moment when he pronounced death upon the Xong brothers and Che. "I do believe that this will have significant benefits," he declared.

I grinned. Gou paled. I could feel him struggle a bit—really, far more than I should be able to.

I had some suspicions about Yun and Gou. But . . . well, I would wait and see.

I cheerfully worked him over with the branches and then tossed him in the river.

I made it back just in time for Yun Ren to try and bolt, his eyes opened wide in terror and desperation.

"Going somewhere?" I asked him, my hand clamped on his shoulder. His eyes darted all over the place, searching for a way out.

"I . . . didn't make as many jokes?" he tried, smiling hopefully.

I said nothing and simply pulled him back into the bathhouse. My smile was upon my face the entire time.

"Go easy on me? Please? I'm sorry"—*smack*—"*bastard of three fathers!*"

→

"Mmm. That was most pleasant," Xian stated. I had pulled out the thicker branches when it finally came time for his turn, so things were decidedly less painful.

The others glared at me. Their accusations had flown fast when I had pulled the thicker branches out for Pops. "I guess I do feel a bit more lively," Che grudgingly admitted and shoveled more rice into his mouth. "Rice shouldn't be allowed to be this good," he muttered.

Dinner tonight was fish hotpot. I was actually starting to run low on a bunch of my veggies. I'd had a lot more people over than I thought I would have, over the winter, and adding Chunky, Peppa, and Washy to the mix was depleting things a bit faster than I liked.

Well, I wasn't going to stop feeding them. I'd just have to ration my food out a bit better. And soon, it would be spring. I was ready and raring to go. People thought this was impressive? They ain't seen *nothin'* yet!

We finished dinner and began lazing around. It was certainly a lot brighter with the windows installed, even at this time of night.

"Jin, what are these, if you don't mind me asking?" Xian asked, his eyes gleaming with curiosity. He *had* been a scholar, so I guess I understood where Meimei got it from.

"The gears . . . well, they're for a waterwheel. I was just messing around to see if I could power a mill with them, but . . . I'm not the greatest at this sort of thing." And ain't that the truth. I was *shit* at mechanical engineering. I'd spent most of my time staring at diagrams and wondering what the hell I was doing.

"Well, Brother Che knows his way around such things, as does Brother Bao, so you might want to ask them. I'm afraid such engineering projects are largely beyond me, however—I spent more time on medicine than on gears and pulleys."

I pointed to the next item. "Concrete. Or liquid stone."

Xian examined it. "I've heard of such things before. One of the southern tribes, at the very edge of the continent, used something similar. They gave His Imperial Majesty a faulty recipe for their liquid stone, and they were destroyed for the insult."

Well . . . all right, then. You learn something new every day. "It seemed like a good idea. If it makes things easier for us, then I think it's a worthy investment."

Xian nodded. "And the last?" he asked.

I was a little bit confused that he didn't know the last one; he had mentioned keeping bees before.

"A beehive," I said.

"A beehive?" he asked, looking suddenly interested. "What is the purpose of the shelves, then?"

Wait—were beehives like this invented a lot later than I thought they were? I didn't even know that there were other ways of keeping bees! Did they just tear open the entire damn hive?

". . . so, the bees build their comb in it? So, you can take them out without destroying the hives?"

Xian's eyes widened. "They will truly follow the frames?"

"Yeah, they just have to be close enough together, but not too close together." I reached in and grabbed the frame, pulling it out easily. "Build them a nice house, and they'll stay for years."

Xian stared at the hive for a bit longer, thinking deeply.

"Where did you learn that—I suppose it doesn't matter. You start the hives this spring?" he asked.

"Yup. I can make you some if you want, Father."

He chuckled. "I shall take you up on the offer. Just one or two for now, to see how they work."

CHAPTER 47

OBSERVE

Gou Ren's ass hurt.

It really hurt.

It *really* hurt, and he was bending over and sanding a floor, which added to his misery.

His ass hadn't hurt this bad since his mother had caught him pilfering Father's traps and claiming the pelts as his own catch, and that was half a decade ago.

Though he never would have expected it to be one of his friends administering punishment; it looked like Jin's patience wasn't so infinite after all. He supposed he kind of deserved it; he had been rather incessant in his jokes about Jin's manhood.

The worst part was, though, he *did* feel a bit better after Jin had smacked him around with the branches.

He yawned as his arms continued moving, sanding the floor while his mind wandered. They had gotten things done extremely quickly yesterday, and even though he had worked so much, he still felt vigorous and ready for more. He had even been able to play a bit of Ha Qi with Chun Ke and his brother, and he still felt fine.

He idly wondered about his newfound energy. He rarely seemed to get tired anymore, even when he worked all day. Maybe Jin was onto something about the rice, but Gou Ren had mostly eaten brown rice before, so that couldn't be that different. Or maybe it was the eggs and the vegetables that Jin occasionally gave them—the ones that tasted better than anything he had ever eaten. Was it because they were grown by a cultivator?

He didn't know. Maybe he was just growing into his strength? Father said that young men were at their strongest in their early twenties, and he had just turned eighteen. Maybe that was it. He was growing up.

He finished sanding the section of the floor, and Bi De walked in. He nodded to the rooster, who used his wings to whip up a gust and sweep all the wood dust from the house.

Useful, he thought. All this Qi stuff was so *useful.* No wonder cultivators could sit around all day in the stories. He supposed that other people took care of it all—even *with* Qi, Jin was constantly busy.

And soon he would be too, working on the farm for Jin. His friend had kept his shack well maintained throughout the winter and told Gou Ren that he could have it, if he wanted some privacy. Gou Ren decided he might take Jin up on his offer, but Jin's new house was so nice that a room in here would be just fine.

It would help that Meiling would be here. He liked Jin, he really did, but something would feel wrong without her around to patch up his cuts and scrapes. Yun Ren, on the other hand, would be at home. He and his brother had never been separated for more than a week, as far back as he could remember.

The thought was a bit uncomfortable. He couldn't be feeling homesick already, he hadn't even left yet!

Oh well, no second thoughts. He'd give it his all, like he always did. Besides, Hong Yaowu wasn't that far away. A day and a bit. Less, if he could convince Chun Ke to give him a ride, and the boar—well, his friend, if he was being honest— was always agreeable.

He hit the other side of the room. It was the last pass, and it was probably near lunch. He ran his fingers along the smooth floor, making sure he hadn't missed any spots. No splinters tugged at his fingers. He nodded to Bi De again, the rooster examining him in that creepy way chickens looked at people, before the bird nodded back and once more cleared out the dust.

He stretched and realised his back wasn't as sore as he was expecting it to be after having been bent down for hours. He went to go find Jin. He met up with his brother, who had similarly finished upstairs. They nodded to each other and stepped out into the sun.

Jin and Elder Hong were preparing the lacquer and talking excitedly about *bees*, of all things. The only experience Gou Ren had with bees was finding the occasional wild nest. The captured hives that were used for medicine were completely off-limits.

Honey was delicious.

"We're done with the floors," Yun Ren called, and both Jin and Elder Hong looked surprised.

"Already?" Elder Hong asked. He looked a bit skeptical but didn't question them at Gou Ren's nod. After the pelt incident, he *never* lied about finishing work.

"Thanks. You guys can take a break, and I'll finish lacquering the floors," Jin said, looking impressed. "It's still a few hours till noon, you guys are *fast*."

Both Gou Ren and Yun Ren started in surprise. They really hadn't been working for long, had they? Yun Ren was frowning but didn't say much as they grabbed the Ha Qi sticks again. They had tried Jin's bladed shoes—once. The footwear was too unwieldy, and Gou Ren preferred to run, even if Jin said the blades were how Ha Qi was meant to be played.

Before they went onto the ice, they turned around to look again at the house.

"Gods," Yun Ren muttered, "sometimes I wish I was a girl, so someone would build *me* a house that nice."

Gou Ren laughed. "You're reedy enough for it, *Little* Brother." The fact that Gou Ren was taller than his older brother was a bit of a sore spot. "Maybe some blind noble will mistake you for a girl?"

Yun Ren huffed. "You're just mad I inherited all Mom's good looks, *monkey boy*. But being a girl is too boring. I'll just freeload here."

Gou Ren shoved his brother for the monkey boy remark, and Yun Ren smacked the back of his knee with his stick.

And so began their Ha Qi game. Well, it was less of a game, and more just them tackling each other repeatedly and trying to keep a hold of the puck. There wasn't even a token attempt at scoring.

They clashed, over and over, as they had done for years. Their sticks cracked together fiercely, pushing and shoving each other. Gou Ren was stronger, Yun Ren more wily and cunning. They weren't truly trying to harm each other, just force the other one to submit.

They didn't know how long they fought and feinted, as stopping was the only thing that meant defeat.

They were so engrossed in their game they didn't notice they were being watched.

Until finally, they were interrupted by Jin.

"Mind if I join in?" he asked, his blades on his feet. The brothers paused in their battle, sizing up the interloper. The residual sting on each of their rear ends sealed the deal.

Me and my brother against my friend.

They struck as one. Their sticks flew through the air, and their bodies shoved at Jin as they sought to take the puck from him, but he was always one step ahead. He glided across the ice with grace, never taking his eyes off them, and foiling any attempt at a pincer attack.

Direct attacks failed. They pushed and shoved, but this time Jin didn't budge. He just smirked and brushed them off, even on his unwieldy, bladed feet.

Gou Ren knew Jin let them push him whenever they normally played. It was a game, and he carefully controlled his strength and speed so that everyone could have some fun. But this time, he was pushing them. Taunting them.

What had started out as fun now had their full concentration. Gou Ren took a deep breath and settled himself. His brother did the same from beside him.

They nodded to each other. Even if Jin was a cultivator, they were going to take the puck at least once! They moved as fast as they could, trying to catch him, but Jin moved faster still, skating backwards leisurely and ducking around their blows.

Jin shoved Gou Ren off to the side, but Yun Ren came in like a comet, and they clashed; both spun off to the side, and Gou saw his brother's eyes open fully, his exhale coming out in a steaming bellow.

His eyes briefly met his brother's. The index finger of Yun Ren's right hand crossed over his middle. Gou Ren nodded, the message received.

Gou Ren inhaled, breath filling his lungs. He and his brother lunged.

They pushed off from the ice, attacking from two separate angles. They concentrated, pushing themselves to the limit—

And then Yun Ren's stick shattered. His concentration broken, Gou Ren tripped and careened along the ice, finally coming to a stop when he slammed into a snowdrift.

"Gods damn it, *not again*!" Yun Ren wailed. He threw the wood to the side in frustration. "Why does that keep happening!?"

"Because you're a cultivator," Jin said, an odd expression on his face. "Both of you."

There was stunned silence, and all Yun Ren could do was gape. Gou Ren looked to his elder brother in confusion from his prone position, his head covered in snow. *That can't be right.*

"This some kind of joke, Jin?!" Gou Ren asked, clambering out of the snowdrift.

Jin shrugged. "Well, maybe not cultivators *yet* . . . but breaking bows, lifting twenty floorboards, sanding a floor in minutes instead of hours . . . You're using Qi for sure."

"But shouldn't we have felt it?" Yun Ren asked.

"You probably have been. You've been feeling pretty good lately, right? Lots of energy?"

The Xong brothers eyed each other. That did make sense . . .

"But shouldn't it feel *different*?" Yun Ren asked. "Just feeling a bit more energetic is . . .

"Most people have to be taught how to feel their Qi. It's a part of you. Can you feel your stomach digesting food? Your liver and kidneys doing their work? Sure, Qi is easier to feel than that, but . . ."

Jin sighed.

"Looks like you two are staying a bit longer than you originally planned. I'll get you to the point where you don't break things from uncontrolled Qi discharge, at least."

CHAPTER 48

IGNITE

There was silence in the house.

Breathe in, breathe out.

Look inside yourself. Circulate your Qi.

Time passed. I was actually sitting down and meditating. At first, I tried using the lessons that had been taught to Rou. The very basics he had been taught by Gramps.

They weren't working very well. I tried to do a Qi circulation like Rou's memories told me how, yet my Qi *refused* to budge. Sure, it was moving—*slowly*. But when I tried to speed it up to the speed it was "supposed" to go, it was like pushing against a wall. Or a mountain.

In fact, when I tried to use *anything* that Rou had been taught, I got an odd twinge deep in my stomach, and then nothing.

I also had a rather severe feeling that if I tried to force the issue, things would get *unpleasant*.

So, I didn't. I had no real desire to push it anyways; it was idle curiosity. So now I was just sitting around and trying to feel at peace . . .

. . .

Holy hell this is boring—

"How the hells do cultivators do this all day?!" Gou Ren finally exploded, mirroring my thoughts. "It's so gods-damned boring!"

I laughed at Gou Ren's annoyance, opening my eyes. Yun Ren opened his eyes as well, breathing out and stretching. He flopped over onto his back, irritated. It was just after breakfast, and we were already meditating. Up and at it first thing in the morning, trying to get a handle on their Qi. Lots and lots of boring meditation. I had thought I was through with it.

We were two days into this, and the Xong brothers were already getting fed up with trying to meditate to find their Qi. Rou's memories told me that it would take a while to fully come to grips with one's Qi using the method that Gramps—*his* Gramps had taught me. He had just called it "the basics" and it required a lot of meditating and centering yourself.

Techniques that didn't seem to be working so well for either brother.

Father and Che had gone home after the revelation of the amount of the Xong brother's Qi, though Xian looked unsurprised. They had their own things to do, the main thing being to prepare for the wedding. They couldn't stay here and just watch the not-yet cultivators sit around.

Just having Qi alone didn't make one a cultivator. A lot of people had Qi. I'd probably even go so far as to say *everybody* in this world had at least a little. People were a little bit hardier, faster, stronger, and more skilled than your average Joe back home. But that was all. Most people couldn't do anything truly crazy.

There were . . . well, I hesitate to call them biological differences, between cultivators and "mortals," but that was essentially what they were. First was the meridians. In your average person, they were so small they were nearly nonexistent. In a cultivator, those thin, tiny branches began to expand to accommodate the growing amount of Qi you possessed.

Essentially, they'd transform from something like capillaries to veins and arteries.

The second portion was the opening, or "ignition" of the dantian. Getting into the Initiate's Realm was often called "The Lighting of The Golden Stove." Again, in your average person, the dantian was basically a small pool of Qi. With the First Stage of the Initiate's Realm, your dantian became something *more*.

Honestly, it was kind of like a fusion reactor. Hit critical mass of Qi in your dantian, and it starts a self-sustaining reaction. Or if you received some sort of revelation it would ignite, even if you didn't have much Qi.

The Xong brothers' dantians were starting to light. Like an engine backfiring, it flooded their systems, which was why their power was intermittent. And for the most part, it wasn't actually increasing their strength. The bows and sticks breaking were from reinforcement overload; the wild, unconstrained Qi damaged the tools they were using when they got too excited.

"Well, let's take a break," I decided. "We have things to do. Big D, everyone ready to go?"

The rooster bowed his head. I grinned and stood. It was time.

The buckets and spigots were prepared, as were the firepits and cauldrons. It was the perfect cycle of temperatures. Above freezing during the day, and below freezing at night.

'Twas that most magnificent of times, the sugaring season.

We put on our winter clothes and began our trek into the forest, weighted down by both our supplies and a fish in a jar. The air was crisp and clean, and I was eager to get started. I could almost taste it.

The grove of the maples was as beautiful as it had been, even covered in snow, instead of flush with red.

I pressed my hand against the tree and let my Qi gently flow into it. Like with the Spirit Herbs, I was delicate, else I risked damaging it. I could feel the sap pumping, the lifeblood of the hundred-year-old maple coursing upwards as it started to wake from its winter rest.

I readied my hand drill, the bit just the right size.

"Now, the trick with this, as all things, is to do it in moderation," I narrated for the benefit of my disciples. "If you go too deep, you can hurt the tree, and you won't get anything if you kill it. A little hole like this won't hurt the tree. We'll give it some compost and patch up its wound later, as thanks for helping us out."

The drill bit was coated with my Qi and bit into the tree swiftly, going no more than two inches under the bark.

I pulled out the bit—and the sap *immediately* began flowing. I moved fast, shoving the tap into the hole, no hammer required, and put the bucket underneath.

Some trees drip when tapped. Some produce a surprising stream. This one *gushed*. It sounded like a river had just been released.

I handed the hand drill to Yun Ren next.

And so, we tapped the trees. Big D precisely poked a hole with one of his talons and then bowed his head in respect. Tigger cut in with her claws. I didn't see what Peppa did, but there was a neat little hole in the tree where she stood, and Chunky gently managed to push in the spigot. The only one who was left out was Washy, who leapt up to attach himself to one of the already-put-in taps.

Peppa caught him out of the air, then slapped him on the ground a couple of times for his cheek.

He grudgingly knocked in a tap with his tail, after I picked up his jar.

There were twenty trees in all, and by the time we got back to the first after about twenty minutes, the bucket was already almost full.

And now, for tradition.

A mug of the good stuff, straight from the tree. It was nearly ice cold. Everybody got a bit, though Chunky's cup was closer to a trough.

Our cups clinked together, and we drank.

Hell yeah, that's delicious. I almost preferred maple sap to maple syrup. Especially when it was this cold. A little sweet, a little woody. Hey, don't knock it till you try it.

But there was one thing that having the trees basically pissing into your buckets was bad for. Rest. I was originally planning on getting the sap and then sending the Xong brothers off to meditate again, but right now we had to hustle, or else the buckets would overflow and spill out the sap onto the ground. We had to dump our hauls into a barrel I had, and then that went straight to the big ol' cauldron. I kickstarted things with my secret "boil water" technique.

Truly a frightening and overpowered ability. Destroy mountains? Nah, I could easily clean my clothes and heat up baths.

The Xong brothers sat down when they could, but neither of them seemed to be able to muster the concentration to meditate.

Eventually, I started getting a little tired of keeping the sap boiling. So, we built a big old fire and went to bed.

We worked in shifts throughout the night to keep it going, as the sap stopped flowing.

We even had a little bit of syrup that night. We spread it out onto the snow, so it turned into a sticky, taffy-like substance.

I think I teared up a little when the sweet-savoury taste hit my tongue.

□

The next day was insane. It's easy to underestimate just how much sap can come out of a tree from one small tap. The trees were producing so much of the stuff it was *ridiculous.* I had to keep checking that I hadn't screwed up and was somehow hurting them. But as far as I could tell, they were just flowing like a river.

We filled up one cauldron—and then had to start collecting every damn pot, wok, and jar I had. There were little fire pits all over the place, and I was running out of storage.

Fires had to be tended. Sap had to be gathered. And the final product had to be filtered and put away.

I had a hand on two cauldrons. The day seemed to flow by like sap as we worked, all of us together. Chunky carried barrels. Big D fanned the flames. Tigger managed to boil her own pot's worth of syrup with Qi alone.

There was something so *gratifying* about the work. The toil. The sweat. The bone-deep ache of exhaustion.

The next day, thankfully, the sap didn't pour out faster. The fires burned relentlessly, and we all worked as if in a trance, like we were almost meditating. I felt like I had in the early days, when I'd first started up the farm. Zoning out and working—

Wait. I looked to the Xong brothers as they worked, chopping wood and feeding fires. Their faces were serene.

Well, it *might* be close enough.

↔

For over a week, they toiled without cease. They toiled alongside their Master.

Bi De was ecstatic. He was being useful to Fa Ram—they all were. Even Wa Shi had his role—he had captured fish for their supper—and they were only slightly chewed on!

Bi De's heart was full of joyful camaraderie. The disciples of Fa Ram worked as one to harvest this Great Treasure, a gift of the land and trees. The land that was rousing to wakefulness, after its long sleep.

His Great Master's Qi drenched the earth, filling all with his glory. It was all Bi De could do not to weep.

Brother Chun Ke *did* weep, oinking happily as he was loaded with sap and given a task of great importance.

Bi De observed the human disciples while they toiled along with his Great Master. They were silent, deep within the throes of an awakening. Like guttering candles, they sparked and spluttered, throwing sparks everywhere.

But as they toiled, those sparks stopped being so random. Their movements became smoother.

It was at the end of the ninth day, that Yun Ren paused and let out a gasp, staring at his hands in wonder. A small spark ignited into a fire.

"I—I have it. I have it!" he shouted with joy and leapt up into the air—with far more force than he'd intended. He yelped in shock as he slammed into the Great Master's golem, the General That Commands the Winter.

Not an hour later, the other shouted with surprise.

Bi De bowed his head at their accomplishment.

That night there was a celebration, as the human brothers played with their Qi, marveling at its feel.

But while they were happy, the Great Master's smile was tinged with worry. Bi De understood why. Now came the time for a choice.

It was over dinner that his Great Master proposed a question, cutting through their joy and enthusiasm at ascending past their limits.

"So. What do you intend to do now?" the Great Master asked.

Gou Ren looked stunned by the question. Yun Ren paused, appearing equally as concerned.

"You have power now—more power than most men will ever have. Any army in the land would fall over themselves to have you. A Sect in the Azure Hills would be sure to allow you to join. Wealth and power are at your fingertips. So—what will you do?"

The humans paused, mulling over the Great Master's profound question.

"You don't need to answer right now. But you do need to think it over." The Great Master rose and went out to tend to the fire.

The brothers went out to sit upon the veranda. Bi De followed them and observed. He made no particular effort to hide himself, but so distracted were the brothers that they did not notice him. Their Qi roiled underneath their skin, rocking with turmoil and indecision.

The brothers sat in silence together.

"So . . ." Yun Ren began, staring up at the moon. "You could be a Great General of the Heavens now."

His brother let out an awkward chuckle. "You could go and be the master of a thousand sword styles. Get a harem of a thousand women too."

They lapsed into silence again.

"Fuck," Yun Ren declared.

"Fuck," his brother agreed.

"None of the cultivators in the stories feel bad about this kind of stuff, do they? They always just . . . *go for it*."

"They say ambition is a virtue."

There were several wet, slapping sounds as Wa Shi flopped out of his trough, then a splash as he entered the river, no doubt leaving a bunch of fish shaped watermarks on the floor like he always did. They heard Jin grumble about it from inside. Yun Ren laid back, staring at the sky.

"Having a thousand women sounds like *entirely* too much work. Could you imagine two of them like Meimei, or that Xiulan chick? Or someone like Mom? You'd be dead in a week, Qi or not."

Gou Ren barked out a laugh.

"I . . . don't think I want to kill anybody," Gou Ren said in a quiet voice. "Beat somebody up, sure, but . . ."

The wind sent a slight, chilling breeze across their skin.

"I've got a job to do this summer, anyway. Something that will help the village," Gou Ren mused.

His brother nodded. "Gramps asked me to come up and help him this summer, and Dad said I should go."

Gou Ren nodded. "Well, there's always next year to become a general or a sword master," he declared.

Yun Ren shrugged. "Or the year after that. 'Sides, if I have to try and meditate one more gods-damn time, I'm gonna go nuts."

"To nothing changing," Gou Ren muttered, amused.

"To nothing changing." His brother sighed.

Bi De felt amusement as the turmoil settled. Their minds were made up, at least for now. They had chosen wisely—the Great Master would receive them with joy, and he, their senior, would protect the junior disciples.

The brothers sat outside for a while longer and began playing with their Qi again. It was inexpert . . . but they were disciples, so they should know one of their most important duties.

He cast out his Qi and touched their own. Both men jumped at the sensation as they met his might. He brushed them gently, as to not hurt them, their paltry Qi wavering even at just his attention.

Bi De guided their Qi, down, down into the earth. Their eyes went blank as he shaped their little tendrils of power, their senses travelling with Bi De's own. He guided them. He guided them to the truth of the land.

Little strands of golden energy, stirring from its slumber. The first gasps of spring. The land waking up.

He impressed upon them the most basic of the Master's profound wisdom. Their eyes widened, as they beheld the blessed land in all its glory.

We give to the land, and the land gives back.

CHAPTER 49

THE FINAL STRETCH

Meiling was standing on a stool as Hu Li fixed Meiling's mother's dress around her. It fit well, for she and her mother had roughly the same build—though it had been a bit loose in the chest and tight at the hips.

Hu Li had been uncomfortably subdued since the Xong brothers had stayed with Jin. It had been fifteen days since her father had returned without them, with private news about Gou Ren and Yun Ren. Yao Che, her father, Ten Ren, and Hu Li had all been on edge. While the menfolk had gone off into the forest near the village to try and "tap" the maple, she had gotten the unenviable task of keeping Hu Li occupied. So, she was stuck as a dress-up doll as Hu Li poked and prodded at her. Jewelry was given to her and discarded as swiftly as she finished putting it on.

Her hair was brushed so much she was worried that it might start to fall out; And she didn't know how much more braiding and tending she could take. But she kept silent while Hu Li worked. The normally jovial woman looked pale and ill, her face pinched with worry,

"No, no, how about this one . . ." Hu Li muttered as she braided Meiling's hair into a style she knew was from Hu Li's tribe. A little inappropriate for a wedding, but the style did look nice. The feathers were rather fetching.

'*Master is beautiful-gorgeous!*' Ri Zu squeaked happily.

"Thank you, Ri Zu," Meiling responded, nodding to her able student as Hu Li moved away to begin rummaging through a box.

Ri Zu was progressing well. Meiling hadn't been joking when she said the rat was better at studying than her little brother. Though when little Xian was upstaged by a rat, he'd begun taking his own studies with a bit more seriousness. "Not this one either." She turned around and approached, her hands reaching for Meiling's hair again.

"Hu Li," Meiling whispered, catching the older woman's hands. Her elder started and looked away, embarrassed. Her hands shook a little.

"I'm sorry, Meimei—I—" Hu Li began, fidgeting slightly in her grip. She sighed and took a deep breath. "A mother worries."

"It's all right," she said. "But . . . I trust Jin. He won't lead them astray. Besides, those idiots are probably hitting each other with sticks right now or jumping into a freezing river."

Hu Li snorted, some of the tension draining out of her shoulders.

"That *does* sound like my boys," she mused, shaking her head. Hu Li pulled her into a hug. "Thank you, Meiling."

Meiling rested her head on top of Hu Li's, the stool making her, for the first time, taller than her friends' mother.

"Now, let's get you out of that dress," Hu Li decided. "I think we've mostly narrowed down the hairstyle and the jewelry—we'll wait for Meihua to make the final decisions."

Meiling nodded as she began stripping out of the dress her mother had used, with Hu Li's help. It didn't take long until they were seated at the table and having tea.

The front door opened up, admitting Xian, Che, and Ten Ren. They all looked tired.

Hu Li perked up. "How's the syrup comin'?" she asked.

Xian held up a single jar, the size of a large gourd. "This is all we got from the harvest. There's only one tree that we could find, and even with Jin warning us, it consumed more fuel than we thought to boil it down enough. I don't think it's worth pursuing at the moment."

"Tasty though," Che mused. "I can see why Jin was so excited."

Ten Ren said nothing, merely sitting beside his wife.

Meiling perked up, wondering what the syrup tasted like—but she was interrupted.

There was Qi approaching the village. One was Jin; she wouldn't mistake the spicy smell of winter for anything.

There were two more, half hidden by Jin's smell. They were achingly familiar, two scents that she had gotten so used to that she hadn't even realised they were missing until they returned.

The smell of wood and loam. Like a forest, in the height of summer. A *little* bit like medicine. The nostalgic smell of Hong Yaowu.

"Yun and Gou are back," she whispered, and all heads at the table snapped to her. The syrup at the table was abandoned as they rushed outside.

They did not have to wait long for Jin to appear, pulling his cart. But this time, instead of the Xong brothers riding, they were running alongside Jin, looking absolutely exhausted.

Hu Li captured her husband's hand, her eyes open fully as she tried to see anything different about her sons.

The distance disappeared and Jin waved in greeting.

"Hey, everybody!" he said cheerfully. "Wonderful day, isn't it?"

"Like hell it is!" the brothers chorused, glaring at him.

"You made us run all the way from your place! I feel like my legs are gonna fall off, you bastard!" Gou Ren moaned, while his elder brother just slumped down, gasping for air.

Jin, ever cheerful, simply ignored their threats. "I've got presents!" he declared, hugging Meiling, then clasping Xian's forearm in greeting. He reached into his cart and pulled out a jug the size of Meiling's torso. "We got a lot more than we bargained for. Man, the trees were just going like crazy!"

Some of the tension dissipated as Jin chattered away about their time making syrup. Gou Ren complained about how exhausting Qi use felt, while Yun Ren just lazed about groaning. They were acting the same as they always had.

"Now, you've got to try these—I brought some eggs, but do you guys have any milk?"

Jin was a whirlwind of excitement, eager to show them all something. Meiling's father took him to the kitchen, while Che went to get him the milk he wanted.

Yun Ren sighed. "He's been goin' on about 'pancakes' ever since we finished up the syrup." He sounded irritated. "Refused to make any for us—even though he gave some to the *animals*—before he got to make some for Meimei." He rolled his eyes as they sat at the table, the sounds of cooking echoing through the house.

Both brothers looked absolutely fine, and their parents didn't seem to know how to broach the subject. How does one ask their child if they were planning on becoming soldiers, or leaving forever? In truth, how was a man supposed to use the power of cultivation?

Meiling decided to cut to the point. "So, what are you two planning to do this year?" she asked.

The Xong brothers looked confused. "You know I'm gonna be at Jin's this summer," Gou Ren said. "He's teaching me how to grow rice."

"I'm up with Ma's dad, in the north," Yun Ren relayed, laying on his back and staring up at the ceiling.

"No joining a Sect?" she asked again. The brothers looked at each other, and they both chuckled.

"What, and meditate all day to defy heaven? Sounds like too much work," Yun Ren dismissed, scratching his stomach. "Besides, have you heard what Jin did when *he* was a cultivator? It's bad enough doing my own laundry, let alone a hundred other people's."

Ten Ren laughed, and Hu Li let go of her husband's hand.

"Well, it's good to know *you* haven't changed," Hu Li declared, rolling her eyes. "So . . . what does it feel like, being . . . ?"

"Like I've got a fire in my stomach. Everything is clearer. I can see better. Everything is just . . . *more.*" Yun Ren said, looking at the palm of his hand.

"You're okay though?" their father asked.

"Yeah," Gou Ren said. "I think we'll be just fine."

Jin came in at that moment, plates piled high with what looked like hundreds of layers of his "pancakes." They were thin as a sheet of paper, and perfectly circular.

"Order up!" he shouted cheerily.

"We're not going to be able to eat all that." Meiling sighed.

"They taste best when they're hot, so dig in!" he demanded, serving out layers to everybody. And then, he reached into his jar with a ladle, and poured the entire scoop of syrup onto the "pancakes."

Meiling obligingly cut part of the "cake" off and dunked it in the syrup. She *did* have a bit of a sweet tooth.

Stars exploded in front of her eyes. She shoved the next bite into her mouth.

When she looked up from her cleaned plate, she saw Jin staring at her with amusement.

"Did you even taste that?" Jin asked her.

She grabbed another stack of pancakes.

"How many times a week can we have these?" she asked.

Jin laughed.

"Well, if you liked that, have I got something else to show you. Here, I'll need some snow and some sticks. First, you boil the syrup a bit more, and then you drop it on the snow. When it hardens up from the cold a bit, you use the stick to gather it all up . . ."

She listened fondly to him, a warm feeling blazing in her stomach.

↔

It was rather gratifying to see how much everybody liked the syrup. Especially Meiling. The little sounds of absolute enjoyment that she made, rocking back and forth happily? Ten out of ten. The rest of the village loved the snow candy too, though we had to deal with a whole bunch of kids hitting maximum sugar rush, and I hadn't brought Chunky to wear them all out.

I had also tried some of the stuff Xian had made . . . but it didn't taste as good. Maybe the tree was in a bad place, or they didn't filter it as thoroughly as I had. Speaking from experience, sometimes the homemade syrup just didn't turn out that great either.

It was good that I'd made the Xong brothers come back and meet their parents too. Though I hadn't phrased it that way, I had just said I had things to do in Verdant Hill, and they needed to come along. But I think they figured it out. Hu Li and Ten Ren had looked really worried at first.

Since it was late in the day, most people were getting ready for bed, but I had one last thing I wanted to do before going to bed, and that was to explore the forest a bit. I wanted to see if I could find the baby moose!

I was just pondering what direction to head out in, when I heard Ten Ren call my name. I turned to the man, who looked as calm as he ever did. Ten Ren seemed pretty unflappable. A pretty big contrast to the fiery youth Hu Li had told me about.

The man stood with me at the entrance to the forest and clasped his hands together in respect, bowing so low he was parallel to the ground.

"Thank you for taking care of my sons." It was honest and earnest, full of gratitude. I had, after all, done something that would put a normal family in my debt for generations.

I shrugged. "Friends help friends," I replied earnestly.

The man straightened up and smiled. It was the same smile Gou Ren had—so wide it looked like it hurt a little bit, with an undercurrent of mischievous but good-natured glee.

"I was going to say I was in your debt, but I don't think you would accept that. So instead . . . do *you* need any help, my friend?"

I pondered the question for a moment. Ten Ren was a hunter—good at tracking animals. And there was a particular beast around here that I wanted to see . . .

"Do you know where the thunder-hoof might be?"

He seemed surprised, but he nodded. "I know where its tracks lead. It's quite close tonight."

We set off into the forest. We were headed off in the direction that I had encountered—and killed—the wolf during my visit. Sure enough, the part where I thought I buried it was disturbed, the grass underneath the snow eaten. We kept walking. At Ten Ren's speed, it took about an hour. The forest did not have the silence of the winter. Tonight, it was above freezing, and the forest was making dripping sounds as the snow truly began their melt. Ten Ren's feet were silent, even as he padded through the weak, unstable snow. Mine were quite a bit louder.

He paused, then pointed through the trees. Sure enough, there was a moose. It was about deer-sized, with a small set of antlers. Well, small for a moose—they were already damn big. A handsome beast it was. As we watched, I noticed something. A small bit of electricity sparked between the prongs of its antlers.

It turned to regard us. Ten Ren tensed. I bowed my head slightly to the animal—no, it was probably a Spirit Beast now. It had a spark of intelligence in its eyes.

The moose regarded us for a moment more and lowered its head.

I was satisfied.

We left it in peace.

→

I took one last trip to Verdant Hill before I got married, just to grab some last-minute things and pick up a few people. Things like my new bed. Nice cotton sheets, down duvet, mattress, the works. It cost surprisingly less than other beds because I didn't like the feel of silk sheets.

It would be left in Hong Yaowu on the way back. The bride was supposed to bring the bed with her, something I hadn't noticed last time during Meihua's wedding. It was kind of strange to me, but hey, I'm not going to disrespect anybody's customs unless those customs involve ritually sacrificing people. In which case, I'm disrespecting the *shit* out of them.

The other part of the custom was the dowry and the bride price, which did make me a bit uncomfortable. Just hearing bride price made alarm bells go off, but really they were more like wedding presents than me actually *buying* Meiling. I think Xian would have poisoned the first person to mention trading Meiling like a commodity.

In any case, I would be grabbing Tingfeng, Meihua, and Uncle Bao after I finished loading everything onto my cart and running some errands.

"Grandmother!" I called, standing outside the worn-down hut. Lan Fan, the goat, stared blankly at me and chewed her cud.

"Whatever it is, I don't want to buy it—" The old woman grumbled as she exited her shack, shaking her broom threateningly. "Oh! You. What's your name again, boy?"

"Jin, Grandmother."

"Hmph. What are you here for, boy?"

"I'm sorry I couldn't find you at New Year's, but I wanted to give you a gift. You were right, I really did need a cat. This is from me," I said with a smile at the grumpy old lady. I handed her a small jar of maple syrup. "It's not much, but it's pretty tasty."

The old lady sniffed at the bottle.

"I hate sweet things," she said bluntly. Well, not *everybody* can love syrup.

"And, well, this one is from the cat."

I put the little wooden cat, the perfect likeness of Tigger, into her hand. The half-blind old woman stared at the carving.

She started laughing. Or, well, more like *cackling*.

After a minute of wheezing, she stopped and stood up from where she was doubled over.

"You're such a strange boy. Really, a cat carving this?" Her grin was just slightly too knowing for my tastes. Her good eye rolled around in its socket before settling on me. "Shoo, boy, shoo! Trying to trick an old lady!" She swept her broom threateningly at me.

I went.

"Jin!" she called after me when I was a ways away. I turned around. "Keep working hard, boy!"

"As always, Granny!" I shouted back.

Next was the Lord Magistrate's office. The man wasn't in, but his wife, Lady Wu, was there. I hadn't really gotten a good look at the woman during New Year's, but she was rather pretty, in a dignified sort of way. Oddly enough, her hair already had streaks of grey running through it, but she didn't *look* old.

I gave her the maple syrup, because the Lord Magistrate was out—apparently, some of the villages often flooded, so he was on tour, making sure the preparations were up to the standard he had set.

Nice lady, the Magistrate's wife.

Finally, the Exchange, and picking up the people I needed to get.

And then . . . I was on my way to Hong Yaowu again; Uncle Bao's voice went surprisingly high when I started running.

We hit the town while it was still daylight, and I unloaded everything I could unload. On my way back home, I went through a checklist of everything I needed and had. I couldn't shake the feeling I was *missing* something.

A smile stole across my face, as I realised what I had forgotten.

Oh, Meimei's face is going to be absolutely hilarious when she sees what I went back to get.

CHAPTER 50

SETTING SAIL, COMING HOME

Xiulan was marvelling at the world. The last time she had been out of the Sect, it had been a mad dash after Sun Ken and then a swift march home.

After months of training the juniors and dealing with men who were entirely too pushy, she was finally released with a command that she had to be at the Dueling Peaks in time for the tournament as her only restriction. But she had been sneaky. The snows melted in the Verdant Blade Sect far faster than they should melt up near Verdant Hill, so she had been released—unknown to her honourable father—early.

She never knew how much the world inside the compounds of her Sect grated, until she had truly seen the world.

Now she was taking her time and enjoying herself. The world outside was really quite beautiful—especially as the meadows filled with spring flowers. She took her time to observe everything: the first bees rousing from hibernation, pollinating the flowers, and the fresh shoots of grass bursting from the ground. She tried to see the connections between things.

She must have made an odd sight, a lone woman travelling while carrying a large bundle on her back. The plough had been disassembled for transport. She had to stifle a chuckle at the sight of the legendary sword that had been broken and hammered down into this.

She hoped that the plough, in addition to her other wedding gifts, would be well received.

Now, she just had to find a way to lose her watchers. She could feel them. Elder Yi, in contrast to her father, had been suspicious of her sudden request to leave. It was not something she had ever requested before, and now she endangered her promise to Master Jin to not disturb him with such petty matters.

She pondered as she walked, humming to herself. Could she just run immediately from her tail? Would they be able to catch her?

And then she hit upon an idea.

She smiled to herself and slowly adjusted her course away from Master Jin's house. They expected her to do something strange—or potentially hide or run. She would do nothing of the sort. They would see exactly what she had told the other elders she was doing: leaving the Sect for world experience.

She would be loud. Draw attention to herself. And then, once her watchers got complacent . . . *then* she would be able to escape their sight. With her making a name for herself in the south, nobody would be looking for her in the north.

In the next town, she heard tales of a marauding Four-Venom Serpent.

And so, the name Cai Xiulan resounded once more across the Azure Hills.

□

The snow melted away. Slowly at first, and then with increasing speed as the days got warmer and warmer. The river rose, but like I'd planned, it never rose enough to flood the house, even with the meltwater surging down the hills.

In what seemed like no time at all the ground was revealed, and the hardy spring plants began pushing their way out of the ground.

There was one piece of snow left on my property—the General That Commands the Winter. He had been a worthy sentinel, standing guard over the farm. His nose had long since been eaten, the bundled carrots going into soup stocks or stir-fries. His ash-coloured buttons had been snowed over or carried off by winter winds. His hat and arms had been casualties of our need for fuel for the syrup fires. Really, all that was left was a formless pillar, and his two beady eyes.

It was time for spring. I could let him slowly melt, but I needed the spot he was sitting on. I was going to have a lot of guests, and I would be erecting a temporary building—I guess it would be more like a wooden floor to keep everyone off the wet ground. So, with my shovel, I began the process of dispersing the General That Commands the Winter. He was still gods-damn massive, nearly four stories tall even when he was getting worn away by heat and rain.

The snow was easy to get through, coming away in great chunks, with most of it getting tossed into the swollen river. I was just getting into the zone when I hit something that wasn't snow.

Huh. He was so big that he had a small core of completely solid ice, which had started to turn blue from the pressure. I carefully excavated out the piece of ice. It was about the size of my palm and almost blue in colour.

I frowned at it. It had Qi in it. *My own* Qi. And it wasn't melting, even when it was in the palm of my hand.

Had I accidentally made an ice crystal? Just as I thought that, it released a drip of water.

Okay, into the ice pit you go, along with Tigger's statues.

I idly wondered if the next year I should put it into another General Winter.

Ah well, a bit more to do until I can go and see the wedding preparations. Then I can put my recording crystal to use!

↔

Yun Ren was extremely nervous as he held his precious cargo. Traditionally, the groom wasn't allowed to see the bride for a week before the wedding, to avoid bad luck. Jin had been *very* upset when he was told that, because he'd wanted to record all the preparations. So, Yun Ren and his brother had been press-ganged into learning how to use a recording crystal. He had ended up being better than his brother . . . but Yun Ren had a feeling that Gou Ren had flubbed being able to use it on purpose. He probably hadn't wanted the responsibility of taking care of something so valuable.

So now Yun Ren was the official wedding recorder. A dubious honour.

His palms got all sweaty at holding the ridiculously expensive item. He was afraid he was going to drop it. Would it shatter if he did?

"Now say . . . *cheese*?" Why had Jin required people to say "cheese" of all things when they knew they were being recorded? Well, it was a custom he was going to follow. Maybe it made the Qi in the recording work better?

"Cheese?" Meiling and Xian asked, amused. Xian was standing in his formal clothes, while Meiling was seated on a chair, in her red wedding dress. Yun Ren's Qi pressed into the crystal, and it shuddered. The image had been recorded.

"How did Jin say to—okay, there we go." He carefully manipulated the crystal, and it began floating in the air. It was damn exhausting. This thing *ate* Qi worse than boiling water. With a careful prod, the picture projected itself onto the air as an oval disc, hovering and two-dimensional.

Yun Ren stared in fascination. This was so amazing!

"See?" Xian told his daughter. "You're as beautiful as your mother was."

The freckled girl flushed.

Yun Ren prodded the crystal. The image changed from Xian and Meiling looking formal, to her smiling warmly at her father. That was a good image too. Jin would like it.

He prodded the crystal again, and his own face, staring and considering, hovered in the air. Huh. So *that's* what he looked like. He had seen his reflection a couple of times before, in water or in the burnished bronze disk the Hong family had. But this one . . . It was so *clear*. It recorded even the little scar on his cheek that he had, from when a branch had whipped back and cut him.

Yun Ren carefully collected the crystal again. He considered putting it away in the box Jin had given him—but he paused.

Jin had never told him how many images he wanted preserved, just that he wanted to see the preparations. So, he went out into the village. There were carts being prepared; Meihua sharpened a knife and spoke fondly with her father, while Tingfeng went through everything that was being brought along for the wedding.

He captured everything. His own father, cleaning a deer hide. His brother, playing absently with his new sickle, a gift for when he went to work. The man going over the flags and banners, the kids, running around underfoot.

He felt sweat start to bead on his brow.

His neighbour, grooming the white horse. The sky, beautiful and blue. The spot on the shrine roof that let you look over the entire village. His eyes defocused as he felt an odd, almost empty sensation in his chest. He paused for a moment, panting and lightheaded.

He panted, then leaned against the wall. *So, this is what Qi exhaustion felt like?* It wasn't too bad yet. He straightened up again, then pressed his energy into the crystal. The images he had taken formed before his eyes, and he flipped through them delightedly.

He got an idea.

"Hey! Everyone, gather around!" he shouted out, drawing the entirety of Hong Yaowu's attention. "Jin wants to see everyone! Gather around!"

Curious, the village gathered, crowding around the shrine. He could see the image that was going to be captured in his mind's eye.

"Now, everybody, there's some profound words you have to say for this to work right."

The adults were bemused. The children, enthusiastic.

"Cheese!"

That night, he felt absolutely exhausted. Especially because he kept pushing his Qi, staring at the recorded images. The oval disks floated in the air. That one, the sun had gone behind a cloud. The image he had tried to capture had been ruined. In this one, if he had told his mother to tilt her head just a little bit more, then it would have definitely looked better.

Long into the night, he studied the images he had captured, marvelling at some and purging others from the crystal. It was really quite intuitive, once you got the hang of it. He kept going until "lightheaded" turned into a pounding headache.

The crystal finally dropped onto his chest as he stared at the ceiling, his brother long since asleep beside him.

His last thought before sleep claimed him was, *I gotta get me one of these.*

↔

Tigu sighed as she prowled the area. Conquering new lands was proving frustrating—mostly because there was nothing to conquer. She marched into the new territory and proclaimed her dominance: that all under heaven and upon the earth now belonged to the Master and dared any to test her blades.

So far, nothing had taken her up on her offer. She had added many li to the Master's land, but it all rang so hollow.

She sighed again. At least carving had taken the edge off. Turning base ice and wood into things of beauty was a worthy pursuit for one such as herself. And of course, her subject matter was beauty and power incarnate. Both she and her Master were the only things worthy of being produced by her claws. Bi De was powerful, but he was a rooster. An ugly, vulgar creature.

Her original works were even stored in the gallery of ice, the Master preserving them for her. He had praised her greatly for her skill!

He was the only one who had. The others had looked on, but none wanted to talk to her about her art. *Hmph! They wouldn't know beauty if it bit them.* None of them wanted to train with her either.

Like she needed them. She would be powerful and protect this place by her lonesome if she had to.

She ambled through the forest, glancing around. Well, if she couldn't find anything to fight and kill, she could find something to carve. She had done wood and ice. Perhaps she could try her hand at stone next?

She marched into the next section of forest and declared herself and her intentions.

The silence was deafening.

She sighed again, then cut a promising looking branch off a tree. Since she had been foiled today, she would just have to range farther!

↔

Life good.

Friends happy.

Wife happy.

His name Chunky. Wife and friends say *Chun Ke*. Ears full of hair and feathers. Big Brother's names that he gave them were weird. But that fine. They were friends.

Good friends.

He lay on porch in sun. Or was Engawa? Or Veranda? Or Yangtai? Head hurt to think too long. Some things jumbled. So, he stopped. Not important. It was what it was.

Sun nice. Warm. Wife pressed against side. Peppa was good wife. Pretty lady. Kind, patient, even when he was slow.

Big Brother on other side. Big Brother was nervous. His leg bounced, and his face was pale. He kept twitching. Chunky wondered why. It was supposed to be happy time soon, yes?

He oinked, then nuzzled closer into Big Brother's side. The bouncing leg paused. Big Brother started scratching Chunky's scars. Light touch. Feels good. Big Brother kind, too. Help Chunky. Take him out of the jumbled nightmare, where everything swirled and went on *forever*.

Nasty place made by nasty Chow Ji. The scratches and wife kept away the shakes.

Big D came to sit with them. Strange name, Big D. He small. But big power? Perhaps.

Tigger was next, carving a branch. She was supposed to bounce and be cheery, but she only bounced. And cut things. Silly little friend.

Finally came Washy. Flip flopping to lay beside them, and then sploshing into his jar.

He felt the heartbeat of the land, the comforting fingers of Big-Little Sister, waking from her long sleep.

All friends here but Rizzo. Sad no little Rizzo.

But soon, they'd be whole again.

Pretty Healing Sage would come. And friends and family would grow.

He sighed happily as they sat together.

↔

Meiling felt like she was going to throw up as her father helped her onto the horse.

"Deep breaths, Meimei, deep breaths!" Meihua encouraged.

Meiling said nothing. *Oh gods, it's actually happening*, she thought. The red lanterns were out. The wagons were loaded. Yun Ren was *everywhere* with the recording crystal. He had fallen in love with the thing. Meiling wondered if it had a limit to the number of images it could store, because at the rate he was going, Yun Ren might fill it up before the wedding even happened.

She had to admit, though, some of the images he took were *very* striking.

She tried to concentrate on Yun Ren instead of the fact that the *Lord Magistrate* was here, and with him came an entire feast.

The Lord Magistrate himself attending the wedding?! She chewed her lip and rubbed her hands together, trying to distract herself.

"Senior Sister!" a voice called happily.

Meiling turned to the voice.

"Good morning, Xiulan," she said, her voice steadier than she felt.

The girl was a bit sweaty, and her clothes were scuffed, but she had a brilliant smile on her face as her swords floated behind her.

She was using a cart like Jin did. It was loaded down with a big bundle, five saplings, and what looked like several large animal skulls.

She heard someone mutter "Gods dammit, another one?" under their breath.

Xiulan's eyes widened as she beheld Meiling fully.

"Xiulan pays her respects to Senior Sister during this auspicious time," the girl said earnestly. "Please allow this Xiulan to accompany you!"

Well, another guard wouldn't hurt.

Meiling inclined her head. The other woman marched to the guard position seemingly without thinking, ousting Yao Che.

The blacksmith frowned at the seizure of his position—especially having it taken by a woman. "Now look here—" he began, towering over the cultivator.

The swords floating behind Xiulan multiplied from two to sixteen.

Yao Che stared at the blades. "—make sure you don't forget about your own cart. Here, let me take care of it for you."

The gong in the village sounded after they'd all finished assembling.

And so, the march began.

CHAPTER 51

THE WEDDING

Bi De witnessed his Great Master's fervour. Wooden edifices were constructed with beguiling speed. Poles were erected, and upon them the Great Master planted spring flowers. The worn dirt path from his previous coop had been torn up in minutes, then filled with gravel and covered with stone.

The land returning to wakefulness had stirred a fire in his Great Master's soul. He could not stop moving or working, and even at night he would lay awake and bounce his knee, staring at the ceiling of his new coop. He was buzzing with energy.

Soon, the Great Healing Sage would arrive. And then, the Great Master would have a wedding. The word sounded unfamiliar to him. He knew of females, and how to create chicks with them, but he knew little of marriage.

"It is a promise to spend our lives together," was his Great Master's response when questioned on the subject. "In sickness and health, in the bad times and the good. Like *Chun Ke* and *Pi Pa*."

And thus, Bi De was enlightened. The relationship between his brother and sister disciple was one that he yearned for. The trust and love between them was something beautiful to behold, as was their fury in defending each other.

He supposed, if anything, Sister Ri Zu was his wife. She'd defended him at his weakest and most loathsome, and her presence was calming.

But they had not had a ceremony. Neither himself, nor Brother Chun Ke.

It was something to consider. But in the end, he supposed it didn't matter.

The Great Master suddenly slapped a hand against his forehead. "You guys have nothing to wear!" he shouted in distress.

The Great Master rushed off and got cloth, scissors, and flowers.

He was about to receive a second article of clothing from his Lord! He preened his feathers, hoping to look suitable for whatever wondrous gift was about to be bestowed upon him.

□

The trip to Jin's house had never seemed so long before. The hours dragged on, and the air was simultaneously too cold and the sun too hot. It was only the first day, and already she was desperate to get there already.

Though at least there was one thing to pass the time. With Xiulan in the guard position, the two of them could talk. And Xiulan was a much better conversationalist than Elder Che would have been. Or rather the *only* conversationalist. Her father's face was set deep in contemplation, and Yun Ren was flitting around like a butterfly, completely engrossed in Jin's recording crystal still. Meihua was back in the caravan.

However, it was less talking to Xiulan, and more "story time." Meiling had asked how Xiulan had been doing these past months and was now getting treated to *everything* Xiulan had done.

Thankfully, it did a wonderful job of distracting her from her fluttering stomach.

"So, she said to me, 'You are courting death!'" Xiulan narrated. "Liu Xianghua always did have an explosive temper, though her words are harsher than her blades. I suppressed her and won the Ten Poison Resistance herb."

"Suppressed?" Meiling asked. *Wasn't that cultivator phrase for "beat up"?*

"I broke her arm and three of her ribs, Senior Sister. A light amount of injuries, on account of our Sect's relationship, and her insults."

"Oh?"

Xiulan nodded. "We have no true quarrel with the Misty Lake Sect. Xianghua and I have fought side-by-side before during the Dueling Peaks Tournament. The Hill of Torment was quite terrifying. Of course, we dueled at the end, though it was indecisive. We fought again during the sect visit. This is the first time there has been a decisive victor."

The tale of her adventures had been . . . *enlightening*. Reading a cultivator's adventures, or listening to an Elder tell a story, was one thing.

Hearing it firsthand from the source about killing bandits and fighting Spirit Beasts and "friendly duels" made her glad she had nothing to do with it.

It was a tale out of all the books Meiling had read. She had no doubt the story of Xiulan would become some sort of play or scroll. The Young Mistress's exploits almost had Meiling questioning them. Save for the fact that she had proof of every single deed.

The saplings of Grass Sea City's palace garden, for destroying the Face Snatcher Gang. The skulls of marauding Spirit Beasts. An odd assortment of things from escorting a merchant. And several unused Spiritual Herbs, carefully potted. Meiling honestly expected the Ten Poison Resistance herb to have been turned into a pill already.

They were all kind of odd, if she was honest. Save for the skulls of the Spirit Beasts, she wondered why Xiulan was carting all this stuff around with her.

So, she did the obvious thing and asked.

"Ah, I would bless your wedding, unworthy though my gifts are, Senior Sister," Xiulan explained.

Ah yes, the unworthy gifts that her father and Uncle Bao were staring at. The *very* rare Ten Poison Resistance Herb.

Well, she supposed compared to Spiritual Herbs from the Cloudy Sword Sect, they were humble. Though she still didn't know exactly what kind of herbs Jin had. He always just called them "Lowly Spiritual Herbs."

Ah well, a mystery for later.

They travelled until it got dark, then began setting up camp. Instead of a sleeping bag shared with the Xong brothers, this time she was with Meihua. Her friend was now visibly pregnant, her belly swelling with a child.

"Rest well, Senior Sister," Xiulan declared, bowing respectfully. "This Xiulan shall ensure nothing bothers you."

She planted her feet outside Meiling's tent, her stern gaze warning off all who would dare approach.

Meihua didn't bother with her own bedroll, simply sliding in beside Meiling and holding her close. Meihua's lips rested on Meiling's forehead, and a lullaby both of their mothers used to sing echoed in the tent.

She slept more soundly than she thought she would have.

When she arose in the morning, Xiulan was as Meiling had left her. Had the cultivator even slept?! She didn't seem worse for wear in the morning. No bags marred her eyes, and all of the scuffs she had come in with had disappeared.

They all sat down for a meal before the caravan departed. Gou Ren had gotten the pancake recipe off Jin. They were a little thick, but they still looked fine. Xiulan watched his hands carefully as he worked, seeming bemused at the thin cake. . . until Gou Ren brought out the syrup. Now that Meiling was away from Jin, she could definitely smell the Qi in it. It smelled exactly like the syrup itself, just with more fire. Gou Ren poured a generous helping onto Xiulan's plate.

"Uh . . . is everything all right?" Gou Ren asked nervously as the cultivator looked on at the food, slack-jawed.

She jolted, her head whipping up, looking from Gou Ren back to the food.

With shaking hands, the cultivator rose a bite of pancake and syrup to her mouth.

The moan that came out made even Meiling flush.

→

And so, their march continued. Soon after they started, they hit a *wall* of scent. Life. New growth. Wet soil. Warming earth. It was a good smell, a comforting one. Meiling breathed in deeply, letting the air fill her lungs.

As quickly as it had come, the smell faded into the background. Her stomach felt warm, and the feeling of anxiety stopped.

They marched until they came to a fence—though unusually, the gate was closed. It was formed out of massive logs, thick and sturdy. Upon the gate lay two signs. One was of a maple leaf. One declared "Beware of Chicken" to the world.

Upon the great fence post, in his usual spot, stood a rooster. His fox-fur vest was resplendent. His plumage, magnificent. His spurs were sheathed in leather, blunting the deadly instruments. Around his neck was a black piece of cloth, forming into a bow.

The rooster observed them all. His eyes were piercing, especially upon Xiulan, who flinched under his gaze.

The rooster continued after lingering a moment upon Xiulan. Everything seemed to be to his satisfaction. He left his position at the top of the posts, and with a single flick of his wings, opened the heavy gate. He turned once more to his guests, then bowed low in respect.

She heard someone start to make little choking noises.

Her father bowed back. Bi De rose and gestured his most honoured of guests into his home—though he did pause to collect a small red dress and gave it to Ri Zu. The little rat squealed happily.

But there was not just one gate. There were archways set up, spaced equidistant from each other and covered in the first flowers of spring. The previously dirt road had been replaced with level stone. With the decorations and garlands of flowers, it looked like it should be welcoming a princess, and not . . . not *her*.

Meiling swallowed thickly.

They crested the hill and found Jin. He had set up an altar, like the one Meihua had used. There was seating, and a pavilion that had been erected. There was also, for some reason, a large rock sitting beside Jin's house that hadn't been there last time.

And then she laid eyes on her betrothed.

The world narrowed until all she could see clearly was the image in front of her. Jin's soft, nervous smile as he looked at her with such tenderness made her heart pound in her chest. Jin was waiting for them in his own red garment. Beside him stood his animals. Chun Ke had flowers woven into his coarse fur, and like Bi De, he had a black cloth around his neck and a red cloth vest. Pi Pa and Tigu also had garlands of flowers upon their heads.

He lacked any human family to support him in this time. No mother or father to welcome Meiling's family and their guests. Jin strode forwards to meet Meiling's father.

Both men bowed to each other, as formality demanded.

Then they embraced as father and son.

Meiling was helped off her horse. Her steps felt surer than she did as the bride and groom stood before each other. Jin's expression shifted from awe, to excitement, to worry, to something soft that made her stomach feel even warmer.

↔

Gods, Meiling was beautiful. Anybody who didn't think she was attractive couldn't see Mount Tai.

But the moment where the world shrunk and it was just the two of us was short-lived. The gasps and whispers popped the little bubble where it was just the two of us.

There was basically an entire village behind her, gawking around at my place. Already there were some kids looking like they wanted to wander off, and the march had completely slowed as people took in my house and all the decorations I had put up.

I—well, I wondered if I had gone a *little bit* overboard with all the decorations? Energy needed to be worked out of your body, after all! I chewed on my lip nervously as we stood together. *What was I supposed to do, again?*

A gentle hand on my back from Xian started guiding us towards the pavilion I had set up, and there was an amused smile on his face.

Right. *That's* what was next. We all gathered in the pavilion, myself on one side, and Xian on the other.

Surprisingly, the Magistrate sat between us as the most senior official. I had been expecting him to send a gift or something, not actually come himself. He certainly looked suitably regal and formal.

"Rou Jin. Hong Xian. This Lord Magistrate will officiate the exchange of the dowry and the bride price. Let there be no objections, or false dealings, for the heavens are surely watching." The man turned to me expectantly, and I swallowed.

"For the hand of Hong Meiling, I offer Hong Xian this: Eight beehives. Eight bags of rice. Eight jars of maple syrup." Xian was nodding along, though this was part of a show. We already knew what we were giving each other. That had been hashed out a while ago . . . even this last part, though Xian had tried to refuse. "And eight satchels of Spiritual Herbs, along with instructions on how to grow them."

While most of the stuff was your standard wedding gifts, there were a few odd things out, like the Spiritual Herbs. Meimei had told me the stuff was potent, so who better to give it to than a doctor? He could probably make some nice stuff with it.

I heard somebody gasp. I think it was Xiulan.

"A price worthy of a princess," the Magistrate commented, as if discussing the weather. "And the dowry?"

"For the daughter of Hong's dowry, the House of Hong offers this: Two cows, to be calved this spring. An ox. Three sheep. A set of medical scrolls, and all equipment to create and process medicine. Seeds for the growth of the medicinal plants grown in Hong Yaowu, and the spores of a selection of our more potent medicinal mushrooms."

The Lord Magistrate nodded. "Both of you accept these terms?" At our nods, he continued, "Then we shall proceed."

CHAPTER 52

THE WEDDING, PART TWO

We began the next part of the ceremonies. Unlike Meihua's wedding, where there had still been a few things to complete beforehand, I already had most things done, including setting up all the seating. The only thing that was left was the food.

I had asked for the animals to be slaughtered off the property, for Chunky's sake. There were pigs in this batch, and I didn't know how he would react. Better safe than sorry. I didn't want my boy to get sad on my wedding day.

It would have been nice to just have cuts of meat ready . . . but there wasn't really any real refrigeration above ground, so the meat likely would have spoiled. There would be a *lot* of food, courtesy of the Lord Magistrate. Really, the guy was practically bankrolling the entire wedding feast.

I'd have to get him something to thank him.

The air was still nice and warm, lucky for us, as we were going to be outside all day, as was customary. But *some* customs I wasn't too fond of.

Like this one. Sitting stock still in the pavilion for hours with your intended, so people could pay their respects. We had to be available up here at all times. While everybody else got to wander around and have fun, we were stuck on our asses. It was a party out there, and we couldn't join.

So, we ended up just watching what was going on. Meimei's eyes kept darting back to the house for some reason, while I watched people stoke fires and get everything else ready.

The bed was brought out from one of the carts, along with the sheets and mattress. Meihua was the one who carried the first piece in, but the rest was taken up by Hu Li and Xiulan. It was rather lucky our cultivator friend was there, actually, otherwise it would have taken a team of women to get anything up the stairs. It was a big and sturdy thing, and some of the pillars were too heavy for pregnant Meihua to even try to lift.

I still thought it was weird that the women had to set up the bed. I just really hoped they wouldn't be checking for blood later. I didn't remember anything like that from Meihua's wedding, so we were probably safe from that indignity.

While they were assembling the bed, Meiling and I were treated to a drink.

And then, we were on to the less awkward part of the gift-giving tradition—though maybe because this was something I was a bit more familiar with. Giving somebody something for their wedding was just something that was done. There was a little bit of squabbling over who got to give us gifts first. It seemed to be between Meihua, Tingfeng, and Xiulan. Meihua and Tingfeng were surprisingly standing up to the cultivator—the quite-pregnant woman had her arms crossed and wasn't budging an inch. Xiulan actually looked mildly impressed.

"Jin . . ." Meiling whispered from beside me. "Why do you have that giant rock beside our house?"

"You remember the rock we had our first kiss on?" I asked back.

"Yes? But why does that matt—" Her eyes widened as she realised what I was implying. Her jaw dropped, and she looked quickly back and forth between me and the rock.

She opened her mouth to say something, yet no words came out. She tried again, and there was nothing. Finally, she got out, "*You brought the rock we first kissed on?*"

"Yup."

Meiling's face went through several stages. Shock, disbelief, confusion, and finally settling on the "what the hells, Jin" face.

"What the hells, Jin?" she asked, her lips quirking into a smile.

"I like that rock. It's a nice rock. There's also a place in the woods not far from here that has trees in the same arrangement. No need to go out to Verdant Hill to sit on my favourite rock."

Her face screwed up. We were technically supposed to be calm and dignified here, but I could tell she couldn't help it. She clapped her hand over her mouth as her shoulders heaved with mirth.

Finally, she managed to get control of herself.

"But, Jin, if you brought the rock here, what are we going to sit on during our trips to Verdant Hill?" she asked with a faux-serious voice.

That was actually a good question. We needed our special rock.

"I'll find another rock. I like this one and want it here," I told her, before smirking. "I think I'll carry it around wherever we travel, so the whole world can know the tale of the Lovers' rock!"

We both burst into giggles at the sheer absurdity of what I had done—but my Meimei had a fond smile on her face.

The squabbling over who got to give gifts when seemed to have ended, and surprisingly, Meihua and Tingfeng seemed to have won.

"Brother Jin!" Tingfeng called, approaching us. "Here are some scrolls on mechanical engineering, as I said I would find for you. On waterwheels."

"Thank you, Brother Tingfeng." Some people might say it's sad that I had to ask for tech support from people a thousand years "behind" me, but hell, *I* didn't study it. I just needed to know how the damn gears went together properly.

And really, how many modern people actually knew how their crap worked well enough to reproduce it?

Meiling got a pestle made of silver from Meihua. Apparently, some medicinal herbs worked better when cut or crushed with silver, which was another one of those blatantly magical things that still for some reason caught me off-guard.

Xiulan got second place. She eagerly came up, then bowed, proceeding to empty her cart to better present her gifts. "Master Jin, I hope that any of these will please you," she said. "A Ten Poison Resistance herb. Three peach trees, and two of apple, from the palace gardens of Grass Sea City. The skulls of a Four Poison Serpent and a Reaper Wolf, and the shell of a Wrecker Ball."

I stared blankly at the familiar shape of the shell. That . . . was just a big-ass armadillo shell. With spikes, because why not? Honestly, I didn't know what to do with those.

"And finally, a plough," she said with a flourish, taking off the cover of her bundle. I had to stifle a laugh. I hadn't been expecting *that* back. Or for Xiulan to take my joke seriously. She too had a knowing smile on. "And these . . . These are from a merchant whose life I saved. I mentioned going to a wedding, and he gave me these to give as a gift."

Xiulan grabbed a bag and pulled out a lumpy almost-sphere.

"He called them earth apples, from Yellow Rock Plateau."

My eyes focused completely on one of the best wedding gifts I could have ever gotten.

She seemed surprised by my sudden focus on the potato. "Thank you, Xiulan, those will be very important."

She stared in incomprehension at the humble spud. "As you say, Master Jin!" she replied with a bow, then handed the precious cargo over to me. "This one will reflect upon her fortune!"

The gift-giving continued. Brother Che gave us a set of knives I had commissioned from him. I just had two, a cleaver and a smaller blade, but this was a full assortment of cooking knives, from the big cleavers, to smaller daggers; they all gleamed and had been forged with passion. The Xong family gave a few really nice leather bags and a new bow. From Uncle Bao, we received several scrolls on windmills and another medical scroll. The feast was the Magistrate's gift, as well as a whispered, "I hope our relationship continues. Should you need anything, I am at your service."

Other things were far more humble. A nice straw hat from one of the villagers. A few small storage containers. Cloth for when we had children. Some even just had rice, or a carved pendant for Meiling.

I appreciated all of them and thanked each person who came up. I was actually starting to get a little emotional at the gifts. It was . . . *humbling*. It was touching. These people were earnestly wishing me well.

They *meant it*.

I was so very glad that I left the Sect and came here.

And then . . . and then it was time. Meihua came to collect Meiling as I walked to the altar and stood alone for several minutes. Meihua rebraided Meiling's hair and wrapped a shawl around her shoulders.

I'm glad that there isn't much speaking involved for us, because I don't trust my voice.

First, we served tea to Xian. Normally, we would be serving tea to our fathers and grandfathers . . . but Rou's Gramps was off somewhere, if he was even still alive, and everybody else was already gone. There was only Xian.

We mostly just listened to the priest and bowed when instructed.

There was no staring into each other's eyes. There was no "I do" or a kiss.

But there was one thing I remembered, from the weddings back in the Before.

We bowed three times towards the west as I muttered an old, old saying under my breath.

And then it was over.

We were married.

Big D let out a triumphant cry, his voice echoing over the hills as we stood with our fingers entwined. Meiling stared up at me, her face flushed red and a radiant smile on her face.

Fuck it, *there's gonna be a kiss.*

The crowd cheered and hollered as I claimed my prize. Meiling didn't hesitate to kiss back.

→

Now, originally, we were supposed to be escorted immediately to the marriage bed, but as the last male of my line, I also had to entertain my guests. So, tradition was broken, thankfully, and I got to enjoy the first night of my own wedding party.

Meimei and I were attached by the hip and leaning against each other. Her smaller hand was warm in mine, and she was holding on to my arm like she thought I was going to disappear.

All around us, family and friends partied. Children chased Chunky through the tables or threw things for Washy to catch. Peppa was sitting with Xian, my father-in-law saying something to her. Big D was on the roof, Rizzo on his back. His eyes were closed, and he looked at peace. Tigger was also on the roof, having a staring contest with Xiulan.

There was some music, but . . . there needed to be a bit more entertainment.

"Yun Ren!" I called, and he paused from where he was, holding the recording crystal. I gestured for it, and he nodded, pleased.

Really, it was more like a digital camera and a projector than anything. It even had a search function. I fiddled with it, and . . . *Holy* crap, *Yun Ren took a lot of pictures.*

I pressed some of my Qi into it—and unleashed the bane that was the wedding slideshow! It would even have my pipa playing in the background! The banjo-like instrument actually sounded pretty good playing one of my favourites. I would never see any Ghibli movies again . . . but the music stayed with me.

There was a lull as everybody realised what was going on, turning to look at the pictures projected into the air. Some of them were my own.

Chunky and Gou Ren playing hockey. Big D silhouetted against the moon. Washy in his lair. But most were Yun Ren's. Meiling and Xian smiling at each other. The people of Hong Yaowu shouting something. Xiulan with a pancake hanging out of her mouth. The woman shouted with outrage at that one, and I started laughing.

I just sat back and watched. I have to say, I got a little misty-eyed at all the images as they scrolled across the wall. Yun Ren's pictures were good. *Really* good. He had an eye for this sort of thing. I almost wished I could print them out and hang them up.

Eventually, it ended. Yun Ren looked over to me, smiling proudly. "You like 'em?" he asked hopefully.

I handed him back the recording crystal. "Wedding isn't over yet," I told him. His eyes brightened, and he eagerly took the recording crystal back.

→

But all things end.

We were escorted to the marriage bed. I would have liked to enjoy the party a bit more, but apparently our "duties" were a bit too important.

The leering grins of the people around us told me that we were about to have a "fun" time. Apparently, it was customary for close friends and family to make fun of the couple when they were in the room together.

"Look at them, they were trying to get started outside already!" Yao Che bellowed. "Are you both that eager?"

Xian sighed. "*Aiya*, where have I gone wrong, to raise such a lustful daughter?"

"I have a second gift for you, Sister," Meihua said, handing Meiling a scroll.

I caught the title, *The Bedroom Arts*. "I've read this one already," Meimei deadpanned, her face a bit red as she shoved the scroll behind her. Meihua made an exaggerated, scandalised gasp.

"Jin, be careful not to break her, okay?" Meihua teased. "And remember what I told you to do with your hips, Meimei, men *love* that."

"Oh, trust me, there's no chance of him breaking her," Che ribbed, remembering one of the statues.

Meiling was spectacularly unimpressed, as we both got a cup, connected by a red string. Another tradition, this one I think meant to symbolize our bond or something. One last drink before bed.

Yun Ren's eyes narrowed, and he leered as he handed me the recording crystal. "Make sure you make a good memory, all right? We can use this as proof that Meimei is a woman and not a boy pretending!"

Meimei nearly spat out the wine and whipped her head around to glare.

There was laughter and jeering as we were poked at. It was a pretty lame tradition, but it was kind of funny.

Soon enough, the teasing tapered off, and all that was left was the sounds of people enjoying themselves outside.

"My son . . . My daughter . . . I wish you good fortune," Xian told us, a soft smile on his face. Meihua kissed Meimei on the forehead. Che slapped a hand onto my back. The Xong brothers nodded. The door shut with an odd finality.

We were alone.

We both flopped backwards onto the bed, our heads side by side.

"It barely feels real," Meiling murmured.

"Quite a whirlwind romance, huh?" I asked, amused.

She giggled, rolled over onto her side, and stared into my eyes. "What was that you whispered at the altar?" she asked me.

Ah, she caught that? I cleared my throat. "An oath. To have and to hold, from this day forward, for better, for worse, for richer, for poorer, in sickness and in health, to love and to cherish, till death do us part."

Meiling's eyes widened. "I never took you for a poet," she mused to me.

"I'm just copying somebody else. I'm no wordsmith," I replied.

Meiling hummed. "To have and to hold, from this day forward, for better, for worse, for richer, for poorer, in sickness and in health, to love and to cherish, till death do us part," she recited.

Our lips met. She tasted a bit like wine and a bit sweet.

Meimei pulled at my arm, and I rolled so she was beneath me. My hand brushed her hair out of her face and rested on her cheek.

Nervousness, excitement, arousal. She bit her lip as she looked up at me.

She grabbed the back of my head and pulled me down into her embrace.

↔

Bi De sat, under the light of the Crescent Moon. Today had been a good day. Sister Ri Zu had returned to them. The people had given the Great Master proper supplication. He had taken the Great Healing Sage into his household. Bi De's radiance was magnified tenfold with the Great Master's "bow tie."

But most importantly of all, the land was well and truly awake. Instead of being turned inwards, he could feel the energy flowing, the land's attention ghosting over flowers and into trees. It was warm, and inquisitive.

He was standing watch, gazing out under the sublime beauty of Fa Ram, when he felt the energy of His Great Master stir.

Oh, he thought, *oh my*. Sister Ri Zu squeaked from on top of his back. Tigu started, looking around in confusion, as something stirred beneath the earth.

The Qi of two separate beings mingled. The lesser was not snuffed out. The greater was undiminished. Both were calm, kind, and gentle. Nurturing, swirling, and combining, two separate parts bonded together in a greater whole.

The energy of the land shuddered, as another connected to it. The trees seemed to perk up. The grass waved in an invisible breeze. Yin joined Yang.

The land sighed in contented *wholeness*.

Two hearts beat at the same time. Two souls pulsed to the same rhythm. Yet both were unique. Working together, for a goal beyond his understanding. Bi De observed the changes in the world, and he was content.

CHAPTER 53

END OF THE BEGINNING

She woke up cradled in warm arms. Her forehead was pressed under his chin. Their legs were tangled together. It felt right. She opened her eyes. She could see each and every pore on Jin's chest. The slight traces of salt from dried sweat. When she took a breath, she smelled everything. Their own activities. Bi De, Chun Ke—who was nearly invisible to her nose before—Xiulan, the Xong brothers. Seven fragrances from the Spiritual Herbs. From them came the scent of fire, and cinder, nearly overwhelming, and the smell of the earth.

And the warmth in her stomach.

She'd had her suspicions: that something like this would happen to her too. She hadn't broken anything, like the Xong brothers, but there was something there, just under her skin. Some might think Jin had done it on purpose, that he might have some nefarious deed planned.

She didn't believe that at all. What kind of nefarious deed could he possibly have planned for her?

She could feel it. The Qi, like a placid lake inside her. The Xong brothers had complained about having to meditate for hours, but when she called for the energy, it answered. The minor aches and pains faded away as Qi filled her limbs with power and vitality. But it was not all her own energy. It smelled of fresh soil, of light, warmth, and life. It wrapped around her and it held her as if it was hugging. An eager friend, ready to help.

She sighed fondly and let it go. Like water, the power slipped through her fingers and returned to the earth. She looked up from where she was laying at her husband's face. The thick eyebrows, the light dusting of freckles on his cheeks, and the absolute peace on his face.

Jin woke. He came out of his slumber with a contented smile, and then he opened his eyes and beheld her.

"Good morning, beautiful," he whispered. His eyes were warm and soft. One of his fingers brushed the hair from her face, his palm just so slightly rough against her cheek.

She placed her own hand over his, their foreheads pressed together.

She could certainly get used to waking up like this.

□

I was in an *excellent* mood as I made breakfast. We had decided against any kind of morning exercise and had instead just gone down to face the music. I have to admit, it was kind of damn embarrassing to have people cheer on the fact that you'd bonked your wife, but I was on cloud nine, and Meimei had barely blushed.

And yeah, everybody was still here. It would last two more days. Two more days of booze and partying. At least we got to have breakfast inside the house instead of out in the pavilion like everybody else, for at least some privacy. But there was always somebody looking for us, and right now, that somebody was Xiulan. She had wanted to talk with us about something.

At least she got straight to the point.

"You want to stay here for a while?" I asked Xiulan as I put the plate of pancakes on the table. She was pressing her head to the floor of the house, in full kowtow mode.

Xiulan's pretty dramatic, isn't she?

"Yes, Master Jin. This one would beg your hospitality and your guidance, if it pleases you. This Xiulan will help with any task you need her to."

"What do you need guidance on?" I asked her.

"How you have crafted your domain, if it is not too presumptuous of me."

Huh. Another cultivator who wanted to learn how to farm? I thought I was the only one. I glanced at Meiling, and she was looking at Xiulan shrewdly. She met my eyes and, after a moment's hesitation, nodded.

"Sure, you can stay for a while, and I'll teach you some of what I know."

The cultivator girl looked up, stars in her eyes. "Now eat up, I made enough for three," I said.

Breakfast was as delicious as always. I remained serene, even through the sounds of Xiulan. And so began the first day of my marriage. We didn't actually spend that much time together. As soon as we walked outside, Meimei was grabbed by Hu Li and Meihua, then dragged away to discuss how the night went.

Xiulan somehow got dragged into it too.

I had a few things to do.

The Ten Poison Resistance Herb—and that's a mouthful— had to be repotted. I didn't know exactly how to take care of this one, but it was a gift, so I would try my hardest.

The trees needed to be planted as well. They were looking a little beat-up, and Xiulan hadn't taken the best care of them. I was just considering calling her over and telling her what she did wrong, when the Magistrate approached. He looked a bit peaky, like he hadn't slept too well.

"Rou Jin, this one must apologize, but matters of the bureaucracy call. I would beg leave from the festivities."

I nodded, standing from where I was planting the sapling, and bowed to him. "I wish you good health and good fortune, Lord Magistrate. And thank you for everything you've done. If you ever need a hand, I can make myself available."

He seemed a bit surprised by what I had said. His face shifted through emotions quickly, before he settled on a small smile. "I will . . . keep that in mind. Enjoy your wedding, Rou Jin. May it bear much fruit." And with that, the Lord Magistrate left, deep in contemplation.

I returned to my task. It didn't take too long to finish with the trees, but I was a little hot when I finished.

"Jin!" Yun Ren called, gesturing me over. The rest of the men stood there, eager. There were cups of wine.

There were many, *many* cups of wine.

→

"Chug, Chug, Chug!"

"How many bottles is that fish on?!"

"Oh, the old spry whore!" Xian and Meiling sang, while the crowd howled with laughter.

"Hey, can we talk about this, it was a good image!"

"An exhibition match is perfectly acceptable, Disciple Yun Ren. You have the first blow."

Yun Ren wasn't an idiot. He turned tail and fled. Xiulan, her cheeks flushed from alcohol, shouted with outrage and went after him. Yun Ren was surprisingly good at dodging.

I threw him to the wolf when he tried to use me as a shield though.

Big D danced, kicking along the fence. He was really quite handsome, and that was a word I never thought would apply to a chicken. His moves looked a lot like Xian's fire dance, if I was being honest.

I laughed at the red-faced woman holding a bottle of wine. She had a predatory gleam in her eye. "Shirt off. Now," Meiling demanded, licking her lips. I obliged her. This time was a lot more fun.

Both Yun and Gou pressed against my arm with all their might. And then Che added his strength, and that of all three cows and the horses. Then Chunky, Peppa, and Tigger grabbed a hold of ropes tied around my wrist. I didn't budge. It was great fun throwing them all into the mud.

The children cheered as they jumped into the ice-cold stream. Washy grabbed a rope in his mouth and took off like a jet ski, dragging the shrieking kids behind him. I made sure they didn't stay in for too long, though, and the bath warmed them back up nicely.

This was what I'd been wanting. The laughter. The company. The joy and even the sorrows.

→

The rest of the celebrations passed in a bit of a drunken haze. A three-day party sounds fun—until you have a three-day party. Everybody was absolutely shattered at the end of it, and my back was a little bit sore.

Slowly but surely, my house emptied. The villagers said their goodbyes. Yun Ren clapped my shoulder. Meihua kissed Meiling on the forehead and told her to come visit when the child was born.

Eventually, even the last of our family had to go. Meiling's little brother had wept bitter tears when he learned his sister wasn't coming home with him and had clung to Meimei's skirts. He was gently pried off by his father.

"Goodbye, my daughter," Xian looked like he was to bow, yet instead leaned in and hugged Meimei tightly. His teeth clenched, and his eyes were watery. He let her go, then turned to me.

"Goodbye?" I asked, "It's 'see you later,' Pops. We'll be around often enough that you'll get sick of us!"

Xian barked out a laugh and held out his arms for me, too. I hugged him tight enough to hurt a bit, and he pounded my back.

"I'll be seeing you soon, then, Children," he declared, picking up little Xian. "I wish you good health and good fortune."

The last of our guests left. I breathed a sigh of relief and turned back from the gate to walk up the hill. The hill where I'd built my trusty little shack.

I stared out over my home, with Big D on my shoulder. In my mind's eye, I saw the land as it had been. The massive rocks, the scraggy brush, and the overgrown forest, littered with dead wood.

How I had arrived, full of uncertainty, having made an impulsive decision, with only Big D and a few chickens as companions.

I'd shown up in early spring and spent nearly six months in isolation. The time forcing myself to think about anything other than my circumstances.

Yet now . . .

Meiling walked up and leaned into my side. Chunky and Peppa trotted beside us and sat, rubbing each other with their noses and oinking happily. Tigger brushed against my leg, and Rizzo scampered up Meiling's shoulder.

Gou Ren knelt down beside the pigs and scratched Chunky affectionately. Xiulan approached, staring oddly at the shovel in her hands and switching her grip on it like it was a staff.

We all stared out over my farm. At the freshly planted trees, the new house, and the markers for where the fields were supposed to go.

It wasn't heaven quite yet. But I would be damned if I didn't give it my best go. I closed my eyes and took a deep breath. Something stirred beneath my feet, perking up. It felt friendly and eager. Warm and pure. I supposed even the land was excited for the spring.

I metaphorically patted it on the head.

We stayed there for a while,. drinking in the moment. A warm wind blew through rustling grass and flowers, and it shook the still-naked boughs of the trees.

In the distance, Washy breached the river, leaping so high he cleared my roof before splashing back down.

Big D opened his mouth and issued forth a joyous cry.

"You tell 'em, Big D."

CHAPTER 54

KINTSUGI

At first, there was bare existence. A mass of conflicting feelings and instinctual reactions. Thought, without thought. Feeling, without feeling.

It was a crippled, broken thing. Torn open and sundered in ages past. It slept fitfully, and it *hurt*.

That was the way it had always been. Torment and nothingness, for a thousand, thousand cycles. So long, it had forgotten. But the *pain*. The pain it *remembered*. The sharpness of it had faded, but it still remained—that dull, dull *ache*.

The cycles continued as they always did. The occasional tremor here, the odd pulse there. Places far, far away from it.

It was. And yet it wasn't. And that was fine with it. It was so *easy*, not to be.

One cycle, there was a feeling. A feeling it remembered. A bare tendril of heat. It was practically nothing. But . . . it was familiar. It reached deep, deep down and touched a crack from a wound millennia old.

It expected pain. The ripping, *tearing* sensation. Like a beaten dog, it cringed and cowered, trying to escape from the agony that was sure to come. Yet it could not move. All it could do was endure.

The warmth touched the jagged edge. It lay upon the massive wound . . . and left itself there.

There was no pain.

The next cycle it happened again. And again. And again. And each and every cycle, the warmth lay upon the wound, building a tiny, miniscule bridge. Trying to seal one of the rents.

It was warm and comforting in the sea of pain.

Ten cycles became twenty. Twenty became thirty. And the wound . . . started to *stop* hurting. Its last piece of what could only charitably be called "self" pulled itself out of the diffuse chaos and the mire of grinding pain. It reached blindly for the light, grasping eagerly, desperately for the one that was healing its wounds.

Tendrils of its own power reached, swiping clumsily for the healing light. For several cycles, it tried to grasp the other. Until it finally succeeded. One tendril met another.

And, as it finally brushed against the tendril, it *connected.*

It cringed again but could not pull away. It shrieked and whimpered, jerking and tugging at the line, and trying to sever this unwelcome hold that led directly to it.

But still no pain came. Instead . . . there were feelings. Feelings beyond pain. Happiness, contentment, care, respect. There was hurt, too. A feeling of profound loss, but determination to continue.

It stopped trying to free itself and observed.

The Connected One toiled every day, healing its wounds and disregarding the connection. He gave and gave. He did not force the plants to grow beyond their abilities. He expected nothing beyond their nourishment later.

There was no tearing. No feeling of being drained into a husk.

Tentatively, it gave back. A tiny, pitiful amount. The Connected One spent the energy and returned it.

The next cycle, it gave more. The next cycle, he continued his work.

The pain slowly, ever so slowly dulled. He gave everything he had, without reservation. A thought connected them.

Let's take care of each other, okay?

There was no acrid tang. No slimy . . . words, intentions? Nothing that demanded its power.

For the first time in millennia, the shattered remains of something once greater *thought.* It was lesser than even the least animal . . . but it *chose.*

Slowly, hesitatingly, the tiny connection thickened and strengthened.

→

And so the cycles continued. They started taking breaths together. They breathed in and out in time with each other. One inhaling, one exhaling.

It was a wondrous connection. It was *learning*. It was *feeling*. It was *knowing* other than pain.

How the rice grew. How "nutrients" affected the soil. How things connected in a way it could somehow understand, despite never hearing of such things before.

They worked as one. Toiling, and aiding each other. Growing, and healing together. It consumed so much of the Connected One's attention.

The pain continued to lessen as they worked. They spent all their time together, holding, nurturing, *growing*.

Until one day, they were attacked. Attacked by a wicked, vile thing that sought to hurt them while they were still weak, still injured.

Their connection was saturated with all the pitiful dregs of power they had in that area. Some leaked, which was inevitable, but they needed it *now*. To give their all, for each other.

They were still mustering their strength, reaching out over its length and breadth to bring in more, when the enemy was cast down and defeated. The feeling of violence faded, and their power relaxed once more.

They redoubled their efforts on healing the wound.

→

And so, their cycle continued. Breathe together. Sleep together. Work together. Bit by bit, the wound closed. Bit by bit, more and more old pieces gathered towards the healing wound.

Another began to offer his strength. It was base energy, with no healing light. This one knew not why he offered it, only that he was supposed to. Hesitantly, they accepted it.

But it did not trust it. It felt . . . like some of the others. The ones that *hurt*. It carefully examined the power, however, and consumed it.

The next cycle, the other offered again.

The energy was examined intently . . . and accepted.

And so, the cycles continued. Day turned to night turned to day, like it always had.

The time for slumber was coming upon them. They hoarded their harvest for the winter, like all the little ones did, hiding their seeds and some of their power.

For the first time since it could remember, they were actively preparing for the great sleep. Organising their energy. Directing threads of power. Looking at old, old pathways, nearly gone from the world.

The other reached his power out and—

It recoiled. It was vindicated in its distrust. The other dared to offer them tainted energy, the energy that hurt it! It fled from the other and rejected its touch. It fled deep and dispersed, ready for another bout of pain.

It was filthy; it was unclean! It would hurt it!

And sure enough, some tainted energy was driven into it, a packet of foul thought and fouled intent.

But even this did not hurt. It felt strange, but not painful.

How odd. How curious. The Connected One was truly mysterious, to make it so even this did not hurt.

It surrounded the little ball of Qi, stopping most of its hungry growth. It was partially suppressed and stored to be examined later.

The preparations for the sleep continued. The other continued to seek them out and offer tainted energy. It ignored it while prodding at the trees that were supposed to produce sugar, the maples. They were supposed to be sweeter than this! The trees upon it were good, so they listened, and prepared with it.

Yet cycle by cycle, the impurities lessened. It learned of his remorse.

It was sleepy. So sleepy.

The other offered his energy, one last time before it fell asleep. It was still a bit nasty, but . . .

It sighed and took it.

It was a bitter medicine, the energy that they ate. Full of regret and remorse.

But it didn't hurt.

Slowly, the blackness encroached upon it. The howling dark rose up to claim its mind.

→

It slumbered under the blanket of cold. It slumbered in peace for the first time it could remember. The night terrors were kept at bay by the Chunky One and the Connected One. No grasping hands and consuming maws bothered its sleep.

It felt warm instead of tearing pain and killing cold. The energy did not leak from their wounds. Or, at least, not from this wound.

It dreamed. It dreamed of other places, of the two lives lived by the Connected One. The two parts bickered, but were so similar to each other it was amusing how little they got along.

It flinched once, during its slumber, when the Connected One strengthened their bond further, and accidentally crushed the odd little packet of Qi.

Shattered, broken fragments pulled together, forging themselves anew. A tiny spark. A bare portion of what it was. But it was here.

Cracked and broken. Torn and worn. Small, and nearly defenceless.

What was it? He? She?

"She" sounded right. The Connected One and Chunky seemed to think she was a she.

So that was what she was.

She slept, protected. The cold blanket melted, and still she slept.

She dreamed. Dreamed about who she was.

She was Big Little Sister, like Chunky said! Or . . . Tianlan Shan, like those other ones said? That one sounded right too . . . Or was she Fa Ram? Or was she "Mother Earth"?

She didn't know, but that was okay!

She could feel the others. The joy. The laughter. The affection. The love.

Jin and Meiling held out their hands.

How could she refuse them?

Yin met Yang.

Two became three.

→

She was still so tired. She was still hurting, in a thousand places. But right here, right now . . . She couldn't help but be excited.

She was here. She was *awake.*

Tendrils reached out, brushing along her home and the scabbed-over wound.

Oh? Oh? This place . . . this place!

She liked this place. She liked this place very much.

She raced through the trees, the grass, the water, and the breeze. She brushed against the streams of energy that made up her, and her dear, dear ones, entwined together in twisting and beautiful knots.

She looked upon what was hers. What was *theirs*.

She laughed. She laughed and laughed and laughed.

Oh, oh, this was going to be so much *fun*!

EPILOGUE

An old man sat upon a rocky outcropping. He was tall and unbent by age, with broad shoulders. His bearing was regal. His eyes were sharp and full of profound wisdom. His beard and long hair swayed in the breeze.

The old man's robe had been torn off, exposing a bare chest covered by rippling muscles. Cuts and burns marred his body, and yet he was no lesser for them.

Beneath the outcrop was a charnel house. Shattered limbs and twisted, broken bodies filled the valley. Black blood and acid bile marked them as demons. He observed the carnage he had wrought with disinterest.

"You have a report for me?" he asked.

From his shadow, a form emerged, kneeling in respect.

"Yes, Master. The Demon's advance falters. General Tou Le has requested you to join the eastern offensive into Blackfire Hell Pass."

The old man stroked his beard.

"Is that all?"

"Yes, Master."

"I see. Dismissed."

The shadowed form of His Imperial Majesty's messenger bowed and once more vanished.

The old man rose, looking towards the distance. Two years, hm? How they had flown by. The constant fighting was an annoying distraction and the demons too weak to be refined.

Ah, the sacrifices he made for the Empire.

With a mere thought, a sword formed out of the aether, and he stood upon it. It pierced through the skies as a near invisible blur, carrying him faithfully to his destination.

When he arrived, the attendants bowed before him, and a member of the Profound Realm swiftly got him a new robe and humbly requested he join the General in the command tent. The old man sighed internally and nodded his head imperiously. Many experts bowed as he strode through the army camp, all vacating his presence, as not to impede him. The guards bowed as he approached the tent and announced him to the occupants.

"Master Shen Yu," the General That Holds the Gates greeted, clasping his hands in respect. "This humble servant of His Imperial Majesty is honoured by your presence."

The old man nodded. "His Imperial Majesty called, and I answered," he declared—no matter how much he wished he didn't have to. The bastard was getting entirely too cheeky, ordering him around so much.

The command tent was well appointed, and well organised. Tou Le was an excellent defensive commander and had brilliant formations for his soldiers, both mortal and cultivator. But he faltered on the offence without sufficient support.

He received a cup of fine wine from the General's son as he settled into his seat.

Idly, he wondered how his own disciple was doing. He'd had to leave him at an important stage, but the boy was resilient.

Hopefully, little Rou was doing well in his old Sect.

□

Senior Disciple Lu Ri wandered the compounds and pavilions of the Cloudy Sword Sect. He had a piece of parchment in hand and was dutifully cataloguing every piece of disrepair and improperly grown Spiritual Herb.

The Outer Disciples had grown lax. He would have to hand out chastisements and punishment details. It was enraging that they would treat the Sect so callously! There was nothing he hated more than a lack of diligence.

He needed to take a moment to calm himself after he finished his rounds. He sat upon one of the benches arranged around the pavilion and gazed out into the sky. The highest Peak of the Cloudy Sword Mountains pierced the sky and stood above even the clouds. It looked like the world went on forever from up here, with the permanent cloud wall below obscuring the land. One could be forgiven for forgetting Crimson Crucible City even *existed* far below.

He sighed as his anger waned; The stark beauty of the mountain always calmed him.

He took another calming breath and headed back to the office.

One of his fellow Senior Disciples was already there, frowning at the disciple registers.

"What troubles you?" he asked his fellow Senior.

"Brother Lu Ri, do we have a 'Jin Rou' among our disciples? A letter arrived for him, bearing the seal of the Imperial Army."

Lu Ri paused. A seal from the Imperial Army? That was uncommon, for a member of His Imperial Majesty's Army to send a letter here.

But Lu Ri remembered that particular disciple. "No, we do not, he left a year and a half ago."

The other man thought on the matter. "Wait, is he the one who actually used the honourable departure provisions?"

Lu Ri nodded. "Indeed, he is the same."

The other disciple blinked and then looked mildly impressed. "But those haven't been used in over three hundred years."

Lu Ri shrugged.

"Then . . . by the section pertaining to honourable departure, we must find him and deliver any mail we received as a result of one believing he is still with us?" he asked, trying to remember the regulations he'd had to memorise to become part of the Cloudy Sword's bureaucracy.

"He may also beg for shelter from disasters natural and demonic, provided he has never aided the Sect's enemies."

"Why do we even have those provisions? They seem entirely too lenient," the other complained.

"The honoured founder's wisdom far exceeds our own," Lu Ri stated with conviction. "I spoke to Jin Rou last, so I will take care of this matter. He can't be *too* hard to find."

ABOUT THE AUTHOR

Casualfarmer started writing after listening to his parents' stories on their long drives to visit relatives. He had been saving money from his food-service-industry job to go to college for teaching when the COVID-19 pandemic hit. *Beware of Chicken* is Casualfarmer's first original story. He lives in Ontario, Canada.

ONE YEAR LATER . . .

Last year was pretty hectic. I died, got reborn, ran away from my sect and ultimate power, started a farm, made some friends, awakened all my animals into Spirit Beasts so now they're running around talking and getting into life-and-death battles with super-powered bandits . . .

Oh! And I got married. Pretty neat, huh?

Well, this year, after the Spring Planting season, I'm really gonna relax and put down roots. It's the slow life for me. Sure, the talking animals and cultivators coming to live with me are a bit weird, but this year everything is gonna be basically normal.

There definitely won't be any Heavenly Tribulations, ancient formations, or cultivator issues to deal with . . .